*I must find a way out of this
or we are all doomed.*

A numbness had traveled from their feet to their hips, and was coursing inch-by-inch up their bodies. As soon as it reached their eyes they would be unable to close them and they would be trapped.

Shunlar sent a thread of her awareness up to hover over the scene. She could see herself standing between Cloonth and Alglooth. Her strength was beginning to wane just as she noticed something outside the circle that had entrapped them.

"Look!" Shunlar shouted. "There, beside the water, an object shines!"

From the shining thing, blue and gold flecks of light spiraled upward in the air. Within the moving lights a form took shape. The ground beneath Shunlar's feet seemed to turn to liquid and she felt as though she were sinking.

She screamed. And fainted.

THE GATES OF
VENSUNOR

Book One of THE SHUNLAR CHRONICLES

CAROL HELLER

AVON BOOKS • NEW YORK

This is a work of fiction. Names, characters, places, and incidents either are the product of the author's imagination or are used fictitiously. Any resemblance to actual events, locales, organizations, or persons, living or dead, is entirely coincidental and beyond the intent of either the author or the publisher.

AVON BOOKS
A division of
The Hearst Corporation
1350 Avenue of the Americas
New York, New York 10019

Copyright © 1997 by Carol Heller
Cover art by Donato
Published by arrangement with the author
Visit our website at http://AvonBooks.com
Library of Congress Catalog Card Number: 96-95181
ISBN: 0-380-79078-5

First AvoNova Printing: May 1997

AVONOVA TRADEMARK REG. U.S. PAT. OFF. AND IN OTHER COUNTRIES, MARCA REGISTRADA, HECHO EN U.S.A.

Printed in the U.S.A.

RAI   10   9   8   7   6   5   4   3   2   1

PROLOGUE

THE CITY OF STIGA ONCE SPREAD LIKE A VAST sparkling jewel for all to see and envy. Centuries ago it had been carved into the side of the mountain known as Stigantval by the hands of its inhabitants. Beginning at the bottom, they had progressed in steps, up and up, to the topmost peak. Indeed, precious gems, gold, and silver ran in thick venous ribbons everywhere they carved. The largest gems were removed from the mountainside and used to adorn the inhabitants' homes, their bodies, and their clothing. Gold and silver were coined or made into jewelry, spun into the finest cloth, turned into goblets, plates—whatever the people's hands could fashion. The thinner veins were left in the rock to become part of the walls of the city.

Cascading over the top of the mountain and down through the middle of the city, coursed the mighty river Thrale, which the inhabitants tamed and piped into each building. From deep within the core of the mountain a hot spring bubbled up. This they also plumbed. Thus the people had hot and cold running water in their homes.

Little by little they carried earth and plants up to their dwellings, and terraced gardens were planted. Soon flowers and trees adorned the mountain that had once been barren rock. Green life sprang up everywhere.

The vast plain that stretched out before the city was blanketed most of the year with lush grasses that fattened the flocks of sheep and the goat herds, as well as the herds of cattle. Those tending the animals never ceased to marvel at the way the city glittered in the light of day and sparkled into the dark of night.

Uppermost, at the crest of a small peak, the Temple had been constructed in the shape of a wheel, and it overlooked the entire city. Carved of white marble with veins of gold running through it, at night, from the proper vantage point, if you stared at it long enough, the Temple spun.

Sacrifices were made at the proper times of the year. The people worshipped equally the stone of the mountain and the Great Trees and the Cauldron of the Great Mother and the sun, all in the same Temple.

The dragons were gone, or at least they were reported to be, and the city-dwellers' world was at last secure. Guilds sprang up: weavers, masons, tinkers, tailors, farmers, drovers, goat and sheepherders, butchers, bakers, wine and ale-makers. All forms of trade were invented and pursued. Foremost among those trades, however, were the scholars. Everyone learned to read and write, both female and male. Scholars were held in highest esteem, especially those who pursued the study of wizardry and the magical arts. Prosperity reigned.

Until, that is, one greedy wizard decided he would live forever and rule with absolute power. His skill at weaving complex spells enabled him to manipulate with cunning subtlety. Somehow a quarrel started between two of the merchant houses that had a long history of evenhanded dealings with one another. One night a death occurred, quickly followed by another to the opposite house. Revenge became war.

But it was not so simple as that. Wizards were recruited by every house, and terrible weapons were created. The foulest of these weapons caused the mountain to tremble and the very stone to smoke, bringing certain death for any who inhaled it. The smoke seeped into the stone and there it remained for years, poisoning all living things. In the end, thousands of deaths later, the remaining few abandoned Stiga.

One group found the Valley of Great Trees, another the Sacred Mountains, another wandered off to the desert of the everpresent sun, and the fourth, who worshipped the Cauldron of the Great Mother, founded Vensunor. So it happened long ago.

ONE

STANDING IN THE DARKENED ROOM THAT SMELLED of candle wax, burning oil, and sour wine, Shunlar considered how her luck had changed in the past weeks. The summons from the Lord Mayor had been most unexpected. After the last fiasco, against which Bimily the shapechanger had forewarned, she had hardly expected to be hired for more than mucking out stalls the rest of the year. It seemed that her luck as well as her money was running out.

"This is a different matter, Shunlar," Mayor Althones said, his dull hazel eyes squinting in her direction.

Shunlar was well aware that Mayor Althones made no move without first consulting the Numbers. She could tell by the way he spat out her name that success had been foretold. Chance, however, always plays havoc with success, and the six-pointed Star of Chance was prominent in her birth Numbers; thus the meaning of her name in the Old Tongue.

Taking a deep swallow from his goblet of wine, the mayor continued to scrutinize her with his drunken gaze. Shunlar stared boldly back at him, her green eyes mocking in their intensity. As she waited, Althones looked her over, inch by inch.

She was quite lovely, in a handsome way. Her auburn hair, neatly braided in the female warrior style of one long braid starting at the crown, did not hide the streaks of gray at both temples, a feature unusual in one so young. Her lips were set in a straight, determined line. Her sleeveless brown leather tunic tightly covered full breasts that moved up and down imperceptibly as she took small, controlled breaths. Her hands were delicate yet muscular. Close inspection revealed several scars on her tanned forearms, along with the white outline of the dagger sheath that had been removed from her wrist for this audience; Althones took no chances. He drank in the paleness of her skin on that part of her arm. He remembered then that her hair was bound in brown leather, signifying Shunlar to be a highly-skilled fighter. Desire seemed to dance across his sallow face as he licked his lips and blinked.

"There have been rumors of an unusual stranger within the city walls. Someone who is known for stealthy tracking is required, and your qualifications take precedence over my better judgment. My advisors concur that you, Shunlar, are that person. What am I to do but bend to the wisdom of Numbers? The stranger is to be followed and his business dealings made known to me by periodic reports."

Shunlar stood in the meeting chamber brazenly staring back at the paunchy official, thankful that she had remembered to close her mouth. In truth she was biting her tongue so that her disgust for Althones would not show. From the way his greasy brown hair clung to his balding head, down to his ankles, where the bottoms of his trousers folded over his boots, she could tell that this was a man who over-indulged in all manner of food, drink, and intoxicants. All in the city knew Althones to be mayor in name only. The real power in Vensunor was the dreaded merchant, Lord Creedath.

Realizing Althones was staring at her breasts, Shunlar decided to speak before the room became even more uncomfortable. "I thank you for the summons, Lord Mayor," she said, bowing lower than was necessary, "and I gladly accept this duty to you and the citizens of Vensunor."

"Hurrumph," or something like it, escaped his lips. "Some of my men await to provide you with information. My steward will take you to them." He called loudly for the steward as he waved her out of his sight.

Only after the door closed behind her did she dare inhale deeply. The man's sour smell had tainted the air. "What an unpleasant interview," Shunlar mumbled to herself as she followed the servant down a gloomy corridor, thankful for the fresh air.

She sensed a dark presence behind her. Her neck hairs rose as she felt something brush up against her back. Shunlar's reaction was immediate. She crouched and whirled around, a small dagger glinting in her hand. But the presence was gone, if it had ever truly been there. The sound of someone clearing his throat made her turn again to see a severe frown on the face of the servant she had been following. He glared with disapproval at the dagger in her hand, sniffed at her in disgust, then turned and continued to lead her down the hall.

Shunlar shrugged and tucked the small silver blade away in its secret sheath at her side. She followed him into the anteroom where earlier she had been reluctantly relieved of her other weapons. The servant waited impatiently for her while she belted on her sword and then the wrist dagger sheath, before he led her down the corridor to the open courtyard.

Several men leaned against the courtyard wall, involved in a game of dice. As Shunlar stepped through the door into the daylight, two others who waited in the shadows raised their heads, making her feel as though she had stepped into a giant spiderweb. She shuddered as one of them stepped out of the shadows, the ragged pink scar on his left cheek vivid in the light of day.

"And who might you be?" he asked, smiling so that the scar crinkled even more.

"I have orders from Mayor Althones to find a stranger within the walls of Vensunor. I was given to believe that one of you might know of him and where he was last seen. Who of you knows where I might find such a person?" Shunlar gripped her sword's pommel, hoping her knuckles weren't white. She exhaled deeply and settled down within herself, into what appeared to be a more relaxed stance as she waited for a reply.

The dice game had been interrupted, but none of the players answered her. They just stared at her in silence. After an interminable interval, the man with the scar answered her, a faint hint of curiosity in his voice.

"That would be me that knows. I've seen a man who is light-skinned. His eyes are brown, light brown, and he has brown hair. He sports a brown cord in his braid, but so do you, I fancy. He's quite a bit taller than me. His ear is pierced, desert fashion, I should think. He's an outsider and asks a lot of questions."

As eager as he seemed to be to give a physical description of the man she had been hired to find, his companion chose to remain in the shadows, still leaning sullenly against the wall. When he spoke, his voice reluctantly rasped, "It's the Dragon's Breath Inn where he was last seen by me."

Something about that voice filled her with an urgency to leave. Still firmly gripping the pommel of her sword, Shunlar thanked the men and withdrew from the conversation as hastily as she could. None of them had gotten close enough to touch her, but Shunlar felt a great need for a bath. As the gate of the courtyard shut firmly behind her, she began a fast trot away from the Mayor's palace and toward the inn.

Before her boot steps became an echo, another servant came for the man with the raspy voice, who still waited in the shadows. Keeping his face hidden by his cloak, he was ushered into the audience hall, but this time another waited to interview him, as well as Mayor Althones. Only Althones spoke, however. The other man merely sat, quietly attempting to pierce the thoughts of the mercenary standing before him, whose face he could not see. What he saw, once he had entered the man's mind, was a fearful individual who drank and gambled far too much. The man also had memories of a severe master, the reason for his fear, and also the reason for his being known as trustworthy.

Mayor Althones asked, "You have seen the woman. What do you think? Can you manage to follow her and deliver her in one piece when I give the order? Understand, she has no small reputation for her ability with a sword, but a very generous reward should reduce the sting of any wounds she might inflict."

"Masters, I am merely a servant for another who, I can assure you, will not fail you." His voice was eerie. There was a persuasive quality to it that set both men at ease.

Althones smiled nervously. The dark man sitting near Mayor Althones held his fingertips pressed together against his lips, a brooding frown covering his face. He crooked a finger of the hand nearest Althones, a gesture for him to come closer. The mayor leaned closely, placing his ear near the dark man's lips. Instructions were whispered. Althones nodded then sat upright in his chair again.

Clearing his throat, he directed, "Bring your master here to us for a private audience . . . say late this evening, after dark. We will, of course, want to see his papers or any letters of recommendation. You are dismissed."

With a very low practiced bow, the cloaked man left the audience chamber. As he followed the servant down the hallway to the outer courtyard he seemed to glide, making no noise at all with his feet. This soundless walk made the servant extremely anxious. Once in the courtyard the mercenary spoke a few words to the man with the scarred face, who shook his head in agreement, and they parted company. Then the cloaked man left the palace, to report to his master.

Two

THE DRAGON'S BREATH INN WAS A POPULAR STOP for travelers as well as a comfortable tavern for the locals who frequented it each evening. Entering at early afternoon, Shunlar found the inn to be nearly empty. She quickly scanned the room, but her quarry was not to be found. She sat and ordered a mug of wine; when it arrived she was pleased to find it tasty and only slightly watered down.

On the spit over the huge firepit several haunches of meat were being turned, as well as what appeared to be an entire flock of ducks. The smell of the cooking herb- and garlic-covered meat made her mouth water. If she waited long enough she could have a fine meal, and it was nearly the end of the day. Perhaps she could afford to stay here a couple of nights. After all, hadn't she just been hired by Mayor Althones himself? Soon she'd have more coins in her purse; why hold on to the few she carried now? Her decision made, she drank down the wine and ordered another.

Three days later, her purse now quite empty and the man she had been hired to find and follow still eluding her, she decided to return to her home well beyond the gates of the city and send for help.

As soon as she returned to her tidy cottage, she released the messenger dove. Only one word was written on the note: Come.

*   *   *

They neared the cottage as the sun was getting low in the hills. Alglooth reached out with his mind, scanning the area to make sure no eyes would see them as they approached. When he determined that Shunlar was alone, he beckoned for Cloonth to come to his side. Silently she joined him, slipping her hand into his as their feet touched the ground. They walked the last distance together.

Tall and slender, with a long, angular face framed by thick, straight, shoulder-length white hair, Alglooth's yellow-amber eyes were his most startling feature. Cloonth, his mate, also had white hair, but hers was a mass of curls that framed her delicate face and cascaded down her back. Her eyes were a darker shade of yellow—very nearly gold—and almond-shaped.

Their leather clothing was dyed in forest colors to blend in with their surroundings. On top of their leathers, soft woolen cloaks draped across their shoulders, the hoods thrown back casually. These were the two who had raised and educated Shunlar, the fire-beings Alglooth and Cloonth. They were the sole descendants of a wizard's experiment that had gone awry: the only attempt at cross-breeding a dragon with a human. The only persons alive who knew of their existence were Shunlar and Bimily the shapechanger.

They had the gift of flight, along with a lot of green scales. Confined for the most part to their upper arms and legs, the scales were also scattered across their upper torsos. Alglooth stood nearly three heads taller than the average man; his iridescent green and blue wingspan was twice his height, it being necessary to carry his frame. Hers was a more delicate span of green and gold, she being only two heads taller than most.

Of the two, Cloonth was more reluctant to speak aloud, perhaps because she could barely control her fire-tongue. Smoke continually wisped from her delicate nostrils, whereas her mate exhaled smoke only when he became excited.

The moment Shunlar felt them land, she added another

log to the fire and lowered the spit so the cooking fowls would begin to crisp and brown. Though the distance for them was short as the crow flies, courtesy compelled her to have food and drink ready. Not to mention, of course, the fact that she had summoned them.

Her mind felt Cloonth's familiar touch as the couple approached, and Shunlar answered with her thoughts, true happiness coloring her reply. *So soon, the birds are just out of the nets! The jug is untapped!* Sometimes it was best to pretend one wasn't ready for company as a sign of good manners—especially when a favor needed asking.

Shunlar turned the spit another full turn, then pulled the stopper from the clay wine jug. Pleased with her choices for the meal, she smiled and poured the clear golden liquid into three silver goblets that waited on a small table of polished wood. With a sharp smack from the heel of her hand, she replugged the jug, then turned to open the door of the cottage for them. After embracing both of her guests, Shunlar offered them wine, which they delightedly accepted.

"Sit and refresh yourselves while I rescue our dinner from the coals before it is too late. I assume the distance you have traveled has made you hungry?"

"Do I suspect more than a routine information passing?" Alglooth asked as he savored the contents of his goblet.

"Please my whims, yes, special matters need addressing," came Shunlar's reply in Old Tongue. She spoke in the formal language to impress upon them the need for secrecy.

"Cannot this wait? I fear our fowls might become cold and disintegrate before our eyes," said Cloonth. When she was hungry Cloonth could be ruthless. Already sparks and flame were escaping from the corners of her mouth as she waited for their reply.

"Of course, Cloonth. We will eat first and discuss matters after our meal. Excuse my poor manners. Come, eat." Shunlar set the platter of steaming fowl before them.

Cloonth and Alglooth made quick work of the roasted

birds, proof that they were indeed hungry. When they had finished, Shunlar removed the platter that was now piled with bones, and replaced it with a bowl of warm water for washing their hands, and with towels to dry them.

"Please my whims, but our hunger now being sated, my thoughts return to the question of moments ago. What information passing is requested of us this day?" Alglooth asked Shunlar in Old Tongue as he dried his hands.

"The Lord Mayor has employed me to follow and observe a stranger within the walls of Vensunor and to make periodic reports. If I trusted him or any of his 'advisors' I would not have troubled either of you. But since you also know the character of the mayor, I need your assistance."

A curious look crossed the faces of Shunlar's dinner companions. Then, as she watched, a small cloud of smoke passed their lips, drifted up before their eyes and took form over their heads. As excitement took hold of them, their internal heat rose. They sat facing each other, rapidly blinking and exchanging information directly from one mind to another. Long ago they had initiated Shunlar in this unusual skill.

Cloonth turned toward Shunlar first, as tendrils of smoke rose from her nostrils. Alglooth turned and spoke, his words interjected with smoke.

"Five days ago my respected mate followed the heat tracks of a person she thought peculiar. She noticed he had entered the city by the South Gate so she suspected he was summoned, but his tracks led back to a small camp on the riverbed not far from here. Since they were not closer to you and whoever it was had returned to Vensunor, Cloonth felt you were safe. She assumed, as I did when she told me of finding the track, that the person was an initiate of the Temple on a solitary quest. Cloonth was sure you would be able to detect a presence if he came nearer. Also, you weren't home for her to inform you," he concluded with a final spark.

Cloonth's choosing to let Alglooth answer for her meant that she was embarrassed at having been discovered checking on Shunlar's safety. She carefully watched the younger woman and smiled as smoke continued to drift from her nostrils and lips.

Knowing tactful words had to be used in this moment, Shunlar replied softly, "I thank Cloonth for her watchfulness. I would not have questioned a questing initiate's encampment by the river. But then, none of us knew of potential danger from a stranger within Vensunor. Please show me the campsite on the river that you backtracked to." She was pleased at her choice of words and so was Cloonth.

To prove it, Cloonth answered out loud, spewing soot and flame into the room. "Yes. Follow me!"

They all laughed, happy to release the tension of the moment, and rose from the table together. Cloonth and Alglooth drew their cloaks around their bodies and covered their folded wings. Only a trained eye could detect the waver of image-casting that surrounded them. To an ordinary observer, they appeared to be an ordinary man and woman of normal height. The trio stepped outside into the twilight; there remained just enough daylight left for them to travel by.

As Cloonth led them down to the river the three moons rose, casting bright pearly light. Shunlar and Alglooth followed Cloonth in single file along the bank, toward the sounds and smells of rushing water. Shunlar reached out with a special awareness. As she did so her breathing changed, a pale greenish tint washed across her forehead, and from deep within her eyes leapt a green spark. Soon there appeared before her faint traces of a heat track suspended upon the air in the dim light. The heat track had a sinuous, catlike quality. Knowing that her companions saw it also, Shunlar remained silent, observing the heat track as she continued to follow Cloonth.

Cloonth grew more agitated by the minute, and sparks once more spewed from her lips. Mind to mind, she communicated with Alglooth and Shunlar, *Truly the pattern is different now. Something about it has changed since I dis-covered it days ago.*

Hidden within a cleft of rocks near the riverbed lay the charred remnants of a fire, a few small animal bones mixed within the ashes. Shunlar felt a slight tingle at the back of her neck. As her neck hairs rose, she stared at the remains of what had been someone's camp. Instinctively she began searching six inches above the ground in a quick backward and forward pattern. With a sudden inhalation of breath, she realized that unusual hex signs had been placed on the rocks and trees around this shelter. And something about the circular arrangement was compelling Cloonth and Al-glooth to stare at it, unable to step closer.

A numbness had traveled from their feet to their hips, and was coursing inch-by-inch up their bodies. As soon as it reached their eyes they would be unable to close them and they would be trapped. Cloonth and Alglooth quickly linked minds with Shunlar. *Send your awareness up to look at this scene from above and tell us if you see a way to break the trap that has ensnared us*, both voices whispered to her urgently.

Shunlar complied instantly, sending a thread of her awareness up to hover over the scene. She could see herself standing between Cloonth and Alglooth and felt a numb-ness slowly seeping up her legs. For some reason the numb-ness moved more slowly through her body than theirs, but already her feet were frozen to the spot upon which she stood.

I must find a way out of this or we are all doomed, she thought to herself as she quickly blinked and looked away. It was becoming increasingly difficult not to stare at the hex arrangement, and Shunlar began to breathe harder with the effort. Her strength was beginning to wane just as she noticed something outside the circle that had entrapped them.

"Look!" Shunlar shouted. "There, beside the water, an object shines."

Her shout broke Cloonth and Alglooth's fixed attention

long enough for them to blink, but they still had to strain with the effort of turning their heads to look in the direction where Shunlar's hand pointed. Once they averted their eyes, feeling returned to their bodies and they were able to move. Something glinted on the ground, but when they turned their attention back to her, Shunlar was now staring, unable to look away, trapped just as they had been seconds before.

From the shining object, blue and gold flecks of light spiraled upward in the air. Within the moving lights a form took shape which began to move and speak a strangely accented language that reverberated within her skull. The ground beneath Shunlar's feet seemed to turn to liquid and she felt as though she were sinking. She screamed and fainted.

Two pairs of strong hands grasped her arms and half carried, half dragged Shunlar behind the shelter of a pile of large rocks. They splashed river water in her face. Very slowly Shunlar became aware of the smell of smoke, and she coughed. She inhaled deeply, which induced more coughing, but it brought her back to consciousness.

"Whaaat haap . . . happened?" she stammered, leaning her head back on the boulder behind her.

"It appears our stranger has left a message behind. We were trapped by it momentarily, and you nearly passed from our sight. Explain please what you experienced," said Alglooth. The concern on his face, along with the smoke that billowed from his nose and lips, let her know just how serious the situation was.

Both Alglooth and Cloonth sat waiting, their smoke subsiding as their excitement calmed down.

Shunlar began, "I saw a bright object from which a spiral of lights rose, turning in the air. Within the spiral the form of a man appeared and began to speak. The voice rumbled so loudly that it shook the ground and opened it up. I saw the river mixing with the ground and I began to sink into one of the chasms." For a few seconds she wondered if in fact she hadn't sunk a few inches. One look at her mud-covered boots confirmed her suspicions. Cold drops of sweat dotted her brow. Within minutes her clothing was soaked. As waves of nausea and shock began rolling through Shunlar's body, Cloonth and Alglooth sat on either side of her, their firm yet gentle hands gripping hers until the shaking subsided. Then both mind-linked with her and as their awareness slid into hers, Shunlar regained a sense of calm.

Once again in control of her faculties, she unfolded the vision and experience directly into their minds. This talisman they had stumbled upon was very powerful. Whether it had been left by accident or design they could only guess.

What intrigued them the most was that no words that had been spoken by the apparition could be understood by them. That is, until Cloonth's eyes began to twinkle. "Truly this is a fine puzzle. Please my whims, but may I see again that part of your memory when the man began to speak?"

Shunlar closed her eyes. This time as she felt Cloonth's familiar touch entering her thoughts it was easier to review the memory without fear. The firm feeling of Cloonth deep within her brain allowed her to actually face the sparkling male. The vision's face emanated a look of pure power that would be difficult to counterfeit. Even in this third viewing of what had passed before, Shunlar felt her strength ebb as the man's eyes again held her frozen in that moment in time. The apparition's last spoken word enticed a chuckle from Cloonth, who listened and watched from the mind-link deep within her brain.

"Aha, trickery. Wizard's trickery." Cloonth laughed. "He not only speaks another language, but it is locked in a code as well. That is why his words cannot be understood. But whoever he is, somehow he suspects that a person, or persons, with our sense of heat trace sight might chance upon this place and his message. But that would mean he knows of my mate, myself, or you, Shunlar. How can this be?"

How indeed? As her companions helped her back to the cottage, the three remained in nonverbal communication, conveying images, emotions, and memories—as well as words—directly to each other's minds.

Shunlar asked, *Why did you not experience the same terror of the ground pulling you into it? And how was it that I was the only one to see and hear the man within the spiral of lights? And just what was that thing?* she asked, leaving no space for answers between questions.

Cloonth and Alglooth answered silently, intertwining phrases and words into sentences.

Somehow the vision was made for your eyes alone, Shunlar. Only by probing your mind's memory were we able to see and hear him. If it had not been for your watchfulness we could have been seriously harmed or ensnared or both. We are indebted to you, child. Their somber response conveyed the pride and deep love they felt for her.

Before they knew it, they had retraced their steps and were again at the door of her cottage. Upon entering Shunlar scanned, as always, for signs of intruders. There were none—except the familiar mice. Shunlur and the fire-beings sat before the fire and continued their mind exchange, until even Alglooth admitted he could no longer continue. As yet, none of their questions had been answered. The puzzle became more difficult to understand the longer they tried.

"The conclusion I am drawn to is this: It is a trap, and a highly sophisticated trap at that. Placed this close to your cottage, it can only be for you, Shunlar. But by whom was it placed? Can the Lord Mayor be behind this? I do not feel he has much of a mind for intrigue," Alglooth hissed quietly, a puff of smoke curling from one corner of his mouth. In the crackle of the fire it was impossible to tell who was emitting more sparks.

"If people of 'fine breeding' are setting a trap for you, Shunlar, what could be their purpose?" asked Alglooth.

Those words continued to ring in her mind long after the fire-beings had flown back to their home. Later, as Shunlar lay half-sleeping, she recalled the apparition's voice droning its indecipherable message within her brain, along with the words of Alglooth's last question. Suddenly she opened her eyes wide and sat up in bed. As her mind continued to repeat Alglooth's words, the bell-like tones of the sparkling man began to make sense. A correctly worded question is the key that unlocks the code, and in his unknowing wisdom Alglooth had handed her the key.

"Know, you who will understand my words, that you are in grave danger," rang the voice. "There is one who knows of your ancestry and would have you for dark purposes. I apologize for the discomfort you experience in receiving this message, but you will see it was necessary. Be warned. And be very careful, young one. We shall meet soon." The message ended there.

Young one! The message was for me, but who is he? And what does he mean by "your ancestry?"

Knowing that she must inform Cloonth and Alglooth, Shunlar got up to find writing paper and send the messenger dove. Suddenly the hairs on the back of her neck began to rise. Shunlar quickly scanned the approach to her cottage to discover several men in the distance approaching on foot. *Now why would anyone be about in the woods at this hour, and so near my door?* she asked herself.

The deciphered message would have to wait. The men were far enough off to give her a slight advantage of time. The new day was hours away, and she knew that before dawn so must she be. With a sigh Shunlar began to dress in the dark, belting her sword at her waist, strapping her wrist dagger in place, and draping her warm russet cloak over her shoulders. Lastly she collected a few necessary belongings and hastily put them into a pack that she slung over her shoulder. She slipped soundlessly out her door and into the forest.

It was easy to lie still in the underbrush as three noisy, foul-smelling goons trampled past her. As a satisfied smile began to form on her lips, the skin on the back of her neck tingled and her neck hairs rose with a sharp jump. Turning her head ever so slowly, she glimpsed two shadows creeping up to her hiding place. Acting with pure instinct, she pulled in her physical barriers, changing them to match the

size of a small woodland animal. As the two men passed
her she recognized their heat trace paths. They were the
men who had spoken to her from the shadows of Althones's
courtyard, the man with the large scar on his left cheek and
the other who had never ventured from the shadows.

*This becomes even more intriguing. Is Althones setting
me up, or do those two men work for another? Well, the
best place for me now is in the city, doing my job for the
Lord Mayor. Besides, it'll be at least two days before those
witless pieces of human refuse realize I'm not coming out
of the cottage.* Shunlar spoke to herself, the last statement
pure bravado in a halfhearted attempt at cheering herself
up. Truthfully, the last two men had startled her. She
calmed herself with a few deep breaths, then turned her
mind and steps toward Vensunor, keeping quietly to a path
that she knew well in dark or daylight.

Three

HIGH IN THE LEAFY CANOPY OF TREES, HE stretched out on the thick limb and said a silent prayer of thanks to the Great Trees. Being stationed to guard the northern part of the valley at this, the hottest time of the year, was considered a treat by most. He thought of his younger friends and chuckled at the memory of his own first years in the heat of the southernmost guard posts. There were few trees and not much shade due to the rock formations at that end of the valley. Initiation rites were hard on the young.

Even though he was at rest, Loff remained alert, scanning the approach to the valley of his birth with his mind as well as his eyes. As he did so, his thoughts wandered again to his dream of the last few nights. He could hardly call it a dream, though. Waking in a pool of sweat to haunting visions and voices was not his idea of a dream. This particular dream began the same way every time. There he would be, dropping to the ground from a tree in slow motion, while off in the distance a person strode toward him at a fast clip, a tall walking staff in his hand.

Loff's reverie was interrupted by a large insect buzzing close to his face. As he swatted it, he lost his balance. The next thing Loff knew he was falling, and to his dismay he was falling in slow motion, just as in the dream. The limb on which he had been resting was nearly four times his height, yet he landed ever so gently on his feet, barely raising dust. Straining greatly, Loff finally managed to lift his head. It took even more effort to open his eyes. He blinked and focused on a person in the distance with a walking staff in his hand coming toward him. Loff tried to speak, but every sound he uttered was distorted, just as in his dream. Not only were his movements being stifled, so was his voice. Loff felt as though he were pushing his body through honey, as though a tremendous weight pressed in on him from all around. Panic seized him as the stranger closed the gap between them with his fast pace.

Though it pained him to move, Loff knew he had to signal his people. Sweat dripped from his face as he raised the ram's horn to his lips. At that moment he felt the hand of the stranger touch his arm. The touch released Loff from the heavy weight of the air and he found himself face to face with the man from his dream.

"Imagine the luck of finding you at this post, Loff. I have been reaching out to you in my dreams. Don't you recognize me? I am Gwernz, your uncle, returning to my valley and my family. Please do not fear me," he said reassuringly.

It had been fifteen years since Loff had seen his mother's brother. People were certain he had long been dead but here the man stood, nearly out of breath with excitement and very much alive. As Loff stared into his uncle's black eyes, he felt as though he were looking into a reflecting pool. There was no mistaking the fact that they were related, though one of them had more gray hair and the other had the well-muscled body of a young man of twenty years. They were the same height, and their hair had the same auburn sheen and waves. Gwernz had a beard that was specked with gray, while Loff's face was colored with several days' growth of dark reddish-brown stubble.

"Uncle, is it truly you?" Loff asked, grasping his arm. "We thought you dead these many years. Where have you been? How is it that you come back to us now?"

Physical contact between the two men sent a flood of memories and mind pictures directly into Loff's consciousness. What he saw clearly indicated this could only be his uncle Gwernz, yet the man standing before him was changed. The strangeness of their encounter compelled Loff to open himself to depths within in a way he had never done before. Easily reading the older man's thoughts, he became aware of the magnitude of power his uncle now possessed and attempted to pull away from the man. But before Loff could feel the slightest bit of discomfort, Gwernz seemed to drop a wall of smoke across Loff's mind. Released so suddenly, Loff staggered and raised his hand to his forehead as he caught his breath.

"I am sorry to have to do that to you, Loff, but you need more training if you are to continue to open yourself up to others so deeply. Does anyone yet suspect how strong your abilities for opening are?"

Loff blushed. It was not often someone complimented the young man, and his face seemed to be on fire. "No, Uncle. I am even unsure of what you ask. I have had no training in this opening you speak of. Because I am unable to project my thoughts forward, I have been told I have small talent for mind-speaking."

"Hmmm, we shall see about that. But you have asked me many questions. Let me begin this way." Putting his hands on Loff's shoulders, he began his tale.

Gwernz had been reputed to be the greatest storyteller of the Valley, and now as he passed information directly into Loff's awareness, careful not to allow his nephew to open any deeper than was safe, his eloquence seemed honed to needle sharpness. Every once in a while he would interject a bit of technique to Loff, which the young man quickly understood and put into action.

"Listen with only part of yourself. Never allow your internal barriers to completely dissolve," the older man gently instructed. "Like this, and you won't tire easily, understand?"

"Yes, I feel that," answered Loff. "Ah, so that's what you meant."

Gwernz told in words, pictures, and thoughts of how the

early winter storm fifteen years earlier had taken his hunting party by surprise. Blinded by the sudden blizzard conditions, he had fallen in an ice-filled pass and been knocked unconscious, thus closing off his mind to all who scanned for him. The rest of the hunting party passed him by, not knowing where he was or that he was lying so close to those who searched for him, buried beneath a blanket of snow. Later, as night was falling, he was rescued by a caravan of traders returning to Tonnerling, home of the Cave People, as they were called. The translation of Tonnerling meant, in Old Tongue, people of the water caves. They were primarily a seafaring folk who had lived in the natural caves that bordered the ocean when they first settled there. Now stood great stone houses, carved from the rocks.

For many days, while delirious, Gwernz "told" those people who had physical contact with him the past events of their lives. A heated debate followed between the men who had found him and their leaders. Most were wary of the stranger who could put ideas into their minds and either wished to let him die or put him to death. But luckily for Gwernz, they were won over by a powerful benefactor, a kindly wizard named Vinnyius, and Gwernz was placed under his protection. He taught Gwernz many new skills, the most valuable being wizardry. Gwernz was a natural, or so it seemed. However, none of the Cave People knew the technique of mind-touch that was common knowledge to the people of the Valley of Great Trees.

As the years slipped away, Gwernz gained much renown among his captors. By their law, only the death of his benefactor could set him free, and that is how he came to be walking into the Valley on this day. The old man had taken ill and after long days of nursing from the healers as well as from Gwernz, his time had finally come to die. While Gwernz worked over the man in a healing trance state, he had contacted the members of his family in their dreams. For all the fifteen years of his captivity Gwernz had never shown the old wizard the true depth of his mind's powers. The old man died happy, for he also participated in the mind-link. Upon feeling the emotions passing from Gwernz to his sister, Vinnyius advised Gwernz to return to the valley of his birth so that he could someday act as liaison between their two worlds.

"Peace between the Valley and Cave People has long been my secret dream," were Vinnyius's dying words to Gwernz.

As the final scenes of the mind-link trailed off, Loff saw the image of a woman for the briefest of seconds. Remembering his duty, Loff sounded his horn, signaling that a known visitor was entering the valley by the north path. Since it was two days before Loff was scheduled to be relieved from his guard post, he rapidly blew another signal, asking to be relieved early.

"This might take a few hours, Uncle. You may wait or go on ahead. Do you remember the way?" Loff asked with a sly smile.

"The way into our Valley is forever burned into my heart. Tell me of your mother. Does she still bake the tastiest pastries in the Valley? How you've grown, Loff . . ." Myriad questions crowded his thoughts as tears in his eyes revealed his deep happiness. The two men spent the next hours verbally and nonverbally asking questions and answering them, getting reacquainted.

Meanwhile, the Valley was caught up in a blur of activity. Rumors had been flying for days, ever since the dreams had begun. Marleah knew the instant she heard Loff's signal who the "visitor" was. Her eyes glistened as she felt her brother drawing nearer and her hands flew, mixing flour and eggs and butter and the perfect amount of spices. Her head filled with memories of Gwernz the small boy, caught stealing pastries from the pantry, chin and lips smeared with butter and spice, shaking his head "no" when asked if he had eaten the cakes. Laughter filled her kitchen. How wonderful to be able once more to gaze deep into the eyes of her brother and also deep into his mind. It was Gwernz who had first awakened her gift of mind-delving. Until he had, no other could budge her mind open. Stubbornness was a quality she relied on even to this day.

As the aroma of pastries filled the air, neighbors arrived at her door with food and drink and sincere congratulations. All the people shared their wealth in this Valley, and soon roasts were turning on the spit and garlands of flowers were piled and hung everywhere in the communal hall. It truly would be a homecoming feast of the kind that hadn't happened here for many years.

The torches were lit by a runner as Gwernz and Loff entered the gates of the compound. Both recognized the honor being given this returning son; it was still several hours till sunset and torches were seldom lit except after sunset and on ceremonial occasions. People lined the way, their faces smiling and their hands outstretched. Gwernz shook hands with them all—with Loff at his elbow, attempting to hurry him along. Finally he stood at the doorway of the family home. He knew Marleah was inside waiting by the fire. Gwernz stepped over the threshold and took his place beside her at the hearth.

She handed him the wick and spoke. "Welcome to your home, my brother. I have kept this fire burning for your return, as our parents asked."

He took the offered wick from her hands and answered. "My sister, this house and all in it now belong to you, as custom demands. You do me great honor in offering it to me. I ask for nothing more than shelter under your roof until I find another."

"Gwernz, brother, I have kept your old room for you, just as you left it. Loff and I are alone here now. Please talk no more of other shelter. This is truly your home too. Besides," she replied with tears threatening to overflow her glistening eyes, "just try to get rid of us after all this time!"

With tears and laughter the reunited sister and brother hugged each other, while most of the inhabitants of the Valley tried to squeeze into the house.

"Mother, Uncle, enough of these tears," Loff finally interrupted. "We have days of feasting to begin and I'm famished!"

Four

SWEAT TRICKLED DOWN THE MIDDLE OF HIS BACK as the young guard hurried down the dimly lit corridor past sputtering oil lamps. He carried a message in one hand and had to keep reminding himself not to crush the scroll with his grip as he repeated his instructions over and over to himself.

1. Carry this message to Lord Creedath immediately.
2. DON'T speak to him.
3. Wait for a reply.

He swallowed drily as he showed the guards at the door the message he had to deliver. Being well-trained themselves, they spoke not a word, but each took hold of the great brass handles of the heavily burled double doors. One man pounded twice, a sound that echoed down the hallway, and then together they pulled open the doors, the air making only a slight sucking noise. The young guard's boots made a hollow echo as they crossed the wooden floor, soon muffled by plush woolen carpets. The sounds stopped as suddenly as they had begun as he snapped to attention.

Creedath raised his head from the papers spread across his desk and glared at Ranth, the young guard. "What is this interruption? I gave orders that I was to be disturbed only for an emergency. This had better be one."

Ranth's knees felt as if they had suddenly turned to putty,

26

and there seemed to be demons flying around his head, yet he remembered himself suddenly and, bowing low, went to one knee with his outstretched fist offering the scroll. He trained his eyes on the pattern of the carpet and dared not raise his head. Almost as soon as he knelt, the visions stopped and he breathed a bit easier. Now he focused his thoughts only on being released from such close proximity to Creedath.

Lord Creedath rose from his chair and walked around his desk to stand before the young messenger. He snatched the scroll from the upraised hand and with an amused smile said, "Excellent poise in one so young."

Ranth continued to concentrate on the carpet and the tips of Creedath's boots just inches away from his head. He had to work hard to control his breath as he felt the master of the castle appraising him intently. A small involuntary shudder washed over him, but he regained his composure.

"You may stand and wait for a reply," Creedath informed him in an absentminded tone.

Ranth slowly stood, keeping his gaze downward.

"Inform the chief steward to come to me at once. And instruct the awaiting servant to tell his master, yes. Understand?"

A nod and a low bow was his silent answer.

"Dismissed," came Creedath's reply through a sinister smile.

With another snap to attention, Ranth suddenly felt a buoyancy return to his body and was aware of feeling released as he bowed again, turned and retraced his steps, extremely relieved. Delivering this message was the most difficult order he'd been instructed to carry out since he had been placed at the post of personal guard to Lord Creedath, as well as the first time he had ever had to stand directly before him. Several men had died in face-to-face discussions with Creedath. Ranth could now understand why. If he had been the slightest bit neglectful of his training or instructions he might have met a similar fate.

Ranth was a slender young man with an olive complexion, black curly hair, and an elegant carriage that set him apart from others. He had no recollection of his family, having been raised by the monks of the Temple from infancy, as was the custom with unwanted children. The story was told that he had been found on the Temple steps early one morning with no sign of family or clan marking on his body or his clothing. Someone had taken great pains to make sure his parents couldn't be traced.

At the proper time he chose his name by picking a number from the Great Cauldron of the Temple. Ranth was his choice, a name that brought a smile to the lips of most of the monks. Many years would pass before he would come to know that *Ranth* meant *changeling* in the Old Tongue.

The Temple monks had educated him well, with much love and compassion. Ranth learned quickly to read and write. His understanding of the meaning of numbers, as well as his grasp of languages, was a constant source of amazement to his teachers. Indeed, he seemed to absorb each new subject that was taught him and hungered for more knowledge. Spending so many years engrossed in study had produced a maturity in Ranth beyond his years. The monks suspected that someday he would take his place as one of the Masters of the Temple, and in their wisdom about such matters—although without Ranth's knowledge or permission—he was being groomed for the job.

Recognizing his value, the monks also hid him from sight when the head servants of the great houses came to look over foundling boys or girls for indenture into servitude. Many preferred to leave the Temple, though Ranth could never understand why. Everyone was not cut out for a life of learning and meditation. They needn't have bothered to hide him, though. Ranth was a small child and he grew more slowly than others his age. His size alone kept him in the undesirable category.

He was several years past his fifteenth birthday when he was first sighted by the merchant Creedath. On that particular day Ranth walked along beside his eldest teacher, Master Chago, carrying a basket filled with purchases, drinking in the noise and bustle of the clothsellers' market. He hadn't a care in the world. Master Chago had long ago taken a personal interest in tutoring Ranth. They were constant companions, and Ranth looked upon the older man as his father.

"Ranth, my son, do you feel as though you can manage to carry this entire roll of cloth?" asked Master Chago.

"Of course, Master. The sun is nearly set and our basket is all but empty," he answered.

As he finished speaking, Ranth became startled by a touch that felt like the sear of a hot knife across his back. When he turned to see who this bold attacker was, his gaze fell upon a tall, commanding presence astride a large roan stallion. It was the merchant called Creedath, Lord Creedath to everyone who knew and feared him. Attempting to appear feeble-minded and hide the look of recognition on his face, Ranth spoke louder to his teacher than necessary, "Have no fear, Master, my back and legs are strong."

It didn't work. Once more Ranth felt the talons of the horseman rake his back, clawing through his defenses. Years ago Ranth had mastered the art of weaving a protective barrier around his body. Once properly woven into place, there were few who could penetrate it; until now only his teachers had managed, but never so savagely. Somehow this brooding stranger had done so twice with such force that Ranth fell to his knees, gasping for breath, leaning heavily against the basket he had been carrying.

Master Chago, aware of what was happening, knelt at Ranth's side, supporting him with his arm and soothing words, his mind straining to help Ranth reconnect his inner shield of protection. He had met Creedath many times in the past and was aware of his treacherous, often painful tactics. The man was a menace. Suddenly Chago found himself fighting to keep the merchant's strong psychic shards from penetrating his own shields.

"Boy," Chago whispered low, "act as though your very life hung on a thin wire. Keep secret all we have taught you from this day on, for I fear I will not see you again in this lifetime. If you manage to break free, return to the safety of the Temple immediately.''

In a whirl of motion surprising for one his age, Master Chago turned and stood with his staff poised and ready, his cloak falling on the ground behind him. His motions were graceful and efficient but not swift enough to deflect the arrow that pierced his heart. In numb fear Ranth looked upon the body of his friend and protector as the last breath sighed from the monk's lips.

Though Ranth tried several times to move, he remained frozen on all fours. Disbelieving what was happening, a great trembling seized his body but it wasn't shock. Someone, something, had taken control of his limbs and he began to spasm in an effort to stand. Ranth finally found himself standing, trembling, as a large shadow passed across his face. At that moment a compelling voice pierced his head from the inside and he felt his body snap to attention.

"Excellent," Creedath said. "We will take this young lamb with us. I have need of a trained body servant, and I can tell Master Chago and his pack have done a fine job on this one. I will deal with the monks later.

"Guard," he ordered, "deliver the body to the Temple and if anyone asks, explain that he acted in a manner most unwise." Riding away, Creedath muttered to no one in particular, "When will they learn that nothing can remain hidden from me?"

Blackness began to descend upon Ranth as he heard a voice from far away ask, "What is your name, boy?"

"I am called Ranth," he heard his voice reply from what seemed to be a very deep chasm.

"Catch him as he falls so he doesn't bruise that fine young face," came a snarled command across the black abyss. Ranth was only slightly aware of being thrown across the back of a horse and jostled for a time.

Meeting Lord Creedath that day in the marketplace was to change his life. No one had foreseen in the numbers the murder of Master Chago or the abduction of Ranth. Only the blackest of wizardry could be involved.

That had been years ago. Somehow Ranth had survived. Being cut off from everyone and everything he had known had had a very sobering effect on the young man. The people under Creedath's roof were kind enough to him, for the most part, especially the women. He had never seen so many women so scantily dressed in all his life. There had been women in the Temple, of course, but everyone there dressed alike. And Ranth was a constant source of amusement to them, as he often stared with his mouth agape. But the men treated him with a distant sort of respect, as if they knew the secret of his fate and weren't allowed to disclose it.

Each day in the palace seemed to open a new wound in Ranth. At sunrise he would be roused from his small bed along with the others in the barracks, by the sound of the trumpet. An hour of work in the stables was followed by another hour of workout in the yard with the sword and staff. At least in this he was treated as all the other young cadets, but most were four to five years younger than he, a fact he wisely never disclosed. After breakfast there were hours of combat practice, then the baths, then lunch and time in midday for rest. For him afternoons would be spent learning the correct etiquette befitting a servant in the palace. In this he was separate from his companions of the yard.

At night, exhausted, he would sometimes sneak out and climb to the top corner of the palace walls and if the wind was right, he would just barely hear the slight whisper of chanting floating on the breeze from the Temple on the other side of the city. How he longed for the cool solitude of the Temple, remembering the hours spent over manuscripts, quiet meditations beside the pool in the Temple courtyard, nights listening to the ancient teachings as the wind played its music with the trees. Reading and writing were not taught to cadets or servants here in the palace.

"Keep secret all we have taught you from this day on . . ." The voice of Master Chago echoed in his memory. Each night he secretly practiced the mind protections that kept his thoughts and feelings barricaded safely from the touch of those around him. Each night he was aware of the touch of his abductor at the edges of his mind, and Ranth carefully projected the picture of a frightened young boy for his new master to see. As the years and his training hardened him, Ranth less and less often projected fear. Whether his boldness betrayed him or time just plain ran out Ranth could never guess, but one day the housekeeper, Mistress Ranla, sent for him.

Changes occurred rapidly. Ranth's status vastly improved. He was assigned his own room, which contained more than a mattress and box for his meager belongings. There was a small fireplace in the corner. The mattress was off the floor, set on a real bedframe, with blankets and pillows provided in a carved wooden chest at the foot of the bed. A matching tall wooden cupboard sat next to the wall; it contained clothing and even a pair of soft leather boots of the kind worn indoors. His rough training shirt and pants were replaced with the softer, closely cut clothing of the house guard. Next to that was a table with an ornate washbasin, a mirror, and a silver candleholder. Two small drawers contained soap, a razor, linens, and candles. He was massaged, bathed, manicured, and perfumed, and his curly black hair was pulled back and braided warrior-style, bound with only an undyed piece of leather. He had never let his real sword techniques be known to anyone.

One morning, as his duties were recited to him, he stumbled over the instructions again, pretending to be confused. His young teacher, Carek, the servant who had been put in charge of seeing that Ranth understood the basics of table serving, patiently began to repeat the procedure. The game could have continued for weeks if Mistress Ranla had not been eavesdropping in the corridor just outside the door. Both young men snapped to attention and bowed their heads as she entered the room. Neither had to look at her face to see her anger; the room bristled with it.

"Ranth," she bit off his name sharply, "why is this game of wits being played upon Carek? I, myself, have seen you understand more complex matters than this in one quarter of the time. I see no reason for it other than that you are bored and feel the need for amusement. That will change immediately. Report at once to Lieutenant Meecha for extra duty. Both of you!''

"Yes, Mistress Ranla," Ranth and Carek answered quietly as they bowed.

Perhaps a soft touch to her mind will affect her tone with us. As this thought formed in Ranth's mind, he began to send a sliver of telepathic touch toward Mistress Ranla. Sooner than he expected, her face dropped its strained, stern look, to be replaced by a surprised, faraway expression. Startled by the immediate change on her face, Ranth began to retract his touch, but not before he heard Ranla's thoughts loudly ringing in his brain: *Why would the Master seek me with his mind-touch at this hour?*

"Go, Ranth," she hissed between her teeth, "and take Carek with you before I strike."

As both young men ran down the corridor, Ranth questioned whether it had been wise to reach out to Mistress Ranla with his mind-touch. Had she truly mistaken his touch for Lord Creedath's? And could Creedath have been aware of it?

What a fool I've been! This is exactly what Master Chago warned me against. If I am ever to escape from this place, I must use greater caution from now on, he told himself. And he began practicing the secret mind protection techniques over again.

Lieutenant Meecha guffawed at the two young men as they told their story. He had befriended Carek years ago and now, as Carek openly retold how Ranth had been tricking him by feigning stupidity these last few days, laughter mixed with respect began to show in his eyes.

"Well, you'd better act like I've given you something awful to do. Start with polishing all the shields, and when you're done I'll think of more. You two aren't the first bunch I've had to deal with this week. Trouble must be brewing. Ranla usually has her emotions under control, but not this week. Best have a talk with her . . . crazy . . . emotional . . . thinks she can dump her problems on me all the time . . .'' His words trailed off as he stomped away in search of the housekeeper.

Lieutenant Meecha was right. There had been many hands busy here this week. Everything had a brilliant sheen to it already. Holding the polishing cloths in their hands, they each propped a shield next to themselves and leaned back against the cool wall. Both young men blinked at each other in the subdued light of the armory, then doubled over into fits of laughter.

That day seemed years away from the present. Ranth returned his thoughts to the duties at hand as he headed down the corridor to the meeting room where the messenger awaited instructions.

Upon entering the room Ranth felt a lightheaded queasiness wash over him. The chief steward, a dour old man named Derlow, had joined the messenger and they sat together, waiting in uneasy silence. Both men stood and as Ranth approached them, he realized the reason for the queasiness of his stomach: the stranger's image was wavering! He was casting an illusion over his features to change the way he looked.

Why would he do that? Who could he be that he must alter his appearance?

The messenger bowed to Ranth, as he would to an equal, and stood patiently waiting for his orders. Pretending not to notice anything unusual, Ranth nodded his head to the man, then bowed to the chief steward. Protocol demanded that he address Derlow first and not the stranger.

"I have been instructed by Lord Creedath to say he wishes you to report to him at once." Ranth bowed to Derlow when he had finished.

"As my lord wishes. And your message for this one?" Derlow asked through pursed lips. His demeanor was meant to instruct as well as scold. Not bothering to wait for a reply, he headed toward the door.

Ranth's reply was a quick nod. Turning toward the wait-

ing servant, Ranth said, "Lord Creedath has also instructed
me to give you this message for your master: Yes. Only
the one word, yes."

Again the image of the man before him wavered. Ranth
looked at him suspiciously, then shot a quick glance at Derlow, but the old steward had already left the room. As fast
as he could without running, Ranth turned to leave, reluctant to turn his back on the man who still stood there staring
after him. He could feel a prickling up and down his back
as he did so. Whoever this person was, he was not the
servant he pretended to be.

Five

JUST AS THE SUN WAS TURNING EVERYTHING A hazy shade of mauve, Shunlar approached the main road to Vensunor. Yawning, she shifted the weight of her pack and joined others who were traveling toward the city to trade. None knew her by sight, but the sword hanging at her side and the manner in which she wore her hair made her profession known to them. Some people greeted her, while others chose to look straight ahead. Nevertheless, she was in pleasant company for the time being.

Those on foot, like Shunlar, soon passed the heavily laden carts. She looked over the packed wagons, some piled high with food, others with leather clothing and boots, while still others carried items such as pots, bowls, and jugs. She smiled smugly to herself. *Yes, it's market day. With so many more people within and outside the walls of Vensunor, it will be easier to pass unnoticed.*

"Besides," she mused, "I am in need of a new pair of winter boots." As she looked about, she noticed that the familiar heat path of the person who had camped at the river seemed suddenly to come out of the nearby forest, cross the main road that she and the other travelers walked down, and continue up to the South Gate. There it ended abruptly, just as Cloonth had said. She walked onward to the main entrance of the city, her step a little lighter. *This seems as if it's already too easy*, she thought to herself.

She reveled in the sounds and smells of the city at sun-

36

rise. Weavers and tinkers were setting up their stalls for the day's trading, arranging stacks of brightly dyed cloth and leather, beads and ribbons, pots and pans. Farmers were busily arranging their wagons on the level side of the road to sell their fruits and vegetables. Inside the gates, the cooks and bakers of the many inns of Vensunor had been hard at work; meat on great spits had been hoisted onto racks to be turned for hours over the fires while loaves of bread browned in the maws of enormous stone ovens.

To quiet a growling stomach, Shunlar purchased buns laced with pungent spices and dried fruits, and to wash them down, a heavily honeyed mug of tea. Everywhere colors became more vibrant as the sun slowly changed its dawn hues of red and pink to the quieter shades of morning.

She headed toward the Lane of Cobblers, finishing her breakfast as she strolled along. The stalls were just being set up. She stopped to eye a shiny pair of black leather boots, tooled with intricate flower patterns down the sides and across the heels. The cobbler watched her from the corner of his eye, nodding to her as she bowed to his artistry. She knew the man well from past dealings. It wasn't wise to approach him until his booth was completely set up. He was good at his craft, but very temperamental.

Shunlar walked past the South Gate, licking the last sticky traces of food from her fingers as she nonchalantly inspected the fading remnants of heat trace glimmering upon the air. Yes, it appeared the one who had been at the river encampment had entered this way many days ago. *It begins*, she thought to herself as she followed the faint trail.

Initially it was difficult, there having been so many people down these streets in the past five or six days. A heat trace could be washed away by rain, blown away by wind, or just fade gradually. Turning a corner, she saw several more sets of the same pattern; some stronger ones appeared to have been made just this morning. Looking up, she found the sign of the Dragon's Breath Inn hanging overhead. Taking her time to walk through the doorway and select a table took great effort, but she somehow managed to control her impulse to bolt into the room. Once she was seated at the far corner table, however, fatigue began to pull her eyelids down.

Since the tavern was empty except for one or two patrons, Shunlar decided the best thing to do was get some sleep. She had been walking for more hours than she wanted to remember. The innkeeper saw her yawn and she nodded when Shunlar pointed at the stairs. Going up and down the stairs was the heat trace of the person she followed, and it looked as though the freshest trace had been made last night.

Without looking directly at Shunlar, the large blonde woman began climbing the stairs with a stack of fresh towels in her arms. "Would yew be wantin' to bathe now or later?" her muffled voice asked into the towels.

"Later will be fine, thank you, innkeeper." Another yawn escaped as she followed the woman's ample hips down the hallway, the sounds of snoring emanating from behind most of the doors. As they passed the room where the heat trace had entered and left many times in the past week, Shunlar asked, "Do you have a full house at this time of the year?"

"Yes, mistress," was the only answer. The woman showed her into a small, clean room. Shunlar hung her cloak on the peg, removed her boots, and was asleep once her head touched the pillow.

Later that evening Shunlar returned to the quiet corner table, where she could sit with her back to the wall. She crossed her ankles before her as she propped her feet up on another chair and then uncrossed them, pleased to hear the squeak of new leather. The boots would take some time to break in, but they were not uncomfortable. She continued to admire the new boots and even took a piece of cloth to the toes as she waited for her dinner. Although she looked preoccupied, Shunlar knew where every other person in the room sat or stood and what they were speaking about. One lone man, the person whose heat trace she was so familiar with, sat a little to the left of the door, sipping his wine. His thoughts seemed clouded by the drink.

She was hungry and Bente, the innkeeper, placed before her a plateful of delicately seasoned roasted mutton and vegetables. From large pockets, Bente plucked a spoon and a knife and asked, "To drink . . . ?" waiting absently for a reply as she set the utensils down.

"Just water, innkeeper."

As Shunlar ate she asked herself again the questions she had been puzzling over, watching the stranger sitting alone with his pitcher of wine. *Why would he enter by the South Gate? He could have been summoned and been made to enter that way, but by whom?* She quickly became interested in her plate of food again as the man casually looked in her direction.

Her mind went back to remembering what she knew about the South Gate. *Unless a person knows of that gate, it cannot be found. To the untrained eye, it looks like just another part of the walls that surround Vensunor. Without my powers of heat trace sight, the gate would have remained a myth, something with which adults scare small children. Only high Temple officials know how to find it on the two days of the year when it is visible. Enchantment opens it for some, but only with the cooperation of the Temple, and only at dark.*

As she watched the man from the corner of her eyes, she made a startling connection: This was the stranger she had been hired to follow! Why had he made a camp so near her cottage? Her trust in Mayor Althones had never been strong, and now she suspected the mayor of being the person who had set the trap by the river. But how would he know of such things? Althones wasn't a particularly clever man, and he spent so much time intoxicated, she suspected that what little intelligence he did possess was being burned away by all the substances he consumed. Creedath must be behind all this. That thought made her shudder. She looked once more at the stranger who sat calmly sipping his wine and thought she detected the faintest trace of a smile on his face.

There was something so very different about him. As she watched him from the other side of the room, the tiny hairs on the back of her neck rose, then lay down. As she suspected, this involuntary movement predicted his rising, stretching, and walking to the door of the crowded inn. She carefully threw a few coins onto the table, rose, and followed him into the night.

As soon as her boots touched the cobblestones her senses came fully alert, reaching outward toward the man's back. The closeness of the room had insisted she dampen her abilities, which she did easily by making a slight adjustment to her metabolism. Only a person who knew what to look for could possibly detect the change in her breathing pattern that was closely followed by a greenish tint that washed across her forehead. Once again in the open—as if the middle of a town could ever be considered so—she reached out in the direction of his heat path. A small spark of green deep within her eyes jumped forward and signaled the correct path by setting it aglow in the dark street. Each heat path was unique in its pulse and design, and she had been aware of this one for days.

Could he have special powers of sight? Could he be a wizard who opened the gate by enchantment? Shunlar continued asking herself questions about the stranger as she followed him through the streets. Since he had left the inn she had tracked his heat trace down several crooked lanes. Now she realized that she had allowed her mind to wander just a little too far, tracking being such an easy task for her. She realized that she was in the part of the city that was inhabited by the pleasure-mongers but was unsure just where it was she had ended up.

Stopping to get her bearings, Shunlar became aware of the sound of breathing coming from a nearby doorway. She quickly realized that the person in the doorway was not the man she had been following. "Impossible," she muttered under her breath. One building ahead she could see that familiar heat trace turn the corner and vanish from sight.

In seconds Shunlar pulled in her sensing awareness, changed her heartbeat, and pulled alcohol traces from her cells to enhance her breath. She stumbled drunkenly and muttered curses as she weaved down the street. The ploy seemed to work at first, but after a few turns the patch of skin at the nape of her neck began to tingle, followed by the springing up of her neck hairs. "Bucket of manure," she cursed under her breath as she realized that now *she* was being followed.

Shunlar stumbled again, deliberately. Her mind was working fast. *How did I manage to let this one get behind me when I was so sure he was ahead of me? He tracks nearly as well as I do. Damn if I'll be caught.* She swore under her breath and slipped into the next alleyway.

There were piles of trash on one side, and barrels of goods filled a large wagon that sat waiting to be unloaded on the other. Where to hide? She dove under the wagon and pulled her awareness in even closer to her middle. She changed her breath and sped up her heart rate to match that of a small rodent's heartbeat pattern. The hairs on the back of her neck stood on end and tingled.

From beneath the wagon she watched as her follower stood at the entrance to the alleyway. Shunlar felt his mind probe reach out, and she quickly projected the awareness of a small rodent to meet his touch. For a moment he seemed confused, reluctant to enter the alleyway. He retracted his mind probe for a few seconds and, without warning, quickly blasted another projection at Shunlar. Too late, she gasped as the strength of this contact broke through her image. Her next move was predictable; with sword in hand she rolled from beneath the wagon, stood up and faced her opponent.

Standing nearly a foot taller than she was a slim, well-muscled, dark-featured man. His hair was black and curly, braided in an intricate pattern, desert-fashion, and bound with black leather. In Vensunor, black leather in a man's braid meant he was a sword-for-hire and a very skillful one at that. A jewel glinted in his left earlobe. Beneath his long cloak, Shunlar could tell he gripped the pommel of an unsheathed sword. She could sense his muscles relaxing and contracting as they faced one another, both of them carefully controlling their breathing. Because of their prior "contact" she knew he would be aware of her mind touch, and so she reached out with her thoughts and asked, *Now that we are face to face, tell me who hired you, and the reason why, if you value your life.*

His mind touch echoed in a thick accent, *Such bold words for so small a woman. Can you use that weapon or is it merely an ornament?*

Shunlar advanced a few steps and deftly carved the air just under the stranger's nose, untying, not cutting, the cord of his cloak with the point of her sword. As his cloak fell to the ground, with the point of her sword inches away from his throat, she saw that his skin had a dark sheen to it. Again he reached out with his thoughts, though this time they were humbler than before.

Forgive me, lady. I see you are not joking. I meant no harm by my careless words and I have no great wish to die at this time. As he finished he backed up slightly and carefully bowed as one does to an equal, never taking his eyes off her.

This gesture seemed to satisfy Shunlar for the moment, and she returned the courtesy, never taking her eyes off him, never moving the sword that was pointed at his throat. His movements were unusual in their precision. His thick accent made her unsure whether she truly understood the meaning of his words. Something about the accent was also uncomfortably familiar. It was the way he didn't answer her question that bothered her. Lying while in mind contact was virtually impossible; alluding to the answer, however, was a most often used technique. And worse, the hairs at the nape of her neck refused to lay down.

"Where are you from? I've never seen the likes of you before. You are not from this city," she stated out loud.

"No," came his quietly whispered reply, "I am not, as

you say, from this city." And with a wry half-smile, he relaxed his grip on his sword and slowly sheathed his weapon. "Lady, perhaps we can discuss this over a drink. I have lodgings not far from here, and the inn will most likely be crowded at this time of night. You will be safe with all eyes on us in a public place." The stranger turned his palms up in a gesture of open sincerity.

Strong emotions emanated from the man standing before her, feelings that conveyed trust, and Shunlar felt a smile beginning to tug at the corners of her mouth. She bit her tongue to stop it for her eyes in full light would have betrayed her growing fascination. Finally the hairs on her neck relaxed and flattened and she allowed herself a deep breath.

"I accept your offer, stranger. But I will have your name first," she demanded quietly.

"You may call me Kessell," he said softly. "And you are called . . . ?"

"Shunlar," she said, suddenly remembering that she had been hired to follow him, and by whom. Caution crept back into her mood, yet she allowed her annoyance to show as she thrust her sword into its scabbard.

"Retrieve your cloak and proceed to the inn so we can, as you say, talk." She motioned toward the black robe on the ground.

He stepped to the side, never taking his eyes off her, bent over, picked up his cloak, shook it out and, in one fluid motion, placed it on his shoulders. With a warm smile, he gestured with his arm, inviting her to walk beside him. Shunlar couldn't help but notice that her legs were trembling. As they moved out of the alleyway and into the street, the hairs on the back of her neck tingled.

In the evening torchlight he appeared no different than any other man. Yet he cast such a strong illusion about him that no one was aware of what he actually looked like. Shunlar watched in fascination as his heat trace pattern changed to match this different physical shape. That explained how the path she had been following had turned a corner and disappeared, and "another" had turned up in the doorway to follow her. When he changed himself, his heat pattern automatically changed to match the new appearance.

"*Yes, I conceal my true identity while in public view. It would not do for people to know of my existence in their midst,*" his soft voice whispered within her skull. A wave of relief washed over Shunlar as she realized that he was reacting only to the fact that she had noticed how he changed himself physically. He remained completely unaware of her ability to see his heat pattern.

This time a very straight route took them back to the Dragon's Breath Inn. Kessell headed for the same dark corner table Shunlar had occupied earlier. From here every other table could be observed with no obstructions and both of them could sit with their backs to the wall if they sat side-by-side. *How is it that this table is conveniently empty and all the others are full?* Shunlar asked herself, careful this time to shield her thought before thinking it.

Kessell raised his arm and gestured for wine and a piece of roasted whatever was on the spit. The innkeeper soon scuttled forth carrying a tray with a pitcher of cool wine, two goblets, a steaming joint of meat, a sharp carving knife, towels, and bowls of hot water for hand washing. The woman bowed and arranged the contents of the tray before them. She bowed again and left the table. Shunlar stared after her. The innkeeper had never treated her with such respect. Just who was this strange man anyway?

With a bemused look on his face, Kessell poured the wine. "This night will be one of many surprises. I drink to your health and your abilities."

Shunlar raised her goblet and took a long drink. It had been hours since any liquid had passed her lips and she was dry. Setting his cup down, Kessell picked up the carving knife and began to carefully slice pieces of meat from the platter before them with very precise movements. Neither said a word as they quietly observed each other and chewed. To any who bothered to notice, they were merely a man and woman sharing a meal. Their habit of constantly surveying the room surprised no one.

"Tell me, if I may be so bold as to ask, where did you learn to, ah, how do you say it, mind-contact?" he asked with his curious accent.

"That is not what you brought me here for," she began answering sarcastically, but as her thoughts reached out to him, her trap warning, the hairs at the nape of her neck, rose. Suddenly she recognized his accent. "You!" she accused. "You were the one I saw at the river." This time her tone was more discreet.

"Very good of you to notice. I wondered when you would. But be most careful, Shunlar, for I am not your enemy, nor do I wish to be. My regrets for what I must do now. But I also caution you, do not reveal to anyone what you saw at the river."

"Am I captured then?" was all she said.

His answer was a slow, deliberate nod as he rinsed his hands in the finger bowl. From the corner of her eyes Shunlar could see several large figures padding quietly to their corner table.

"I must have your weapons, Lady," Kessell said, offering her a towel. She pulled it sharply from his grasp, wiping the food from her fingers, the fury in her eyes very nearly burning a hole through him.

She sat still for a moment, desperately hoping for a plan to somehow leap to mind. Kessell snapped his fingers and gestured impatiently for her sword. Shunlar unbuckled her sword belt, then angrily slapped her sheathed weapon atop the table.

"I will require your other blade as well," he said, his hand still extended. The hatred in her eyes would have melted a lesser man.

Shunlar took the dagger at her wrist from its sheath and slapped it into his palm but did not remove her hand.

"Return it to me. I will not be your captive. It is the honorable thing to do and I request it formally," she hissed.

"Regrets, Lady, for though I have managed to trap you,

you are not my captive but another's whose work I do this night. I will ask that you be treated fairly but can make no promises.''

Then he stood, took the dagger from her grip and bowed again, this time extending his arm in a motion for her to precede him. A silent trio of scruffy men waiting near their table leered at her as she exhaled angrily and stepped toward the door. People watched in silence as they left the inn, but none interfered. Once they were outside a rope appeared and two of the men began to bind her arms behind her while the third roughly gagged her.

From the shadows just outside the door of the inn, Kessell leaned against the wall, watching with impassive eyes as the men trussed her up. The one to Shunlar's right took hold of her braid and pulled hard, jerking her head back. Looking over her shoulder from this angle, Shunlar recognized something familiar about the way Kessell slouched in the shadows. He had been the man in the courtyard who had given her the name of this inn just two days ago! How could it be? She didn't recognize his heat trace. Then she remembered Kessell's shape-altering abilities.

She also remembered the man standing beside her, who was twisting her head at such an uncomfortable angle. Close enough for her to see the scar running across his left cheek, the stink of his ale breath in her face made her gag. While one hand yanked hard on her braid, his other held a dagger to her hair. Shunlar tripped, recovered and used the stumble to her advantage by sweeping out her left foot, sending the man at her left sprawling onto his back, his head making a solid thunk as it hit the cobblestones.

Stupidly, the man holding her braid let go his grip just enough for Shunlar to pull free with a quick snap of her head and kick out with her right foot. It hit its mark and landed in his belly, pushing the air from his lungs in a loud rasp, as his dagger skittered across the uneven cobbles.

But he toppled forward, not back, and grabbed onto her leg, his whole weight on it as he wrapped his arms around her calf. Falling, Shunlar planted a hard left heel into the man's right temple. He groaned but didn't relinquish his grip on her leg. Shunlar lay there, gasping, the wind knocked out of her, her bound arms aching miserably in the ropes behind her back.

The third man had begun backing away from the scene, but as luck would have it, when he turned to run, he collided with Kessell, who had just stepped from the shadows, sword in hand. Kessell knocked the man aside with a blow that sent him skidding on his stomach across the cobblestones.

"Enough. The games stop here. Up, man, all of you," he growled, hitting the first man Shunlar had downed across the back of his shoulders with the flat of his sword. The man was sprawled on his side, rubbing the back of his head. In another motion Kessell scooped up the fallen dagger and dropped to one knee beside the man who lay trying to catch his breath, still clutching Shunlar's leg.

Holding it against his throat Kessell promised menacingly, "Attempt to touch her again and I'll set her free and give her a weapon. I expect she's better with her hands than her feet, judging from this display. Arm yourself, and let go of her leg so we can deliver her. If he wishes her braid removed, it'll be his pleasure, not yours."

The man clambered to his feet, and with the merest hint of a bow to Kessell, resheathed his dagger, muttering curses under his breath as he did.

Kessell bent and pulled Shunlar roughly to her feet. "No more tricks, Lady," he warned. They started down the street once more, and this time Kessell followed with his sword trained on all their backs.

SIX

ANOTHER PERFECT MOONRISE MARKED THE BEGIN-
ning of the harvest season in the Valley of Great Trees. For
generations these proud people had protected their valley
from intruders with techniques of mind-projection. The valley was surrounded by old-growth forest, but centuries ago
a powerful leader had shown them how to project an image
of dense, impenetrable forest around the valley, and even
today the custom remained.

Twenty sat in a circle, minds linked, for five hours at a
time. They were relieved precisely on the hour by twenty
others, and so had they done for generations. The work
never tired those of the Circle, but rather strengthened
them, so long as the five hour limit was strictly observed.
Those young people who showed promise were asked to
join the Circle of Protectors. It was a great honor that
rarely, if ever, was passed by.

As a young man, Gwernz had been asked to join the
Circle of Protectors. He had been in the fourth level of his
training the year of his disappearance. This evening it was
his intention to ask the eldest member and leader of the
Valley if it would be possible for him to rejoin the Circle
and resume his training. Beside the fire sat Gwernz, Marleah, and Venerable Arlass, beneath the light of the rising
triple moons. Pale yellow Daleth had appeared first, closely
followed by tiny red Andeela. The largest, Malenti, was a

pale blue-green orb that was farther away than usual from the others this night.

"Truly, Gwernz, your proficiency at wizardry shall have given you many skills that surpass the knowledge necessary for one of the Circle," said Venerable Arlass, her abundant white hair glistening in the flickering firelight. "I would be inclined to think you would become bored or impatient with this work. I will honor your previous interrupted training. I do remember, however, the clarity with which you approached your training years ago. I myself will supervise you in the final stages. Come, sit beside me here and allow me to observe some of your innermost images so I may comprehend all that has happened to you these many years." And Venerable Arlass patted the spot next to her on the bench with her small, nearly transparent hand. The power of her office rested gently on her slight frame. Arlass had been the spiritual leader of the Valley for over eighty years.

"Good Arlass," Gwernz began, as with a grateful smile he slid closer to her, "I remain your most humble student. During the years of my exile I kept a memory of your kind eyes upon me, as they were when you first extended the fellowship of the Circle to me. I am ever thankful to the spirits of the Great Trees for the chance to sit here once more under your watchful gaze. It is true, I have learned many things that I am very willing to share with you, but you must also be strong of heart to look upon some of the mysteries I have learned. The Cave People have customs that you may find distressing."

"Yes, I am aware it may be unpleasant, Gwernz; there are, however, mysteries of the Circle that are also unpleasant." She paused here and gazed deeply into his eyes, then continued. "I have been carrying the weight of this office for many years now. It has been revealed to me that you, Gwernz, are to be my successor. In order for you to understand the importance of this office you need to see all sides of the situation. I have had very strong dreams about this moment we are approaching. Both of us will change for it. There is even the possibility that you may die from exposure to the knowledge of the Great Trees, but there is no other recourse.'' She sighed, ''If it be the will of the Great Trees, that I soon join the part of my family that has gone before me, you will become the head of the Circle. That, of course, would put a tremendous burden on you who have been gone so long. To place such responsibility on your shoulders so soon . . .'' Her voice trailed off.

Arlass's wistful gaze followed the path of the moons as they hung in an arc, pale in the sky, all three in a row. ''I have sat and observed these three maidens well past ninety years now and never have they seemed to be more radiant. Perhaps this is a portent that all will be well. In two weeks' time, at dawn, we will consult the Circle of Great Trees to see if the time is correct. If it is, we will proceed with your initiation. I must give you my knowledge first, just in case.'' Arlass smiled as once more she gazed at him in the firelight, her dark eyes enticing.

''I shall bow to the will of the Great Trees,'' was his whispered reply.

Near the fire, quietly observing this scene, sat Marleah. Her brother's reappearance had rekindled a spark of life in her that she had long ago put aside. The years had given her much sadness. She had stopped looking for reasons why she alone seemed to be singled out when disaster struck. There had been a time when she wondered if a sign had been painted on her back that said, *Choose me*. The Great Trees had offered little consolation, or so Marleah felt. Their only message, time and again, had been, *Patience. The time for mourning is not at hand.*

This same message was repeated when she lost her first-born daughter, then her brother. When her parents died in the following winter, the Trees had cried with her. But their message retained the same piercing quality when she asked for a sign about the child and Gwernz. *The time for mourning is not at hand.* Her response was to shut away a part of herself, as if closing a door to a room. She decided that a part of her must be walled off, the part that allowed her to remember her feelings for the daughter and brother she had lost. When her son, Loff, was born she needed to give him love—but in order to do that, she knew she must never think about the child or her brother. Memories of them stayed behind the strong walls she had built.

But patience was not a virtue easily embraced by this strong-willed woman. A baker by trade, Marleah was also quite good with her hands when it came to fighting. She could fell anyone, woman or man, with a skill that brought instant respect. Perhaps her fighting skill, coupled with her sharp tongue, was the reason she never married Loff's father. It seemed to her to be quite ridiculous to marry someone she could so easily defeat in a contest of wits or in a fair fight. To marry for love was not an option for someone who had walled her feelings off so very meticulously.

As she sat across the fire from Gwernz and Arlass, staring into the glow of the crackling embers, Marleah turned her thoughts toward the old wounds deep within. She envisioned herself unlocking a long unused, dust-encrusted door. Once open, she scraped away the layers covering her emotions and indulged herself by feeling her loss for the first time in years. *Does my daughter live?* she asked once again. Never had she really felt her death. Though it would have been difficult to feel the death of a child so young, she was certain she would have felt her firstborn's passing.

As Marleah reached back into the memories of the past, she remembered being the young, headstrong person she was, as she relived the day she had taken the child along with her while she made the rounds of her guard post. She had fed her and left her safely—so she thought—in a hidden place high up in the trees. The babe had been so young. For a moment Marleah could see her small face and she swallowed hard, fighting back the tears that threatened to begin. She relived the terrifying moment of finding the empty cradle. Though she searched for hours, there was not a trace left by whoever had abducted her child. A short distance away, however, the shredded clothing and jewelry had been found stuffed into the hollow of a tree. The only thing missing was the smell of death.

Abruptly, Marleah was brought back from her memories. She became aware of Gwernz's hand on her shoulder. The physical contact enabled him to see the memory from the past, and he patted her gently, his way of telling her that he understood her fear and pain as well.

"Do you think it possible she lives?" Marleah asked, her voice sounding far away to her own ears.

"Perhaps the time has come to find out, my sister," was his whispered reply.

Marleah shuddered with a chill, then looked around to see the last embers of the fire glowing in the dark. The moons sat low on the opposite horizon, and Venerable Arlass was gone to her bed. Marleah had been so involved with her memories that hours had gone by. Gwernz helped her up and they started off down the path to their home.

She leaned heavily on her brother's shoulder once they entered their cottage. For the first time in many years Marleah allowed herself the privilege of tears. As Gwernz held her tightly Marleah sobbed away the pretense of fearlessness and cold calculation. She allowed hope to seep into her bones, at last.

SEVEN

THE LONE CANDLE FLICKERED IMPERCEPTIBLY, casting distorted shadows that barely wavered on the wall. Hours ago the last of the torches of the city had been lit, and through the open window Ranth watched a long line of flames burning lazily in the still night air. The city had been in the throes of an unseasonable heat wave for three days and nights. With no air moving, he wondered how such strong dung smells were able to rise to his room from the stables below and invade his nostrils with their acrid scent. Choosing heat over the aroma, Ranth rose from his bed to pull the curtains closed. As he did so, he noticed a small group of people, civilians from their manner, bringing a bound and gagged prisoner in through the side gate. Soldiers met this unusual group and secreted them inside with very little noise. Even so, the stillness of the air amplified every scuffle across the stones of the yard.

Ranth constructed a thin tendril of mind-probe and very slowly sent it in the direction of the group below, scanning them for information. He watched as the prisoner, a woman by her movements and stature, turned her head in the direction of his window, obviously able to feel his carefully constructed touch. Instantly he withdrew the probe and retreated behind his curtains. If he had waited and watched a few seconds longer, he would have seen one of her captors also turn in his direction.

Shaken by nearly being detected, Ranth began to design

another shield around himself in his continued effort to keep Lord Creedath from discovering his talents. As he sat on his bed configuring yet another layer of protective ward around himself, calmness settled over him and Ranth once again felt able to breathe a sigh of relief. He undressed and stretched out naked atop the covers of his bed. Sleep captured him, and Ranth dreamed of the solace of the Temple, as always.

Several hours later, when he rose from his bed to quench his thirst with a drink of water, a loud voice suddenly boomed inside his head. It was Creedath, summoning him—with a decided chuckle of satisfaction to his tone. Ranth slowly began to dress, dreading another encounter with the master of the castle. Ranth put speed to his footsteps only when he approached the dark corridor that led to his master's wing of the palace; this was to be their second face-to-face meeting in as many days.

Armed guards opened the doors for Ranth as he approached, and then stepped across the threshold into a large, well-lighted room. A remarkably long, highly polished wooden table, upon which sat five blazing candelabra, covered practically the entire length of the room. At the opposite end of the room two men stood leaning against the mantel of the large fireplace. Since it was so warm, only candles burned on the mantel; no fire had been set. The unmistakable voice of Creedath could be heard questioning a very tall man whose left earlobe glistened in the candlelight. Even from as far away as the door, Ranth could tell that this man was using a very sophisticated technique to mentally barricade himself from the unsuspecting lord of the palace.

"Approach us," Creedath's voice boomed.

Ranth obeyed instantly. Keeping his eyes cast down, he strode the length of the table and, standing off to the side of the two men, bowed low and went down on one knee. For several seconds Ranth waited. Then he began to feel and hear a light thrumming sound that got louder as each second crawled by. It was unmistakable now; a very strong pulsation was being sent from this stranger toward him. What's more, the consistent sound seemed to be penetrating his carefully constructed shields. *No, dismantling them is more like it.*

In his mind's eye, Ranth saw himself standing behind a brick wall. As he watched, the bricks were pulled out one at a time from the opposite side. When enough had been removed so that he could see through, the dark face of a man peered in at Ranth from the other side. The man was smiling at him and appeared to offer no threat; in fact, he beckoned Ranth closer with a sinuous gesture of his hand. Confused but curious, Ranth stepped closer to the wall and looked through the hole. What he saw astounded him: A woman with dark hair and skin nursed a tiny baby. There were faces and whispered voices ... softness ... words mumbled, long forgotten, the smell of milk and the feel of loving eyes looking into his own.

Daring a quick glance, Ranth raised his head slightly, then dropped it just as fast. The stranger had been observing him with a benevolent smile. Ranth realized that his mouth was hanging open and as he snapped it shut a voice with an oddly familiar accent spoke inside his head.

I believe it is possible that you are my son, taken from the arms of your mother by our enemies. It was before you were named. What do they call you now?

Ranth was the name I picked from the Great Cauldron. But how can you ... ? and he was cut off.

You are only to answer my questions. Are you willing to return with me to the place of your birth? whispered the accented voice.

Cutting off the communication and still unaware that it was happening, Creedath spoke. "Ranth, you are to entertain our guest." He hissed the last word. "His every desire is to be fulfilled. Is that understood?"

Just before Creedath turned his attention away from Ranth and back to the stranger, a look of extreme satisfaction crossed his face. "Do report to me if he requires more training. You will find him extremely bright and perhaps a bit of a surprise. I bid you a good night, Kessell.'' With that, Creedath rose to leave the room, bowing curtly to the man called Kessell, who returned the bow as an equal would.

Ranth felt his cheeks red hot as he kept his head down, bowing low on one knee while Creedath left the room chuckling to himself. *So this is the special duty I have been prepared for*, he thought to himself, panic rising in him. His only consolation was that the man he had just been "given" to was professing to be his father.

"My name is not Kessell," he heard a gentle voice say. "It is Benyar sul Jemapree. Stand and look at me, my son."

With his cheeks still burning, Ranth stood up and looked into the face and eyes of the man before him. He could see the same high cheekbones, the very similar full lips, the same black eyes and curly hair. How had Creedath not seen this also?

"This is how I looked to him," said Benyar, reading his thoughts again. Instantly the man standing before Ranth transformed himself into a fair-skinned man with thin lips, hazel eyes and brown hair drawn back in a warrior's braid. The impression was so genuine there was not the slightest waver of image-casting to be seen.

"Let us return to my quarters and give Lord Creedath something to dream about while we talk. I have a dangerous proposition for you. It will require much courage. I have turned an innocent woman over to him tonight and we must help her escape."

"Brought in tonight, sir? I saw someone from my window," said Ranth aloud while to himself he was thinking, *Why should I trust him?* Then he realized he was again seeing images from years long forgotten. There was the sound of laughter, music, and a woman's voice singing a lullaby.

Blinking back tears, he faced Benyar and boldly demanded, "These memories, if that's what they are, must stop now. I cannot tell if they are real or false images you are placing in my head."

Ranth was confused but quickly realized he had spoken as no servant should to a lord. He sucked in his breath, bowed his head and apologized, expecting some sort of punishment.

But the soft, accented voice only replied, *These memories are mine and they are most real, my son.* He approached Ranth, put a loving arm about his shoulders and held him for a moment. Together they left the room and entered the corridor that would take them to Benyar's apartment. Benyar kept his arm over Ranth's shoulder as they walked through the palace. While maintaining physical contact, it was possible to freely enter each other's minds and have no one else see or overhear them. Ranth was frightened at first by the magnitude of power in Benyar, but the man soon quieted his fear.

Your abilities are very strong for one who has been raised in this place, said Benyar as they walked to his quarters.

But I was not raised here. I was raised in the Temple. Taught by the monks. One day in the market Lord Creedath saw me and my teacher. He killed Master Chago and abducted me. Until this day I had no idea what he truly intended me for. I will not stay here, a prisoner to be placed in others' beds at his whim.

You are right, my son. Your place is with me. I have much to teach you and precious little time. Once we are within the privacy of my chamber, I will begin by teaching you a sleep spell. Then, I suspect you have hundreds of questions to ask as to how I came to be here. I will answer all of them and more, whatever it takes to convince you that I am truly your father.

Ranth had no choice but to accept this offer to explain what was happening to him. The words were coming at him so fast he barely had time to think, but he trusted this man more than he had trusted anyone in a long time.

Once behind the closed door of his quarters, Benyar settled himself comfortably into a chair and invited Ranth to sit near him. The older man closed his eyes, slowed his breathing, and then wove an impregnable ward around them, so that their conversation could not be overheard. Then he began humming a high-pitched tone. After a few minutes he encouraged Ranth to join him, explaining, "We have many plans to make this night. I will begin with this cover." He began weaving a great tapestry of sensuous lovemaking that once again brought redness to Ranth's cheeks.

In his chambers, Creedath paced, stopping occasionally to sip the brandy from the goblet he carried. Why was he not visiting his newest prisoner? He had been so aroused when the steward had announced her delivery by Kessell, the man he had hired, that he almost had her brought to his chambers instead of taken to the round dungeon. *No*, he told himself. *There will be time enough for those special visits later. Besides*, he cautioned himself, *the woman does employ herself as a sword-for-hire and I want her to be docile, not ready to kill. A few days in the damp underground will do much to cool the temper I suspect she has.*

Creedath found himself wishing he had been at the scene when she was captured. He wondered if the woman had figured out that the very man Mayor Althones had hired her to follow had been the one who had captured her.

He laughed aloud, very pleased with himself, and yawned. Great waves of tiredness began to envelop him and the only thing he desired was sleep. He decided to forego having anyone undress him, there being no one's face he wanted to see at this hour, except perhaps the servant, Ranth, whom he had just given to Kessell for the night. Once Creedath settled himself into bed he decided to try searching with his thoughts in the direction of the guest quarters. Kessell had requested a young man to warm his bed, not a woman. That thought aroused him even more.

Soon Creedath was observing the scenes that Benyar was purposefully transmitting as a cover for himself and his son. *Ranth is proving to be a most useful and amusing servant after all. Perhaps he will warm my chambers some night,*

Creedath mused to himself as he was lulled to sleep by the intriguing images. This night was no exception; like all others, he slept alone, trusting none of the countless numbers of people whom he took to his bed. Never did he allow anyone to remain in his chambers once he tired. He carried one scar on his back to remind him of that folly.

Sleep took him and he drifted into his own vivid dream. Creedath lay once again in the arms of the woman. He felt his entire being ache with longing for her touch and he once again watched in horror as she stabbed him in the back with his own dagger while he slept. Suddenly, he was jolted awake as the pain in his back flared white hot. Bathed in sweat, he sat up, half awake, still mostly in the dream. Again he remembered the reality of how he had strangled her with his bare hands before the guards were able to respond to his call. They found him collapsed on top of her, the dagger still in him. It had taken nearly a year for him to recover his strength; the dagger had been poisoned.

His breath was ragged in his throat, but now, just within his range of hearing, a compelling high-pitched sound was lulling him back into a deep sleep state, showing him the visions of another tantalizing dream: two glistening male bodies moved in the candlelight. Pulled down into the dream, watching the scenes of lovemaking that were being broadcast from the visitor's wing, Creedath was asleep in seconds.

Hours later, every man, woman, child, and animal in the palace was sleeping.

EIGHT

THE CONSTANT SOUND OF DRIPPING WATER DID nothing to brighten Shunlar's mood. She had been thrown into a small dark cell that in many ways she was happy not to be able to see much of. It wouldn't have helped to observe the vermin hard at work in the corners. She had carefully cleared out and marked one corner as her own. It wasn't too difficult: Thrust the image of a cat here, a hawk there, all the proper predators these creatures would stay well away from.

"What could I possibly have done to be captured and thrown in here?" The words echoed off the stone as, too late, she realized she was talking to herself again. Shunlar knew the place she had been taken was deep under the palace, which meant tons of stone and no chance of digging out or of sending a telepathic call for help. A message would never make it through so much granite. After what seemed like hours she finally came up with a plan, though it seemed rather silly.

I will have to make an ally of one of these creatures and send it on its way to Bimily. She seems my only hope of rescue at the moment.

A loud squeak and a scurrying noise brought her thoughts back to the cell and the escape plan. Two eyes glowed from the near wall, and she sent off a small mind probe to meet it. The rat was fairly large but not so big that it couldn't fit beneath the door. Enticing it closer with a few seeds from her pocket, Shunlar mentally constructed the image of a friendly rat to bring it even closer to her. While the rat hungrily chewed on the seeds, Shunlar gave it directions to Bimily's cottage outside the city.

"Better eat all of these, little friend. You'll need your reserves for this journey." When she saw that it understood its purpose, she also instructed it to leave the cottage once its message was delivered. That was one sure way of ensuring Bimily's assistance, as well as of keeping the rat alive. Shunlar then set a barricade around the rat's mind so no one with the ability to read would suspect it. Then, much to the dismay of the guards, she shooed it loudly out beneath the door.

"Hey mistress, keep your pets under control," came the muffled, shouted command through the door, accompanied by a lot of pounding. Loud laughter followed.

Shunlar didn't bother with a reply but went about trying to make herself comfortable on the pile of straw that was supposed to be her bed. She tossed the sour-smelling rag of a blanket to the other side of the cell. She made herself as comfortable as she could, in the circumstances, pulled her cloak tightly about her arms and, exhausted, fell asleep listening to the squeaks and noises of ownership disputes over the blanket.

Morning was announced by a loud racket; the guards pounded on the doors as they brought in breakfast. A bolt clacked, followed by a sliding sound. A shaft of light appeared at the bottom of the door as a slot opened, through which was pushed a tray containing a small bowl of steaming, thin porridge and a mug of bitter-smelling tea. The slot closed almost as quickly as it had opened. Since the tea smelled suspiciously like thinker's bane, an herb that caused one to lose the ability to concentrate at all, she decided quickly not to drink it, choosing instead to spill it into the gutter in the corner. The porridge was greasy and for the most part tasteless, but at least it was warm, and Shunlar knew she must keep something in her stomach if she was to have any strength.

Once she had swallowed what she could of her meal,
Shunlar began her daily training ritual by slowly stretching
out her aching muscles. The damp stone floor had been a
wretched place to sleep, and she was stiff. Since there were
no weapons to practice with, she began a series of kicks,
punches, and blocks. She wondered what had happened to
her sword and dagger and imagined the man Kessell standing before her. She moved in to strike with a sideways leap
that became a deadly kick to his head. *Should have done
this to you the first moment I saw you,* she told herself,
envisioning him sprawled out on the stones of the alley.
But the words gave her only empty satisfaction.

All this was done in silence so as not to alert the guards.
*No use letting them know anything about me that will put
me at a disadvantage,* she decided. Finishing at last, Shunlar sat and quieted her breathing. *Time for some news about
what they intend to do with me.*

When she was finally settled within herself, Shunlar
reached out carefully into the room with a shielded mind-
probe. It circled directly above the heads of the guards as
they sat huddled around a small charcoal brazier, the only
source of heat. Remembering the shape of this place to be
round, she wondered if there were others imprisoned in this
part of the dungeon. The mind-probe settled itself within
the wisps of smoke hanging near the ceiling.

A smile turned her lips upward. *Nice aroma. I don't want
to get too involved with this stuff, though. Better to let the
guards get like a bunch of giddy girls.* They were smoking
dragonweed.

Inhaling deeply and holding it until his eyes began to
water, the first guard coughed and handed the pipe to his
friend. "Best put this out soon. If the master finds out, we
won't be much more than fodder for the fields," he said as
the second man took a deep draw on the pipe and broke
into fits of laughter.

A third man sat glassy-eyed and said, "We hardly be
more than horse dung now. What difference could that
be?" And he too broke into loud guffaws.

Jolly group, this, thought Shunlar as she split her awareness and sent the thinnest thread of probe to search for signs
of life in the other cells. There were ten in all, hers included. Most contained young women, although three held
young men. The field around the prisoners felt thick and
viscous, and a bitter smell hung in the air. *It seems they
have been drugged. The tea, I'll wager. Speaking to them
now will do no good. Perhaps later when the effects have
worn off somewhat I'll come back and attempt to speak to
some of them*, Shunlar thought to herself and abruptly
stopped probing further. One of the women had felt her
scanning and was reaching out to Shunlar with her mind,
in a very uncontrolled telepathic send.

Shield your mind, Shunlar commanded in a firm, yet gentle tone. The young woman seemed very confused at the
suggestion, as if she did not understand the language, and
withdrew her awareness. Shunlar's full attention was drawn
back suddenly to the noisy guards, who were now rolling
on the floor in spasms of laughter.

"Maybe we should get this breeding program off to an
early start," one of the guards said as he chuckled at his
own words.

"Aw, gurron, you couldn't pleasure a sheep in your condition," hollered another over his shoulder who, as he
turned around, pointed at his very flaccid penis, hanging
out of his pants. "I could hardly get it to empty just now."
That brought on more hoots and coughs and great slaps on
the back from the other two. "Besides, I'm used to havin'
this fella right here between my legs," he said, patting himself, and then pulling up the laces of his breeches. "If the
Master was to find traces of our juices inside any of these
little cows here, I'm afraid we'd all be talkin' with much
higher voices before the day was over." More loud laughter.

"Well, I'm not particular. Let's see one of the little studs
then." This brought an uneasy silence and some nervous
glances were exchanged between the other two, until the
man who made the comment couldn't hold back and fairly

roared at the hilarity of what he was proposing, bringing on laughter once again from his partners.

"A genuine genius we have here," said the man as he rose, walking to the key cupboard.

Good, show me where the keys are kept, demanded Shunlar as she slipped quietly into his mind. For a moment the giddiness of the dragonweed pulled at her seductively, but she managed to push it aside. The light in this corner of the dungeon was very dim. Shunlar accustomed herself to the dark, looking through the guard's eyes as he stumbled to the cupboard and fumbled for the proper key. Having noted the whereabouts of the keys, Shunlar made his hand jerk with a sudden spasm so that he knocked all of them from their hooks. The guard jumped back, as if he had been bitten, as ten keys clattered to the floor. All three men were instantly on their knees, grabbing, trying to read the numbers on each, hanging them back as fast as they could. Satisfied that she had the information she needed, she slowly pulled her awareness from the mind of the guard. A cold shudder ran through him as she did so. The men silently returned to their places around the meager source of heat.

"Things like that gives me the shakes," was all that was said as three now very somber, sober guards huddled under their capes in the damp stone room where the only noises were once again the drip of water and an occasional hiss from the charcoal embers.

Shunlar retreated into herself to digest what she had overheard. What could he have meant by "get this breeding program" off to a start? Did Creedath intend to sell them all for breeding stock? *Someone will lose body parts before that occurs*, she vowed, shuddering in the damp. Her thoughts turned to sifting through what details she could from the jumble of information collected from the guard. She was slowly beginning to understand.

NINE

RUNNING, I RUNNING, TO PLACE OUTSIDE GATES OF city. I see path. Protect myself all'a times. Keep running. Message. I carry much important message. Bimily. I call you. This was how the little Rat spoke to herself as she scampered along under the cover of bushes and shrubs beside the packed dirt road. It had been rough going for some hours now, and she had traveled all night and most of the day. She neared her destination as the sun began to set.

Suddenly from nowhere the shadow of a large bird loomed across her path. Rat froze in midair, landing with a dusty thump in the dirt. Without warning a black eagle landed just in front of her with a shriek to its mate, circling up above. The second eagle banked and started back to the aerie, answering the signal.

For a moment the air sparkled and shuddered, and the eagle was replaced by a rat. The little messenger Rat was still trembling as she became aware of a voice coming from this newly appeared rat, calmly saying, *There, now, just who are you and how do you come to this part of the world broadcasting a message for me?*

Send by Shunlar. She is capture by Creedath. Must rescue, Rat squeaked.

Well, at least her timing isn't bad. I only have my mate to consider and not a brood. Come then, little friend, back to my home under the trees. We have some planning to do, and you must tell me any details you can of where it is we

65

will be going. And the air once more sparkled and shuddered as the rat form was replaced by the human form of Bimily.

The little messenger Rat began to tremble harder. Never in all her life had she seen shapes change back and forth. Once more Bimily spoke to her, but this time the voice was not inside Rat's tiny skull. "Be still, little one. I'm your friend and am indeed the person you were sent on this journey to find. It will be safer if you climb onto my shoulder and ride the rest of the way. I'll bet you're tired and won't mind riding, huh?" And she patted her shoulder as she knelt down on one knee.

Satisfied by the reassuring tone of her voice, Rat leapt onto Bimily's shoulder. The shapechanger stood up and began walking rapidly to her well-hidden cottage in the woods. "I'm sure you thought you were dinner when you saw the eagle drop from the sky in front of you. There are two very good reasons I choose to spend most of my time these days as an eagle. One is, that I'm very fond of flying and the other is"—they stepped through the entryway of her cottage, dust flying at the opening of the door—"I hate cleaning house."

Both Bimily and Rat began to sneeze. Bimily covered her mouth and nose with her scarf, then opened all the windows and let the breeze blow through the house, encouraging it with a few soft-spoken words. Rat clung to her shoulder through all this, maintaining her balance as best she could, having never ridden on a human's shoulder before. Bimily worked fast once the dust was gone. She closed the windows, set a spark in the fireplace, drew water from her well, and set the kettle over the fire for tea. In minutes she had water for Rat and even some tasty seeds that had been sealed away in a jar. Then Bimily set Rat down on a small table and sat in the chair beside her.

Rat ate and drank hungrily as she observed the human in front of her. Bimily had gray-green eyes that seemed to sparkle in the firelight. With the hood of her cape pushed back, Rat saw Bimily's hair was the color of dark copper, and she had it combed back sleekly and braided in several long plaits down her back. Her smile and soft voice reassured Rat as she took a long drink of the cool well water.

"Now that you are fed, you can tell me what you know of Shunlar and how you come to be sitting in front of me. I am going to enter your mind once more so that I may also see the pictures as you supply the words."

Rat wiped her whiskers and readied herself for the touch. It happened quickly, and this time she was composed as her tale unwound itself. She showed Bimily the round dungeon and the door that led to Shunlar's cell. She showed her the ledge she had hidden behind when she had slipped under the door. Even the foul smell of the place was transmitted to Bimily. When all was told, Bimily removed her touch from Rat's mind, and both of them sat looking into the fire; one feeling what could only be described as homesickness, the other planning.

After several long minutes Bimily spoke: "First we will rest and wait for cover of night. I don't want anyone to see us as we return to the castle. I must give some thought as to what shape I will use once inside the dungeon. Will I be animal or elemental? Whatever I choose must be done with the greatest caution, however. This fellow Creedath is proving to be quite dangerous. Here, come and climb upon my lap, little one. Be warm and sleep while I plan." Rat climbed cautiously at first onto Bimily's warm lap and nestled into the folds of her skirt. Never had she experienced such kind treatment from a human.

I like, she thought to herself as she drifted off to sleep.

"I like too, but you cannot stay. There might come a day when my eagle self gets hungry and I can't control it. You do notice that there are no others of your species living here. Clever of Shunlar to firmly plant in your mind the message to return to your home, even though it is a dungeon. You'd not last long here."

After several hours had passed Bimily woke Rat. Both were rested and it was night. "Wake now. It is time to begin our rescue. You will ride upon my back to the gates of the city. I will be in the form of a large dog. Be very still and unafraid. If I smell fear I cannot be sure what I will do to you. I will then change into the shape of a rat and together we will enter the gates of Vensunor. Are you prepared for a fast run, little one?''

Rat picked up several large seeds and stuffed them into her cheeks. *With food here I be not afraid*, and she eagerly climbed up Bimily's arm to her shoulder.

As soon as they had crossed the threshold of her house, the air sparkled and shimmered and Bimily was a large copper-colored dog with gray-green eyes and a rat upon her back. *We're off. Hang on tightly Rat.* Wind rushed past them as the dog fairly flew into the night. The road to the city was traveled heavily in the daylight hours, but superstition and safety kept everyone except the dangerous or the patrol soldiers off the paths to Vensunor at night. This night was no exception. Only once did they pass a person, and that was a solitary guard sleeping upon his horse. The dozing mount jumped as the large dog streaked by. The guard yelled a curse after them for having startled him awake.

Once Bimily was beneath the shadow of the gates of Vensunor, she transformed herself into a rat and followed her companion under the gates. Then they sped on their way, covered by night, to the palace.

TEN

THE NIGHT HAD BEEN AN EXCEPTIONALLY LONG one for Ranth. They had sat facing one another for many hours, Benyar soundlessly passing stories and a great deal of love to his son—directly from his mind to Ranth's.

Benyar described to him how, after searching these many years, he happened to find Ranth by accident. He had been living in Vensunor for several months, under various disguises. Changing his looks enabled him to travel in many different circles, and he knew that the more groups he infiltrated, the better his chances were of finding his son. He had very real letters of introduction written for him by a rich merchant from a distant, prosperous city. The rich merchant, was in truth, Benyar himself, in the guise of yet another person. These letters spoke of the man Kessell in generous terms and described in great detail how he had served as a loyal bodyguard and hired sword. After reading them, Creedath had hired Kessell to find and capture Shunlar. The reason she was hunted had not been told to Benyar. Reasons were seldom disclosed. She was wanted and gold—a lot of gold—would be paid upon her delivery. In order for Benyar to continue his search, he needed gold.

On the day Benyar had been hired, he had come to Creedath's palace, altered his looks, and appeared to Creedath and Mayor Althones as a mere messenger. As he told of that day, Benyar changed himself in front of Ranth, to look like the messenger. Ranth recognized him at once as the man to whom he had delivered the one-word answer only days before in the palace, believing him to be a servant.

"I did see a waver about you, but never would I disclose that I could tell you were casting an image."

"Yes, I know," replied Benyar. "When I realized that you were able to see the wavering of the image I projected, I knew you had abilities beyond those of a mere guard. That and the strong mind-shield with which you protected yourself made me begin to suspect. I began asking several of the guards discreet questions about you, making it known that I was a lover of men. None were entirely co-operative, but I was able to read some of their thoughts about you. It seems several of them suspected that your master had already taken you to his bed. Fortunately, when Creedath hospitably offered someone to warm my bed, he did not scoff at my request for a man. When he realized that you were the person I wanted, the thought of it aroused him in a most peculiar way. He very nearly said no, but I believe his near refusal stemmed from jealousy. I had to manipulate his mind to change it. He is very cunning and dangerous, my son. And, of course, your face told me who you were."

Ranth did not need a mirror to know what Benyar meant by that last remark. He resembled his father down to his chin.

"And you did send out a mind touch to my prisoner when we came into the yard last night," Benyar continued. "Your scan was thorough, but I caution you against using such a strong one again. To ensure your safety, let me show you a more subtle technique." Benyar masterfully extended a part of his awareness to touch Ranth's mind. Once touched, Ranth realized that he had only been peripherally aware of this part of himself. Suddenly a new spaciousness opened to him. He felt, rather than understood, how to reach out with a part of himself and split his awareness. Not since he had been abducted from the Temple had Ranth received any new mind techniques, and he leapt upon this lesson, eager for more.

His father—for Ranth now truly believed this man to be his father—laughed with delight at how rapidly Ranth understood the tiny nuances of this new approach. When Benyar was satisfied that Ranth could duplicate the process to perfection, he removed his touch from his son's mind and sat back with a satisfied grin.

"For such a good student a reward is in order." He slapped the arms of the chair, rose, walked over to a low table and opened his traveling bag. After a bit of digging, Benyar retrieved a leather pouch, from which he produced a gold chain with an amulet attached. He hung this around Ranth's neck, kissing him on each cheek as he did, saying, "If we should be separated, go to the land of our ancestors, my son. Take this amulet to the high priestess. She will know what to do. I pray nothing will separate us now that I have found you. There is so much I have to tell you, but now is not the time. This roof under which we are sheltered conceals much treachery. I dare not risk telling more than I already have for fear of being overheard." A faraway look crossed Benyar's face as he touched his chest.

Ranth sat quietly, unable to find any words of thanks, aware of the weight of the chain that hung around his neck. When he finally found his voice, he could only whisper a quiet, "Thank you, father," with his head bowed.

Then, after a few uncomfortable minutes of silence, something sparked the anger buried deep within him. "I have been living under this roof for five years now, subjected to the whims of the mind of the man I must call master. His power is absolute here. I have witnessed and heard tales of the cruel strength of his . . . 'talent,' " Ranth tersely spat this last word. "But you, my father, overshadow his abilities. How is this so?"

Benyar answered, "My son, did you not suspect that Lord Creedath has never been formally trained? All of his techniques are self-taught. If he ever trusted anyone enough to allow them to teach him, his power might become unstoppable. As it is, I manipulated him without him knowing it, to bring you to me. There are many techniques he has never learned. Without his knowledge, I was able to scan his memory until I saw you and learned your name. Then I planted the suggestion in his mind, ever so carefully, that he should make a 'present' of you to me for the night. Tomorrow, when you come to me again, we will once more put all in his castle to sleep and rescue the woman. Now, we need rest.'' Benyar smiled and patted Ranth's arm affectionately. ''Go now and sleep, my son.''

Both men rose, yawned and embraced once more. As they separated, a small jolt of energy jumped between them, which made Ranth feel giddy. An embarrassed laugh escaped him. Benyar smiled, recognizing the feeling, something he hadn't felt since he was a boy. He quickly explained to Ranth that it was the effect of the new techniques he had learned. It also confirmed to Benyar that he was correct: Ranth was his son; there was no mistaking it. But even their excitement couldn't keep them awake any longer.

At the open doorway, Ranth bowed to Benyar. ''I bid you a good night, sir,'' he said, for the ears of the guard who stood watch. He closed the door carefully behind him and walked to his quarters, in the same wing of the palace, pretending not to notice the guard, who was shaking himself awake. If anyone knew that he had fallen asleep at his post, he would likely pay for it with a very nasty death.

Returning to his room just a few hours before dawn, Ranth was exhausted. He pulled open the curtains and then the shutters, to allow some fresh air into the chamber. In the last few hours the temperature had fallen, and the cool air felt refreshing on his face. With new hope running through him, Ranth undressed and slipped into his bed, shivering until his body heat warmed the covers. He clutched the amulet, the present from Benyar, that now hung around his neck from a thick gold chain. A smile remained on his lips as he drifted into grateful sleep, dreaming, remembering the night of planning with Benyar.

The next day Ranth somehow managed to stumble through his work, and much later that evening, long after his duties of the day were over, as he lay napping, he was again summoned to the same meeting room, this time by a guard. It was with great relief that he saw Benyar also waiting for him. Benyar and Creedath sat at the end of the long table, discussing something in discreet tones. Creedath raised his arm and motioned for Ranth to approach. Ranth stepped toward them, bowed, went down on one knee and remained waiting with his head held low, careful to avert his eyes.

"Kessell tells me you have pleased him greatly. What am I to do but grant him your company yet another night?" Creedath said with a self-satisfied grin.

Suddenly Ranth began to tremble. He fell to both knees as droplets of sweat beaded up on his forehead and ran down his face. He continued to shake as his breath came in large gulps. He groaned and fell over onto his side at Benyar's feet. It appeared that Creedath could aim his mind power at an individual when he chose to. Benyar, though, startled at the sight, pretended not to be able to "see" what Creedath was doing to his son. He jumped from his chair, staring in disbelief at Ranth.

"Master Creedath, it seems the lad is not well. Perhaps I should summon a physician for myself as well as him. Since I have had contact with him, I may be at risk of suffering some strange ailment. Even you, my gracious host, might be at risk." Benyar backed away from Ranth as he spoke, pretending fear for himself, when in reality the fear he showed was for Ranth, who now lay in real pain, gasping for breath.

As if on cue, Creedath called out, "Guard, summon the physician to me immediately. Kessell, you will excuse us. I will tend to the boy myself." Creedath stood over Ranth, who continued to writhe in pain on the floor.

"What could be the matter with him?" Creedath asked in mock concern.

Then turning his attention back to Benyar, he pronounced, "There is little need to worry for the boy. He is a valuable servant and I promise he will be in excellent care. The physician will see you shortly, if you wish. Please go to your own quarters now and await him.'' His voice grated against Benyar's ears, compelling him to turn and leave the room.

Ranth tried, unsuccessfully, to stand, finally giving up the effort to just lay on the floor groaning, with his arms wrapped about his head.

A look of very real concern was on Benyar's face as he was escorted through the doorway. Hastening down the corridor toward his room, he sent a secret thread of a message to Ranth's mind. *Hold on and be brave, my son. I will protect you as best I know how. The man's renegade power seems to have taken hold of you for now, but I vow that I will never let him harm you again.*

Creedath turned his full attention on Ranth, easing up his iron grip on the young man's prone, shaking body. The trembling and sweating stopped as abruptly as it had begun, and Ranth was able to sit up. He continued to hold his head as several guards entered the open door behind Creedath, planted their feet, and remained impassively, waiting for orders. None would look at Ranth, yet he was acutely aware of their contempt for him.

"No, my boy, we will not allow you to enjoy the company of Kessell tonight." Creedath's sneer broke the uncomfortable silence. "I had nearly forgotten how well you responded to my touch until this moment. No, I have other plans for you that are much more important. Guards, take him to his quarters and see that he does not leave. The same for our visitor. See that extra guards are posted outside his door.''

"Yes, Lord,'' one man answered.

The guards roughly scooped Ranth up off the floor by his armpits and proceeded to escort him to his quarters. As they half-carried, half-dragged him down the corridor, he began to come around, aware of a pervading tone in his head. It was the same tone Benyar had taught him the night before, and it gave him strength. He continued to behave as though he were in extreme pain and groaned loudly as the guards deposited him like a sack of flour onto his bed. After they left his room, Ranth began to duplicate the sound in his head, and as he did, a feeling of power began to well up within him. He lay upon his bed as waves of sound washed gently over him, giving him strength.

Several hours later, the spell of the resonant toning that Ranth and Benyar continued to weave reverberated throughout the palace. The soothing tones of the sound had become words that said: *Rest, close your eyes, sleep.* Guards fell asleep at their posts, cooks at their ovens, servants in the midst of their duties. Throughout the palace, people suddenly yawned, sat down on the nearest piece of furniture or leaned against the wall, and were soon fast asleep. Even the animals in the stables and courtyard fell into a deep, peaceful sleep. Indeed, it seemed all of the palace was sleeping.

Benyar was out of his room first. As he stepped over the bodies of the guards sprawled in front of his doorway, he sent forth a mind-call for Ranth to join him. Ranth armed himself with sword and dagger, then cautiously pulled open his door and stepped from his room, careful not to disturb the guards who snored loudly where they sat, slumped against the wall like some child's forgotten toy. Ranth had slung a saddlebag with a change of clothes and his personal belongings over his shoulder.

He joined his father, noticing that he carried saddlebags over each shoulder, as well as another sword and dagger. Ranth suspected they belonged to the woman. As they walked soundlessly along the dark corridor, Benyar handed the extra sword and dagger to Ranth, then pulled a large amber crystal from beneath his shirt. Held tightly in his fist, it cast a soft yellow glow, providing them with enough light to wind their way around the maze of the palace.

As they approached the stairway that led to the round dungeon, a feeling of dread washed over Ranth. In the eerie stillness, he had seen most of the castle's inhabitants sleeping; many snored contentedly right where they stood. That had been eerie enough, but something about this dungeon was making his skin prickle as well.

"Father, do you feel it?" he whispered.

"I do. Draw your weapon and cover my back," Benyar answered, as he began slowly to descend the spiral stone stairwell.

Their descent was accompanied by the sound of dripping water as they made their way down the stairs. Once at the bottom, Benyar held up his hand for Ranth to stop.

"My son, there is something covering this entrance. Perhaps Creedath is more proficient than I suspected. Step no farther and I will see if I can manage to contain it so that we may pass through it and alert no one in the process. I will need silence to work, but if you wish to learn what I do, touch my mind at the edges and watch carefully."

Ranth nodded to his father and put forth a delicate mind-touch. He saw what Benyar saw instantly. A web—a dark, blood-red color—did seem to cover the entrance. Benyar used the crystal he held in his hand to touch a junction where two threads of the web crossed. It caused the web to shimmer for a second or two and then stop, as a tiny point of amber light appeared. He touched another junction, then another, continuing until he had made the pattern of a doorway in the web. Holding the crystal against the centermost threads, each spark of amber light began to run along the webs and the color changed, from blood red to amber, the color of the crystal. Very slowly, Benyar reached up and pushed the strange door open with one finger.

Ranth was fascinated. He had hundreds of questions but Benyar just held his fingers to his lips. Speaking directly to Ranth's mind, he asked, *My son, remember the feeling on your skin as we approached the stairwell?* Ranth nodded his head, yes. *Remember it well. It will save your life one day. Soon, very soon, I will be able to answer all of your questions. Have patience, for now we must rescue the woman. Come.*

They walked through the strange doorway and cautiously

began to circle the room. With Ranth at his back, Benyar sent a silent mind-to-mind touch into each cell until at last they found her.

Shunlar answered them with a cautious, very tentative touch to the edges of their barriers. That is, at first she did. Then, seconds before she could react, Benyar threw a stronger shield over himself and Ranth. For several minutes both men endured the strong mental barrage of anger and rage that she directed at the man she knew as Kessell.

Cutting off her words, Benyar ordered, ''Stand away from the door. I have come with another to rescue you. There will be time for anger later.''

The mention of the word ''rescue'' calmed her foul mood instantly and Shunlar answered, ''Behind the pillar near the brazier is the key cupboard.'' Ranth immediately went in search of the key cupboard, happy to be away from her for the moment.

Apart from the amber crystal that Benyar held, the only source of light was one hanging oil lamp and the charcoal brazier that cast its orange glow onto the floor and ceiling. There were three stools near the brazier, one of them toppled over, but no sign of any guards. Ranth grabbed an unlit torch from a small pile on the floor. He touched it to the lamp and, once lit, used it to illuminate his way as he walked along the wall, still looking for the keys.

The whisper of steel being drawn from its sheath told Benyar that they were no longer unnoticed. Three guards were advancing from the opposite end of the dungeon. Obviously the spell of sleep hadn't penetrated this far down into the stone of the palace.

The first man shouted and attacked Benyar immediately. His two companions hung back for several seconds, but then realized that their friend needed help, and they also came at Benyar.

My son, free the woman first. I can hold these three off easily, Benyar instructed Ranth with a mind-contact.

Ranth obeyed reluctantly. As he ran to Shunlar's cell, his movements were automatic. He dropped the torch, pulled her sword from his belt, unlocked the door, threw it open and tossed her sword into the dark cell practically in one motion. He spun around and ducked as he unsheathed his weapon, just in time to avoid a sword swipe much too close to his head. Several quick jabs, a roll to the side and he was behind his portly opponent. One well-aimed stab to the back felled the man.

But as Ranth whirled around to assist his father, it was just in time to see Benyar lose his footing on something in the dark corner. Momentarily thrown off balance, he took a deep thrust in the left shoulder, much too close to the heart. Benyar staggered, dropped his sword and fell to the ground, groping with his left hand in what appeared to be an attempt to pick something up. Without thinking, Ranth ran. He leaped through the air at his father's attacker, a scream escaping his throat as he did. Dropping his sword in midair, Ranth pulled his small dagger from its sheath as he landed on the guard's back. One hand covered the man's eyes as the other slit his throat. Ranth was at his father's side before the body hit the floor.

The third man hid, crouching behind a pillar. He had turned away from the fight, being no swordsman, and now stood watching in horror as his friends died. When he wheeled around, looking for a place to escape the same fate, he nearly ran into Shunlar's sword.

Having spent several days in the dark, the light of the torch that lay guttering at her feet was enough to nearly blind her when she stepped from the cell. Her eyes were becoming used to the light just as this dolt who had laughed at her and spat curses at her through the door stumbled into her, inches short of impaling himself on her sword. She was as surprised as he, and their near collision took her off balance.

Though not a skilled fighter, this guard had managed to survive so far by his wits. He ducked low as her sword swung over his head. From his low crouch he completed a lucky upward thrust that raked Shunlar's rib cage as it cut a deep gash in her left arm. With an enraged scream of pain, her right arm swung the sword down across his neck. The strength of her swing severed his head; as it toppled from his shoulders she staggered backward, struggling to remain conscious. The body fell heavily onto the torch and snuffed it out with a loud whump as the head rolled past her toes into the wet gutter of the dungeon.

"Now that's a fitting final resting place for a mind like yours," she managed to gasp.

Holding her wounded arm against her blood-soaked side, she knelt to wipe her sword on the dead man's cloak. Shock numbed her from feeling the pain, but she regretted at once the fact that she knelt because it meant that now she would have to stand up and the room had begun to spin. Not bothering to sheath her sword, Shunlar looked around the dimly lit chamber for Kessell and whomever it was that had accompanied him on this rescue. Across the room, she could just make out the figure of a man who appeared to be kneeling on the ground, holding another to his chest.

She staggered toward him calling out, "Kessell, if you're rescuing me, we must leave now. There is no time for mourning. Come *now*!" she demanded. Staggering closer to his shoulder, she recognized the deathly pale face of the man being held as Kessell, her captor, but chose to ask no questions. Escape was the only thing on her mind. There would be a time for questions later. For now she closed her eyes and grimaced, waiting for the pain to subside so she could begin the climb out of here.

Ranth gently placed Benyar's head on the wet stone floor. He resheathed his dagger, took Benyar's from the sheath on his lifeless wrist and tucked it into his belt. He crossed his father's hands over his breast, bent over him and kissed him on each cheek. The tears blurred his vision, and he failed to notice the amber crystal that had fallen behind a pillar on the cold stones a few feet from them.

Ranth wiped his cheeks quickly with the back of his hand. In response to her command to leave "*now*" he stood stiffly and turned to face the woman who was responsible for his father's death. He swallowed the bile in his throat as he bent to pick up their saddlebags, struggling to keep his face impassive. "Follow me quietly if you want to live. We go to the stables, then out the back gate."

Shunlar followed him to the stairway as the hairs on the back of her neck rose. Once she had stepped through the doorway Benyar had made in the web, her neck hairs laid back down. Her pain kept her from immediately recognizing that she had passed through some sort of barrier. Only after beginning her climb did what she had seen register. The vivid colors of the webbing were what grabbed her attention, but she released the thought of it just as quickly. She was bleeding heavily and her breath was coming hard as they climbed up the stairwell. She needed to concentrate all of her energies on escape.

Accompanied only by the echo of their boots bouncing off the surrounding walls, they climbed up, out of the depths of the castle, Ranth in the lead. Shunlar and he held their swords ready for attack, but none came. They made their way cautiously through the castle, passing people and animals still sound asleep.

At a doorway leading to the courtyard, they stopped and waited for someone or something to move. There was an entire length of courtyard to cross before reaching the stable. Still, not one person or creature stirred. Ranth stepped up, opened the door and cautiously stuck his head out, checking side to side. Several inches away on each side of the doorway the guards leaned against the wall, fast asleep. He pulled his head back in, turned and nodded to Shunlar, and they both stepped through the doorway.

Halfway across, two dogs who claimed this part of the yard as their territory slept with a bone between them. Ranth and Shunlar cautiously crept past on tiptoe as one of the dogs' noses twitched. The only other movement seemed to be the flames of the torches that danced lazily in the still night air.

Once inside the stable, Ranth became a blur of motion. He found a pack that contained lengths of cloth bandages and threw them to Shunlar. Then he chose two sturdy horses and hurriedly threw saddles on them while Shunlar leaned against the wall, struggling with the bandages. She managed to wrap her arm and staunch the flow of blood but could only stuff a piece of cloth through the slice in her shirt and try to hold it against her side with her elbow. She'd been biting her lip so hard to keep from passing out that now it was also bleeding.

Ranth led the horses toward her. One look at Shunlar's white face told him her wound was serious. "Mount now. Can you ride?" he asked in a whisper.

Shunlar winced with the effort of pushing herself off the wall and then walked unsteadily toward him. Her glazed eyes were his only answer. He held her horse steady as she climbed up. Once he made sure she was securely mounted, Ranth led both animals through the stable. At the storage room he grabbed what provisions he could: waterskins, packets of travel rations, bags of grain for the horses. He stuffed as much into the saddlebags as he could; the rest he slung over his shoulders to secure later when they were beyond the walls of the city. Blankets and cloaks were quickly thrown over the saddles. As he worked, Ranth duplicated the sleep spell sound within his head, making it reverberate throughout the castle. It continued to do its magic.

The guards at the gate snored loudly as Ranth pushed the gate open without a sound. He led both horses through and then closed the gate behind them. Once outside the walls of Lord Creedath's palace he placed a rope around the neck of Shunlar's horse and then tied it to the pommel of his horse's saddle. He mounted and led them on their way to a little used gate of Vensunor, which he knew was left unguarded. They passed through in silence.

"Can you manage a hard ride?" he asked her in a quiet voice.

"Yes. Give me the reins. I'll not fall while the horse is moving," she answered, although the effort nearly made her pass out.

He gave her the reins but didn't remove the rope from her horse's neck. Shunlar never noticed. Soon they urged a gallop out of their mounts and began putting miles between themselves and Vensunor.

ELEVEN

BACK IN THE DEPTHS OF THE SLEEPING PALACE, two rats cautiously appeared from a chink in the wall near the last steps of the only entrance to the foul-smelling round dungeon. Four very still bodies lay sprawled on the stone floor. After several minutes passed the rats ran down the steps, passed through the threshold, and crossed the room to finally race into the open cell where Rat had last seen Shunlar.

This the place Shunlar 'sposed to be, Rat squeaked.

Breathing very hard, Bimily answered Rat, who was also panting with exhaustion. "It appears we are a little too late. Now I must find out how Shunlar escaped and who all those dead people are out there. Your job is over, little Rat, and mine begins. Thank you and good-bye."

Once again the sparkle and shimmer filled the air, and Bimily was once again in human form. As she hurried to the side of the only man in the room not dressed as a guard, Bimily stopped abruptly. An unusual glowing amber light seemed to pulse from behind a nearby pillar. She peeked around the pillar for the source of the light and saw a large amber crystal laying on the stone.

Transfixed by the object, Bimily sat down, picked up the crystal, and held it in both palms. Her eyes closed as she allowed her breathing pattern to match the pulsing of the crystal. The air shimmered again as Bimily became a statue the exact hue of amber as the one she held. The

crystal opened to her mind and showed all that had transpired within the dungeon minutes before. She recognized
the man lying at her feet as the owner of the crystal, but
had no idea who he or the young man who accompanied
him were. The only thing she could discern was that they
had come to rescue Shunlar.

Bimily was just beginning to recognize the power she
was holding in her hands when a tinkling voice said: "I
am the Lifestone of Benyar sul Jemapree. Return me to my
owner or he will be lost forever."

The air crackled for a moment as Bimily the shapechanger transformed herself back into her human form and
jumped as she did, nearly dropping the Lifestone. It did
seem to have a life of its own.

"Is that man lying there Benyar?" she asked the Lifestone, nodding to the still form nearest her.

The Lifestone glowed brighter in response, beginning a
more insistent, rhythmic pulsation. Again the voice came
to her ears, this time instructing Bimily precisely what to
do. Holding the Lifestone, she went to the side of the man
closest to her, knelt down, and laid it gently upon his chest,
placing the pulsing stone across the bloody gash.

Rays of intense light fanned out in an arc from the Lifestone as it began its work. From its depths rang a high
piercing sound that seemed to shake the walls of the round
dungeon. The still body of Benyar stirred. He inhaled—a
liquid sound—and he coughed up blood. His hand moved
to his chest, clutched the amber crystal, and held it in place.
Bimily watched, fascinated, as the blood ceased to flow
from the open wound.

Realizing she must get this wounded man to safety Bimily quickly changed into the form of a large man. But, as
she bent to pick him up, Bimily heard whispered warnings.
She tried reassuring the voice that she was a friend and
reached toward Benyar. Instantly Bimily became rigid,
stuck in a half bent-over posture. She was freezing cold
and unable to move. Enclosed in ice, her body trembled as

she felt as well as heard a powerful voice warning her to stay away.

Still frozen in place, Bimily said, "You've been seriously wounded; left for dead, I think. You've lost a lot of blood. If you'll let me, I will take you to the healers of the Temple. Your Lifestone trusted me. I recommend you do the same."

For several heartbeats, a quick whispered conversation could be felt at the back of her mind, and in seconds the frozen feeling left her body. Able to move again, Bimily gently picked up the man called Benyar.

Had he been a weaker man, as soon as they made physical contact, Bimily would have seen inside his mind. However, Benyar had a strong protective mechanism firmly engaged to prevent such a thing happening. Bimily was made aware of the strength of the power Benyar possessed and the depth of the Lifestone, but she was shown only a glimpse.

As Bimily turned toward the stairway she saw what appeared to be a red and amber webbing partially covering the doorway. The amber section was shaped like a door and it was standing open. She had passed through it minutes ago in the form of a rat and seen nothing. Now, with Benyar in her arms, his sight amplified by his Lifestone, their physical contact enabled her to see the "door" the Lifestone had made in the trap and she prepared to step through it.

"You are female. You are a shapechanger. I will trust you and thank you . . ." The faint voice of Benyar trailed off as he inhaled painfully. "My son; has he escaped with the woman?"

"Hush now. Shield your mind. We are yet within the walls of Creedath's palace. Yes, they are both gone, as we must be. Tell me: Do you think you are capable of riding?"

"I will attempt it. Is the ride far?"

"No, I don't think so," was her reply as she carried Benyar out of the dungeon and up the stairwell by the amber-hued light of the Lifestone. After they passed through the amber "door," it slowly closed. Once they reached the open courtyard, Bimily again adjusted her physical form. She changed only her eyes to those of the eagle, the shape she was fondest of. Then, she followed her nose to the stables. It seemed very odd to her that no one challenged them as they crossed the courtyard. But her keen vision showed her what another might not have noticed in the surrounding darkness. Every person and animal was asleep.

Reaching the safety of the dark stable at last, the air again shimmered and sparkled as Bimily transformed herself into a sleek roan mare, saddled and bridled. She knelt as Benyar, pale and shaking, managed to climb into the saddle and sit, a groan escaping his lips as he did so. She made her way to the gate, where Benyar manipulated the guard into a wakeful enough state to open it. As soon as they were beyond the gate the guard fell back into a deep sleep, slumping where he stood.

Bimily stepped into the night. Once she got her bearings she picked up the pace, taking care to keep her gait smooth. She was aware of the Lifestone pumping vitality into Benyar. Because it required strength to stay in the saddle, however, he weakened with each step.

Once in sight of the Temple, Bimily spoke mind-to-mind to Benyar: *We have safely arrived. Because I do not want my identity as a shapeshifter known in this city, I cannot wait until you are within the gates. We will meet again soon. May the Cauldron of the Great Mother see fit to heal you.*

The roan mare knelt for Benyar to dismount. Somehow he made his way to the gate. He pulled on the rope and heard the urgent summons of a bell ringing on the other side of the massive, ornately carved gates. Soon the sound of running footsteps could be heard. Leaning against the wall, he turned and whispered, "How are you called?"

Bimily, echoed a voice in his head. Then the horse backed away into the shadows, where the air shimmered and sparkled. Instead of a horse, a large black eagle stood hidden from view. As it spread its expansive wings, rising beyond sight in a matter of seconds, one shimmering feather landed on the stones next to Benyar.

He was found unconscious when the gates were at last opened, clutching his Lifestone to his chest with one hand and holding a black eagle feather with the fingers of the other, and thus was he gently carried inside the gates.

Circling far above, Bimily made sure that her charge was safe beneath the roof of the Temple before turning her thoughts to the task of finding Shunlar.

TWELVE

SAND SEEMED TO STRETCH IN EVERY DIRECTION. There had been only sand for hours and hours—nothing but dry, hot sand. Eight days' ride southwest, had been the only instructions his father had given Ranth the night before as he placed the gold chain around his neck. Then Benyar had touched an object on his chest beneath his tunic that hung from his neck by a chain similar to the one Ranth now wore. He recalled the faraway look that had passed across Benyar's eyes, as if he had heard something or someone. Feeling for the piece around his neck, Ranth let its weight and warmth give him a small amount of comfort.

"So soon? Father you are gone from me so soon?" Tears ran down Ranth's cheeks, precious liquid that evaporated quickly in the heat. Realizing he was crying, he stopped, then shook his head, straining to listen.

Don't waste your water on the dead, rang a voice inside his head in a familiar accent. It seemed Benyar had not left him altogether alone.

"It must be the heat," Ranth mumbled to himself. He turned in the saddle to see how the woman behind him was faring. So far, true to her word, she had managed to stay on her horse. This woman was now his responsibility. She was badly wounded, and continued to lose blood. The constant motion of riding kept the gash on her side from closing altogether. He knew they must find water and shelter from the sun soon.

Ranth reined his horse to a halt, and the woman's mount stopped as well, connected to Ranth's saddle by the rope. Checking his companion, he could tell she was using all of her reserves just to sit astride her horse. Her lips were white, as were the knuckles of her right hand that tightly gripped the pommel. Ranth had helped her bind her left arm to her side with a piece of leather, but blood still dripped from the wound, down onto her mount. The smell of blood made the animal's eyes search about nervously, and its flanks quivered.

Ranth offered the woman some water from a skin, but she refused it with a shake of her head. Both knew they needed to find shade soon or they would perish in the desert heat. Ranth hung the waterskin back over his shoulder and nudged his horse forward with a touch to its flanks, offering a silent prayer of thanks as he did so for choosing these mounts. They were young and energetic animals, and so far had responded eagerly to his every demand. As the day wore on, though, much of their youthful enthusiasm drained away.

Once more they stopped for a drink of water, and this time the woman managed to swallow a small amount. She looked even more pale than before, if that was possible. Her forehead had a strange greenish tint to it. As Ranth scanned the horizon, he cursed under his breath. Off to their left he spotted a sandstorm steadily making its way toward them. Ranth pulled a hooded cloak over his head and managed to cover the woman just as the storm hit.

The two sturdy horses braced themselves against the wind as it began whipping up the sand into whirlpools of stinging pellets. Both animals turned their backs into it and stretched their necks out, alternately sniffing the air and sneezing together. After much head shaking and pulling against the reins, Ranth recognized this as the moment to give them their heads. He loosened his control on the reins and urged his mount in the direction in which it was already straining. The tired animals picked up their feet and plodded on. The woman remained astraddle, practically motionless now, rocking stiffly with the rhythm of her mount.

They traveled blind for some distance, and Ranth lost track of the hours. Finally, as the wind subsided, he peered out from beneath the edge of his hood. In the distance there appeared to be an outcropping of rocks and a few trees. The horses smelled water, and they began a hard, bouncy trot, then a canter, and finally they ran full out. Ranth watched to see that his charge didn't fall from her horse as they galloped to water and safety, leaving the stinging sandstorm behind.

The oasis was very real, and a quick scan proved it to be empty of anything other than plant life. Heady smells of ripe fruits and blossoms filled the air, but to Ranth and Shunlar, the strongest smell was the water. The horses stopped only after they had walked into the very middle of the large pool up to their bellies, where they stood, sighing and drinking deeply.

Ranth dismounted and was at the woman's side immediately. She let him catch her as she slipped from the saddle and into the water. Her side burned as water and sweat seeped into her wounds. She grimaced, refusing to cry out, then lay limp, floating, held gently in his arms. She turned her head to take small sips of the water, and it seemed to give her enough strength to speak.

"Take me to dry land and bind my side tightly to stop the flow of blood." Then the exhaustion and pain were too much and she lost consciousness.

Ranth carefully carried her from the pool and laid her upon the sand. Then he remembered the horses and ran back into the water for them. They'd be in bad shape if he let them drink too much too soon. He had to resort to blatant manipulation as he plunged into the minds of both horses. They finally let him lead them to shade where he tied their reins firmly to a tree, grabbing one of the bedrolls as he hurried back to the woman he'd left lying on the sand.

She was still unconscious, thankfully. He unrolled the blanket and laid her upon it as gently as he could. He untied the leather binding that held her left arm to her side and lifted up the edges of her leather shirt to examine the wound. There was a long, clean slice covering nearly all of her ribs on the left side, as well as a deep gash into the muscle of her left upper arm. As he moved her arm, Shunlar groaned in pain. It didn't appear that the blade had been poisoned, but the wound was deeper than he'd suspected.

His hands touched her side, and he was startled to feel a searing pain along his left side and arm. Touching the wound somehow had transmitted her physical pain into his body. From somewhere deep in his memory he recalled a healing technique, learned at the Temple, of sending a visual probe within her body and repairing the damage from the inside out. Bandaging would stop the blood after a while, but it would take so very long to heal, and there were sure to be search parties sent after them. They might be on the run again before this night was over, and she had lost so much blood, it was doubtful she could ride farther. There was no alternative.

Ranth settled himself into a comfortable position and put his hands over her forehead. Never having done this before—having only learned about the technique—he remembered how it should work, in theory, and shuddered as he began. He reached within her mind and was at once aware of a quality of thought not unlike his own.

She not only welcomed him but encouraged him as well. It was as though she recognized him and knew his touch. Puzzled by this at first, Ranth set to work, setting aside any questions he had about that until later when he could ask her. There were so many severed blood vessels to bind together, so many sliced muscle fibers. He plunged into this work as though born to it, all the while being gently encouraged by Shunlar. Their minds worked together perfectly. No questions were asked. None, that is, until he was nearly finished and began to repair the bottom rib. He should have been alerted by what appeared to be bright lights flashing behind him.

The woman suddenly awakened, screaming, "What are

you doing in here? Who gave you permission to touch me like that? *Get out!*''

Ranth grabbed his temples, gasped, then lost consciousness, toppling over in a dead faint.

Suddenly awake, Shunlar realized that she had lashed out with a bolt of raw energy meant to do what . . . stun . . . kill? She couldn't remember. Nor could she remember where she was or how she got here. She touched the nape of her neck and found no familiar prickle of warning. When she awoke to find him so intimately embedded within her body, her natural instinct for self-preservation had taken over and she had reacted aggressively.

She pulled herself up onto her right elbow, sucking her breath in sharply as she moved her left arm. It was bandaged! Her shirt was open and she looked down at a long red scar in the beginning stages of healing that ran the entire length of her ribcage. Memories of the fight in the dungeon, of killing the guards, of the death of the man Kessell, and of their flight into the desert ran through her mind. She shook her head, trying to clear away some of the grogginess, and turned to look at the man lying next to her, face down in the sand. With a trembling hand she grabbed his warrior braid, pulled his face out of the sand and flung him onto his back in a single movement that left her panting.

She crawled closer to him, shaking from shock and anger. Was he breathing? Yes, but, several slaps later he was still unconscious. She screamed at him, "What gave you the right, son of a sheep! Who taught you manners, some dung farmer? No one invades me that way." But she was screaming to herself. Her strength ebbing, she fell onto her left side and gasped at the pain that washed over her. Venting at him did no good, not in his condition. *Certainly doesn't improve mine either*, she thought to herself, gasping for breath.

Shunlar looked him over carefully as her breathing slowed. He was not visibly bruised and he certainly was not hard to look upon either, she noticed for the first time.

With a sigh she pushed herself into a sitting position, near his head.

Very carefully she reached out with her awareness toward his mind. To her surprise, she encountered no one. Instead she appeared to have stepped into a gray, lifeless plane. This was much worse than she had imagined. Out of the corner of her mind's eye she saw someone move, but when she turned to see who it was, he scurried away, a shadow of the man she sought. After several attempts she was finally able to catch up to the faint shadow, but there was little awareness left, and it was becoming fainter by the second. Only raw emotions seemed to be emanating from him, but not much else of the personality of her rescuer remained.

Another stab of pain quickly made Shunlar remember her own needs. In this dimension of mind-to-mind contact she was able to see inside her body with very little effort. A look at the wound showed her that the blood vessels near her last rib still needed reconnecting. Without thinking, she split her awareness, continuing with the tissue reconstruction where he had left off, as she called out to him: *Come back. If you can hear me, follow the sound of my voice and come back. Please, it's not as safe here as it appears.* It was difficult to tell if the man had heard her. Sound did not seem to carry in this place.

Annoyed by her weakness, annoyed by having to rescue someone when she needed to rebuild her own strength, she continued after him, the sweat running down her temples. It was dangerous for her to allow feelings to color her thoughts as she approached him. Remembering that, she put her emotions on hold and continued to call out to him, but tentatively this time, prepared for retaliation.

ThirTeeN

CREEDATH AWOKE WITH A START, SCREAMING FOR the guards before his feet touched the floor. Fully clothed the man was impressive; naked he was even more so. His tall, well-muscled frame was taut. There was no fat on him. A rigorous schedule of combat practice and swordplay each day plus a diet of lean meat, grains, and vegetables kept him fit and trim.

With a forceful yank, Creedath pulled open his door, causing the sleeping guard to fall to the floor at his feet, his armor clattering as he did so. Waking so abruptly, the guard began to sputter as he tried, unsuccessfully, to stand. Then he realized the naked form standing over him was Lord Creedath—and worse, Creedath had his foot planted firmly on the guard's chest. The sword being held to the guard's throat was beginning to cut off his wind. Wide-eyed, he could only stare up at Creedath, motionless.

"This is how you guard me?" were the last words the hapless man ever heard as the sword plunged into his throat.

Creedath pulled the blade out, stepped over the body, and yelled once more, this time coupling rage with the awesome power of his untrained telepathy. The shout shattered the dreams of each living being in the palace. Shrieks of pain could be heard emanating from every corner, inside and out. The sound of footsteps came next, as people scurried everywhere, some moaning loudly from the pain, holding their heads.

Mistress Ranla approached. With hands at her temples and tears running down her cheeks, she fell to her knees before Creedath saying, "Master, I implore you. The pain is unbearable."

By this time his face was crimson. He took a deep breath and pulled back the crippling force of his mind. "Do you think I care about your pain? My guard was asleep at his post, as I believe was everyone else under this damn roof. If I could, I'd put them all to the sword, but then I'd have no one left to guard me. Have someone take this away," he snarled, pointing with his sword at the still form of the guard he had just killed. Then he turned and stepped over the body that blocked the entrance to his chambers.

"Send someone to dress me and restart the fire in here," he ordered over his shoulder. Then something made him turn and stare at Ranla in an unusual way. "No, better yet, you dress me, Ranla," he said, as a curious smile barely turned up the edges of his mouth. He turned and went back into his chambers.

Still kneeling, Ranla raised her head and forced herself to look at the corpse before her. She had known the man and liked him well. He left behind a wife and two children. But none of that mattered now; all that mattered was to stay alive and keep everyone out of Creedath's way. Ranla forced herself to be calm as she realized Creedath had just ordered her to dress him.

It had been years since Creedath had allowed Ranla into his chambers. He actually liked this woman and knew she had once felt an attraction to him. But that was then. Now he knew that fear had replaced any desire for him, a deep fear that controlled her completely. Never would he let anything that smacked of love or emotions interfere with his control over a person. Once he had let down his guard and trusted; the scar in his back burned at the thought. Hadn't he just dreamed of that night? Somehow he was unable to remember. His head felt fuzzy and he rubbed his temples.

Ranla was on her feet at once, hurrying to the doorway, as two guards rushed down the corridor toward her. "Mistress, has any harm come to you or the Master?" asked the first man.

"No, but take this poor wretch away quickly and quietly or you may be next. Send a young maid, *not* a pretty one," she emphasized, "with hot cup and coals, to the master's chamber. Take care to replace the guard here immediately and tell every man you see to have his sharpest wit about him today. Go at once," she commanded. Taking a deep breath as she stepped into the chambers, Ranla closed the door quietly behind her.

"You have handled another crisis with a clear head. That's what I admire most about you, Ranla: your clear head." And something like gentleness crossed Creedath's dark brow for a moment. Saying no more, he stood, waiting for her to come closer. Ranla stood at the door, eyes cast down at the floor. "What are you waiting for, woman? I told you to dress me."

"As you wish," was all she said as she walked across the room to stand before him. "In what shall I dress you today, sir?" Ranla asked, still refusing to look him in the eye.

Creedath reached out and cupped her chin in his hand. Slowly raising her face to his, he pulled her closer, his cold gray-blue eyes penetrating her depths. He bent over and tenderly kissed her on the cheek. The caress was pretense; physical contact enabled him to read her mind, and he checked the thoughts racing through Ranla's mind.

"No, we will not be lovers," he whispered to her. "I need you to run my house and train my servants. You I prize above all others. Do no more thinking along those lines or you will regret it." With that warning he quickly pulled away his hand.

For the briefest of moments she had had the fearful thought that he might force himself upon her, and he had seen it! Ranla shook her head to regain possession of her own thoughts and realized her body was trembling.

"Do you wish the brown leathers today, Lord?" she asked, forcing composure to take hold.

"They will do. Hurry; I grow impatient. I must learn just what transpired under this roof last night. Summon the stranger, Kessell, and that little pup; what's his name?"

"Ranth?" she reminded him.

"That's it; Ranth. But don't bring him to me until after I've seen Kessell, and only bring him after I've eaten. I don't wish to spoil my appetite with that pretty boy and his newly found pet." These last words he spat out. His temper had returned, and Ranla hurriedly dressed the man she called lord.

Years ago Ranla had hoped to one day share his bed. However, with each passing day her hope was crushed by his cruelty, until it had been completely replaced by fear. But today—today had given her an unexpected sense of apprehension. What if he were truly changing his mind and pretending otherwise? She shuddered at the thought. Fear made her mind race. Perhaps a song-spell would help. With fingers flying over the laces of Creedath's tunic, Ranla began humming a song. The effects were immediate. Under the leather Ranla felt her master's muscles relax, and as his breath came and went with a deep slow rhythm, hers calmed also.

The guard's knock at the door announced a pretty young maid carrying breakfast and hot coals for the fire. A self-satisfied grin crossed Creedath's face as he watched her carefully place the tray of hot tea and food on the table and then see to the task of stoking the embers in the fireplace. A quick, fearful look touched Ranla's eyes.

Creedath sat at table and proceeded to eat very calmly, outwardly relaxed, inwardly plotting his next moves. His eyes were curiously glazed as he ate his breakfast.

As he had ordered her to do, Ranla stood near his left shoulder, humming the calming tune over and over just within the range of hearing. Once his breakfast was consumed he instructed Ranla to gather up his guest and ready Ranth for his turn at questioning. As she turned to leave,

Ranla noticed that the young servant girl was standing closer to the calculating, brooding master of the castle than was prudent, an innocent blush on her cheeks. At the door Ranla observed what she feared: Creedath's eyes hungrily assessed the young bosom. He snapped his attention in Ranla's direction momentarily and waved at her to close the door. She obeyed instantly, fearing his wrath if she delayed.

Sweeping through the corridors, Ranla questioned every person she came upon. All had the same story to report of mysteriously falling asleep at their posts or wherever they stood. The frequency of the distressing story made her forget her fears for the young servant girl left alone with the master.

Ranla pounded repeatedly upon Kessell's door. When no answer came she ordered the guard to unbolt it. The bolt slid open with a loud click and another mystery presented itself. He and his belongings were gone! The thought of explaining the mysterious disappearance of this strange man to Lord Creedath sent cold waves through her body. Ranla whirled on her heels, nearly knocking over the guard who was standing close behind her. Recovering her composure, she began to question this unfortunate who had been posted outside the door and who, she knew, would be held accountable for the whereabouts of Kessell.

"Mistress, I did not see him leave. I swear I never left my post. I . . . I . . . cannot remember anything about last night, not beyond hearing a strange noise, that is. I woke this morning leaning against the doorway with a stiff neck, Mistress," reported the now very uncomfortable guard.

Ranla assumed the most severe expression she could, and ordered, "Remain guarding this door until you are relieved. See that no one enters or leaves." Beneath this hard exterior she began to worry in earnest.

Knowing this guard might suffer the same fate as the one who had been posted outside Creedath's door, Ranla decided to tell the master herself, stopping first in her chambers to quickly splash water on her face, change from a nightdress into one that showed off her ample bosom and run a comb through the thick blonde hair that cascaded in waves about her shoulders. Though young, just twenty-five, Ranla had been chosen for her position on her physical appearance, which she was well aware of. Being intelligent, her self-preservation instincts were high. She knew that Creedath might respond better to the bad news she bore if she took the time to freshen herself. She sent another servant to have Ranth brought to her for questioning before being sent off to Creedath. Learning he was not in his room either, the knots in her already tight stomach constricted again.

To muster her courage at Creedath's door she began humming the calming tune before the guard knocked to announce her. Once inside the room she bent to one knee, bowed her head and began to deliver the bad news.

"My Lord," she said, not daring to raise her head, "it seems the man Kessell is not in his room. I also have men searching the castle for Ranth, who has disappeared as well." She waited, continuing to stare at the floor.

Footsteps told her Creedath was approaching her. He nearly knocked her over as he stormed from the room. "Guard, follow me." His booming voice trailed off as he rattled each new man he encountered at his post along the corridor, questioning, demanding answers.

Ranla just stood and stared after him. There hadn't been time to tell Creedath about the strange sound the guard had mentioned, and now another sound caught her attention. She turned and looked toward the bed on the other side of the room. The pretty young maid she'd left behind many minutes ago was huddled in the middle of it, clutching the covers, her torn clothing on the floor.

"I hate him . . . I hate him . . ." was all she repeated over and over again under her breath, between great sobs. Ranla came to her side, fighting off the feelings of guilt running through her for having left her alone with him. Gathering up the remains of the dress, she gently wiped away the girl's tears and encouraged her to leave the blankets of the bed and dress herself. With the extra skirts they managed to cover her young shoulders where the dress had been none too gently ripped from her body.

"Hush now, my girl. I never should have left you alone with him in such a temper. Are you hurt?"

"No," she managed through her sobs, clutching Ranla's shoulders. Pride had made her lie. One of her cheeks was turning purple, and a trickle of blood coursed down her chin from the corner of her mouth.

Her sobs stopped in mid-breath, however, as Creedath stormed back into his chambers with a retinue of armed guards close at his heels. "Remove that immediately," he pointed at the young maid, "and see, Ranla, that I never encounter her again," he commanded. Both women were hurried from the room by two guards, breathing only after the slam of the huge wooden door echoed off down the hallway.

Creedath sat listening intently to the story of one of the unfortunate guards before him. He had chosen these men at random, waking one at his post, the others picked from the courtyard where they were stumbling around in bewilderment.

"Lieutenant Meecha, proceed with the interrogation," he said, cold eyes boring holes into the men standing before him.

Each in their turn told how they had been aware of a sound that had evidently put all of the castle under a spell of sleep. At the first mention of this strange sound, Creedath sucked in his breath. He too remembered, now that it was brought to his attention, a high piercing tone just at the edge of his hearing. His sleep that night had been unusually deep as well. So, it had been a spell, he quickly deduced. But who could have cast it? Surely not the stranger who called himself Kessell. His thoughts were interrupted by another loud knock on the door.

"Enter!" he screamed, causing all in the room to jump.

"My Lord, we have found the bodies of three guards in the lower dungeon. It appears one of the prisoners has also escaped: the woman brought in two nights ago by the stranger. There are traces of blood that lead from the round dungeon to the stables and out the back gate. Also, my Lord, two horses are missing," reported a guard, bent on one knee before him.

Creedath remembered the web he had placed over the entrance to the dungeon. It enabled him to see, for an instant, any who walked through it. He recalled seeing, moments ago, this same guard and others as they crossed over the boundary of it. It appeared to be in working order. But, if a spell had caused him to be profoundly deep asleep, as he was last night, he might not have seen anyone crossing it!

"Meecha," came the voice, icy cold this time, "find the best trackers in the city. Take the men you most trust and go after them. Do not return until or unless you find them. Is that understood?"

Lieutenant Meecha nodded. Aware that his life had just become expendable, he asked, "How many are we searching for, my Lord?"

"How many indeed?" was the only reply.

FOURTEEN

THE RUINS OF AN IMMENSE CITY SPREAD ACROSS the horizon. Once a highly developed society had thrived here, loving, creating, building. High atop a tall, nondescript stone structure that showed obvious signs of repair, someone sat, looking out across the expanse. Tendrils of smoke escaped from a delicate nose. Stunning yellow-gold eyes scanned the distance, well beyond the buildings of broken stone. Turning at the sound of footsteps behind her, Cloonth looked upon her mate, Alglooth, approaching, his long white hair casting a nimbus about his face.

"Waiting longer would be folly. Two days has it been since we sent the dove with its message. Many more days than that have passed that Shunlar has been gone from her cottage. My senses tell me there is danger. Come, we must fly now, my lovely one."

Alglooth extended his pale slender hand to Cloonth. As she grasped it, his concern flooded into her awareness and brought tears to her eyes. Both of the delicately boned persons poised for a moment on the ledge, extended their wings, and were lifted away by an updraft.

Soaring in an upward spiral, they surveyed the ruins of their home city Stiga beneath them, turning shades of mauve in the pink light of dusk. Choosing to fly at this time of day assured them privacy—not that anyone would invade these tremendous crumbling bastions.

Alglooth thought back over their years together. In their

youth, secrecy had not been sought. They had lived a very public life and were treated like royalty, even paraded before the crowds of the city on special holidays. As they grew older, the public displays grew more and more tedious, even uncomfortable. Tempers flared, as well as tongues. Sometimes the curtains burst into flame, once the talent for flame-speaking was learned.

Eventually they were left alone, their living quarters being in a secluded part of the city that few frequented. People gradually forgot about them, and stories of the half-dragon, half-human boy and girl became the stuff of legends. With the passage of time everyone they knew in their youth grew old and died, but Alglooth and Cloonth continued to grow more beautiful and wise and strong, never suspecting that some of the inhabitants still secretly spied on their every move. They learned to cling to one another in every way and, when the time was right, performed their bonding ritual in the privacy of their secluded home. The years passed, and when the child they so much desired was born it was to cling to life only for a few precious hours.

Perhaps it just was not strong enough. Perhaps it was the poison that continuously seeped into the stone from the wars. The people of the city, in their lust for power, had resorted to magical weapons. Magical warfare caused irreparable damage to the living, and thousands died from the poison, the rest from the fighting. The remaining few fled the rubble of what once had been a proud, beautiful city. No one knew that the two half-human, half-dragon people had been left behind in the ruins, alone with their grief.

Alglooth in his terrible anguish flew from the side of his mate to look for signs of life in the city. Cloonth had finally fallen into a deep sleep after days of crying. It was his intention to find someone to blame and punish. Instead, he found nothing but the bones of the dead. His rage at having no one to inflict his horrible sorrow upon pushed him over the edge, and he destroyed what would burn with gigantic balls of flame. Exhausted and numb, he flew from the smoldering ruins to the great forest.

The early dawn light found Alglooth perched in the branches of a towering pine. From this vantage point he could watch the people of the valley and not be seen. He had no plan. He sat, observing the comings and goings of whoever walked near his hiding place.

Into his field of vision came the very familiar form of a small, muscular young mother, nursing her baby as she walked. Moving quickly along the ground through the trees she arrived at her post. She secured the sleeping baby in her cradle in the branches of a tree and left to scout the area. Alglooth's gaze followed her path, remembering their meeting nearly two years before at the dark of the moons festival. She had thought he was one of her kind. As was their custom, they met in the dark and made love in the treetops until she fell into an exhausted, satisfied sleep.

As Alglooth observed her, he became aware that numbness was rapidly being replaced by pain, especially in the area surrounding his heart. He saw the face of his beloved mate and knew what he must do. Swiftly, silently, he swooped upon the babe. He picked the child up gently, trying not to waken her, but she opened her eyes and laughed at him. She reached upward and touched his chin with a tiny hand, her green and gold–speckled eyes looking trustingly into his. In the moment physical connection was made, Alglooth knew she was his child. Their minds opened to each other, and he saw the moment of her conception. Yes, he remembered that night. He recognized his daughter.

His next move was to carefully remove, then tear the clothing she wore and hide it nearby. Nothing she was wearing must return to the city with them. He removed her tiny earrings and bracelet and hid them with the small torn garments. He tucked her safely within the folds of his tunic, and cradling her to his chest, he flew soundlessly into the dawn.

The next months were spent settling the three of them

into a safe environment. Cloonth was so preoccupied with having a child to nurse and care for, she was practically useless when it came to planning a move. Everything in her being was poured into this little person, whom they called by many pet names. The child would choose her own name when she was older. Nowhere on her body were to be found any trace of scales, nor did she have wings; however, as she grew older, a large birthmark at the nape of her neck took on a bright greenish tint. Her hair was straight, shimmering copper in the sunlight, with one or two strands of white at her temples that were to become thicker streaks as she grew older. Her eyes danced in a most pleasant way when she saw her father enter the room.

They lived for many years in the large, comfortable cave that had once been the home of their great dragon mother. They had found her bones deep down at the bottom of one of the labyrinthine tunnels. In a few years, when parts of the city were again fit to be lived in, the family moved back, this time taking up residence in the ruins of what had once been the heart of the city, the Temple. It was there that Alglooth and Cloonth learned the circumstances under which they were brought into the world. One man's greed was at the bottom of it all. They chose not to tell the child.

From the scrolls, tablets, and books left behind, all manner of knowledge became available to them now. They found out that their ability to read each other's minds was not limited to their kind, but could be learned by anyone. They learned also that they possessed a special gift. This was not discussed in any of the texts, though their search went on for many years. It seemed only they could see the path left by others, best described as a trace of heat in the air. And the child possessed this gift also.

She chose her name one day from the numbers of the Great Cauldron. It meant "chance" in the Old Tongue. Shunlar, the six-pointed star.

These memories flooded their thoughts as they flew toward Shunlar's cottage. She had never been told the truth of her parentage and had never asked. Alglooth had chosen not to speak of it all these years. Now he faced, with more regret than he had felt in his lifetime—this being a considerable number of years—his decision not to speak of it. Whenever the subject had been broached he could read in the child's mind her denial based upon their physical appearances. As she grew older, the question of who her parents might be no longer mattered. She had been raised with so much love, trust, and understanding, it was taken for granted that these two beautiful creatures were all she needed for parents.

Cloonth landed first. She inspected the cottage, finding faint heat traces of several men who had waited just beyond the first stand of trees. Inside the cottage their heat paths were easier to see, having been left relatively undisturbed in the building. When the men had finally entered the house, they had ripped it apart in anger at finding no one there. Seeing that nothing had been permanently damaged, Cloonth and Alglooth again took flight.

Gliding silently upon the breeze, they followed the even fainter heat trace of Shunlar to the walls of Vensunor. Knowing they must keep their true identities secret, they landed in a thicket of small trees far from any probing eyes. Wrapping their cloaks tightly around their wings once they landed, Alglooth and Cloonth reassured each other with silent glances. Because of her inability to control the perpetual smoke emanating from her nostrils, a pipe was a necessary item of camouflage for Cloonth, and she pulled one from a deep pocket and clamped it firmly between her teeth. Both covered themselves with an illusion so as to blend more easily into the crowds of the city and travel unnoticed. They began the walk to Vensunor in silence and passed through the gates, just two of the many anonymous travelers.

Once inside the city their suspicions were confirmed as they observed Shunlar's heat path first entering and then leaving the Dragon's Breath Inn twice. Cloonth removed the pipe from her mouth and chuckled out loud at the name. Both noticed that the second set of heat trace paths had signs of unusual perturbation, the most noteworthy being that a larger group left the second time and there appeared to be signs of a scuffle, although after so many days it was hard to be sure.

At the wall of the merchant Creedath's palace they found the same to be true. The first heat path was fainter, while the second showed haste in leaving. Shunlar was upon horseback the second time, and they recognized the trace of blood in the second heat path. In their haste, both of them failed to recognize the shimmering trace of Bimily, but they had never known her to take on the shape of a rat or a horse.

FIFTEEN

RANTH WAS ONLY MINIMALLY AWARE OF SOMEONE calling to him. He had finally succumbed to the shock of his years of loneliness and loss; first his friend and mentor, Master Chago, and now his father had been cruelly taken from him. Being hit with the flash of energy loosed by Shunlar had been like an explosion upon the barriers he had so carefully built and maintained for years. Behind those barriers the lonely young man had no voice with which to answer, only emotions. His body shook as he lay on the sand, eyes closed, hardly breathing, as tremors passed over him. He was no longer in control of his mind's reactions, no longer aware that a deeply instinctual part of his training, learned many years ago at the knee of Master Chago, had come into play.

Shunlar continued to try to reach him, her strength ebbing. She thought she was making progress, but was in no way prepared for the sound that tore itself from her throat when his defenses reached back and touched her mind. After what seemed like several minutes she stopped panting.

What in the remains of the pyre was that? By the moons, he must have learned something while under that gods-cursed roof.

Halfheartedly she attempted to reach him again. Each time she approached his mind with a sliver of a mental probe, bolts of lightninglike current crackled and made her skin itch. A final exasperated effort nearly knocked her unconscious. She sat for several minutes trying to decide what to do. If she left him alone now, the chance remained that he might die. The only alternative, it seemed, was to keep trying and risk weakening herself further.

I'll rot before I get so weak that I can't defend myself. She lay back onto the sand, reaching into the recesses of her awareness to gather her strength. Deep within her belly she found the wellspring of her power and as she nurtured the sensation and watched it grow, she felt sparks of it through her torso, legs, arms, and head. For several minutes she lay there, a faint golden glow spreading throughout her body. When she opened her eyes, several minutes later, she felt balanced and stronger.

Thirsty from her efforts, she rose and walked the short distance to the water's edge for a drink. She bent over to cup water to her mouth and a touch of dizziness, probably from loss of blood, made her lose her balance and nearly fall into the water. A sudden movement behind her made her turn her head in time to see the man struggling to stand, as if in anticipation of her tumble.

By the stars, he knocks on death's very door and yet something compels him to protect me. Dare I test him to see if he will come to my rescue? Well, why not? she decided. She lowered herself into the water, walking into the middle of the large pool until she stood, waist deep, flailing her arms and legs and yelling, "Help! Help me, kind sir!" in a mocking voice. She didn't have long to wait.

Instantly he clambered onto his feet. Running with jerky, awkward steps to the rocks he dove in after her. Waiting for him on the other side of the pool, Shunlar could tell she had the advantage. He may have jumped into the water to save her but his eyes were still glazed over and there was no hint of expression behind them as he swam to her. She ducked beneath the surface just as he reached her, and as he sputtered, she pulled him under. With her arms and legs wrapped around his torso from behind, they sank to the bottom of the pool. Her mind pulsed a tentative, slow message to him: *Listen to my voice. Rebuild your barriers and live!*

Next she began projecting pictures to him, never actually touching his mind, just sending mental images to him of what this thing called a "barrier" looked like. Curiously, it resembled a brick wall.

Slowly, very slowly in suspended time, Ranth responded to her instructions and began to build a wall of bricks, putting one brick upon another. Satisfied that he was no longer in danger, and badly in need of air, Shunlar released her hold on him. Together they pushed off the bottom, gasping for breath as they broke the surface of the water.

An awkward silence followed as they swam across the middle of the pool back to dry land. When their feet touched the sand, a fiery, lightninglike current snapped through their bodies. The jolt brought a simultaneous cough of surprise from their lips as they moved quickly apart and stood facing each other, dripping, feeling uneasy.

Shunlar was the first to speak. "Have you always had this effect upon others?" she asked between breaths.

"What effect can you mean, Lady?"

"I'm no lady. And I mean that bolt of energy that you just threw at me. Who are you? Who taught you these things—that monster, Creedath?" She spat after saying the name.

"But I assumed you did that," he answered quietly, eyeing her suspiciously.

They both raised one arm and reached toward the other. Another bolt ran up their arms, leaving them gasping for air, as if someone had punched them in the stomach. Once they regained their breath they looked up at one another to see that they were both doubled over, rubbing their arms.

"There must be some explanation for this. I have never felt the likes of this before. Could it have something to do with this oasis, or could it be the effects of the water?" Shunlar asked out loud. She turned to walk away only to realize that her knees were buckling and she was falling. At her side before she landed, he eased her to the sand as yet another bolt of energy ran through them. Curiously, Ranth noticed that he felt stronger the closer he was to the woman, once the effects of this strange energy jolt washed over them.

"Please, just lie here while I collect kindling for a fire. Night is coming and we don't want to be wet and cold." Ranth rose looking for anything that would burn. Passing the horses, he spied her saddlebag and brought it to her.

"You might want to change into dry clothes," he mumbled as he tossed it to her, careful not to get too close, to avoid her eyes.

She didn't want to admit it, but she knew he was right. The sun was beginning to set, bringing cold night with it, and she shivered in her wet clothes. Though it took great effort, she pulled her saddlebag to her and took out her other pair of leather breeches and a dry tunic with sleeves. Sadly, she pulled off her new, quite thoroughly soaked, boots. She wrung out her wet clothes, and then flattened them on the sand beside her. Unfurling her bedroll, Shunlar lay down and covered herself. Exhaustion took her quickly, and within two breaths she fell into a troubled sleep. She dreamed of a wizard with white hair. In the dream she asked him what could be done about this strange bolt of energy they were both experiencing. The wizard laughed and advised, "It is simple, young one. You have met your match, and you must take him to your bed before you both loosen teeth over it."

"But," she protested, "he is untouched. I prefer a man who has had some experience, some polish to his sword." She laughed rudely at her last comment.

The loud clatter of dried palm branches dropping to the ground woke Shunlar with a start. She didn't have to ask to know her dream, especially her rude protest, had been broadcast to him. The cold fire in his eyes told her that and much more. Too late, Shunlar slammed down the barriers to her mind.

Ranth managed to keep distance between himself and this strange woman by digging a shallow pit in the sand

and starting the fire. Once it was burning, he hurried to the horses to change into dry clothing, keeping the animals between himself and the woman as he did. It seemed that staying on opposite sides of the fire kept them from jolting one another with the strange lightning.

With a start, Ranth realized he was ravenously hungry. He rummaged in his saddlebag for a package of dried meat and hard travel bread. He tossed these to her after taking a portion for himself, then sat on his bedroll on the opposite side of the fire. The food stopped the rumbling of their bellies.

Shunlar looked around her for the first time as they sat eating. The oasis was sheltered by huge rock formations. If anyone searched for them, however, they would be easy to spot, especially by firelight. Sitting up, she scanned the surrounding area. No one approached from any angle, but that could change at any time. The fire would have to die, but at least her hair might dry and she had the luxury of dry clothes. Things could be much worse. She sighed heavily. The silence thickened as the fire popped, spitting embers onto the sand.

Through half-closed eyes Ranth watched her unbraid her hair and comb it out to dry in the warmth of the fire. It felt unseemly and highly intimate for him to do the same. He merely squeezed the remaining water from his braid as he watched her. Deciding it was time for sleep, Ranth opened his bedroll and pushed the sand into more comfortable piles for sleeping. Both were jolted once more, however, when he accidentally got a little too close to her.

Breaking the silence first, Ranth announced, "Lady, I am here to protect you and pose no threat to you. Can you please stop . . . whatever you call this fiery touch. It is becoming painful. My first priority is to find my father's people and there, I am sure, you will be treated fairly." A dark frown furrowed his brow as he examined his arm for scorch marks.

"Stop calling me lady. If you must address me, my name is Shunlar. I don't recall asking you for any protection.

Besides, who said I would travel your way? You have done well healing my wounds. For this I am grateful and in your debt, but our ways part in the morning.'' Thinking out loud, she remembered, ''No, consider this: I brought you back to the land of the living, so my debt to you is cleared.'' A very smug look crossed her face as she combed back her mostly dry hair to braid it.

''You were the one who nearly took my life by lashing out at me as I was tending to your wounds. As I see it, you are still indebted to me.'' He was angry, frustrated, and suddenly very aroused. He licked his lips and continued, ''I have a request that you, indebted as you are, cannot deny me, Shunlar.''

Shunlar felt a faint trace of sweat dance across her top lip, then disappear in the heat cast by the fire. Hearing him speak her name made her pleasantly uncomfortable. ''Speak then. I'll be the judge of whether or not I can deny you,'' she whispered, her throat suddenly dry.

''If I am, as you say, untouched,'' he cleared his throat nervously, then continued, ''why don't you change that?'' As soon as the words were out of his mouth, Ranth's face turned crimson. He rubbed his forehead, asking himself, *How have I become so bold to ask a question like that?*

Shunlar stared at the dark, handsome young man who sat across the fire from her, considering what he had just asked of her as payment for the debt of which he spoke. His black, almond-shaped eyes had the most alluring effect. Young though he seemed, he was not undesirable. She stopped looking at him, busy with putting away her belongings in her kit bag. When she had finished, she raised her face to look at Ranth again. Shunlar's gaze softened as she stared into his eyes, her decision made. *Perhaps the white-haired man in my dream is correct. There is only one way to find out . . .* she mused to herself.

Answering in a quiet voice, ''May all my future debts be so pleasurably fulfilled. You have my name; tell me yours.'' She reached a hand out to him.

''Ranth,'' he said softly.

"Ranth," she whispered the name. "Come closer."

Her eyes said the rest as Ranth approached, and they endured, this time eagerly, the jolt of energy running through them accompanied by waves of heat. Beads of perspiration covered both of their bodies as with shaking hands they undressed each other by the firelight. Shunlar was amazed at the urgency surging through her. There had been times when she had let her animal drives take over; times when passion drove her on. This was different. Great shudders pulsed through her body.

Never had Ranth felt such desire, nor had the opportunity to fulfill his need ever been so close. He had only seen women in the palace; none had been allowed to even speak to him. No one had ever touched him in this way. His hands tingled as they caressed her shoulders.

It must be the water in this place, she told herself as their hands explored.

No, Lady, came a soft whisper within her skull, Ranth's voice saying, *This is a fire from within that we cannot contain.*

Feeling Ranth's awareness in her mind caused Shunlar to tremble as the fire in her groin spread throughout her body. Long into the night they stayed with this fire, their bodies turning, tumbling, moving together in their dance. Stopping for a drink of water, they touched, and the flame seemed to leap up and consume them once more. Nothing existed for them except this moment in time. Hours later, sleep took them.

Perhaps that is why it took them so long to hear the nervous sounds of their horses as dawn cast its rosy light on the sand. Shunlar was the first to open her eyes, finally choosing to pay attention to her trap warning signal—the tiny hairs at the back of her neck that now stood firmly on end. There, far off in the distance, a band of people on tired mounts was making its way to the oasis.

As her hand lightly touched Ranth's shoulder to shake him awake, a small spark leapt up her arm and a sensual shudder reverberated down to her feet. She could feel most of her muscles aching painfully from the night's pleasure. A deep breath and a sigh from Ranth told her that he was feeling the same. Shunlar put her hand over his mouth and pointed. Following its direction, his eyes rested on the standard the riders carried. Although the group was nearly thirty minutes' ride away, they recognized the crest of Lord Creedath.

Crawling on their bellies, they buried the ashes of the fire, along with any signs of their presence, gathered their bedrolls and clothing, and crept through the underbrush to the rocks where the horses were hidden. They spoke to them softly until the animals' nervous shifting nearly stopped. Giving care of the horses over to Ranth, Shunlar picked up several branches that were lying on the ground and in a low squat began covering their tracks, following behind him and the horses. Making sure her mental barriers were secured tightly in place, she spoke directly to Ranth's mind.

Because it is near dawn and they ride, the only advantage we have is sleep, though not much, she remembered. *We can hide from them on the far side of the water. If we have to we will bury ourselves and the horses in the sand.*

There looked to be a cave on the other side of the water. I saw it while gathering firewood last night. Follow me. With that, Ranth hurried their mounts between rocks that did in fact form a small cave. But with two people and two horses there was no room to turn around. The horses seemed to like it though, and instantly relaxed in the dark coolness, as did their human companions. They slipped grain bags over the horses' heads, and both animals fell into a satisfied half-sleep as they chewed. While the animals ate, Shunlar and Ranth dressed.

"Stay with them while I check on our visitors," said Shunlar as she squeezed past Ranth. This brushing against his body caused her to add, "Please. I go because I am better skilled at stealth. I know you can handle the horses."

If Ranth could have seen her face fully, he would have done more than nod assent. Their touching the night before had created a bond between them, the strength of which neither had imagined possible. Their hands met, then separated as Shunlar stepped into the dawn light. Already she could hear the jingling of harnesses and orders being shouted as the straggling group of soldiers and mercenaries approached.

Under the cover of rocks and plants, Shunlar lay, watching them drink and refill their water skins. There were two women she recognized, fellow mercenaries she considered friends. They looked at the covered over remains of the camp in the sand but did not speak. Their eyes gave them away as they carefully pretended not to see what was so obvious to a skilled tracker.

One of the women spoke to her companion just loud enough for Lieutenant Meecha, commander of the group, to overhear. "Well, guess we're off the track all right." He summoned them to him and together, in hushed tones, they discussed their next move.

Counting twenty-two members of the party as they rode away some time later, Shunlar slipped back into the coolness of the cave and the arms of Ranth. He greeted her by covering her with hungry kisses, as they both felt the fire growing again.

"We're alone again. I recognized two of the women trackers. For some reason they led the soldiers away," she managed to say between caresses. The horses snored as once more the dance began. "Ranth, what have you done to these two animals?"

"I don't know. It seems now my powers include spelling horses to sleep." They laughed softly.

"Lady, there is only room to stand in here. Can we go outside?"

"No, it's not safe yet," was all she said before her mouth hungrily covered his.

If they had been out in the open, they might have observed a speck in the sky circling in an ever-expanding spiral.

Sixteen

HE WATCHED SILENTLY, SHIVERING IN THE PRE-
dawn light, as the small procession wound its way toward
him into the Circle of Great Trees. Clad only in a leather
loincloth, Gwernz sat upon one blanket, another wrapped
around his shoulders. According to tradition, anyone asking
to be accepted by the Great Trees must spend one week
alone within the sacred grove. His lonely vigil and fast were
now over.

Arlass, the eldest and spiritual leader of the valley, came
first. Six members of the Circle of Protectors came next,
followed by Marleah, and then her son Loff. Each person
carried an elaborately tooled leather bag that contained a
ritual branch from the sacred trees. The branches were
limbs of the Great Trees that had fallen to the ground.
Never were any of the branches touched by saw or knife.
Each limb was approximately three feet in length and had
been chosen for its straight line. They had then been carefully stripped of bark and rubbed until they were smooth;
finally, each branch was covered with gold.

As the group entered the natural amphitheater formed by
the Great Trees and took their places around Gwernz, each
person reverently removed the golden branch from its bag.
As a soft chant began to fill the silence around him, Gwernz
stood and bowed ritually to each member of the Circle.
Starting with Arlass, he took the branches from each person, carefully placing them one by one on the ground,

pointing toward the center of the circle. When all the branches were in place, he returned to his spot in the middle.

The chant became a loud thrumming drone, and as it gained in volume it carried all the participants into a trance. Soon the ritual branches began to glow brightly and shudder until each one stood on end, forming another inner circle. Standing upright, shafts of light poured from the branches onto the lone figure in the center. Soon the grove of the Great Trees was throbbing with light, and Gwernz was especially brilliant. His body was bombarded with pulsating, glowing rays. His hair stood on end, and though his eyes remained open, he was temporarily blinded by the brightness.

Arlass spoke the ritual words of greeting and was answered by a cascade of golden sparks falling around her body. Everyone in the group recognized this as a sign of acceptance. Delight spread quickly around the Circle. Since the beginning was the most critical part of the ceremony, everyone felt that a positive outcome was assured.

Not only had Gwernz been accepted, but the Great Trees had amplified the trance-inducing drone that summoned all the inhabitants of the Valley. As the ceremony continued, people ran up the hill to the grove to encircle, but not enter, the sacred enclosure. The morning sun cast slender shafts of light upon the nine members and Gwernz who stood within. Then, as the entire population of the Valley stood and watched, Gwernz was lifted up. Suspended high above their heads, he rotated slowly while being bathed in blue, green, and golden lights. The Great Trees had, it seemed, accepted him as the next leader of the Valley. As his body gently returned to the ground, the swirling lights subsided and the drone slowly quieted. The ritual branches trembled and lay themselves down upon the ground, and as the lights receded, Gwernz knelt in the midst of the circle blinking, overcome with utter joy.

As silence released the nine who encircled Gwernz from their trance, they picked up the sacred branches that lay on the ground before them, respectfully placed them in their leather bags, and then seated themselves closely around Gwernz.

Arlass approached him with the ritual cup. She said prayers over it, asking for further guidance from the Great Trees. Marleah covered his shivering shoulders with a blanket as he drank the bitter herbs, and sat close beside him with a concerned look on her face. The inhabitants of the Valley also found comfortable places to sit to watch. The strong potion began to take effect. Gwernz's eyes glazed over; his hands trembled. With a thick tongue he began to share the vision the Great Trees had shown him.

"I traveled to a time in the past, to Stiga, when abominable magical weapons were conjured and wars ravaged the land."

The mention of the city their ancestors had fled sent murmurings of trepidation passing through all assembled.

Gwernz waited for silence and once it was quiet, he continued, "A lone female dragon, the last of her kind, lived deep within the mountains. She had witnessed the needless deaths and devastating wars and lay waiting, a terrible hope in her heart. Her hope was that all the men would finally die at each other's hands.

"The evil wizard Banant had overpowered the wizard Porthelae, by creating a spell that ensnared his mind and changed him into a dragon. This evil enchanter's plan was to begin a race of people that would be his mindless slaves, a race of fearsome half-dragon, half-human creatures that would control the minds of those they encountered, thus performing his will."

Another murmur of excitement went through the crowd at the mention of Porthelae. The ancient mystery surrounding his death had never been revealed, though many suspected Banant had been behind it.

"The dragons met. So powerful was Banant's spell that they flew instantly into the air to mate. All would have gone well had the ensorceled wizard's human awareness not returned momentarily to him while in the midst of mating.

The mating completed, the dragons separated, and he flung himself against the rocks. Dying, Porthelae's body returned to its human form.

"The female dragon was furious, for she too had learned the truth of her consort's identity at the moment of mating. She sought out the wizard responsible for this foul deed and, as she reduced him to ashes, felt the stirrings of life within her. She laid but two eggs. When they hatched a mere nine months later, she knew a special breed of beings had come upon the land. Giving birth at her advanced age, however, had put a tremendous strain on her heart. Knowing death was near, she placed her children where they would be found and taken by the people of Stiga to be raised in the city of our ancestors.

"The Great Trees have shown me that one of these half-dragon beings visited our Valley. In fact, he left his seed within my own sister at the Darkest of the Moons Festival. The child has been mourned as dead all these years, but she lives and has grown into a woman who is now being sought by a descendant of the great evil one Banant for the same purpose: to breed a race of beings, descendants of the dragon, who will control others for him."

More murmurings passed through the people, and Gwernz waited for them to become quiet once again. The last bit of information now had Marleah's full attention.

"I have been chosen not to seek but to guide another to find this young woman, my blood, and return with her to our Valley, back to the Circle of Great Trees, so that the truth of her ancestry can be told to her. Loff has been chosen by the Great Trees to go in search of the sister he has never met. Know that he is assured a safe return. Finding her will lead to the destruction of the last living descendant of Banant, thus ending his line forever."

Gwernz paused and gazed out at the people gathered around him. "Lastly, I was shown that the children of the dragon still live."

The mention of the dragon's half-human descendants caused a startled outburst from many in the crowd.

Calling for silence by raising his hand, Gwernz concluded by saying, "They are our ancestors, ancient beings who came to life because Porthelae—whose blood many of us in this Valley sprang from—was spell-cast and mated with a dragon."

Spent, and breathing shallowly, Gwernz closed his eyes and leaned heavily against Marleah. Her face was impassive as she looked upon nothing and no one in particular. Marleah traveled off in her thoughts as she allowed the impact of Gwernz's message to settle in. Her daughter lived; she would be reunited with her. Marleah knew she would meet the strange father of her child.

The revelations of Gwernz's vision seemed to hang over everyone like a spell. They sat and stared as Marleah rocked her brother in her arms like a babe. After many minutes had passed one thought ran through the entire group like a single breath: *His hair has turned completely white!* And, indeed, it was true. Gwernz's hair and beard were now totally white.

Slowly, people began to rise and straggle away, leaving Arlass, Marleah, Loff, and the six members of the Circle of Protectors to their final duties. As a group they offered thanks for the vision Gwernz had been given. Also they prayed for the speedy return of their new leader's strength, although it would be many months before Arlass stepped down so that Gwernz could assume his duties. Their prayers finished, two men appeared with a litter on which to carry the exhausted Gwernz home.

Rest was what he needed most now. Precious sleep took Gwernz as soon as he was laid upon his bed, although he tossed and turned, waking often from his very vivid dreams. Through the day and evening Marleah stayed by his side, trying to get him to eat or drink something each time he woke. But he refused each offering. Finally near midnight she was able to cajole him to drink a bowl of hot broth. He slept peacefully after that.

Dawn came too soon. Gwernz had not been prepared for the vast amounts of pure energy that had surged through his cells. There were no words sufficient that could describe what the experience was likely to be. The Great Trees seemed to treat every person differently, according to the moment. Several people had died in this process, simply because their constitutions were not capable of handling the extreme forces coursing through them.

A strengthening elixir was given to Gwernz several times each day. When he had the energy, he ate ravenously; afterward he would fall into a deep, restful sleep. The remainder of the week, he knew, must be spent making preparations for Loff's journey. Upon awakening he would call Loff to his bedside and give him specific instructions for his journey. With their minds linked, Gwernz showed him the visions from his trance. Loff saw the city of Vensunor, inhabited by thousands of people. He heard the language of that city, and knew that he must speak it in order to pass for one of its inhabitants. Concerned, he questioned how he could learn another tongue in one week's time. His uncle repeated that he must place all of his trust, unwaveringly, in the wisdom of the Great Trees.

The young man sat most of his waking hours by his uncle's side, learning all he could. Each night Loff slept within the Circle of Great Trees. His dreams were vivid retellings of what Gwernz had shown him during the day. Each day Loff changed. His speech acquired an unusual accent; he carried himself differently. By the morning of his departure, Loff was speaking a language that only Gwernz and he understood. He waved a long good-bye to his mother and uncle and slipped from their sight through the trees.

Soon after, he came upon a horse, as his dreams and instructions had told him he would. Loff slipped a bit of his awareness into the horse's mind, caught it easily and slipped the blanket and saddle on its back. The horse was a huge beast, with a surprisingly easy gait for one so large.

But the talent of reading or touching another human or animal's thoughts was one of the things Loff had been cautioned to conceal well. He was no longer safe within the confines of his beloved valley, where everyone thought freely to one another. Outside of the valley his very life would be in danger for that type of behavior. In this world he must remain perpetually on guard.

The mysteries of what had transpired in the last week remained fresh in Loff's mind. As his horse put many paces between himself and home, Loff marveled at the changing landscape. He had never been so far beyond his valley. The new rock formations, colors, and smells gradually grew more unfamiliar as he climbed higher into the mountains.

In time he sighted the ruins in the distance, as his uncle had foretold. The sight of the massive dead city of Stiga sent long shivers up his spine. How could people have lived there, piled up one upon the other, like the stones from which their homes were constructed? There were no trees, no greenery to cover the rock. The dark magic of the long-ago wars still gripped the mountain. On the air floated the strong smell of cold, damp stone. As he rode past the ruins, his only thought was to reach the safety of the forest.

When Loff camped each night he carefully placed a circle of hex signs around his campsite, as Gwernz had instructed. These kept away even large animals. The larger in size the form that ventured to cross the path of the hex sign, the stronger the energy jolt it received when it did. Even though he was completely enclosed in protection, Loff still preferred to sleep high up in the boughs of the trees.

Just after dawn, Loff awoke to his horse's nicker. He saw a startled bird fly out of the underbrush, and he assumed the cause was a fox or some other small predator at the hunt. All seemed very normal. He breakfasted on water and some dried fruit, not making a fire for safety's sake, keeping alert for ambush. Once he finished packing up his bedroll and saddling the horse, he removed the hex signs he had placed the night before and mounted.

Then it happened: Three men were upon him. One of them grabbed the reins while another jumped up behind him on the horse, wrapping his arms around Loff in an attempt to pull him off his mount. The third took aim and threw a large rock that bounced off the side of Loff's head with a painful thud. Loff fell to the ground and they were on top of him before he could get his hands on a weapon. Another blow to the back of his skull ensured that he wouldn't move at all. When he woke, he was bound and gagged, and had a filthy rag tied over his head.

Never would he have suspected that he would fall prey to capture from the likes of these men. Even now he marveled at how such huge ugly brutes could have been so stealthy. As they plodded on hour after hour his head ached where the rock had struck. The leather thongs that bound his arms behind his back began to cut off the circulation to his hands. He tried to get the numbness to spread to the pain in his head, but it wouldn't work, what with the horse jostling him. All he could do was grip with his legs and hope to stay mounted. He knew that if he fell they'd just place him astride the horse and continue, caring little whether he was bruised or not.

Even if he could have seen where he was being taken, Loff never would have believed it. When the rag was finally pulled off his head they were within the confines of the walls of a great castle. Before him, upon a large roan horse, sat a dark, imposing man, painfully bombarding him with a cruel lash of mind-probe energy. In his weakened state Loff could not defend against it and he passed out, falling from his horse. From there he was carried and unceremoniously dumped into a cell in a round, damp dungeon at the bottom of the castle.

SEVENTEEN

MUFFLED SOUNDS OF ACTIVITY WOKE BENYAR. Dawn was barely beginning to color the serene walls of the courtyard garden beyond his window. His senses absorbed the scent of incense, the faint tinkling of small bells in the breeze, the brush of bare feet moving across polished wooden floors, while away in the distance the music of many voices chanted together in delicate harmonies.

One particular set of feet made its way across the courtyard to his room. A young man knocked on the wooden doorway, then drew aside the heavy curtain. He carried a tray with hot medicinal tea and soothing porridge. His calm, gentle smile reminded Benyar of the son he had known so briefly. What had happened to his son? Did he yet live? Had he truly escaped with the woman? He had fought so bravely . . . there had been so little time. . . . If only he had taken the time to explain to Ranth the powers of the Lifestone, they might be together still. But he'd made the decision not to risk making that explanation while under Creedath's roof.

The monks of the Temple were greatly skilled in the art of healing, but the fact that Benyar's strength was so slow in returning was a puzzle to them all. His recovery should have progressed further in even the short time that had passed. They did not know about the dreams that haunted his nights.

Today, realizing that the dreams were robbing him of

vital energy, Benyar decided it was time to speak. He startled the young monk attending him by saying, "I request an audience with the heads of your order as soon as possible. It is most urgent." Had Benyar not been in such a weakened state, he would have been aware of the language he used. Still feverish from the wound, he spoke in the sacred language of the Temple, Old Tongue.

Although his eyes betrayed him, the young monk remained calm, remembering his training, bowed and left in search of the wise masters, Delcia and Morgentur. He did not understand the words that had been spoken to him, but recognized the ancient language. Delcia and Morgentur should be the first to know that this strange wounded man was speaking it.

Centuries ago it had been decided by a particularly enlightened leader that the Order was to be led by an oathbound couple, most often male and female. As was the custom, when the couple had been chosen, they made a blood pact on the day of their investiture to remain together forever. There was no chance of separation while they lived, and the death of one was followed within days by the natural death of the other, by mutual desire. That is how it had been for generations.

In the minutes before his audience Benyar lay with the Lifestone on his breast, directly over the wound, thinking. If he had had the Lifestone in its pouch or upon his body, death would never have occurred. Using the Lifestone for a torch as he had done, he had placed himself in great jeopardy. The intense joy he had known at having found his son after years of searching had made him reckless. Now in this time of healing, there was nothing to be done but lie and wait for his strength to return—the strength that was being robbed from him each night by the mysterious, recurring dream.

Benyar could sense Delcia and Morgentur approaching. No audible sound they made, no rustle of their garments announced them; their mutual deep love and trust for each other made their arrival known. They moved as one, as surely as their minds spoke with one voice.

The young monk who had summoned them knocked on the doorpost, then drew back the curtain for them. Delcia entered the room only slightly before Morgentur. Each stepped together, their hands entwined, etheric and regal. When Benyar attempted to rise in their benevolent presence, both tilted their heads and raised their free hands in exact rhythm; eyes beseeching and without speaking, their voices in unison bade in the Old Tongue:

"No, do not stand for our sakes, brother. You must preserve your strength. Please our whims. Tell us your story, but only so long as it does not deplete your precious life's energies."

The young monk propped up Benyar with pillows, and then brought two chairs into the small cell. When Delcia and Morgentur were seated, the young man left as silently as he had come, as Benyar began his tale, touching the minds of the couple directly—once he had placed an impenetrable mind shield around the three of them, for secrecy's sake. The old language doubly ensured that what he was about to disclose would not leave these four walls.

As a young man I found my destiny was to one day become leader of my people, he began. *When I found my wife, she became linked with me to share the same destiny. What neither of us had foreseen was her near fatal wounding during an enemy raid. The numbers had not foretold this disaster. What the numbers had predicted was far stranger. Both she and I possessed a Lifestone, as is our custom. Hers was torn from her at the time of the raid, as was our only son. My wife was found unconscious, suffering from a head wound. The Priestess determined that if the Lifestone could be returned, she might live again; at least so said the numbers.*

For years I searched not only for the Lifestone, but for our son as well. My search brought me here to Vensunor many months ago, where I have been living under disguise. I gained the respect of the mercenaries of the city and one day I was recommended to a powerful man for a most un-

usual job. *Let me briefly say it involved sorcery and deceit and the entrapment of an innocent person. On one of my visits I discovered that this same powerful man had enslaved my son as his servant. When I found my son, he told me he had been raised by this Temple. I ask you now, was a Lifestone upon the child who was later called Ranth, when he was discovered?* He then formed a picture in his mind of Ranth for Delcia and Morgentur to see.

Of course they knew him. *Both of us loved Ranth as our own. He was found on the Temple steps, wrapped only in a blanket. Yes, we were present when he was discovered and taken in, but no, sadly, there was no stone found upon him.*

The most astonishing part of Benyar's story was told next. *The body of the child's mother, my wife, Zeraya sul Karnavt, has been kept preserved in stasis by the Priestess of the Temple all these years. She awaits the touch of her Lifestone to breathe life back into her body so she may take her rightful place beside me once more.*

This part of the tale astonished Delcia and Morgentur. *Can these crystals of yours truly restore life after so many years have passed?* they asked, their two voices perfectly echoing each other. *Lifestones are believed to be only legend in this part of the world.*

Yes, came Benyar's immediate reply, *they have the power to restore life; however, I plead with you on your honor never to disclose this part of my story to anyone. That is why I have covered our conversation with a strong shield and further ensured that no one understand by speaking in the old secret language. I have taken you into my confidence and ask for your vow of secrecy, as is my right. This particular configuration will also safeguard your dreams.*

This last item, that their dreams would be protected, sparked their curiosity. *If you will but teach us how to shield dreams, we would be most grateful. And, as is the custom, you have our sworn vow of silence for all you have*

*told us here today. But rest is what you need now. Please
quiet yourself.*

His breath coming in hoarse gasps, Benyar instructed
them how to weave an impenetrable mind-shield that
guarded dreams. *I must tell you this*, he added. *I dream
each night of a wizard from a far-off land who speaks of
the Great Trees. Because of my wound, I cannot maintain
my mind-shields while I sleep, and somehow this dream is
sapping my strength. I ask for your protection until I am
healed so I may recover.* Exhausted from the exertion of
his audience with Delcia and Morgentur, Benyar fell back
upon his pillows and lay waiting for his breath to calm. He
withdrew his mind-touch from them so that he could concentrate all of his energies on his healing process.

Speaking aloud, Delcia and Morgentur's soothing voices
said, "We could not understand why your healing progressed so slowly. Now the mystery is solved. Rest now,
friend. We will send the healers to you. Of course, you will
receive our protection while you sleep. You have merely
to ask and it is given." In silence, Delcia and Morgentur
enclosed Benyar's mind as well as his body within a bright
impregnable light, then rose and left the room.

The monk who had attended to Benyar earlier was waiting outside the doorway. "Honored Pair, how can I best
assist this man?" he asked, very concerned.

"Bring hot and cold compresses for his head and see
that he is always warm. Tonight have a brazier of hot coals
brought in. For now, young Fadin, please summon the master of herbs and his assistants."

Fadin bowed to them and ran to do their bidding.

Together, concern furrowing their brows, Delcia and
Morgentur seemed to glide as they walked toward the room
of the Great Cauldron. This stranger, whom they now called
friend, had presented them with many mysteries, and they
knew the only way to learn the truth of what he told them
would be to consult the oracle. As they approached, attendants to their left and right pulled open the two large doors,
which were intricately carved with scenes of Temple rituals.

Only Delcia and Morgentur had the authority to enter the room unattended at any time. As their feet crossed the threshold of the sanctuary, the great doors closed behind them, stirring the air and causing the lamps to flicker.

The sanctuary, a triangular room, was lighted by oil-burning lamps that hung from the ceiling and walls. Respectfully, Delcia and Morgentur approached the Great Cauldron. It hung, suspended from the ceiling by three thick gold chains, over a large opening in the seamless, polished red marble floor.

Taking their places on either side of the oracle, Delcia and Morgentur spoke their ritual greetings aloud, in unison. White vapors began to curl up from the opening, coiling around the Cauldron and then sending fingers toward the two seekers of knowledge. The vapors wrapped around their middles, down their legs and feet, and extended across the floor, disappearing in wisps behind them.

In Old Tongue they asked questions about the wounded man, questions that would validate what he had told them. Each question was put to the oracle, and after a few moments vapors would bubble up from within the Great Cauldron itself. Ancient symbols glowed with a yellowish light, appearing and then disappearing on the sides of the suspended sacred pot, signifying that the answers were available. Delcia and Morgentur took turns extracting the tablets from the bubbling, mist-filled Cauldron.

Was his story true? For this question they drew the number fifteen, the Male Wizard. Who was he, for he had not spoken his name to them? They drew number twenty-eight, Horse and Rider.

Did the Lifestone he asked about exist? They drew the number nineteen in answer to this question, called the Lifestone. If so, where was it? Number three, Mother Bear, was the answer.

Was there truly a woman being kept alive by the Priestess, waiting to be reunited with her Lifestone? The number twenty was drawn, the Fire-Bearer, in answer to this question—that and forty-six, the Oxen, with a yoke around their neck.

Was it true that Ranth had at last escaped his slavery under Creedath? For this one they drew number fifty-two, the Windstorm, with number twenty-nine, Horse without Rider.

When the last question had been asked, each held a handful of tablets. They began the ritual of thanks and closing—but surprisingly, the Cauldron had another tablet for them, one that no question had prompted. Thick vapors continued to curl about them, letters glowing, lights moving on the sides of the suspended pot, indicating that they were not yet done with their task.

Exchanging quizzical glances, Delcia reached in with a delicate hand and chose a tablet, number seventeen, the Six-Pointed Star of Chance. The Cauldron continued its bubbling, indicating another tablet was waiting. This time, Morgentur reached in. He chose number one, the Female Dragon. Only then did the vapors disappear.

Curious was the word they echoed to each other, mind to mind. Together they spoke the words of thanks and closing, turned from the Cauldron, and walked to a table in the corner of the chamber.

There the venerable couple sat, brush pens in hand, making delicate strokes upon paper. They recorded their night's work first on paper for themselves, then made a second copy—the permanent record for the Temple archives. Their work of deciphering would keep them awake long into the night. First the ancient symbols were recorded; the translation followed. Though they sat for hours, neither tired. This was part of the gift of the Oracle; strength and sustenance seeped into their bodies. When at last they had finished their task, both folded up their papers and sealed them with wax.

Only their eyes showed a bit of weariness as they strode confidently toward the doors that would put them back into the world once more. Together they pulled the cords of the bells that would announce their readiness to be released from the chamber. In response to the bell chimes, attendants pulled open the doors, and Delcia and Morgentur stepped across the threshold into the late night air. They had spent the entire day at their work, and now it was approaching midnight.

Their smiling faces announced success to any who were awake, though most of the inhabitants of the Temple were fast asleep at this hour. As they turned the corner and entered the public wing of the Temple, they were surprise to see Lord Creedath himself waiting, with a retinue of armed guards in attendance.

He stood and bowed to them. "I have important business that we must discuss in private."

"Of course," they softly replied together. "Please follow us to comfortable quarters and refreshment." The three of them, with several guards in tow, wound their way through the Temple to the private apartments of Delcia and Morgentur.

Once in their chambers, Creedath paced, the fingers of his left hand worrying his gray-specked beard. He claimed he had come to request an audience with them and the Great Cauldron. But in truth he had come searching for the man he knew as Kessell, for Ranth, and for the escaped female prisoner.

A young student entered the room with a tray containing tea, bread, and cheese. "Thank you for your kindness," spoke Delcia gently, for there were no servants in the Temple. The young woman, feeling Creedath's eyes upon her, bowed and left the room, happy to be away from him.

Creedath realized he must use tact and assume a gentle voice when speaking to Delcia and Morgentur, for his demeanor would greatly influence their willingness to speak to the Oracle on his behalf. He stopped pacing and took the chair offered to him at the table, as Delcia poured the tea and Morgentur cut slices of bread and cheese.

"Honored Pair," he began, "I come to you seeking information about a stranger, someone who could, perhaps, be a grave danger to us all. The name he gave me was

Kessell." In his most trustworthy, most cunning manner, Creedath hoped to beguile Delcia and Morgentur, to sway them to his purpose. But his honeyed words were spoken to no avail. They knew he relied upon treachery as most would a friend. Beneath their exterior of concern, the minds of Delcia and Morgentur became one as they took in the story being woven, and as quickly sifted through it with their synergistic capacity to know truth.

"I have reports that such a person was left at your door several days past, and I have come to claim him, if that be the truth," Creedath continued. "He pretended to be my ally, and I befriended him and gave him my hospitality, but then he set loose a dangerous prisoner and stole one of my servants as well, killing three guards in the process. It may be that the young man is with him as well. His name is Ranth." Creedath's mouth turned into the mockery of a smile, which he just as quickly dropped and replaced with a look of utter bewilderment. In his haste, Creedath had forgotten the circumstances of Ranth's capture so many years before.

At the mention of Ranth's name, Delcia and Morgentur looked at one another, then turned their gaze on the man before them, with an unreadable expression upon their faces. Under this calm exterior their minds relived the memory of Ranth's capture by Creedath, as well as the horror of Master Chago's death. The stranger under their roof had just that morning confided to them that Ranth, one they had loved as their own, was his son.

"We have a wounded man in our care," spoke Morgentur, "but he is near death and it would be unwise to disturb him. He gave us no name, in his condition. But tell us, what did the man you are pursuing look like?" he asked, knowing it was very unlikely that he had shown his true appearance to any one of them.

"He had brown hair, hazel eyes and fair skin. I received him in good faith, accompanied by letters of recommendation from a merchant who claimed to know him well. I suspect the man had some degree of talent that he hid from me," said Creedath earnestly. Thinking he might be close to his victim, he allowed his excitement to show.

They listened intently, between bites of food and sips of tea. When their guest had finished, the couple spoke. "There is no one of that description under our roof. It was an older man—no warrior, but a farmer with weathered skin—as we recall." Speaking thus, as if with one voice, it was only the truth that could come from their lips. It also indicated they had no wish to be questioned further.

Creedath knew from past experience with Delcia and Morgentur that pressing the matter would only close the subject more quickly. He wanted to keep the Temple friendly because he had need, and only for that reason. Foolishly, he did not fear them. He rose to take his leave, bowing carefully.

"I thank you for your audience, Honored Pair," he said, just barely hiding the malice he felt toward them with his manner of speaking and his careful bow. He seemed to be in a hurry, and forgot his request of an audience with the Great Cauldron.

"Master Creedath," they began again, "we wish to give you a message from our audience within the Cauldron's chamber this night past." Eerily, their voices blended together as they continued to speak: "The Cauldron of the Great Mother gave us a message tonight and we were puzzled by the meaning of it. We now believe the message to be for you. It is this: the Six-Pointed Star of Chance. It will be your downfall."

"Chance? This means nothing to me. I am an exceptionally careful man. Never do I take chances, and now I will be doubly careful. I truly thank you for this gift of warning, however cryptic you may think it to be." This time the voice and bow were genuine as the dark, brooding man knit his heavy brows together and left.

"Did we do wrong, my beloved, to fail to mention this rune had the female-dragon glyph associated with it?" questioned Morgentur.

"I believe we did all we could in the circumstances, my

dear one. Come, let us rest now. Other matters can wait. He has put a tremendous strain on us both," answered Delcia. Quietly, in one motion, they rose and crossed the room to pull back the curtain that led down a small corridor to their bed. True weariness had settled upon them.

Eighteen

"EVEN WE MUST SLEEP SOMETIME, MY PRECIOUS one." Alglooth smiled wearily. Cloonth nodded, putting her pipe to her mouth in an automatic gesture. They had followed Shunlar's heat trace only to find that it had been obliterated by the desert storms.

The trail gone, tired and hungry, they had returned to Vensunor to learn what they could from the locals and had taken a room at the Dragon's Breath Inn with the sole purpose of spying on the men- and women-for-hire who frequented it. The inn was a well-known meeting place for mercenaries, and Alglooth recognized several who sat at the corner table nearest the door. Frequently he and Cloonth would sell information to them, for a low fee. It kept them involved in the world of Vensunor, but also allowed them to watch over Shunlar, something their daughter was well aware of.

While forming a plan, they sipped on their favorite cactus alcohol beverage. This fiery liquid was the only substance that calmed Cloonth and dampened her omnipresent smoke. "Ah, the Desert People do possess a priceless gift when it comes to certain plants," she said, admiring the clear greenish liquid in the firelight. Cloonth calmly put her pipe aside.

"We need a plan. If you have a better one, we will choose it, but this is mine. We will begin with the illusion that I am a woman with 'services' for sale, and you her seller. I will manipulate one of these young men to succumb to my enticement. He will follow me up to the room and there I will pick his brain for information. Does that sit well with you?''

''It is a plan, my dear one, but which of these in the room do you wish to entice?'' answered Alglooth.

''I think the young one who talks with those two women. He wears the uniform of a guard of the House of Creedath, and by the neutral color of leather in his braid, I can tell he is inexperienced. Also, I overheard him mention a mission that is underway. He seems the least seasoned; therefore he might be the easiest to deal with. Besides,'' she grinned, ''he has been drinking for hours.''

Alglooth turned his head slightly to get a better look at their fish and to determine if he agreed with his mate. This was a game they had played before, and both knew their respective parts very well. He nodded his assent, looking deeply into her eyes. ''Easy prey—but be wary, as always.''

''Yes,'' she smiled warmly, ''I will remember to take every precaution, my dearest one.''

Banging his cup on the table then, Alglooth announced loudly, ''Woman, you know your job—get to it!'' The room quieted for a moment, all eyes on their table. In the next instant Cloonth was laughing.

The liquid tones of her laughter seemed to flow across the heads of all around her, encircling the head of the young guard who was desperately trying his luck with two women. He turned and noticed the most bedazzling jewel of a woman staring at him, smiling, beckoning with her eyes. He thought he could hear her speaking to him, whispering in his ear with urgency, her breath hot upon his ear, and he reached to touch it. Seeing that gesture, Cloonth rose. She shook her head and the hood of her cloak fell back, revealing rich golden tresses. The young man rose and followed her up the stairway to the room at the back that was provided for this type of activity, entranced by the swaying of her hips.

Alglooth remained downstairs at their table, ordering more drink and food with gusto, for all the room to see. The sounds of the inn returned to normal as heads turned back to their own business. From somewhere in the corner came rude laughter.

Once inside the room upstairs, the real work began. Cloonth put the young guard into a deep trance as soon as their lips touched. His mouth fell slightly open and his eyes glazed over. His hands fell limply from about her waist to hang at his sides. Her fingers quickly unbuckled his leather armor and unlaced his leather breeches, he being no help at all. Naked, he sat on the edge of the mattress and lay down, as she bade him, drawing the covers over himself. Then Cloonth began weaving an illusion of lovemaking for him to remember long after this night had passed.

Though his mind was clouded by the cheap wine he had been gulping the entire evening, there was intriguing information behind the heavy curtain of alcohol. It took some time, but as soon as she had her information she released her hold on his mind, placing him in a deep slumber.

Sitting on the floor next to the mattress, Cloonth breathed a sigh of relief. Now at least she knew Shunlar had escaped and was probably still alive. The fact that she was wounded and being pursued by Creedath's men and several hired killers disturbed Cloonth greatly. Taking the pipe from beneath her cloak, Cloonth blew smoke at the face of the sleeping young guard. In the midst of a snore, he coughed and awoke. After a few moments he sat up. A look of utter confusion crossed his face when his eyes met those of the lovely blonde sitting patiently at the foot of the bed, and he began to scramble for his clothes which lay in a heap on the floor.

"There is the matter of payment, kind sir," she cooed, pretending to avert her glance as he dressed hastily.

"Yes, ah . . . payment. How much . . . ?" He emptied his purse onto the mattress, his embarrassment at having fallen asleep and the effects of too much alcohol showing.

"That will do," was her honeyed reply.

The young guard stepped out the door and stumbled down the stairway, all eyes upon him as he staggered out into the night. Before his steps became an echo, all eyes turned back to the stairs as Cloonth floated back to her place at the table across from Alglooth, looking as fresh as morning dew. She deposited a handful of coins on the table for everyone to see and ordered, "Drinks for all!" in a merry voice.

Alglooth was the first to laugh out loud. A hearty, "That's my girl!" from him brought another round of laughter from everyone in the room.

Alglooth lifted his cup to Cloonth. Their arms entwined in a toast and they drained their glasses as they entered each other's minds. Their illusion of physical identity holding for all the room to see, they rose together. She preceded him up the stairs to their rented room. Once inside, with the strongest barriers set, the telling and receiving of the information that had been gleaned from the young guard passed between them.

Cloonth had learned of Shunlar's escape as well as that of the two men. Seeing into the young guard's mind, Cloonth had obtained an image of these two men to show Alglooth. This particular guard had been one of the men on duty the night Shunlar had been captured and brought to Creedath's dungeon. As they looked upon the scene of Shunlar being delivered to Creedath's palace, they recognized the heat trace of one of the men. It was the same as the person who had camped on the riverbank and whose heat trace had somehow entered Vensunor by the South Gate. The very man Shunlar tracked had been her captor!

We knew a trap was set for one or all of us, but not by whom. Now we can be certain that Creedath is behind it. Tomorrow we must check the South Gate from the inside to see if the track we followed leads us back to Creedath. Alglooth began to emit sparks from the corners of his mouth as his anger rose and his cheeks colored.

As they resumed reviewing the contents of the guard's mind, Alglooth observed what had happened when the young man learned of the escape and subsequent deaths in the round dungeon. One of the men killed there had been his uncle. Though he had never set foot in that particular dungeon, they felt the tremendous fear that rose up in his mind at the thought of the place: a memory of terror and unspeakable acts.

What could a merchant like Creedath be doing there? And why had he hired someone to capture Shunlar? they asked one another. At this point their only consolation was knowing that Shunlar had escaped, and if she escaped she lived; of that they were certain.

Before dawn they must be gone, to continue with their search. Now that they knew who their enemy was, a greater sense of urgency pushed them forward. But rest was what they needed most. Making sure the fire would keep them warm until a few hours before dawn, they lay entwined in each other's arms. Knowing what little they did eased their minds enough for sleep to fall upon them after some time had passed.

Nineteen

LOFF WOKE TO THE SOUNDS AND SMELLS OF DAMP and decay. One moment he was burning with fever, the next bone-chilling shivers wracked his body. He tried to remember a time when he wasn't cold, but thinking just made him shudder harder. The last memory he had was of someone or something smashing down the barriers that shielded his mind. So great was the power, he had nearly succumbed. Loff rubbed his temples with both hands in an attempt to ease the pain.

Voices and keys clinking beyond the door were not enough to arouse Loff's curiosity. This time, however, the guards were not dropping off food. His door was thrown open and a torch preceded the man carrying it. The guard was lean and wiry, and his eyes peered at Loff with pity.

"Come on, lad, and stand, or I'll have to drag you out. You've been summoned and *he* don't wait. I'll wager by the time this day is over you'll be cursing the skirts that dropped you into the world."

Loff pretended not to have heard even after the guard had drawn his sword.

"Hey, I need help with this one," he yelled over his shoulder. In the next minute the doorway filled with an immense presence that made Loff take his hands from his head and look up. Muscular, shirtless, bald, and greasy, this second man took one step toward him and Loff was on his feet. He lurched as another shiver made his teeth clatter and he nearly fell, but he did not sit down again.

"That's better, lad," said the smaller man in a quietly urgent voice. "Out the door with you now. I wouldn't try anything fast. Remember, we're right behind you, especially my little friend here." He chuckled.

Loff stepped onto the wet floor of the dungeon on trembling legs that threatened to pitch him over at any second. He could see by the light of torches that all the other cells were being opened and one by one the inhabitants were being urged out.

They were a miserable looking group. All of them badly needed to bathe and wash their filthy, matted hair. On their painfully thin bodies hung the rags of what had once been clothes; some of them had foul-smelling blankets draped over their scrawny shoulders. All were young—under twenty, about Loff's age—and he was aware at once that this group was unique. They were all very strong telepaths, and all were untrained. Their thoughts virtually screamed inside his head, and the pain, because of the damage he had sustained to his protective barriers, brought him to his knees, gasping. One of the young women screamed and grabbed her temples.

Loff was beginning to realize that he had been seriously injured. Spending so many hours alone in his cell, separated from other people, he had had no way to gauge the damage. Now, with his head banging from the noisy chatter of those unshielded, unprotected minds, he cried out loudly in the tongue of his people for help. Consciousness left him as he crumpled to the stone floor.

Everyone who heard his outcry turned pale as a splitting pain forced its way into their heads. Most of the young prisoners began to retch or faint. So powerful was the cry that Creedath, at work in his great library stood up and grabbed his head. On his feet and at breakneck speed, he ran toward the round dungeon, a smile of glee on his face. "At last, at last," he repeated over and over to himself, rubbing his temples as he ran.

Approaching the bottom of the stairwell, he muttered a

long string of words. The air before him seemed to waver for a few seconds, and shades of deepest red and amber flashed ever so slightly. He stepped through the archway and into the room, unaware that the web he had placed there so many months before had been tampered with by Benyar when he and Ranth had helped Shunlar to escape. The web had been a device to signal him of anyone's comings and goings from this place, nothing more. It was something he had stumbled upon in the book of spells from the wizard Banant. A vision of the person who touched the web would appear in his mind's eye, thus enabling Creedath to see who passed through it. Had he not been excited to the point of distraction, Creedath would have remembered that only the color red should appear for the briefest moment when it was removed.

In the midst of the chaos, Creedath gave his orders. He ordered litters brought in and all the prisoners laid on them. They were taken to private quarters that adjoined his wing of the castle. He summoned the physicians and loudly called for Mistress Ranla as he hurried back to his rooms, a string of red-faced guards following in his wake.

When Loff awoke, the first thing he was aware of was that he was naked, though very comfortably warm and clean; someone had bathed him. The second thing was that he was not alone in the room. Pretending to sleep, he moved a bit as he moaned. As he suspected, it brought people to his bedside. The third thing he realized was that his head had, at last, ceased its throbbing. Once his breathing returned to the rhythm of one in a deep restful sleep, the attending doctor and his assistants left the bedside and returned to their speculations.

"And look at the weave of this cloth," said the voice of the one who held Loff's shirt.

"I have never seen such a design as this," said another. Their hushed speculation and murmurings lulled Loff into a peaceful sleep.

Hours later he was wakened by the shake of a gentle, urgent hand upon his shoulder. This time it was dark.

Through a bank of tall, narrow windows in the stone wall, too small for anything but a hand to reach through, he could see stars in the night sky. A warm fire crackled in the corner hearth at the end of that wall, its light casting shadows across the room.

"Come, sit up if you can. Easy, easy," urged the woman's voice. Ranla offered him a blanket that smelled of fragrant wood, and his heart ached as he thought of home, wrapping the thick cloth around himself. He was dizzy, and the exertion of sitting up caused his temperature to rise.

"Now stand, young sir. Over there is a container for you to relieve yourself." Gently she urged him and turned her back politely until he had finished.

"Over here, if you please, is food and drink to strengthen you and heal your hurts." Ranla offered him her arm and walked him slowly to the table. Only when he had seated himself and begun to reach for food hungrily did she turn to leave.

"Don't go," he pleaded, pulling back his trembling hand from the food before him. "Where am I? Lady, at least tell me who I am captured by and for what reason," he continued in a hoarse voice.

Ranla returned and faced him across the table. "I am not at liberty to speak of such things. When the time is come for you to know these answers, my master will inform you. Until then, rest; regain your strength. My time is not my own. There are many other mouths to feed, and all of my staff is busy as well. After you have eaten, I will return to see if you have any other needs." He could see the concern on her face as she turned again to go.

"Lady, please sit with me while I eat. I hunger not only for food but for human companionship as well." Loff's dark eyes pleaded with her.

Sensing the fear behind his brave words she turned and pulled up a chair near the opposite end of the table, then sat down. Her next thoughts were those of comfort as she began to hum a calming spell-song to this young man, who succumbed to its effects. Loff smiled a thank you to her, nodded politely, took a deep but calm breath, and began to eat.

Ravenously hungry, Loff reached for the bread first and dipped it into the stew set before him. The stew was hot, thick, and very tasty. The herbs in it that would drug him to sleep were flavorless. After he wiped the last bit of gravy from the sides of the bowl with the bread, he took a long drink of the cool water. *It tastes like the water of home*, he thought. Only after he had drained the goblet did he begin to feel the effects of the drug. In panic he pulled himself to his feet. Looking at Ranla, but not able to see her, Loff staggered blindly and threw himself on the door, pounding it with his fists until they bled, blinking back hot tears of rage. Then the drug overcame him and he slid to the floor in the midst of a sob.

Ranla stood slowly, turning around with her gaze down, knowing where she would find him. She knelt next to Loff, gathering up her skirts in one graceful movement as she did so. Her hands felt for his pulse; she made a grimace of disgust when she saw what damage he had done to his hands on the door. Pulling his body away from the door so that it could be opened, she called loudly for the guards. The bolt clacked in instant answer to her summons and two guards with drawn swords entered, nearly stumbling over Loff in their haste.

"Lift him carefully and place him on the bed," Ranla ordered in a hushed voice. They sheathed their swords, bent to pick Loff up, then deposited him on the bed.

"Now, quickly summon one of my women to assist me." Ranla spoke again, this time her voice a bit louder, containing more urgency. "Have her bring hot water and bandages. Hurry."

The younger of the guards made a curt bow and hastened from the room, leaving Ranla and the other guard standing next to the bed. Within a short time the other woman arrived with hot water, bandages, and salve. Together they washed Loff, cleaned and bandaged his bruised hands, covered him, and left him alone to sleep off the effects of the herbs.

He dreamed of Gwernz and was troubled.

TWENTY

SHUNLAR AND RANTH HAD DECIDED TO STAY AT the oasis until she had regained her strength. There was plenty of water, and the trees provided them with fresh ripe fruit at this time of the year. Besides, they didn't want to risk running into the band of mercenaries and soldiers that was searching for them. A few days more and it would be safe to continue on their way; so they told each other. Truthfully, they had forgotten about escape. The only thing on their minds was each other.

Shunlar panted in the midst of her training practice. She had missed five days thus far due to her injuries, and would not allow herself to miss another. More than ever, her life now depended on her skill. Though Ranth occupied her thoughts almost completely, she would not let him distract her in the midst of training.

Ranth watched, mesmerized by her motions. He had had no idea she was this good.

With one hand then the other, Shunlar carved a circle in front of her. Next with each hand she carved a triangle. *See the triangles within the circles. Where are the angles?* she asked herself. *Now see the circle divided into three.*

Three. The number of action. Begin to move now. The triangle is strong. You can do things with it. Carve patterns in the air. See the heat trace. Carve a triangle in the air. Stand and take in the angles of the upright triangle. It is control. Solid and stable. Dependable.

Voices within her head echoed these words from her training long ago as she carved the forms in the air with her hands.

She could hear the voices of Alglooth and Cloonth instructing her, remembering the first time she learned her unique gift of seeing a heat trace was something she could strengthen and use. *Once you project your own heat trace outside your body, then you strengthen your ability to read heat traces around you. This is how you begin to differentiate, by learning to filter out and read what you're looking for.*

She carved these forms in the air with her hand again, remembering the instructions, knowing these practices had saved her life, many times. Only by repetition did she fully understand the hidden meanings. *With the right hand, trace the upright triangle. With the left hand, trace the downward one. To unify the energies, do them in a series. First right hand and then left, and back and forth. Every once in a while pause in the middle to recapture all of you. And begin again.*

She lost herself in the practice series of the six-pointed star of Chance. *Chance: Being able to influence things to happen. Opening oneself up to being influenced. Riding the winds of chance. Neither being buffeted by it nor grasping it so tightly that it cannot move.*

Chance: Where the mystical meets the ordinary.

Breathing harder, Shunlar continued with the series of exercises to the end. The whole time Ranth studied her closely. When she finished, he politely asked, "Shunlar, will you instruct me in your art?"

"Of course I will. But first, show me the strength of your sword arm. I haven't tried *this* sword of yours yet and I'm anxious to feel it as well. Come at me with your equipment and let's begin," she invited with a sly smile.

Ranth blushed when he realized what she meant. Although he was slowly getting used to her directness, he doubted if he would ever grow accustomed to the way she seemed to compare everything to sex. He began to wonder if it would wear on him after a while, quickly realizing that he was speculating about being with her in the future. As he thought more about it he knew it was true: He wanted her in his future. Pulling his sword from its sheath, he decided to play her game. With a most tantalizing smile, Ranth called out loudly, "I come with my sharp sword this time, lady, not the blunt one. This sword is not kind."

Shunlar hooted with laughter and met him, steel to steel, as she taunted, "You call that a thrust? I have felt more strength than that from your blunt sword."

They trained for hours, always wary of each other, learning from each other, the air punctuated with grunts, laughter, the ring of steel, and the occasional slap of a swordflat on a backside. In Ranth she found a worthy partner. His years of Temple training, as well as the combat skills he had learned at the palace of Lord Creedath, were not so different from her own early years.

By midafternoon they called a halt to their exercise. Both of them were winded and in the heat of the day the best place to be was in the water. They hurriedly stripped in front of each other, which made Ranth uncomfortable. Watching her undress aroused him, and his face turned a darker shade of red. Seeing him blush so brightly—along with the reason for his embarrassment—brought another huge grin to Shunlar's lips.

"Thank you," was all she said as she allowed herself to let her eyes lazily drift up to admire his flat, muscular stomach and his well-proportioned chest and arms. She inhaled deeply, turned, and sprinted for the pool, Ranth close at her heels. Soon they both floated on the surface of the water.

"Ranth, surely while you lived in the palace you learned something about the round dungeon." Her words echoed against the rocks. "Tell me what you know about the people held captive there and what was to become of them."

He found a boulder just beneath the surface of the water and sat on it, then leaned against another. The rocks in this part of the pool seemed to form a gigantic chair. Shunlar swam to his side and joined him.

"I knew of the place only from palace gossip. One night when I was assigned to serve dinner in the guards' dining hall, several of the men were drinking more than usual and discussing a rumor that Lord Creedath was going to begin a breeding program. They spoke about bringing some young boy before Creedath, and a test that he had been put through. Because I only heard snatches of their conversation I don't know what happened to him, only that afterwards these same men carried him to the round dungeon. My guess was that their job was so distasteful, they needed to drink to forget what they saw. Several days later I remember Lieutenant Meecha reprimanding them. They were still slightly drunk, and no one would tell me much of anything. After all, I was in training for something special, something they all knew about and I didn't." Ranth looked away and frowned.

"I had never seen the place until I stepped into that wretched hole myself to rescue you. Yet I remember feeling an awareness, something 'different' that I cannot describe coming from behind the doors of each of the cells." He stopped talking and took a deep breath. The palace and Creedath all seemed like a bad dream, a nightmare that Ranth was determined never to have again.

Shunlar waited a few minutes for him to continue. When he didn't she cleared her throat and said, "I know it troubles you to remember the past, but I must ask you questions if I am ever to understand why Creedath wanted me."

A nod of his head and more silence followed. Finally she asked, "What can you tell me about Kessell, the man who captured me?"

The question startled Ranth into understanding for the first time that Shunlar had not made the connection that Kessell and his father were the same person. Perhaps all the pain she had been through had made her unable to see the truth of it. Though very puzzled by this, he chose not to reveal his secret for the moment. His breath caught as he sensed the feelings of hatred and frustration that boiled beneath the surface of Shunlar's calm exterior.

Hearing his breathing pattern change, Shunlar quickly masked her emotions. Her level of trust had become such that there was very little she did not reveal to him. But this last show of personal emoting had been, she felt, discourteous.

Ranth, in turn, carefully put a cover over his thoughts before questioning himself, but his reasons were different. *What will happen when I tell her her captor was my father in disguise? Will she attack me—or worse, turn her hatred on me and leave? Will she think I was somehow involved with her capture? I can't risk the truth yet so I must either lie to her or tell a half-truth.* He sighed heavily, mulling over his words, his decision made before he spoke.

As calmly as he could, Ranth began to explain, all the while praying he would be able to closet his secret behind the protection of his mind's barriers. "Kessell . . . um . . . told me he was from a desert tribe and had been hired to search for me by my father. He told me I had been stolen from my mother's arms by enemies but never disclosed who those enemies might have been. It seems Kessell had infiltrated a ring of mercenaries and was at Creedath's palace to gain access to me. All he explained to me the night before we rescued you was that Creedath wanted you and that a lot of gold had been paid for you. He admitted that he regretted using you to get to me, and that's why we came to release you. You must remember, he died trying to rescue you from Creedath and whatever fate you were destined for. He gave me hope for a short time that I might find out about my past and who my parents were." Ranth stopped there, looking carefully at Shunlar to see if he could read her emotions. Did she believe the truth within the lie?

He breathed a sigh of relief when she answered him tenderly. "Ranth, I am sorry that he died and that you suffer because of it. You've explained Creedath was behind my capture, but not why he wanted me. Can you please tell me what you meant by 'different' when you talked about the others who were held captive?" Shunlar whispered.

Ranth held out his hand to her; upon physical contact both of them opened their minds willingly to each other. Shunlar's voice urged, *Show me what you felt.*

From his mind came pictures of the moment he first stepped into the round dungeon. She could smell the damp, dark stone and felt the awareness of the minds of all who were imprisoned there. But neither Shunlar nor Ranth was ready for what occurred next. Before each door, including the door she had been locked behind, wavered a transparent image.

"What is that?" she whispered.

"This was nothing I saw before, I swear to you. This has to be happening because of you," he accused. Ranth pulled his hand away and closed his mind off to her. "Who are you that images suddenly appear where they were not? You are no mere mercenary or tracker for hire, Shunlar." He moved away from her, waiting, hoping, for some sort of answer that might explain the cause of the apparition.

As Shunlar was about to speak, the familiar call of an eagle pulled her attention in another direction. "Bimily!" she cried as she pushed off the rocks, swam to the other side of the pool, and climbed out of the water. Ranth followed close behind her. They ran to where they had dropped their clothes in a pile, and Ranth continued to eye her suspiciously as they dressed. She pulled on breeches and sleeveless leather shirt, he breeches only. They walked to meet Bimily.

A large black eagle landed with the barest whoosh of feathers behind an outcropping of rocks that hid her from their view. The air shimmered and sparkled as Bimily took on her human form. She stepped out from the rocky shelter, smoothed her hair into place, and looked about urgently. Seeing Shunlar and Ranth, Bimily rushed toward them.

"Shunlar, I have been searching for you for days. Your little messenger reached my cottage and told her tale, but by the time I reached the dungeon, you had been whisked away. Tell me, has the flight been a good one thus far?" she asked, mischief in her tone as she placed her full attention on Ranth, who stood openmouthed, a look of disbelief on his face.

Pretending to ignore the way Bimily's eyes wandered up and down Ranth's body, Shunlar addressed the shapeshifter in Old Tongue. "Up to your old tricks again, I see. Well, keep your hands and eyes to yourself. This one is special and I refuse to share him. Please my whims, but do you have information as to the whereabouts of a search party that passed through this oasis? We are anxious to avoid them."

At the sound of the formal language being spoken by Shunlar, Ranth slowly turned his head toward her, then toward Bimily, arching his eyebrows even higher. Both women took his expression for shock or curiosity, not guessing that he might be able to understand them. He pretended ignorance and listened intently, not even bothering to hide his thoughts behind a veil of confusion; his face did that.

"The band following you ran into another storm and has turned back this way again. Please my whims, but you must introduce me to your handsome young friend before I continue further." It was all the information Bimily would divulge as she stood waiting for an introduction.

Shunlar, well aware of her friend's physical prowess, let her annoyance show. "Bimily, may I present to you Ranth, late of Lord Creedath's personal guard," she said—through clenched teeth—in the standard language.

"Ranth," said Shunlar, "may I present Bimily. Our guide out of here."

He acknowledged the introduction by bowing deeply and saying, "I am honored, Lady Bimily." For the moment he seemed to forget that the woman who now stood before him had just minutes ago flown down from the clouds in the shape of an eagle.

Bimily curtsied to Ranth, bestowing a seductive smile upon him as she did. She managed to bat her eyelashes in a most peculiar way. She recognized him as the son of Benyar, whom she had recently delivered to the Temple for healing, but she did not tell him that. She was having fun watching Shunlar's anger build and continued to act the coy young maiden for that reason alone.

Easily falling back into Old Tongue, Shunlar began to explain to Bimily how she and Ranth had escaped and found this shelter. Bimily listened intently, traces of the eagle's posture and movements lingering around her head and shoulders. Her eyes darting from one to the other, Bimily laughed aloud when Shunlar began telling her how the bolts of energy had wracked their bodies, and how the act of lovemaking had been the only thing that stopped the pain.

"Ah, now I understand the reason for such venom in your introduction. Do you think I pose a threat to you and your young man?" Bimily cooed. She was about to tell them about her rescue of Benyar but was stopped suddenly by Ranth.

Ranth could take no more. He burst into laughter, doubling over, holding onto his sides. Both women watched and waited for him to regain his breath and explain what he found so uproariously funny. Shunlar began to suspect that somehow he had understood everything she and Bimily had said.

As he wiped the tears from the corners of his eyes with the back of his hand, Ranth bowed to them. Out of breath, he spoke in Old Tongue, and started to laugh again as he said, "Please my whims, but do you intend to fight over me?"

Neither woman could believe her ears. Shunlar and Bimily first exchanged glances, and then they turned on him. Ranth's laughter stopped in mid-breath. He began to back away as both women inched toward him. Behind him, Ranth knew, was the water, his only escape. He spun around and broke into a run, scrambling as fast as he could in the sand. At the rocks at the water's edge he dove into the depths of the pool, only seconds before the two women did the same.

Bimily chose to torment him in the shape of a very large

fish. The air sparkled and shimmered as she ran and as her clothing crumpled to the ground, just at the edge of the water, as a huge fish sailed through the air and broke the surface with an enormous splash. Under the water, Bimily the large fish bumped and probed Ranth with her nose in a very unladylike fashion.

Shunlar's mind lashed out at him with questions. *How do you know this language? What other skills do you possess that you haven't told me about? Who are you?*

He countered with, *I could ask the very same of you*, as he was roughly pulled under the water again by the huge fish.

Lady Bimily! his mind screamed, *I must have air.*

Both females pushed and pulled him to the surface and released their hold on him. Coughing up large mouthfuls of water, Ranth swam to the side of the pool nearest the horses. As he clung to the rocks, choking, he noticed the wind suddenly whipping up sand and throwing palm tree limbs about. Off in the distance, riders could be seen coming at top speed, a wraithlike storm roaring at their heels. Doubtless they had been seen in the water.

"Shunlar, they come and bring a storm with them!" he called out, attempting to hide as he climbed out of the water.

Shunlar heard him and signaled to Bimily. Underwater, the fish suddenly became a woman who emerged from the water with Shunlar. Both hid behind any rock or shrub they could, scrambling to find Bimily's clothing. The horses had been tethered just beyond the small cave, and Ranth ran to hide them inside. At the entrance, with the wind whipping sand in their faces, Bimily stepped aside.

Touching Shunlar's arm, she said, "The cave won't hold all of us. I'll hide in the rocks in the shape of a small lizard. Don't worry; we won't be caught." This last part of her message was all bravado. Luckily, Shunlar could not see the fear in Bimily's eyes.

With the horses nudging them in the cramped quarters of the small cave, Shunlar and Ranth finished dressing.

Their only armor was the hardened leather shirts and thick breeches of the guards that they had taken as they fled the castle. With memories of the past several days flowing through her mind, Shunlar stopped her hands from the task of buckling the sword to her waist and reached up to touch Ranth gently on his cheek. His reply was to take her hand from his face and kiss her palm ever so softly. Both were nearly overcome by waves of desire. Outside the wind howled and brought with it the soldiers. Their passion and their questions would have to wait.

TWENTY-ONE

DUSK BROUGHT THE SAME TREPIDATION AS THE night before. Gwernz had been sitting for hours, trying in vain to contact Loff's mind. Sitting near the hearth with her brother, watching the fire as it crackled, Marleah could sense the fear and guilt that enshrouded him like a dark cloak.

She chose to speak anyway. "Brother, you cannot take all the blame. Loff knew the dangers he had to face. Because I can feel the spark of him within me, I know he lives. As his mother and as a warrior of the Valley, I claim the right to go in search of him."

Gwernz could not deny her request when it was asked in this way. "We will go together to find your son. But I warn you, the road is a difficult one, and you must be able to speak the language, if only rudimentarily. With your ear, though, it should not be difficult and," he raised an eyebrow mischievously, "you *will* have ten days to learn it."

Marleah accepted the challenge, saying, "The language is inconsequential, brother. Begin now and I shall have eleven days. Besides, I intend to pick your brain every inch of the way to Vensunor."

"Yes, Marleah." He smiled wearily and turned his thoughts once more to the task of finding the awareness of Loff. So far he had only succeeded in touching the edges of the mind of the same man he had mysteriously reached several times before. This time, however, strong barriers protected that mind. Unconcerned for his own safety, Gwernz probed further, willing to accept that it might sap his strength. As he continued to reach out with his awareness, the strong, peaceful presence of two other minds opened to him. Upon entering the field of their unified consciousness, a deep sigh escaped his lips. Soft, warm velvet seemed to envelop him, making him feel safe and actually strengthening his already overtaxed system.

The clear minds asked, *Who are you that you intrude on the mind of a seriously wounded man? Your presence is interfering with his healing process. You must discontinue this invasion if he is to regain his strength.*

I am Gwernz, Protector of the Valley of the Great Trees. I have been searching for my nephew for many days. Perhaps this man's awareness has called forth to me because I, too, am recovering. Please my whims, with whom do I have contact and where are you? he asked in Old Tongue.

We are Delcia and Morgentur of the Temple of the Great Cauldron, the City of Vensunor.

Honorable pair, forgive my intrusion on your privacy and that of a wounded man. We ask your assistance, my sister and I. In ten days' time we can be at Vensunor, for that is the name of the city to which my nephew was journeying. May we enter by the South Gate for the sake of secrecy?

There was a moment of silence before the reply was received. *Asked thus, we cannot refuse you, Brother and Sister. In ten days the moons will be full and at two hours past midnight an escort shall be waiting at the South Gate. Please our whims to be as silent as the breath of birds. There is danger, and strong shields may not sufficiently hide us from prying minds.*

In ten days, then. May the Great Trees protect us all. Ending the conversation with those words, Gwernz slumped forward unconscious in his chair.

Before he could fall, Marleah was standing over him. As soon as her hand touched his shoulders to prop him up, she knew all that had passed between Gwernz, Delcia, and

Morgentur. Hot compresses and another blanket soon revived him. He thanked her silently with his eyes.

"Rest well tonight, my brother. Our journey will be hardest on you. Dream with the Trees." She touched his face lightly and slipped out of the house to prepare for their journey. There were horses to barter for from beyond the Valley, and provisions to pack. *The cold nights will be harder on him than me. I had better pack the winter breeches and cloaks*, she told herself as she walked, making a list in her head.

Crisp cold air pulled color to her cheeks as Marleah approached the guard post at the edge of the village. "Hello the guard!" she called out to the figure in the dark. She quickly made her needs known for two saddled horses to be left for them. A runner streaked off in the direction of the high meadow with the request. Horses taken care of, Marleah next made her way to the main kitchen, where she packed two separate travel bags of dried meat, fruit, bread, and cheese. She filled waterskins and took wineskins as well. She set aside minimal amounts of grain for the horses, since there would still be plentiful grass for them to forage, it being only the beginning of harvest season.

The next stop was the great common house that stored the travel clothing. Marleah chose long fur-lined waterproof cloaks, soft fur-lined leather breeches, and shirts. The weather at this time of year was unpredictable; best to be prepared for everything. Since no one in the Valley had need for personal swords—the bow or dagger being the weapons of choice—swords along with staffs and shields were stored in the common house. Marleah chose two swords from the weapons rack and tested them for their weight and balance. She gave a start as she turned to leave, for she had not heard Arlass enter.

"So it is true. Both of you go," came her sad voice across the room.

"Arlass, it is the children. I must find them," Marleah blurted out, her voice breaking.

"Yes, you must. I have only come to give my blessing

and to assist in any way I might. How fares Gwernz?'' she asked, deeply concerned.

"His strength has been sorely depleted with worry and effort these last days, but his spirits are up and ready for the journey. Arlass, can you help him? He is so weak, I hardly recognize him,'' Marleah said, beginning to cry. Years of being proud, years of being strong, fell away as she stood there crying, arms filled with clothing and weapons. Arlass came to her side and picked up the saddlebags of food.

"Dry your tears, my child. Of course I will help. Let us return to Gwernz. I have brought an elixir for him. Since he is chosen by the Great Trees, this potion will strengthen him. I will instruct you both in its use.'' Together the two women made their way back to the cottage.

Gwernz was in a deep sleep before the fire, just as Marleah had left him. He did not stir when the women walked in and deposited their bundles on the floor. Arlass went to his side and very tenderly shook him awake. "Gwernz, I bring you good news. You will have strength for the journey.''

He smiled at her and spoke in a voice that already seemed stronger. "Yes, I have just dreamed the very same thing. What do you bring for me?''

Motioning with her hand for Marleah to come closer, Arlass sat down and slipped the strap of her leather pouch over her head, placing it on her lap. Marleah settled herself on a stool on the other side of Gwernz as Arlass opened her pouch and produced another, smaller bag that contained a brown powder.

"I cannot tell you the ingredients because I, myself, do not know. It was made while I was in trance. Tonight you must mix a small measure of it with hot water and drink it. The rest you will take each day, as many times as you need for strength. Marleah must not sample any of it, for to her it would be poison. Only you and I can drink it and live. Do you both understand?'' They nodded.

Arlass continued, "Your journey will not be easy, but

this powder will ensure that you live. For Marleah I have only this.'' She produced another bag, from which she proceeded to extract a large amber crystal. "Allow no one else to know you possess this. I was told to have you present it to a wounded man. That is all I know."

"Arlass, many nights have I reached out to Loff, only to find another whose mind is strong, a match for mine. I have only just learned that this man is recovering from a serious wound. Is he the one we are to give this stone? Do you know who he is?" Gwernz asked.

"Alas, I was given no name or reason, just instructions for Marleah to present it to a wounded man," Arlass answered apologetically.

"Do you recognize the names Delcia and Morgentur?"

Arlass nodded and was at once relieved. "I do indeed. If those two souls are involved, then your success is assured. I can tell you no more. Go with the knowledge that you travel with the blessing of the Great Trees." Arlass rose, bent to kiss Gwernz and Marleah on both cheeks, bowed, and left the cottage.

Marleah had not been able to move since Arlass had placed the amber crystal in her hands as she had embraced her in farewell. The stone was vibrating with what seemed to be a life of its own. "Gwernz, it is alive," she whispered in awe.

"My sister, I believe it is merely in tune with you; it shows that you are the one alive," he answered her, laughing.

"No, listen, Gwernz, I hear a voice. It is very faint, but it speaks to me."

Intrigued, Gwernz reached forward and took Marleah's outstretched hand in his. As his awareness slipped into her mind, Gwernz could feel the lifelike pulsation of the stone. The faint voice in the background was female. It whispered, and he also heard it now.

"I am the Lifestone of Zeraya sul Karnavt. Return me to my owner. She is dying without me." This message was repeated over and over as Gwernz and Marleah stared at the stone, then at each other in disbelief. Marleah broke contact with Gwernz first, continuing to stare at the stone as she returned it to its leather pouch.

"Brother, we have been given this stone so that it can be returned to its rightful owner. But how could Arlass not have heard the voice? I must go and question her about this," she said, instantly on her feet. Holding the pouch in one hand, Marleah grabbed her cloak with the other as she ran out the door and down the path to Arlass's cottage.

So many mysteries tumbled inside her head, the foremost being disbelief at how Arlass could have missed hearing the voice of the—what did it call itself—Lifestone? As Marleah approached the gate to Arlass's cottage she slowed her pace and centered herself by concentrating on her breathing. Regaining her self-control, she unlatched the gate and stepped into the yard. Several steps and several deep breaths put her at the bottom of the worn stone stairs that led to the front door. Behind this door was the person who would answer the troubling questions Marleah had. By the time she knocked on the door, her breath had returned to normal and she had ordered her questions. If long years of study with Arlass had taught her anything, it had taught Marleah never to ask questions of Arlass while in an excited state.

Arlass's gentle voice bid her to open the door and enter. The interior glinted with the light of dozens of candles. The eldest's possessions were few, but what she did possess glowed from constant care and polishing. Neatness and order were the rules here. *How can a mind work if there is no order to one's own possessions and surroundings?* These words echoed in Marleah's head as if she were hearing them for the first time.

Arlass sat in her chair next to the fire. She put aside her mending and beckoned her with a weary smile. "Marleah, come and sit. What concerns you at this hour?"

Marleah settled herself into the chair across from Arlass, cleared her throat, bowed her head and began. "Venerable Arlass, I realize the hour is late, but I have need of your wisdom. I formally ask for guidance from the Great Trees before we set upon our journey.''

''Formal asking is acknowledged. Speak to me, daughter, and I shall answer to the best of my ability, aided by the wisdom of the Great Trees,'' came Arlass's ritual response as she fell into a trance. When she had entered into rapport with the life force of the Great Trees, Arlass indicated her readiness by making a sound in her throat that always reminded Marleah of wind rustling the leaves prior to a summer storm.

''From whence came the Lifestone of Zeraya sul Karnavt?'' asked Marleah, shuddering at the memory of the sad, pleading voice of the stone as much as from the boldness of her question.

''It was found many winters ago by hunters, with the frozen remains of several travelers. The wolves had found the unfortunate persons first. The hunters burned what was left of the bodies and brought the belongings here to us. Until two nights ago we had all but forgotten it existed.'' The quality of Arlass's voice took on a deep, rich timbre as the Great Trees spoke through her; a golden glow lighted her features from within.

Increasing awe nearly stifled Marleah's tongue, but she remained firm. Swallowing hard, she gathered herself for the next question. The room began to glow with the power that surged through Arlass. Feeling bolder, Marleah asked another question. ''What can be the purpose of giving this Lifestone to me?''

''You shall be instrumental in returning the Lifestone to its original owner,'' replied Arlass with a frown creasing and then leaving her brow.

''How did Arlass not hear the voice within the Lifestone?'' came Marleah's third question, the sharpness of her own voice startling her just a bit.

''The voice of the stone was never meant for her ears. Yours alone have heard it. Arlass only suspected the powers the stone held, and only once before, with the greatest of caution, did she remove it from its pouch.'' At this point the glow within Arlass began to flicker, and once more a frown crossed her brow.

"My child, can you release me soon?" she whispered. "It is the hour, nothing more." Her attempt to cover up her failing strength alerted Marleah.

Marleah snapped her head up to look deep into the eyes of her old teacher and friend. "May the Great Trees long protect and guide you, Arlass. My questions have been answered. I release you from formal asking." Deeply concerned, Marleah rose and moved quickly to stand at the older woman's side.

Hearing the words of release, Arlass breathed a shaky sigh of relief and raised a trembling hand to her head. She held out her other hand to Marleah, who helped her from the chair and walked her to the bed. Once Arlass was comfortably lying down, Marleah scolded, "Venerable Trees protect us all, how long have these symptoms been occurring?"

"There is no need for concern, my child. My time is passing. Soon Gwernz will take over this work and my weary old bones will finally rest. Have no concern; I will be here awaiting your return. Now go. Sleep. I insist." Already her voice was fading as her head tilted gently to one side and she slept. The faint, glowing light within her face finally subsided as a tiny, unladylike snore escaped her mouth.

"No concern, my foot," grumbled Marleah as she pulled the blankets over Arlass. "Had I known, Arlass, I never would have requested this asking tonight. Sleep well, little Mother." Marleah bent over Arlass and kissed her gently on the forehead. She blew out all the candles as she took her leave of the cottage. Marleah made a quick mental note to inform the elders of the Valley of Arlass's fragile condition before she and Gwernz left. Arlass's health was of the greatest importance to all who lived under her tutelage and must be protected at all costs. She was much weaker than anyone could have guessed.

Twenty-Two

RISING WELL BEFORE DAWN, CLOONTH AND AL-glooth reached for each other in the cool, dark room of the inn. Most mornings they awoke this way, reaffirming their deep bond of love and trust. As they lay waiting for their pulses to return to normal, Cloonth sensed something was different. Her voice was but a hoarse whisper that seemed to bounce off the walls.

"My smoke is gone. What do you make of this?" she asked.

"I can remember only one other time, my beloved, when your smoke ceased. Could it be a child?"

"Let me tell you my dream," she began. "I saw myself sitting at a long table piled high with every manner of drink and food. My plate was full, but the food did not interest me. Suddenly a long line of children, girls and boys of all sizes and colors, ran into the room. With hands linked together, they made a circle around me and the table. As each passed me by they looked longingly into my eyes and said: 'Choose me, choose me.'

"I did finally choose a very tiny, fragile-looking boy. Placing him on my lap and cradling him gently, I began to nurse him. While he nursed, another even smaller girl climbed up my skirt and nestled herself in the crook of my other arm. She too began to nurse. At that moment you walked into the hall. All the other children left by the door you held open, save for the two at my breasts."

There were no words Alglooth could think to say. He continued to stare into the darkness at the place he knew her face to be, propped up on one elbow. The only sound was the occasional plop of a tear onto her chest.

Finally she laughed out loud. "My love, I will drown soon if you cannot turn off that flow."

A sigh escaped his lips, but the emotion of the moment was too great. He began covering her with kisses and caresses until he too could laugh aloud. Then he leapt out of the bed and put a few logs on the remains of the previous night's fire. Kneeling before them, he breathed a stream of concentrated flame that set them ablaze. With a warm glow filling the room, Alglooth ran back to Cloonth and scooped her up in his arms. Holding her close, he twirled her around the room, both of them muffling their laughter, attempting to keep their sounds quiet so as not to awaken any of the other inhabitants of the inn.

Nearly bursting with happiness, Alglooth sat down on the edge of the bed, hugging Cloonth tightly to his chest. "Now I feel certain we will find Shunlar. But we must not allow our joyful news to blind our sight. Let us leave now; each moment we delay is precious."

Cloonth nodded her assent and kissed her mate firmly on the lips before sliding from his lap and standing to stretch in preparation for their flight.

They had taken a room that was at the outer corner of the inn. Below the windows a quiet, dark alley ran along the back of a large stone warehouse. Like the back of the inn, the warehouse had no windows. Pulling back the heavy wooden shutters that had kept out the cold night air, Alglooth scanned the outside with his awareness, then climbed onto the ledge. Once he was certain no eyes would mark their leaving, he held out his hand for Cloonth.

She had unlatched the door to peer into the hallway. She closed the door, letting it click more loudly than necessary, and thought, *if anyone hears, all the better.* After carefully checking the bed and floor to make sure nothing had been left behind that could betray their existence, such as a scale, she joined him on the ledge. Hand in hand they unfurled their wings, which picked up a faint bit of sparkle from the light cast by the fire, and flew aloft, the shutters closing quietly behind them. Flying straight upward, they were well above the inn and the city within minutes.

Asleep, Vensunor seemed so much like an innocent child; no intrigue or guile could be detected upon the winds. Cloonth reminded Alglooth of the mystery of the South Gate. They flew over it and were not surprised to see that the heat trace they had sighted on the banks of the river many nights ago ended abruptly before the gate and could not be seen within Vensunor's walls—nor was there any further trace of it on the outside. It just stopped.

"What do you make of it?" she asked as they changed direction.

"I believe we are dealing with a person who has many powers. If he is capable of just ending his heat trace in such a manner, he is no mere acolyte. If he could leave a message for only Shunlar to see, he has ancient knowledge."

Cloonth agreed, and they climbed higher. As they flew near the palace of Lord Creedath, they observed what appeared to be a loosely woven net of red floating in the air above it. "Some sort of trap?" Cloonth asked. But it was crude, not fashioned with any degree of finesse, and Creedath's pervasive, obviously untrained telepathic abilities could be seen reaching out in several directions by their special vision as well. Cloonth felt it necessary to fly well away from those traces in the atmosphere explaining, "It hurts my head to fly closer. Something must be done with him after we find Shunlar."

Alglooth squeezed her hand in assent, as they increased their altitude, and then their speed. At this height no one would be able to hear the sounds their wings made as they flew into the night sky. Using the light cast by the setting moons, they soon returned to the place where the trail of Shunlar and her companion ended, obscured by the storm. Strong winds—such as a desert sandstorm—or a steady downpour of rain were the only conditions that could erase a heat trace. It was obvious that several sandstorms had come and gone in the last week.

Tears of frustration welled up in Cloonth's eyes. In exasperation she blinked them away and looked upward toward the stars. Several seconds later, a few small sparks jumped from her mouth as she exclaimed, "Look, the trace of Bimily!"

Alglooth's eyes followed the direction of Cloonth's outstretched arm, and there the trace hung in the air. With much lighter hearts they increased their speed and veered off to the southwest, knowing that dawn would soon light the sky. In order to remain unnoticed, they knew they must maintain a much higher altitude after first light; that is, unless they found Shunlar and could land while it was yet dark.

Off in the distance Bimily's heat trace began a plummeting spiral. They stopped together to hover at that point, remaining in mind-contact. Looking down, they observed an oasis and the lights of several small campfires. They decided to separate and began a slow spiral descent on either side of the oasis.

Closer now, they were at last able to see the heat traces of those present. A sandstorm had wiped away all their heat tracks. Cloonth put forth a mental probe and felt the presence of many humans and their animals, most of them asleep. Panic spread through her when she touched upon several corpses. Alerting Alglooth, they hovered and scanned the bodies together. Shunlar was not among the dead. They continued their descent.

Quick to recognize a military encampment, they checked for prisoners. There, near the horses, shackled and chained to a palm tree, was Shunlar. Close by was a man, also a prisoner, chained to another tree. From the looks of them both, they had put up quite a fight.

Cloonth's mind reached out soothingly to Shunlar. Fury and rage seethed in the young woman; that and a good measure of shame at her predicament. Her captors had finally knocked her unconscious with a blow to the side of her skull.

Shunlar drew a deep breath as she awoke and lifted her head, welcoming the accustomed presence within her mind. Even this tiny bit of movement made her wince with pain, which caused her chains to rattle. She swallowed hard and coughed, her throat raw from the stranglehold in which one of the guards had held her just before she was knocked unconscious. At the sound of her cough, the nearby guard jerked his head in her direction and instinctively gripped his sword. His left arm was wrapped in a bloody bandage and his mood was foul from the pain.

An instant later, Ranth barely opened his right eye, the left being not much more than a swollen slit. Blood had dried and crusted on his forehead. He thought he had sensed the approach of two very strong minds, from high up above. Ranth opened his right eye wide, careful not to move any other part of his body. He became fully alert and awake and searched above him with a thin thread of mind probe. Someone or something *was* there. A chill ran through Ranth as the sensation of a very strong protective barrier enveloped him; then the gentlest mind-touch scanned at the edges of his perception. He marveled at the strength of the shield. He began to hope that this meant they would be rescued. All he could do was wait, for he knew he could not penetrate the walls of what surrounded him to contact Shunlar.

Shunlar remained frozen, pretending to sleep as she reached out mentally to the pair who hovered silently overhead. *There seem to be only two guarding us*, Shunlar explained in a rush of words. *The one to my back has anger to keep him awake. I nicked his left arm before they hit me. There is another guard hidden nearby. Do you see her?*

Yes, we see her. This will take a moment, but you don't seem to be in any hurry. Alglooth reached toward the guard at Shunlar's back with a powerful sleep spell and the man slowly sat down, stretched out on his back, and was instantly asleep. The same happened to the second guard. As

Alglooth turned his attention back to Shunlar, he scanned her body. It was obvious that someone had performed very sophisticated healing techniques on her wounded side and arm. Other bruises, though more recent, were minor in comparison, and were already beginning to heal on their own. Minor, that is, except for the bruise at her temple.

Did Bimily do this work on your side, Shunlar? Alglooth asked admiringly.

No, it was Ranth. I have much to tell but, please my whims, include him in our exchange. He will understand us thus. Cloonth and Alglooth exchanged glances at her request in Old Tongue.

Feelings of warmth, recognition, appreciation and what could only be explained as "family" ran through Ranth's awareness as he was included in their rapport. It broke his concentration so that he moved his body, and he felt his many bruises—as well as how stiff he had become from sitting in the same cramped position shackled to the palm tree for so long.

I thank you for including me. I am Ranth, son of Benyar. How may I serve?

Stay still as you have been and you will know the moment to assist, came the strong voice of Alglooth.

Together Cloonth and Alglooth flew to the far edge of the camp and landed. Working very swiftly they put every woman, man, and animal deep into a sleep trance, except for Shunlar's and Ranth's horses.

Cloonth found the keys on the belt of the nearest guard and hurriedly unlocked Shunlar's cuffs. Shunlar's hands were so stiff from hours of immobility that she couldn't remove the chains from around her own body. Cloonth unwound the heavy chains and Shunlar staggered to her feet, leaning heavily against her foster mother, who entered her mind, scanning rapidly to assess the extent of her injuries. After quickly repairing the cells around Shunlar's temple, Cloonth turned her attention to Ranth.

He welcomed the fire-being's touch and sighed when she unlocked the shackles from his wrists and removed the chains. When Cloonth had relieved the pressure around his left eye, the swelling began to diminish. Ranth barely took the time to rub the circulation back into his arms before walking off to search for their saddles and bedrolls.

Meanwhile, Alglooth probed the minds of Lieutenant Meecha and some of the mercenaries. He worked as swiftly as he could, knowing they would all suffer from painful headaches when they awoke. Forced rapport was only used under the direst of circumstances. When he had pulled out all the information he deemed necessary, he returned to where Shunlar stood in the embrace of Cloonth. Each woman was deep within the other's mind, and he waited patiently, hating to disturb them, yet knowing they must leave. Aware of his presence, Shunlar and Cloonth separated, maintaining their rapport.

Ranth held the horses off to the side, ready to go. Shunlar called to him, and he approached with his head bowed. Standing closer, Ranth went down on one knee before them. He shivered in fear. Shock was beginning to take hold as his mind raced with questions. Before him stood Shunlar with two creatures who were taller than any humans he knew, and who could fly.

Shunlar reached out to him with a calming sliver of mind-touch. "Ranth," she called softly, "raise your head and look at us. These are Cloonth and Alglooth, who raised me and taught me. I have just learned the wonderful news that Cloonth is with child. I have also learned the reason for my imprisonment, as well as that of the others in the round dungeon. We must return to Lord Creedath's palace to free those other poor wretches."

"We have information that may be of great interest to you," Alglooth said to Ranth. "A man called Kessell is being sought by Creedath. This band of soldiers and mercenaries was sent after him and two others who escaped Creedath's dungeon." His eyes boring intently into Ranth, Alglooth stepped closer to the kneeling man, saying, "Can you tell me who this man Kessell is and why he captured Shunlar?"

The fact that his father might be alive stunned Ranth and he sharply sucked in his breath. Taking a moment to answer, he stared at Alglooth in silence; then he spoke up boldly, saying, "The name Kessell was just a cover. Benyar was his real name and he was my father, but . . . how can they be searching for him? I saw the life leave his body, as did Shunlar. We left him dead on the floor of that accursed dungeon."

"The information was in the minds of those two soldiers, and a guard we questioned in Vensunor as well. I cannot explain it any further," Alglooth whispered softly. "But now we must move with haste. Dawn is nearly here and I cannot guarantee this group will remain so docile once the light touches their bodies."

Suspicion, then rage, crept across Shunlar's face. She watched Ranth stand, bow to Cloonth and Alglooth, and hurry to the horses, all the while avoiding looking at her. Unable to hold her anger, she followed him, grabbed his shoulder and spun him around to face her. "Kessell was Benyar, your father? Your talk of Kessell and your story of being stolen: Where is the truth in that? Did you tell me those stories so that I would pity you?"

Ranth shrugged and turned away from her to recheck the girths. As she waited for an answer he handed her the reins in silence. She snatched them from his fingers, and Ranth tried to explain in an unsteady voice, "Benyar captured you so that he could free me. That is the truth. I explained that a lot of gold was offered for you and he admitted he needed gold. That is true, also. I know it must not feel good to realize that you were only bait, but he had to free me from Creedath. I was his son. . . ."

She swung herself into the saddle and glared at him. Ranth stood at her knee, his eyes cast down, saying, "It was never his intention to leave you in the clutches of Creedath. He died trying to free you; you must remember that." He turned his face to her, but she would not look at him.

"Died, you say?" Now her eyes cast daggers at him. "Because of him I was thrown into that stinking hole in the first place. I discovered Kessell was capable of changing his appearance just before he captured me, but never did I suspect that he and Benyar were the same man. My fascination with you obviously clouded my judgment.'' If she meant to hurt him, she had succeeded. She watched Ranth's back straighten and his expression change—to what, she couldn't say. After a brief pause she continued, ''Who was he? Or, I should say, who is he that he can die and still be alive?''

''Shunlar, I am here with you, and I am not an enemy. Do you forget how we have known each other these past days? My father's dying act was an attempt to undo the terrible wrong he had done to you. Yes, his joy at finding me, the child he had thought lost forever, did blind his judgment, but he died trying to rescue you. Or, I thought he died. . . .'' Ranth's eyes threatened to fill with tears, and he choked on these last words.

Shunlar softened, and she reached for his shoulder tenderly. He looked up at her, pressed his lips together in a firm line, and then he too mounted his horse.

''We must take all their animals with us. There is no time to gather up their supplies, but without horses, they cannot go far. Can it be done?'' Ranth suddenly seemed to take control of himself and the situation.

Alglooth answered, ''A complicated maneuver, but not an impossible one.'' He took flight, hovering over the herd, awakening it.

''We may also have need of some gold. Let me grab a purse or two.'' Approval flashed in Shunlar's eyes as she nodded at Ranth and dismounted. Quickly she picked the purses of the sleeping soldiers to which she was closest.

When she stood over Lieutenant Meecha a plan began to form in her mind. She looked to Cloonth, who nodded her assent. As the sounds of the stirring horses broke the silence, the noises of coughing and sputtering filled the air, along with a sparkle that could only be Bimily. A lovely woman with copper hair and gray-green eyes appeared before them, doubling over with fits of choking.

"Bimily? Where were you?" Shunlar's surprised voice asked.

"What did you do to me? I could have died or something! I was waiting for the right moment to escape and go for help, and the next thing I knew I was deep in trance. I swallowed half the sand behind this tree...." She continued to cough as her voice trailed off.

Cloonth came to her side and, with permission, slipped into rapport with her. Bimily's face changed after a few moments and she placed her hand upon Cloonth's belly, smiling as she did.

"Bimily, your devious mind is needed to help us form a plan. I will inform you of what we have all learned from the soldiers here as we fly. Hurry; the sun will soon awaken them."

Bimily changed form in front of them, not caring any longer for secrecy. The air shimmered, and she was once again a huge black eagle.

"We will remain in rapport as we fly. Now let us be away from here. Dawn has arrived."

Within the encampment the humans remained in their deep sleep-trance as their animals moved out in single file, beyond the safety of the oasis. Once they were past the last rocky outcroppings, Shunlar and Ranth reached out to the herd, and the animals responded by quickening their pace. Soon they were placing great distances between themselves and the oasis.

As they traveled to the next oasis, the five of them kept in mind contact, planning. With three beings flying overhead scouting, it was much easier leaving the desert than it had been entering it. Bimily took charge of the search for water, while Cloonth and Alglooth took charge of the herd. Ranth's knowledge of the layout of Creedath's palace was most helpful, and by nightfall a solid plan had formed.

Twenty-Three

LORD CREEDATH HAD HAD TROUBLE SLEEPING FOR days, ever since that last prisoner had been brought in. The lad had a remarkably strong mind, even while drugged, and Creedath wanted to know where he had learned his unprecedented control.

There it was again, just at the edges of his perception. Creedath paced in his chambers. Someone within the walls of the palace was actually reaching out with his or her mind, with what seemed to be a call for help. It seemed impossible that this could be happening, yet Creedath could just barely sense it again. Though the message was faint and in a language he could not understand, there was no mistaking the content.

"Everyone has a breaking point," he hissed to himself under his breath.

There was so much to do. More than anything he needed to remain composed. If he was to maintain mastery over this young man and the other captives, his head must remain clear. They were his prisoners, after all, because they showed promise. Creedath had to be sure his spells were capable of controlling their minds completely once the drugs his physicians were giving them were no longer being administered.

He paced to the far wall of his personal chambers, clenching and unclenching his fists. Tired of pacing, he reached for the lantern sitting on an elaborate golden sconce. With his other hand, he removed the sconce, revealing a large hole in the wall. Inside, with a key hanging next to it on a peg, was a hidden keyhole. He plucked the key off the peg, put it in the keyhole and turned it. The lock clicked, and the entire wall moved and could be seen for what it really was—a hidden door. He returned the ornate sconce firmly back into its place on the wall and pulled the door open with it. Carrying the lantern, he entered the chamber and closed the wall behind him.

The lamplight cast an unsettling glow upon the haphazard piles of books and papers. Some of the writings were piled high on shelves and tables, and some cascaded onto the floor. He placed the lantern on a table and, with a taper, lit several other lanterns and candelabrae. Rubbing his hands together, he walked to a table that held a single very large book, and opened the impressive volume.

Now, and as he had always done, he stared at the portrait of the author that covered most of the first page—the Wizard Banant. That face, identical to his, never failed to send a chill along the entire length of his spine. Compiled well over three hundred years ago in the long dead city of Stiga, this book of spells had been given to him in secrecy by his mother. For countless years he had struggled to decipher the strange language. Now the formal script of Old Tongue was familiar to his eyes. Speaking it, however, was another matter entirely. Though he tried, he could not master the language.

Creedath had learned from his mother that many generations ago his ancestor, Banant, had been the wizard who ruled the minds and bodies of the people of Stiga with his iron will. His greatest experiment had succeeded, but afterward he had been reduced to a pile of dust by a dragon. Creedath knew the story, but only from the bereaved widow's perspective. Absolute power was in his blood— and revenge. The men and women of his family had a long history of tyranny, and he intentionally had continued along the same path. Vensunor was Creedath's version of Stiga.

As he turned the brittle, yellowed leaves, he came upon

two pages that were stuck together, amazed that he'd never noticed them before. Unsheathing his dagger, Creedath carefully slit the pages apart. From between them he pulled a folded parchment upon which was drawn the plans for a very large room. Studying it carefully, he found it to be a floor plan for a suite that contained a secret room behind a false wall, not unlike his own. At an encircled spot in the plans he recognized the cipher of what appeared to mean "Crystal of Vitality."

Beads of sweat formed on his brow as he hurriedly leafed through his piles of scribbled notes and explanations. Some of the sheets fell to the floor, but he paid them no mind, so consumed was he by his research. One question urged him on as he worked long into the night: *Could I have found the secret location of the Lifestone of my long-dead ancestor?*

Plans, so many plans he had made over the course of the years. The idea of the breeding program had occurred to him as he learned the secrets of this ancient text. The book was part diary, part instruction into the dark arts his ancestor had learned so well. On one particular occasion he remembered trembling as he discovered the story of the struggle of Banant and his rival, a wizard by the name of Porthelae.

Porthelae had followed the path of the Great Trees and was prone to being too trusting, according to the story. Trust in the wrong man proved to be his downfall, as Banant ensorceled him in a moment of weakness and transformed him into a dragon. The story continued with details of the spell, even down to the moment when two dragons met and mated in the air.

Here the writing had changed to the feminine script of Banant's widow, Malatrese. This part of the story was dated several weeks later and told of how Banant had died. The book continued in sporadic intervals to chronicle the family of Banant and the fate of Stiga as wars raged between rival families. One particular note was of immense interest. The female dragon who had mated with Porthelae while he was in dragon form had borne offspring!

The notes continued to the end of the book, changing script many times. For pages the book chronicled the lives of the two half-dragon children, following them through childhood, adolescence, and adulthood. The pregnancy of the female was recorded, but there the story stopped. It had been at that point that Creedath's ancestors had left Stiga behind, escaping before all were killed.

All these centuries later, Creedath believed that many children of the dragon pair existed and, suspecting this, he had set out to capture one or more of them. He had worked long, arduous hours translating, perfecting a spell that would ensnare at least one of them. This done, he itched to try it out. So, he had sent a message to his network of spies that he had need of a person with unique tracking skills. After secretly watching as Mayor Althones interviewed the numerous mercenaries, he had chosen a man known as Kessell above the others.

Creedath remembered that day well. He had hidden behind a large wooden screen at the back of the audience hall, observing in secret as Althones interviewed perspective mercenaries. It had been his first glimpse of the mercenary known as Shunlar. Something about Shunlar had captivated his attention the minute she began her audience with Mayor Althones. One thing Althones could do was bluff very well, and Creedath was impressed with how he had handled her that day. Just as she was about to leave, however, Creedath took special notice of her features, the color of her skin, and particularly her hair. The strands of white hair at her temples were nearly hidden by the fashion of her braid. The color had jogged his memory, causing him to recall a particular passage from the diary of his ancestors that translated something like:

"*If thee seeks the dragon spawn, be wary of those of white hair.*

> *It speaks of things ever secretly done, unnaturally*
> *fair."*

He told Althones to hire her, but in truth it had been pretense. Secretly he and Althones later met with Kessell and arranged for him to capture the woman. He offered a very large sum of gold and gave no reason for wanting her; none was necessary in dealings such as these. When Kessell insisted that he work alone, Creedath had offered no resistance.

In fact, Creedath secretly liked Kessell. The man had a keen mind and, true to his word, he had delivered the woman. He had had no trouble understanding the trap that Creedath taught him to set. Perhaps that should have alerted him, but Creedath was so used to working with halfwits that an intelligent man was a welcome change. He remembered having to explain only once to Kessell how to place the hex signs and then sprinkle the contents of the pouch in a circle on the ground. It had been a formula from Banant's book that was specifically designed to attract and trap dragons. How delighted he had been when Kessell could repeat the process to him, word for word, and ask no other questions. The explanation that it would trap the woman had seemed to be enough.

When the trap had been in place for several days, Creedath grew impatient and sent some of his men to check it. They returned well after Shunlar had been brought in by Kessell, reporting only that she was not to be found in her cottage or anywhere near the river.

But Shunlar had escaped his dungeon before he had been able to examine her. Who had Kessell really been, to bring this woman to him and then stage such a mysterious disappearance himself? The entire city had been turned inside out looking for Kessell, to no avail.

Creedath had only his giant book to refer to for such answers. Tonight, however, he became consumed by this new intrigue. If a secret chamber existed in Stiga, the city of his ancestors, might there also yet exist the Lifestone of Banant, hidden in the Temple these long-forgotten generations? He began forming a plan for a journey to Stiga. The oil lamps burned long into the early morning hours.

TWENTY-FOUR

THE FIRST HINT OF FROST WAS IN THE AIR AS Gwernz and Marleah silently bid their valley farewell and at last set out for Vensunor. They soon reached the high meadow, where two horses patiently waited at the appointed meeting place.

Marleah guessed that the bay mare was for her and the larger brown gelding for Gwernz. They secured their belongings behind the saddles and then mounted, admiring the polished leather of the tack as they did so.

Brother and sister exchanged smiles as they turned their mounts in the direction of Vensunor. They urged the horses onward and were off at a bouncy trot, both animals eager to break into a run to test their new riders. As they rode past a large enclosed pasture and several horses on the other side of the fence fell in with them, the mare sent out a spirited whinny that was answered by the trotting horses. At this point the road turned away from the pasture, and both animals began to fight their riders. Marleah and Gwernz carefully slipped into the horses' minds to reassure them. Once both animals had settled down, Gwernz carefully wove a spell of protection around them. Peace seemed to fill the air as they rode, and soon their steady climb into the mountains began.

It took the entire day to climb to the top of the first pass. The air became thinner the higher they rode, and they stopped several times to let the horses rest and catch their breath. Nearer the top the road narrowed, so that they were forced to ride single file, and Marleah took the lead. The wind became crueler also, whipping down upon them, tugging at their cloaks so that they had to set their shoulders into the wind, holding the reins with one hand and their cloaks with the other.

As they plodded upward the road suddenly leveled and widened. The wind now seemed to be blowing in two directions. Far off in the distance the setting sun glinted upon something that caught Marleah's eye. She slowed and waited for Gwernz to ride alongside of her.

Are those the ruins of Stiga, my brother? she asked, mind-to-mind, for in the ever-pervading wind, speaking aloud would do no good.

The jewel in the mountain, Stiga in Old Tongue. Yes, there lies what remains of the city of our ancestors. In five days we pass it, but now we must stop for the night. A bit farther down, out of the wind, we will find shelter.

Urging their horses on, they rode until the road began to slope downward and the rocks formed a shelter from the wind. Once below the level of the rushing air, only the whistle of pine needles could be heard overhead. In the twilight, a vision from the Great Trees overtook Gwernz. He turned off the path, following an inner light that led them to a grove of ancient pines. Here they would sleep very well, for layers of needles were heaped one upon another, so thick that the horses fairly bounced as they stepped.

With the wind no longer drowning out every other sound, they heard the sound of rushing water. Exploring further, they found a whitewater stream coursing down the side of the mountain. The splashing water had long ago formed great pools that were convenient for drinking and bathing, if they wanted a good cold dunk. On the banks grew lush grasses as well as thick clumps of lotus tubers and watercress; these would prove a tasty addition to their supper. At this altitude the plants grew smaller, but they were plentiful.

They saw to the horses' needs first, unsaddling the animals and then rubbing their legs with liniment. The gelding nuzzled Gwernz's shoulder gratefully as he rubbed the salve into the tendons of the horse's powerful legs. Likewise, the mare nickered softly with her eyes half closed as Marleah applied the liniment to her horse's legs. Once finished, Gwernz wove an invisible boundary around the animals to prevent them from straying too far as they were turned out to graze.

"Marleah, if you would be so kind as to set out our supper, I will make a small fire so we can warm ourselves with hot tea."

She nodded assent, and both went about their separate tasks.

Gwernz made a small pile of dried twigs on a large flat rock, there being nowhere else safe to have a fire under the pines. He set a small spark to this pile, and put the water bowl on it until it was hot. He made tea for Marleah, and in the other cup he mixed the brown powder that Arlass had given him the night before they departed. The liquid soothed his aching body and added a warm fire to his veins. He knew sleep would be deep and very enjoyable this night.

Their meal finished, Marleah wrapped up the remaining food and repacked it while Gwernz put out the remains of their small fire. He laid out their sleeping rolls. Not bothering to wait for his sister to join him, he climbed between the layers of down-filled cloth and stretched out. Just before dozing off he rechecked the hex signs he had placed all around them earlier one last time, as he was accustomed to doing. He never heard Marleah returning from washing up at the water's edge. So their first night was spent in great comfort.

The next morning they awoke refreshed from a sound sleep in the open air. The sun was just breaking through the trees and the ground had patches of frost scattered here and there. Once they had eaten a light breakfast of dried fruit and travel bread, they called the horses to them.

A quick check of the animals found them to be sound,

with no cuts or bruises or swollen joints. It seemed the liniment had worked on their spirits as well as their muscles. Both seemed eager to be on their way and stood patiently while Gwernz and Marleah saddled them.

They left their secure nest under the trees and continued on toward Vensunor. Their pace was slow and their breathing labored due to the thinness of the air. Nevertheless, both horses kept up their steady rhythm, and on the fifth day, they approached the dead city of Stiga. As they rode near the ruins, Marleah realized that strangely, the quality of the air had begun to thicken. Gwernz suddenly stopped and called to her.

"Marleah, we must enter the city. One of my dreams is unfolding before my eyes. Enter into rapport with me, my sister, so you can understand, but be prepared. I will attempt to shield you from some of the darker visions, but I am weakened. Do you understand?"

"Yes, Gwernz. I will be most careful," answered Marleah as she easily slid into her brother's awareness. Her protective barriers were ready just beyond the range of her inner sight, so that she could leap behind them at the slightest danger.

They rode on, the horses' hooves echoing off the ruined stone walls of Stiga as they approached the main gate. Where proud, massive wooden gates had once hung, the empty hinges now rusted. The remnants of charred logs were all that remained of the immense gates, and these logs were strewn across the gaping entrance to the city. The horses carefully sidestepped around them, the whites of their eyes showing as they snorted and shivered past. Once inside the city, Marleah and Gwernz rode through streets long empty of human occupants.

Birds of all sizes and colors had taken up residence in the eaves of the ruins, and the clopping echoes of hooves sent billows of them flying into the air from the windows high above. Gusts of wind blew around and through the buildings, long absent of doors or shutters.

As they followed the path of Gwernz's dream, they soon

wound their way to the Temple. Well within the walls of the city, the Temple rose majestically on a rise overlooking the dwellings of those who had lived here. Different from the surrounding structures in every way, this building had been constructed of white marble. It was surrounded by an impressive uprising of round steps on four sides and by what must have been an elaborate system of fountains and waterfalls. Once-flowering vines had wound up and around its columns and across the lintels. Now only scars remained where the roots had clung.

Together they rode to the first accessible stairway, stopped, and dismounted. Dropping the reins straight to the ground was the automatic instruction to their well-trained mounts to wait where they stood. Both animals shifted nervously, crowded shoulder to shoulder for comfort.

Let me take the first length of steps alone, Gwernz gently suggested to Marleah, mind to mind. She nodded, and Gwernz began his ascent. Gwernz stumbled and fell to his knees as a force pulled him down, and then abruptly turned and sat down on the steps.

Marleah shouted, "Brother!" and started after him.

Gwernz brought up his hand in a gesture that meant *stop, stay where you are*, while he caught his breath. Slipping out of mind-rapport with her for her protection, he said out loud, "The stones have a power. Give me a moment to feel the story within them and I will be fine. It seems they will not be ignored."

Marleah nodded and silently, trustingly, sat on the bottom of the step while Gwernz allowed the visions within the stones on which he sat to seep into his awareness. The color drained from his face as he witnessed the years of suffering of all who had fought and died here. After what seemed like mere minutes, he regained control of his awareness, and he opened his eyes. He had been in a trance for well over an hour.

"Gwernz, brother, need I remind you that you are still not recovered? Why must you sap your strength in this manner? Could you not have waited . . . ?"

Gwernz cut her off abruptly, "I had no control. The stones demanded my attention, as well as diminishing my strength. No lectures, Marleah. This is neither the time nor the place to bring out your Mother Bear nature!"

Marleah swallowed and took one step backward. The commanding tone of his voice made her realize he meant to be obeyed. She bowed her head to Gwernz. "Forgive me, brother. Worry has once more sharpened my tongue. You were in rapport with the stones for so long, I thought . . ." and she let her voice trail off.

"Perhaps the answer will be found within the Temple. Help me up so that we may enter. The stones here seem to have some very strange powers." His voice was once more his own.

Marleah braced herself and stepped closer to Gwernz. Once she put her foot on the step on which he was sitting, though, she wasn't able to stand. Marleah stumbled and dropped down next to Gwernz. She began to see horrible visions from the past floating through her mind.

With great effort, Gwernz pushed himself off the steps. Once he had steadied himself, he held out his hand to pull Marleah to her feet.

"It appears we are being challenged to pass beyond this barrier. Are you ready, Marleah?" The grin on his face told her that her brother had regained full possession of himself.

Before they began, Gwernz pulled a small, smoothly polished wooden wand from the sleeve of his cloak. He pointed it to the sky, then the ground, and then, in a fluid motion, drew a tree in the air before him. The air tingled with anticipation and the heady aroma of pine filled their nostrils. He quickly tucked the wand away and reached for Marleah's hands. Locking arms this time, they started to climb the stairs of the Temple together, two at a time. Once at the top of the first set of steps, they stopped to catch their breath. They had passed beyond the first threshold. A quick glance to the left and right revealed hex signs that looked to have been placed recently.

"It appears there are current tenants who wish their privacy as well. I wish that I could concur. Stand behind me while I cover us so that we may pass beyond these." Gwernz wove a spell of protection around himself and his sister, choosing not to disturb the protective devices, so that their trespassing would go unnoticed. These and other hex signs they passed unharmed, and finally they came to the top of the stairway. A great sigh of relief from Gwernz told Marleah just how much of a strain the past hour had been on him.

"Brother, I am concerned for your safety. Is it wise to continue? We must remember the reason for our journey."

"Please, Marleah," he told her, "my strength has returned. I am only following the order of my dream, and yes, it is important, as well as wise, to continue. You will understand once we have entered the heart of this Temple," he answered as he gestured for her to take in what stood before them. "Look at these treasures!"

Marleah gasped at the sight of the immense doors that enclosed the entrance to the sanctuary. Never had she seen such fine workmanship. Each door was over twelve feet high, and half again as wide. They were inlaid with semi-precious stones, and ornately carved with scenes of the lives of the inhabitants of the city of Stiga. On the center of both doors was carved the face of a man; his name, written in Old Tongue, was encrusted in jewels beneath each portrait. Marleah whispered the name out loud as she traced the letters with her finger, and as her voice echoed off the walls the doors began to swing open. With a look of surprise, Gwernz grabbed Marleah by the arm and pulled her aside as the path of the doors crossed the spot where she had been standing.

"My sister, take caution not to speak that name aloud again while we are in this city. It seems to have a power of its own, and I do not know what might happen if you were to repeat it."

"I will remember, most certainly, Gwernz," came her awed reply as they both peered into the sanctuary of the Temple.

The round room appeared to be made of gold. Everything in it shone and glinted in the sunlight: chests of gold and silver coins, statues and artifacts of the same metals, tapestries, ornately carved furniture, and shelves upon shelves of books and ancient scrolls. Once inside the room Gwernz turned around and carefully checked it for traps. There were no windows, but nearly three stories overhead was a skylight with the dome completely intact.

"The former owner, whose name I believe you whispered," said Gwernz, "seems to have been quite a wealthy man."

Marleah was busy admiring the workmanship of one of the delicate tapestries that adorned the walls. Seeing that she was preoccupied, Gwernz began investigating the wall near one of the bookshelves. The way he moved told Marleah that he was half in the present world and half in his dream world once more. If she squinted her eyes in a certain way there appeared to be a glow emanating from Gwernz's hands as they searched along the walls, feeling for only he knew what.

She was startled by Gwernz when he suddenly called out, in an excited voice, "Marleah! I've found the secret room, as in my dream!"

She turned around several times. His muffled voice seemed to have come from behind the large tapestry with the hunting scene on it. Looking closer, she was able to see that the hunters woven into the silk held a dragon at bay.

"Call again, Gwernz. Where are you?" she asked in a worried voice.

"This way. I'm under the hunting scene. Pull aside the curtain and you'll find a doorway. Hurry; I need your help."

She followed his instructions and, pulling back the curtain, saw the doorway. The crackle of small thunderbolts could be heard. As she stepped into the secret room and adjusted her eyes to the subdued light she saw Gwernz on the other side, holding a glowing object in his hands. Periodically the object emitted sparks that flew outward in all directions.

"Quickly—link minds with me and help me contain my newfound friend here."

Once in rapport with him Marleah felt the strength of the object Gwernz held.

"Behind me on the shelf is a box," he instructed. "I am frozen to this spot and you must carefully hold the box beneath this crystal. I don't want to risk dropping it on the floor to watch it shatter into a thousand pieces. Whatever you do, don't let the stone come in contact with your flesh. Understand?"

Marleah nodded and retrieved the box from the shelf behind him. It was black and smooth and looking at it hurt her eyes. It tingled in her hands as she picked it up. *What power can the stone have if its container does this to my fingers?* she asked herself, knowing that Gwernz was concentrating very hard, and that it might endanger him to ask questions at this point.

Marleah cleared her thoughts and set herself to the risky job at hand. She came round slowly to face Gwernz and held the tingling box directly beneath his hands. Together they put their awareness into his arms, instructing them to separate, giving his hands similar instructions, to part and so release the crystal. His breath came faster now, and beads of sweat trickled down the sides of his face into his beard. With the greatest of effort his hands pulled apart and the crystal dropped into its cushioned container.

Marleah felt a flash of heat run up her arms, into her chest, and then down her torso. She forcefully willed the heat down her legs and out the bottoms of her feet, and when it left, she could move her arms. She slammed down the lid of the box, hard. Once enclosed, the crystal quieted and the tingling sensations stopped. Breath escaped from both their lips in great gasps, and as they shakily sat down on the floor, Marleah placed the box between them.

They looked at each other, then at the box, and began to laugh. Both were drenched in sweat.

"Whatever under the moons possessed you to touch that thing?" Marleah asked.

"I had little choice in the matter, sister. It lay on the floor and compelled me to pick it up. Once I had done so, I heard a voice that complained that I was not its master, and in protecting itself, it froze me to the floor. Had the Great Trees not already claimed me as one of their own, I might not have survived. As it is, I have become accustomed to large amounts of energy pouring into me." They both laughed a small nervous chuckle of relief.

Shaking his head, Gwernz looked appreciatively at Marleah and said, "It is a pleasure working with one who takes instructions as easily as you, my sister."

"Taking instructions is one thing; adjusting my metabolism to match and coerce yours is another matter. I'm exhausted."

Gwernz laughed until he cried, from relief as well as the absurdity of their situation. After a few minutes they wiped their tears away and stood up on their shaky legs.

"Now let us finish this journey. I long for a proper bed and a warm fire," he said, scooping up the black container as he rose, carefully placing it in the large pouch tied to his belt. Marleah left the chamber before Gwernz and waited as he closed the door the same way he had opened it: with glowing hands, the assistance of the Great Trees.

As Marleah watched her brother, an uneasy feeling began tugging at her from behind. Suddenly she whirled, pulling her sword from its scabbard as she did so. The doors were closing, this time of their own accord.

Gwernz emerged from behind the tapestry to watch with fascination as the massive doors closed silently. "Marleah, what was the name you whispered just a few minutes ago?" he asked quietly.

"Banant," she dared to murmur again, and instantly the doors began to open.

"Gwernz, I don't like the feel of this. Tell me we can leave now. Do you have what we came for?" she asked, looking around the room nervously, her sword poised for possible attack.

"Yes, we can leave. I have what we came for, Marleah." His face was calm, but there was such a look of determination to him that Marleah knew to keep quiet and ask no more questions of him.

To her surprise, he added, "This Lifestone will be the test of a man's strength. I have been shown who is to receive it, but not why. Loff will be there, as well as you and I. The rest is not clear."

Marleah came closer to Gwernz and put her arm around his waist so he could lean against her, his stamina at its limit. Together they stepped across the threshold of the sanctuary and then turned to watch the doors close behind them. They retraced their steps, making their way past the hex signs and back down the stairways to their nervous, sidestepping horses. Marleah sheathed her sword, as her brother heaved himself wearily onto the gelding's back, and then she mounted the mare. They took a few moments to reassure their mounts, and both horses responded to the gentle touch of their heels instantly, eager to leave this place behind.

Twenty-five

BENYAR WOKE FROM HIS DREAM. THREADS OF IMages and feelings were all he could remember. Days had passed. His wounds had healed rapidly once the dreams of the man with white hair had been damped, but the ache of loss triggered his emotions once again. He blinked back tears. His vision cleared; before him he saw the concerned face of his constant companion, the young monk Fadin.

Knowing that the guest's fever had finally broken, the young man smiled encouragingly and offered him a comforting cup of broth. Feeling like a supplicant, Benyar's outstretched hands shook slightly as he took the cup.

"May the Great Mother of us all bless you for all your kind ministrations, Fadin," Benyar said. As he slowly sipped the broth, his focus returned and his mood brightened. "Today I would like very much to bathe and have clean clothes. If that will not inconvenience you too much, will you make that possible?" he asked.

"Sir, I will be most happy to assist you. Allow me to arrange it." Fadin bowed and left the room, to return in moments with another young monk. "If it please, we will assist you to the baths now. This is Jerill, a friend of mine," he said.

A generous smile beamed on Benyar's face as he replied, "It is indeed a pleasure to meet a friend of Fadin. I will be very grateful to be able to bathe myself at last. Until then, I must accept your kind help." He knew that propriety demanded that he tell them his name, after having been introduced and learning their names, but he held back. They helped Benyar to his feet and supported him as he walked down the Temple corridors to the baths. Being in close physical contact allowed Benyar to read their thoughts as they walked. They wondered who he was, but neither dared ask it aloud. Benyar weighed his decision carefully before he whispered, "You may call me Benyar."

It was early morning, and most of the inhabitants of the Temple were already taking the ritual baths. Benyar was nearly at the end of his strength, this being the most exercise he had had since arriving at the Temple nearly two weeks before. Trembling and sweating profusely from the exertion, he was thankful for the two attendants who removed his clothing, walked him to the edge of the bathing pool, and slowly lowered him step by step into the steaming water. Some of the older monks smiled and nodded to him. Others bowed in respect; most tried not to stare. They parted to allow him his own corner and privacy.

He had lost weight, along with some muscle tone. The wound in his chest was now but a fading pink scar. The only thing he wore was the Lifestone that hung about his neck in its leather pouch. As it submerged beneath the healing waters, it cast a glow through the leather, continuing its work of repairing the damaged muscles of Benyar's chest. Neither Fadin nor Jerill thought for a moment of removing it.

Their faces remained perfect masks of serenity as they bathed him. Only their eyes widened as his appearance changed several times while his body was submerged beneath the surface of the water. Benyar was working a powerful healing spell on himself, combining the power of the Lifestone with that of the water. This affected the spell that cast his image, and caused it to waver for seconds at a time. Only these two, who had physical contact with him, were able to observe this phenomenon; none of the other monks in the baths saw anything unusual about the appearance of the wounded man. As Fadin and Jerill washed him, their eyes observed how the illusion faded and his physical appearance changed to that of several different men, yet always returned to the original face. Most curiously, one of the bodies was covered in intricate tattoos.

He allowed the spell to do its marvelous work on him and, with the bath nearly over, his inner voice began weaving another kind of magic. Benyar's song of healing opened his inner vision to his homeland. He remembered the Temple of his people and the sanctuary where his wife's body lay waiting. From that place he drew more power and, as his strength returned to him, he was at last able to stand on his own. Much to the surprise of Fadin and Jerill, he seemed to vibrate with a tremendous rush of energy. They moved aside and allowed him to walk from the pool unattended, remaining close in case he should falter.

Benyar dried himself off, humming a tune as he did so. It felt wonderful to be able to perform just this small amount of activity for himself. He dressed while his two attendants watched silently.

"Sir, if you have no more need of us, we will attend to our other duties," said Fadin.

Benyar turned toward them. "Thank you," he bowed to them. "I am very grateful for all you have done for me, Fadin. And for your help as well, Jerill. I have one last request, though. Please inform Delcia and Morgentur that I wish to speak with them at their convenience sometime today."

Together they bowed, and Fadin scurried off to find the Benevolent Couple.

He waited for them serenely, standing near the bed he had occupied these last days under the care of the healers. "Please enter, my friends," Benyar called as Delcia and Morgentur approached a short while later. He had chosen this moment to show them his true identity. Delcia and Morgentur knew his voice, but not the face of the man standing before them.

All three bowed to each other. Benyar quickly wove a spell of cover around their words. "I know that you will have visitors tonight. I am not certain why, but I am compelled to ask that I be there when you receive them. Now that I am healed, I can give you my name as well as allow you to see my true form. I am Benyar sul Jemapree. My home is the desert of Kalaven. My people are the Feralmon. Please my whims to allow me to be present when the visitors arrive." This last sentence was spoken in Old Tongue.

Delcia and Morgentur answered with a smile, happy to see at last behind the physical illusion with which the man had covered himself. In unison they spoke: "We will receive visitors in our chambers tonight and most assuredly you will be present when they arrive. Our wish is that the secrecy of the moment will be kept by all. No one will be sent to summon you when they arrive. We trust that you will know the moment. Is that acceptable to you?"

"Perfectly acceptable," Benyar replied, bowing lower than needed, a sign of thankfulness.

The Venerable Couple bowed to him in turn and moved to leave the room.

"But, if I may be so bold as to ask," questioned Benyar, "I wish to take counsel of the Great Cauldron."

"Yes," was their reply. "Follow us."

In solemn quiet the three made their way to the hallowed chamber. As before, the doors were opened by the two attendants, and the trio stepped across the threshold onto the red marble floor. The doors closed behind them with the barest whisper of wind. Benyar went down on one knee, bending his head respectfully, as Delcia and Morgentur approached the Cauldron. As the couple began the ritual words, tendrils of white vapor began climbing from the break in the red floor up onto the Cauldron. As the vapor wisped around Delcia and Morgentur, it crossed the floor and began to encircle Benyar, enticing him to stand. The vapors continued, seeming to pull him closer to the oracle itself. When he finally stood between Delcia and Morgentur, the Cauldron began to bubble and spark, fairly spewing forth its contents.

"I humbly ask to know the fate of my wife and my son," his words echoed throughout the chamber.

It seemed the ground trembled for long moments before subsiding. Delcia first attempted to withdraw a tablet, but the Cauldron would not relinquish its contents to her. Morgentur then tried, to no avail. Both looked at Benyar, and he slowly put in his hand and drew forth one tablet, and then another. When he had taken seven tablets, the Cauldron abruptly darkened and the vapors disappeared. Delcia and Morgentur spoke their ritual words of thanks and, with Benyar, they retired to the desk to begin deciphering the tablets.

As before, the female dragon glyph was present. It had been picked as the answer to Benyar's question, along with the glyph of the mated eagles.

TWENTY-SIX

🍂 NEARLY FOUR DAYS HAD PASSED, AND FINALLY THE spires of the city of Vensunor loomed in the distance beyond the last expanse of forest. Shunlar and Ranth shared expectant glances as they urged their tired mounts toward their final destination. It was dusk, and the color of the evening sky was an ever-deepening shade of rose.

Much earlier in the day they had parted company with Bimily, Cloonth, and Alglooth. Shunlar was to meet with them later that evening at the Dragon's Breath Inn. The herd had been left to graze in a high sheltered meadow where the farmers in the outlying villages would soon discover them and add them to their stock.

As Shunlar and Ranth approached Vensunor, their anticipation was fast becoming clouded by sadness. Both had taken to sighing loudly the last few hours, something that Bimily would have teased them about, no doubt, if she could have heard them. Neither was very happy about the prospect of parting. What kept them going was the hope that Ranth would soon be reunited with his father, and their plan to release the inhabitants of the round dungeon.

"I cannot remember a time when I have felt so torn," Ranth said in a sudden rush of emotion. "I know my father lives and I long to see him again, but . . . Shunlar . . . I cannot bear to part from you." His throat was dry as he spoke.

His words brought a blush to her cheeks and quickened her breath. She looked deeply into the dark eyes of this young stranger in whom she had recently placed so much trust. How different it felt to rely on another person, she thought to herself as she answered, "I will return, my love."

"Please, lady, for safety's sake, hide the feelings you have for me in a deep place within. If Creedath should suspect our connection, he will use it to his advantage. We have no way of knowing how much he can do or how much he already knows. We are nearly at the walls and must part as planned, but we must hide our feelings for one another."

"You need not remind me," she said. "It comforts me to speak this way to you now, for it may be a long time until I see you again."

Ranth reined his horse to a stop near hers and they both dismounted. As they reached for one another, they quickly slipped into that place where their minds and hearts met. For a long moment they embraced, savoring the connection. When they broke apart he held her at arm's length, gripping her shoulders and saying, "I wish I agreed more with your plan. That Cloonth and Alglooth are there to protect you gives me courage to go along with it, but it will be so dangerous. None of you know what Creedath is capable of. Please, do everything you can to stay unhurt until I arrive. I will not fail you." He kissed her once more and jumped onto the back of his mount, to ride fast in the direction of the South Gate, as he had been instructed by Cloonth. Shunlar watched him vanish into the trees, still feeling the touch of his mouth on hers.

She mounted and turned her horse toward the city then, slipping a glamor over herself. She had spent hours in mind-link with Cloonth and Bimily, learning how to change her appearance. To all who looked upon her, she appeared to be a grizzled old man upon a very tired looking horse.

At this time of evening, very few people were entering the gates, and those who were chose to ignore the ragged old man and his forlorn animal, allowing them to pass without much notice. As Shunlar rode through the gates of Vensunor, her private thoughts were well hidden behind the thoughts and feelings of an impatient old man. She recognized the familiar heat traces of Cloonth and Alglooth and followed them down the streets. Soon she arrived at the Dragon's Breath Inn and, after seeing to her mount, entered the tavern, shaking off the dust of the road amid much grumpy coughing.

Heads turned and quick glances scrutinized her; everyone in the room was aware of her entrance. None recognized her, however.

"Ale, innkeeper," she demanded, thumping the table with her fist. A smile curled her mouth as she heard her changed voice and watched the effect her appearance had on the young maid serving her.

"Ah, you're a pretty thing," the gravelly voice purred. "Want to make an old man happy?" The old mouth smiled wickedly.

"Here now, none of that. Keep yer paws off my daughter," came the warning of the owner, Bente, as she propelled her large frame through the doorway. Once she was at Shunlar's table her voice lowered to a more discreet tone. "If yer looking for some comfort, it's bein' offered by the likes of the lady at the far table, yew old goat." She nodded curtly in the direction of the couple at the table near the far wall.

Making a pretense of poor eyesight, Shunlar squinted, and the old man everyone saw caused some of the younger men in the room to chortle into their cups. His gaze fell upon the beautiful blonde woman who sat whispering sweetly to her male companion, an equally beautiful man. Dulcet tones of laughter tinkled across the room, and all were instantly quiet as the old man caught her attention and gestured for her to approach. Cloonth rose and swayed to his table. A few polite whispers were exchanged. The room seemed unusually quiet as Cloonth returned to her table and whispered to Alglooth, who nodded and rose. Within moments Cloonth and Alglooth began to climb up the stairs.

The old man got up, stopped at the bottom of the stairs and squinted comically as he looked around the room for the innkeeper. "Madam, I require a large room tonight and a tub filled with hot water. Can you accommodate me?"

"Now what would an old sot like yew be needin' wit' a large room?" came Bente's reply.

He wrinkled his nose and laughed, slapping his leg hard enough to let the coins in his purse jingle. "Just answer yes or no. Can you accommodate me and ... some guests?" he hissed at her. "I feel in the mood for a party."

The sound of money sent her scuttling off to the kitchen, calling out to her daughter, "Gitlen, see our pot has a good fire under it and make haste with blankets and towels and some of that lavender soap. Can I interest you in any food or drink, sir?" she called over her shoulder.

"Food, yes, best in the house. Also whatever my two guests were drinking, and see there is enough for a very thirsty crew," Shunlar called down from the middle of the stairway. As she did so she turned and scowled over the room with a hard glare.

The tavern patrons, all of whom had been staring open-mouthed at the scene unfolding before them, began to cough nervously and talk loudly among themselves. Someone laughed and choked on his wine as his companion clapped him on the back. In the corner a young guard stared menacingly at the stairway, his mind broadcasting memories through the room of a night not so long ago when he had followed the hips of the beautiful blonde woman up the stairs, memories of which only Shunlar, illusion-covered as an old man, was aware.

In the guise of an old man, the hairs on the back of her neck did not warn her of danger and she missed it. Turning, Shunlar felt the guard's eyes upon her back as, shuddering slightly, she continued up the stairs. *Could be trouble*, was her first thought; then she checked herself. *No, this is the very fish we wanted to take our bait. He'll go back to the barracks with talk of an old stranger with a bulging purse. This may all work out better than we had hoped.*

Late into the night sounds of laughter could be heard from the best room of the Dragon's Breath Inn as the jolly group ate and drank and planned. To all who listened, it was a party of questionable appetites.

TWENTY-SEVEN

THE HOUR WAS VERY LATE. BOOTSTEPS ECHOED down the corridors as Creedath, with Mistress Ranla and several guards in tow, made his way to the wing where his "special" guests were housed.

Making no excuses for the hour, Creedath stopped the group before the door of the room where Loff was imprisoned. The bed might have been soft, with a fire constantly warming the room, but this was still a prison. The bolt clacked, unlocking the door, and they entered.

Loff tossed in his bed, disturbed by dreams. Creedath entered the room with Ranla, quietly approaching the bedside. Loff murmured in his sleep, speaking in the tongue of the valley, which both delighted and intrigued Creedath. Without turning his gaze from the face of his captive, he motioned for a guard to bring a chair for him. Sitting, he grabbed Ranla about the waist and plunked her down uncivilly onto his lap.

"Look at him, Ranla," he commanded, whispering in her ear, increasing the pressure of his hold on her mind as well as the grip of his arm around her waist.

There was nothing she could do but obey, and as she gazed at the tortured young man her skin began to crawl. Creedath was using her body to read Loff. Through her eyes and compassion he attempted to see what his own awareness was not able to.

The young man's body was contorted with pain. His

cheeks were red and his skin burned from the poisonous effect of the sleeping potions that were being administered by Creedath's physicians. His dreams were clearly distressing; he tossed and turned, murmuring now and then, calling out in another language. Ranla knew his life was in danger. She conveyed this to Creedath, who understood but seemed more interested in his language.

"What is it he is saying, Ranla? How can I learn his words? There must be a way . . ." and his thoughts drifted off, breaking the cruel grip of the forced mind-rapport with which he held her. Ranla slumped forward at the release and would have fallen from his lap if he hadn't been holding her so tightly.

They sat this way for what seemed like hours. Finally Creedath spoke. "Ranla, stand away. I have decided to stop the sleeping herbs. The physicians will be instructed to give him and the others no more. I want them alert and well fed. By week's end they will all meet at a banquet held in their honor. I will weave a very believable story of how I have rescued them from their fates. From now on they will live with me in the palace. I will be their protector. Yes, their protector. Their willingness to accept my story will make it all the more easy to control them."

Ranla stood beside him as he spoke, barely believing his words and being careful to think no thoughts that would endanger her. Instead she began to calculate the necessities of everyday living with so many more mouths to feed and bodies to clothe. "Shall I have the women begin work on new clothing for them, Master?" was what she asked when he had stopped speaking.

"Yes, my dear, competent Ranla. Do that." He turned his attention away for a moment, then very unexpectedly focused on her again.

"Lieutenant Meecha has not yet returned, has he?" he asked.

Ranla, still reeling from his cruel mind-contact, shook her head numbly.

"When and if he does, I believe I shall arrange for the

two of you to marry. I saw your admiration for him when we were gazing upon our young man here. Yes, I believe a marriage would be good for both of you . . ." and he was on his feet and out the door before Ranla could question this latest pronouncement.

Loff's sudden outcry brought her attention back to reality. "Guard, summon all of my healing women. *Now*!" she screamed.

Loff and the others had suffered at the hands of the palace physicians. This enraged Ranla, and she had no desire to see their faces this night. To calm herself she knew she must immerse herself in her work. She inhaled deeply, then walked to the basin of water and began to wet cloths to place on Loff's forehead. For the moment this small task quieted her, and she began to form her own plans for the care of the other "special" guests.

Soon she heard the sounds of skirts rustling and feet scurrying down the corridor. The group of women filed silently into the room, accompanied by the familiar smells of their herbs. Ranla stood and collected her thoughts. When the last healer had entered she closed the door and turned to them, tightly clutching her hands before her.

She began, "Good women, I need your skills as well as your strength—tonight and for the next several days. Before you pass any judgment, please be reminded that what was done to these poor young souls was done by direct orders of Lord Creedath, and no one person is to blame. We are all to blame." At this point several of the women picked their heads up sharply and stared at Ranla, the Mistress of the House, hardly believing what they heard.

Ranla stood before them with tears streaming down her cheeks. In the five years Ranla had served as Mistress of the House, the most valuable lesson she had learned was how to cover her deepest thoughts. She had no formal training, but her instincts for survival were better than most. Over time she had learned how to drive Creedath from her mind. Details of mundane everyday tasks were what he abhorred most, and so she would fill her head with scenes of the work to be done. He hated lists of medicinal herbs or gardening, anything that required care or compassion. She had learned what his mind touch felt like and was skilled at driving him out within minutes of his entering her thoughts.

For Creedath to have discovered her past feelings for Lieutenant Meecha sent waves of cold hatred through her which she just as quickly covered up. This was the greatest insult she had suffered at his hands. She had no desire to marry, and certainly she would never consent to being coupled with the likes of ''that man Meecha,'' as she privately referred to him. He was such a puppet. Her mind raged.

Ranla nonchalantly wiped the tears from her cheeks and continued. ''This young man is just an example of how ill most of them are, although I have not seen the others in the last two or three hours. The sleeping potion administered by the palace physicians is poisoning him. You are all skilled in your craft, and I need not remind you that these people are most valuable to Lord Creedath. I will tend to this one myself. Now go quickly to the others and report anything unusual to me as soon as it happens.''

The women bowed and left the room, some murmuring to one another. All had concerned looks on their faces.

Ranla resumed her place at Loff's bedside, wiping his face, neck, and shoulders with cool, wet towels. This seemed to help, but he continued to call out in the strange tongue. She went to the table where the herbs were laid out, and chose the ones she knew would counteract the poisonous sleeping potion. By allowing her fingertips to guide her measurements, she soon felt she had the correct amounts. Only once while in the midst of her work did she feel the brush of Creedath peering into her mind, but she would not allow him to break her concentration.

Ranla blended the herbs into a rough paste, to which she added boiling water until she was satisfied with the consistency of the mixture. Then she added more hot water until she had a strong tea. After straining the tea through a fine filter she very carefully propped up Loff's head and poured some of the warm liquid into his mouth. The effect was immediate. He breathed easier and turned his head toward her, his mouth searching instinctively for more. She helped him drain the cup and then stepped back from the bed. After several minutes, Loff's color began to return to normal. Although he did not waken, he seemed to be sleeping peacefully at last.

The hours passed as Ranla, exhausted, kept her lonely vigil. Several times during the night she gave Loff more of the medicinal tea and his body temperature returned to normal. Several times she nodded off to sleep. She sat slumped over in a chair, rubbing her forehead, wishing she had someone to rub her back.

The sound of footsteps at her door announced an unwelcome visitor. With a great deal of commotion Creedath burst into the room. Ranla moved to stand, but he compelled her to remain in her chair.

"No, stay where you are. I know how long you have worked and I appreciate it. To show my gratitude I have brought you this." Servants carried in trays of food and drink. They deposited the food on the table for her and one of them—a young woman—placed a goblet of wine in her hand. The young woman curtsied and all the servants left.

Creedath was standing beside Loff's bed, watching him as he slept.

"Please, my lord . . ." she began, but again Creedath cut her off with a raised hand.

"Before you request it, Ranla, I have already ordered the other women to be fed as well. Believe me when I say I am grateful for the miracles you have done with your berries and weeds." He always found a way to diminish her, even in the midst of a compliment. Turning his attention away from the sleeping man, he clapped his hands loudly.

Another woman servant came into the room, this one carrying clothing. Ranla's curiosity got the better of her as a red and black leather gown was placed on her lap.

"My lord?" she questioned, looking at Creedath.

"Ranla, call it an early wedding present. I must go now

to see personally that all our other 'guests' are in such fine condition." He bowed with an overly grand gesture and left the room, while Ranla steamed with rage. Through the intense anger she became aware of another's mind at the edge of her perception, and she turned to look at Loff lying still in the bed. He was watching her intently and apparently had observed everything that had just happened.

"Young sir, I would advise you to be careful with your talents. My master will use you for evil purposes if he suspects the measure of your abilities."

"I know your name is Ranla, but who is your master and why am I his prisoner?" Loff asked with a husky voice.

"Lord Creedath, the most powerful merchant of the city of Vensunor," was her terse reply.

Well, at least I have arrived at my destination, Loff thought to himself, but he asked her, "How long have I been held captive? Please answer me, Ranla." He could sense her extreme anger and was thankful that he had healed sufficiently that he was able to block it from entering his mind. This was the moment to get anything that looked like help from her—when she was disenchanted with the man she called Master.

"I will answer your questions, but you must promise not to give me any information that he can pull from my mind. I do not want to know where you come from, nor what language you spoke when you were delirious. Nothing that will endanger you or your people, is that understood?" She was standing now, fire blazing in her eyes, a plan forming in her mind as she clenched her fists.

Loff nodded and watched. He was all too familiar with fiery looks behind the eyes of a strong woman.

TWENTY-EIGHT

THE DAYLIGHT HOURS SPENT RIDING HAD BEEN ARduous and overlong, but the nights seemed to stretch on forever. On two mornings in the high mountains Gwernz and Marleah had awoken to find snow on the ground. Now, as they neared Vensunor, the wind seemed to be treating them with a little more kindness. The elixir that Gwernz drank each day did much to improve his health, but he was unable to tell if he was truly back to his normal robust physical condition because of the miles they had traversed. Their muscles ached and they longed for hot baths and proper beds. The horses, too, were weary. They had ridden hard for nine days to cross the mountains, but at what cost? One animal's coat looked dull and ragged and the other's head hung low.

This morning, the tenth and last day, brought them through the final pass and onto the edges of a vast treecovered plain. From their vantage point at the top of the pass, Vensunor could be seen far off in the distance, looking like a tidy pile of children's blocks. As they rode down the steep, rocky trail, the sounds of the many minds of those who dwelt behind the walls of Vensunor danced upon the breeze. The sheer number of voices caused Gwernz to shift uneasily in his saddle. He attributed his discomfort to his stronger telepathic abilities, thinking it was only himself who was affected, until he turned around to check on Marleah.

She just barely managed to stay upright in the saddle. She gripped her forehead with her left hand, rubbing it hard back and forth, as if in an effort to remove something, while trickles of sweat coursed down her pasty, colorless cheeks. Her mouth hung open and her breath came in ragged pulls.

"Gwernz," she whispered hoarsely, the strain affecting her voice, "there is a terribly strong . . . evil mind." She choked suddenly.

Gwernz immediately responded by increasing the strength of the protective barriers he had placed around them, realizing that he hadn't bothered to check them in the last two days, there being no apparent need. He regretted it now as he jumped from his horse's back to hurry to Marleah's side. He touched her hand and as they linked minds, Marleah's face relaxed. The strength of the shields gave her instant relief, and she sighed and took several deep breaths once the pain stopped.

"Thank you, brother," she managed. "Somewhere in the midst of all that, I perceived Loff for a moment. I'm certain he is a prisoner there."

In response, Gwernz reached out to the edges of the shield, where he could touch but not be crushed by the onslaught of so many minds. Together they sifted through the ever so many awarenesses that made their presence known and, safe behind a strong shield this time, they located the mind of Loff. It gave them little comfort when they realized how close he was to the dark, dangerous presence both of them had felt.

"Can you ride to the bottom of this pass?" asked Gwernz with concern. "We will find shelter in the trees and there you can rest."

"Yes, Gwernz. Now that you have softened some of the impact of all those minds, I will be fine." Already the color was returning to her cheeks. Marleah smiled briefly.

Gwernz returned to his horse and mounted, as his sister took the lead with the mare. Their descent was slow going at first; however, the trail soon leveled off and they approached the comfort of the forest. The aroma of the trees,

grasses, mushrooms, and ferns touched their nostrils as
soon as they entered the canopy of trees. The farther into
the forest they rode, the denser the underbrush, until they
found themselves following no trail at all.

At the top of a small rise the horses suddenly began
tossing their heads and sniffing the air, a sure sign that
water was near. Gwernz motioned for Marleah to remain
with the horses as he dismounted. He walked through thick-
ets that seemed to tug at his clothing, and a partly covered
root tripped him. He was taken by surprise and fell headfirst
into a dense bramble bush. When he pulled himself onto
his feet, he parted the brambles and glimpsed a sight so
delightful, it lifted his spirits immediately. Several yards
beyond this opening stretched a beautiful meadow, with
what appeared to be a stream flowing through the lower
end. And there, hidden off to the side, within a small stand
of pines, was a cottage. He scanned for any sign of human
inhabitants and thankfully found none. Since it was too
early in the day to approach Vensunor, he decided this
would be a fitting place to stop and rest. Tonight, when the
moons were full, they would enter the city as planned.

"This looks like the perfect place to spend the last day.
What do you think, my sister?" His voice softened as he
looked at Marleah, who was busy scanning the cottage for
herself. Usually her tongue would be ready to chide him
for his tumble and crashing about in the bushes, but now
her heart pounded. Her awareness was being pulled to the
small cottage. Unusual emotions coursed through her.

"Gwernz, my oldest child lives here. I had not even
named her before she was stolen from me. A mother knows
her child. I tell you, there is no rationale for this, but I
know she lives there." One minuscule tear stood out at the
edge of an eye, but she fiercely blinked it away. She turned
on her heel, ran to her horse Clue, mounted the animal, and
bolted ahead to the cottage, pushing the mare to its limits.

Gwernz followed, urging Echo on after them, and the
weary horse answered his request for more speed with all
it could muster. At the periphery of the cottage both horses

stopped and refused to go farther. Marleah threw her right
leg over the saddle, jumped to the ground and began to
pace.

"I must enter the dwelling and feel for her presence,
alone," Marleah stated flatly as Gwernz arrived.

The edge in her voice caused Gwernz to scrutinize his
sister closely. It was more a demand than a request for him
to stay behind, and Marleah waited impatiently for him to
agree. Once he had done so, she bounded to the door and
pushed it open.

It was apparent to her that another party or parties had
been seeking her daughter, for the cottage had been torn
apart. She overcame the initial shock of seeing the mess,
and Marleah uprighted the overturned table and chairs and
placed the mattress back upon its frame along the wall. She
bent to pick up a piece of broken pottery and as she touched
it, recognition and alienness both flooded through her
awareness like a storm. There was only a small trace left
of the babe she had suckled, but it was enough for her. As
Marleah let her tears flow unchecked, she experienced rage,
longing, confusion, terror, guilt, love, and hate. She vowed
again that whoever was responsible for stealing her daughter from her would pay for her pain.

Meanwhile, Gwernz waited patiently outside, seeing to
the horses, allowing his sister privacy, thankful for some
himself. They had spent every waking hour in each other's
company for the past ten days, and now he too relished the
idea of time to breathe alone. He unsaddled the horses and
set them free in the meadow. Echo nudged him a thank you
and turned to follow Clue, who had already found a large
patch of clover to munch on. Gwernz placed his saddle at
the base of a young tree, sat down with a groan and leaned
back to watch the two bone-tired animals graze, contentedly
flicking their tails.

When Marleah finally called out to him, he had fallen
asleep. Gwernz got to his feet and slowly made his way to
the door. Once he stepped inside the room he could only
agree with his sister. Yes, this was the cottage of his niece,

Marleah's daughter. The unmistakable presence was female, and it reminded him of Marleah in many ways. There was just a speck of the infant he had known and taken to his heart so long ago. Both of them stood quietly for a long while, looking around at the contents of the cottage, taking in the essence of the person who called it home.

Marleah broke the silence first, saying, "I'm tired of hard biscuits and dried meat. Tonight we'll have fresh meat, my brother. While I hunt, unpack and see that the horses are watered and fed." With those instructions Marleah was out the door, only stopping long enough to retrieve her bow and quiver from the saddle.

She certainly feels better, Gwernz chuckled to himself.

His examination of the surrounding area had told him there were no other humans near the cottage. Marleah was aware of that, and he trusted her skill enough to relax somewhat, though not completely. Truthfully, the thought of a freshly cooked meal made his mouth water. He brought their belongings inside. Remembering a particular patch of brown mushrooms he had seen on the ride in, Gwernz took a large piece of cloth with him, retraced their steps and found not only the mushrooms but, to his delight, edible greens that also grew nearby. He piled the cloth with enough greens for a feast and returned with them to the cottage. Next he collected kindling and firewood, which also proved to be abundant. Knowing that Marleah was a masterful hunter and would very soon return with fresh meat for roasting, Gwernz readied the fire.

Relaxation and a solid meal foremost on his mind, his next task was to cut some cloth into small pieces to tie around the horses' feet. They would need these cloths to ensure stealth once they entered Vensunor.

When he had finished cutting the cloth, Gwernz opened their saddlebags and laid flat their clean, more formal clothing upon the bed. He then stripped off his dusty travel clothing, slung a towel over his shoulder and, with soap in hand, walked out into the late afternoon sun toward the river. As he searched for the best spot in which to bathe, he noticed that near a bend in the stream there appeared to be steam rising. Upon closer inspection, he found a hot spring bubbling its precious healing waters from far beneath the ground. What's more, the rocks had been cleverly arranged to form a bathing pool.

A deep sigh escaped Gwernz's lips as he inched himself into the steaming water. Someone had spent hours educating his niece about the finer things in life. He made a mental note to thank whomever that person was when they met, for surely they would meet: He felt it in his bones. But for now he allowed the hot waters to seep into his aching muscles and do its work. Time seemed to suspend itself as he gave way to the pull of the water and sleep.

What seemed like mere minutes later, the crunch of footsteps awoke Gwernz. His eyes opened to the sight of Marleah standing on the riverbank, proudly holding up four fat birds.

"My brother, tonight we feast," she called out to him. Then, turning, she laughed and called over her shoulder, "Enjoy your last few minutes of solitude. I'll be right back to wash off the grime of the road as soon as I spit these hens. You are cook tonight!"

"Of course, sister, it would only be fair," he mumbled, closing his eyes to allow the steaming water to soothe him for a last few precious moments.

Later, with their bellies full of roasted hen, wild mushrooms, onions, and greens, they lay under the stars, savoring the meal and the memory of their long soak in the hot water, waiting for the moons to begin their climb. The three orbs did not disappoint. They appeared on the horizon, one closely following the other, announcing that the hour of departure had come. First came pale yellow Daleth. Close behind came tiny red Andeela and lastly rose, the largest, pale blue-green Malenti.

Marleah and Gwernz entered the cottage for a last time to change into their clean formal clothing by the last dying embers of the fire. Marleah donned her tunic of soft deerhide that had a pattern of turtles and stars beaded onto the front in gold beads and green emeralds. The tunic was dyed a shade of russet she was particularly proud of, one that had taken many years to perfect. She wore a matching leather riding skirt, split like full-cut breeches and beaded down the outside seam of the legs in a precise zigzag pattern. Over this finery she wore her long travel cloak of soft, thick, deepest-green wool.

Gwernz pulled a dark blue buckskin shirt over his head. The color set off the white of his hair and beard and made him look even more handsome. The shirt was resplendent with beads of rose-colored crystal sewn in a star pattern across the chest, and buttons of the same color that started near the neck on the left and continued down the sleeve to the cuff. He pulled on plain black suede pants and black boots, and around his waist he buckled his sword belt, as Marleah had done. Lastly, he donned his long black woolen cloak and snapped the ornate silver clasp closed with a click at his chest.

Marleah and Gwernz were at last ready for the final part of their journey. They silently hoisted their bags upon their shoulders and sent a beckoning call out to the horses, which responded with no sign of reluctance. Rest had made them much more docile than before, and only Clue grunted a bit when Marleah threw the saddle over her back. As before, brother and sister rode toward Vensunor with a protective cover around them and their animals. They passed unnoticed by most of the wild things—and even managed to startle a few on their way, so quietly did they ride.

The moons were hanging brightly overhead like two luminous pearls and a ruby when they reached the break in the trees at the approach to the South Gate. Staying beneath the cover of branches, they dismounted. From his saddlebag Gwernz removed the pieces of cloth which together they tied around the horses' hooves. Muffled this way, no one would be aware of their entrance or their ride through the city's cobblestone streets.

Making sure his head was covered by the hood of his cloak, Gwernz left the shadows and walked alone to the

South Gate. In a barely audible whisper he spoke the ritual words of opening in the still moonlight. As the Gate began to move, he waved for Marleah to approach. Together they watched in awe as in total silence, a portion of the enormous gate slid sideways. So this was how the gate left no trace of opening on either side of the walls! As if it knew when just enough space for them to enter had slid by, the gate ceased its movement.

A group of monks—their promised guides through Vensunor—waited in the dark. Though they weren't visible, Marleah and Gwernz felt the men's minds reaching out toward them with respect, friendship, and urgency. Marleah entered first, leading Echo and Clue behind her. Gwernz followed, and once inside he turned to cover the evidence of their passage. But as he raised his hand to do so, he became aware of the presence of another mind just at the edge of the trees.

The strong mental barriers of the one who hid in the shadows softened for a moment as a thread of mind touch asked Gwernz, in formal Old Tongue, *Please my whims, but I do not know the correct ritual for entering. May I follow you in?*

Gwernz, certain that only he was aware of the question and the person who asked it, returned, *Who asks in formal language?*

I am Ranth, son of Benyar. My life hangs on your decision, came the hurried reply.

Gwernz knew that if the stranger had not given his name, he would not have granted him entry to the city. Nevertheless Gwernz was astonished that the young man had done so. He also discerned that Ranth told the truth because, to his surprise, a trance of great strength was threatening to envelop him. Gwernz knew this was a sign of approval from the Great Trees so he answered mind-to-mind, *Come, but do so in absolute silence. I will explain that you are our servant.*

Moving like a silhouette in the moonlight, Ranth joined Marleah and Gwernz on the other side of the threshold of the South Gate, choosing to keep his physical identity covered under the hood of his dark cloak. Gwernz evoked a gust of wind out of nowhere with a small gesture of his hand, and blew away all traces of the small party's footprints. Again he spoke ritual words, and the South Gate silently closed behind them. Now Gwernz and Marleah were forced to turn their attention to quieting the horses. The animals had suddenly begun shifting and kicking to try to rid their feet of the rags tied about their hooves. Marleah cast sideways glances at Ranth who held back in the shadows, waiting.

"My brother . . . ?" she questioned, touching his arm and thus entering into direct rapport with Gwernz.

Gwernz did not have to reply. Marleah instantly became aware of his trance state and gently removed her hand from his arm, bowing her head slightly as she did so. She knew now was the time to obey and ask no questions. Nodding her understanding of the situation, she gestured for Ranth to approach and take the horses from her.

Ranth was quick to move. He stood before Marleah, bowing as a servant would. He took the reins from her with a practiced hand. As he did so, their fingers tangled together, touching for several seconds. Marleah swallowed hard and bit her lip so as not to betray them with a sound. Her attention had been on Gwernz, but now it swayed and floundered as traces of her daughter were transmitted to her through the touch. This person knew her daughter. Intimately!

Ranth's attention was fixed entirely on the horses, which were responding extremely well to his touch. The animals became as docile as well-fed puppies. After quieting them, Ranth opened the bed rolls, under the scrutiny of Marleah, and proceeded to cover the saddles with them to further hush any creaking of leather as they passed through the streets of Vensunor. Another glance, this time an appreciative one, passed from Marleah to Ranth as he waited for their instructions. He bowed a servant's grave respect to her, unaware of what had passed to Marleah from his brief touch.

Silently, with the barest whisper of cloth, one of the escort approached and beckoned for them to follow, cautioning them to keep to the shadows. Marleah followed Gwernz and Ranth came last, leading their horses into the city. They passed dwellings where sounds of sleep could be heard and dwellings where only silence prevailed. The citizens of Vensunor slept as the small party wound its way through the streets and alleys in single file. Finally they arrived at the back gates of the Temple. They entered as silently as they had approached. Only when the gates were closed tightly behind them did they allow themselves to relax.

Gwernz managed to smile at his sister, and for the moment they forgot all the trials of their long journey. They forgot Ranth as well. He stood behind them, holding the reins, continuing to send quieting thoughts to their two horses.

Off to the right a candlelight procession wound its way toward them. At the forefront, carrying their own candles, Delcia and Morgentur walked hand in hand. When they reached the courtyard the group assembled around them and bowed. Gwernz and Marleah returned the gesture of respect, and as they did so the delicate voices of the Venerable Pair welcomed them in formal Old Tongue.

"You are most welcome. We are Delcia and Morgentur."

"I am Gwernz, soon to become Protector of the Valley of Great Trees, and this is my sister, Marleah."

With a slight nod of their heads, the voices continued, "Please our whims to follow us, and we will take you to our quarters and refreshment. There, be assured, our conversation will be protected. Your belongings will be taken to your rooms by the young ones who willingly serve. Be mindful that they are volunteers and not servants. Also, it is our pleasure to inform you that an honored guest awaits your pleasure."

"Is this honored guest one who recently healed from a

great wound?'' asked Marleah with a hopeful tone to her voice.

"Yes," the voices chimed again in perfect unison.

"Then it is for such a person that I carry a gift from our elder. With your permission," she said, and with a bow Marleah turned and walked to Clue and her saddlebag to retrieve the pouch that contained the Lifestone of Zeraya sul Karnavt.

While the group waited for Marleah, Ranth decided to take this opportunity to come forward. Kneeling before Gwernz, with his head bowed low so none could see his face, he spoke.

"Sir, I ask permission to speak to the Honored Pair of the Temple."

Gwernz looked at the young man before him, then quickly to Delcia and Morgentur. They nodded together and Gwernz answered, "Yes, speak freely, for you are no servant, young sir."

Ranth turned away from Gwernz then and toward Delcia and Morgentur. Still on his knees, he pulled back the hood of his cloak and raised his face to them. Delcia and Morgentur gasped aloud, dropping their candles. They opened their arms to Ranth, who was on his feet and in their arms in the next instant. They wrapped their arms around him, hugging him tightly, while Marleah and Gwernz merely watched the scene with wonder.

"You have returned one of our own to us. Where did you find him?" they asked together, all traces of formality gone from their voices.

"It seems he found us," was all Marleah replied as she stared at Ranth, many questions hidden behind her rigid gaze.

The happiness of the moment immediately changed the tone of their hosts, for soon Marleah and Gwernz found themselves in the midst of what appeared to be a family reunion. Old teachers and friends of Ranth who were in the welcoming party came forward to embrace him and welcome him home. For several minutes Gwernz and Marleah seemed to have been forgotten as they were jostled to the back of the courtyard amid the laughter and hugs.

Manners and respectability soon returned and, as formally as before—though this time their faces beamed with joy—Delcia and Morgentur called their guests forward. Together they led the way to their quarters with the large group following close behind.

As they entered the corridor to the private apartments of Delcia and Morgentur, Ranth felt a familiar awareness emanating from inside the room. When he entered the room, Ranth thought his heart would leap from his chest: His father was sitting beside the hearth. In an instant of recognition, Benyar was on his feet, running with outstretched arms. Ranth ran to him, no longer attempting to hold on to any semblance of decorum in front of the group that had followed him. Father and son held each other in a long embrace, which led to instant rapport. In these brief moments of sharing, all that had happened since they had last been together flowed freely between them, one mind to the other.

Ranth saw his father rescued by Bimily and life returned to him by his Lifestone. He marveled at the power of the stone. He witnessed the healing, saw the dreams, and recognized the man in the dreams as Gwernz, who now stood here in the same room with them.

Benyar was witness to his son's grief and resignation over his father's supposed death, which was soon replaced with responsibility for the woman. He watched in awe as scenes of Ranth reconnecting her severed blood vessels were revealed to him. He saw Bimily and instantly made the connection, recalling how she had rescued him and brought him to the Temple and its healers. A blush covered Ranth's cheeks as his father reviewed a scene of intense lovemaking, for the merest of seconds, between himself and Shunlar. Benyar discreetly refrained from probing further in that direction, but realized how deep the connection had become between Ranth and Shunlar.

Passing their information to one another took mere seconds, and they returned their attention to the group that had now gathered around them. Benyar was first to speak, turning to Gwernz and Marleah. "My profound thanks I give to you this night. You have returned my only son to me. Willingly I am indebted to you. My name is Benyar sul Jemaprée and this is my son, Ranth."

Gwernz and Marleah exchanged a knowing glance. Gwernz nodded to his sister and Marleah stepped forward, offering the leather bag and its contents to Benyar.

"This we believe to be your property. It has long lain in safekeeping in the Valley of the Great Trees. Many seasons ago a group of our hunters found it near what was left of a body. The hunters thought best to burn what was left of the man, but they brought this to our leader, Arlass. I was instructed to return it to a man who had been recently wounded. If you are that person, then this belongs to you." Carefully Marleah placed the bag in Benyar's outstretched hands.

As soon as his hands touched it, a strange glow began to pulse from the bag. The Lifestone that he wore around his neck also began to glow through the leather of his tunic. Next, a spark jumped from the bag to the bright spot on his chest. Everyone in the room witnessed sparks of light jumping from Benyar's chest to the bag in his hands and back again. Benyar stood frozen, waiting for the sparks to subside. Tears overflowed from his eyes and ran down his cheeks, unstoppable. His hands trembled.

When he finally regained his tongue he whispered, "You have just handed me another most precious treasure. One who has not breathed the outside air nor seen the sun for nearly twenty years will now be restored to life. This gift I could never repay in my own lifetime. I am forever, most gratefully, indebted to you." His face wet with tears, Benyar knelt before Marleah and Gwernz, as if he were a servant, clutching the Lifestone of his wife to his chest, overwhelmed with happiness.

This admission of gratitude from Benyar touched a deep chord in Marleah. She heard her voice saying, "I ask this favor of you who seem to be able to find lost children. Help me find my children. One is female and was stolen from me while yet a babe. The other is male and is being held captive somewhere in this city by one with a strong, evil mind.''

Benyar nodded assent and put the pouch with his wife's Lifestone into the full sleeve of his robe. He removed his dagger from its sheath and made a small slice across the bottom of his palm. ''With my blood I swear I will do all in my power to find your children.'' He showed his hand to Marleah, who bowed her acceptance and asked him to stand.

Marleah and Benyar bowed once more to each other. Then she continued, ''I accept your oath. But I also believe that your son has certain knowledge of my daughter. If this is so,'' said Marleah, turning now to speak directly to Ranth, ''please tell me where she is.''

Delcia and Morgentur, seeing that the homecoming had taken an unexpected turn, asked those remaining with them in the room to quietly remove themselves. The several who had volunteered to bring food and drink to the travelers silently ushered themselves out and set to work at once, everyone eager to allow the reunited family members privacy.

As the room emptied, Ranth shook his head to clear his thoughts. Had he really heard correctly? Had this woman just said she was the mother of Shunlar, the woman he loved?

''Ranth, is this true? Do you know her daughter?'' Benyar asked, suddenly bringing Ranth's thoughts back to the room.

''Father, I know only the woman we helped to escape from the clutches of Lord Creedath.'' Then he turned to Marleah, questioning, ''How can you know of her, Lady? I have never set eyes on you until this night and we have not even spoken yet!''

Anger flashed from Marleah like a great spark. Emotion clouded her judgment as instinctively she took several steps toward Ranth. Only Gwernz could stop her, and he came up behind her and gently put his hands on her shoulders. After his touch had soothed her, he said, "Sister, explain to all of us how you come by your knowledge."

Marleah was subdued for the moment. "Certainly, brother. Young man, I have certain . . . ah . . . shall we say *abilities* that perhaps you are unaware of. When you brushed fingers with me earlier tonight as you took the reins from my hand, I was able to see your thoughts. But only for that instant we touched. Believe me that I went no deeper than what your thoughts were sending out. If I had approached your mind, it would have felt like this." Marleah reached toward him tentatively. Feeling her brush against the edges of his mind with her touch, Ranth closed her out with a strong protective barrier.

"Now why didn't you do that earlier? You seem to know about mind-delving. How is it that you were sending messages off into the air? You are too reckless, young sir."

Admonished by Marleah, Ranth bowed his head, color flooding his cheeks. *When will I stop this accursed blushing?* he asked himself.

But Marleah heard that, too, and answered him. "When you are older, believe me, it will stop."

He was very startled, but in spite of his shame, he smiled, contritely. Once he did, the room seemed to lighten and everyone relaxed a bit, even Marleah.

Delcia took this opportunity to speak. "Ranth, please tell us that you have not forgotten all that we have taught you!"

When he turned to her, apologetically, he answered, "Forgive me, Delcia. I cannot explain the why of it. I myself cautioned Shunlar to protect her mind against such unintentional thinking of me. I have no excuse other than that . . . I . . . ah . . . have no excuse," he stammered.

They laughed again, all but Ranth. His father put an arm around his shoulder and explained, "My son, I would take a wild stab in the dark with my dagger and say that you have fallen under the spell of this young woman. I remember her well. Truly, the lady Marleah is her mother, for she was as I recall quite lovely, nearly as beautiful as her mother. It is very understandable why.''

Benyar's charm worked on Marleah, and this time she blushed. More laughter followed, including a loud chuckle from Gwernz. She turned and swatted at him as only a sister can.

''So, young Ranth, tell me, how is—did you call her Shunlar? Above all, please tell me where I may find her.''

''Lady Marleah, she was very well when we parted last night. As for where she is, I await the arrival of one of our companions, Lady Bimily, to tell me that. She was one of the persons who helped us return to Vensunor, along with. . . .'' Here he stopped. This part of the story would take much longer, and he felt there might be some convincing to do. ''Please, let us sit closer to the fire and I will tell you how we met and how I come to be standing here before you. This will take some time.''

''Time, I hope, will be kind to us. I am anxious to meet with her, so please, tell us your story,'' said Marleah.

They sat and Ranth began to tell his tale, beginning with their escape from Creedath's palace and their flight into the desert. When he told of Bimily's finding them, he left out the fact that she was a shapechanger because she had sworn him to secrecy. Only Benyar knew the truth of what or who Bimily was capable of becoming. He told of their fight and capture by the soldiers and hired mercenaries sent after them by Creedath.

Surprisingly, it took little convincing when he told of their rescue and his meeting with Cloonth and Alglooth, the two who had raised Shunlar. As he described them, he noticed that Marleah's face went white, but he refused to ask her questions as he watched her expression change from that of an interested listener to one of extreme rage. Gwernz, however, became excited, and asked if Ranth would be willing to allow him to enter his mind and see what these two persons looked like.

''Gladly, sir. I will show you all if you like.''

The group assembled nodded acceptance of his willingness to do this, and he sat still, allowing their touches to brush against the edges of his thoughts. The sensation was marvelous for Ranth. Gwernz, Delcia, Morgentur, and Ben-yar all had very distinctive differences to them, but what Ranth noticed mostly was the subtlety that hid the strength. Marleah had held back, but as her touch reached him, he flinched, as did everyone else. For one brief second the overwhelming pain of loss was felt by all of them and, too late, she covered it.

The etiquette of all in the room would not allow them to mention what they had felt from her, not even Gwernz. They covered their thoughts with careful illusions of awe for what they were seeing, and Marleah was unaware of what had occurred, so preoccupied was she with the vision of the two half-human, half-dragon beings in Ranth's mem-ory.

After answering several detailed questions from Delcia and Morgentur, Ranth continued; this time, however, he was met with frowns and exclamations of protest, particu-larly from Marleah, when he told them they were willing to become captives of Creedath in order to free the others in the round dungeon.

"This is madness. Who came up with such an idea? Surely it must have been the male and his partner. They are at the least risk here, I think. Have they no concern for the lives of the two women with them?" protested Marleah loudly.

"I regret to inform you that it was Shunlar's idea," an-swered Ranth. "Alglooth and Cloonth tried to talk her out of it, but her mind was firmly set on this course of action. Shunlar explained that it was to free the others held captive. Since she had been a prisoner there, and Bimily and I had seen the horrors of the place as well, we agreed with her."

Marleah had nothing to say; she just sat and steamed. Ranth continued.

"When they are captured, the Lady Bimily will know. She will then meet us here at the Temple, to let us know that our three friends are under Creedath's roof. If you are

willing, Delcia and Morgentur, we ask your help in bringing the other captives here to the Temple for a very short
while, to determine which of them can travel and which of
them must stay on here to be healed. I trust they can be
hidden while they do so?"

"Of that you can be sure. We will send a guard with
you. How many will you need?" they answered together.

"I would think a party of no more than ten will be necessary," answered Ranth.

"We will accompany you, won't we, Gwernz?" stated
Marleah. Her brother nodded his assent. "Both of us will
assist you, be assured."

"And I, my son. Now that we are together it will be
impossible to allow you to go very far from my sight, especially if you are planning a venture back into the nest of
Creedath," added Benyar.

Very concerned, Gwernz asked, "Can someone tell us
more about this person who calls himself Creedath? I dis-
like the danger I am able to feel from the man, and after
hearing your story, Ranth, I fear that Loff is one of his
'special' captives."

Long hours they talked, learning of Creedath, and the
details of the escape plan devised by Shunlar, Ranth, and
the others. But most surprising was the engraved invitation
that arrived as they were deep in conversation. It invited
Delcia and Morgentur to a formal evening banquet at
week's end at Creedath's palace, a mere two days away. A
handwritten message on the back of the invitation declared
that he had a special surprise for his honored guests. Special
surprise indeed!

"This is most auspicious. The deliverance of two or three
people is one thing, but if we are to rescue an entire group
of captives, the comings and goings of so many people at
this banquet should make for an excellent diversion,"
spoke Delcia and Morgentur, their voices in unison. Their
voices unified in the truth-telling mode portended a positive
outcome, however it unfolded.

Twenty-Nine

🍃 DAWN'S LIGHT BROKE THE UNUSUAL PEACE OF THE Dragon's Breath Inn. As the door of the large suite banged open noisily, four occupants stepped forth and descended the stairway. Already the fire blazed in the hearth, and the smell of freshly baking bread permeated the inn. Shunlar, still disguised as an old man—but somewhat cleaner than the night before—was the first one down the stairs. She stood waiting as the two ladies and one gentleman sat down at the table and then seated herself last.

The owner, Bente, stared a long while at the four who sat bright and shiny in her dining hall. Where had the other woman come from? She had vaguely remembered being aware of a fourth voice late in the night, but she couldn't remember letting another woman into the room.

In truth, no one had let her in. The second lady was Bimily. As planned, she had flown into the room in the shape of a bat. Not one soul had suspected her, and that was how she wanted it. She sat in the disguise of a pretty but rather plump brunette.

The four merrymakers beckoned for service, and soon there was food and hot tea all around. They had consumed more of the cactus alcohol than they had meant to the night before, and were quite thirsty. The first pot of tea went down fast and another steaming pot was placed before them and emptied as well. All were ravenously hungry, and soon the hot cakes and syrup disappeared too. Empty plates before them, they sat, bellies full, waiting for the inevitable to happen.

The room began filling up with guards who had just been relieved from the night watch. With them came the same young guard whose illusions of a night spent with Cloonth were larger than life. He looked as if he hadn't slept for days. He circled the room nervously. Finally, amid looks of approval and nods of agreement from the other men, he boldly stepped up to the table where the four sat, drinking their tea, seemingly oblivious to what was happening in the room around them.

"Madam," he addressed Cloonth, "I request a bit of your time." He clicked his heels together and held his hand out to her.

"Young sir, can't you see I am eating my breakfast? Besides, it is too early in the day for such things," she answered, trying to put him off.

"Now, madam!" he demanded in a loud voice.

"No!" roared Shunlar, in an even louder voice, still spell cast for all the room to see as a gray-haired old man. "The woman is with me. I have paid for her time and she breakfasts with me."

The sound of steel rasping from sheaths could be heard all around the room. With so much reinforcement, the young guard became even bolder. "Where do you come by the gold to pay for all this?" he questioned, one sweep of his hand taking in the people, food, and lodgings.

A slightly older guard approached their table now. His sword remained in its sheath, but he clenched the hilt menacingly. "Old man, I would look at the purse in which you hold your coins," was all he said, holding out his free hand.

Shunlar produced the purse. It in turn produced the desired results. Knowing what would happen when it was seen, Shunlar had deliberately taken the purse of Lieutenant Meecha, filling it with the contents of several other purses, before they left the oasis.

As the man inspected the detailed leather pouch, he turned down a fold at the top where underneath was tooled the name MEECHA in small, stylized letters. He looked at the four persons at the table one by one, and in a quiet voice said, "Let's all go for a little walk, shall we?"

Their plan was working perfectly, right on schedule. They rose from the table and were very roughly relieved of their weapons and escorted from the inn at swordpoint, to the palace of Lord Creedath.

Thirty

THE ROOM'S STILLNESS WAS PUNCTUATED BY bright flashes of light as Loff moved across the floor. The day had begun with the sun pouring through the five narrow vertical windows. Loff had been awake for hours, working out his very stiff, very unused muscles. In the darkness of the room he moved between and into the bars of sunlight, which flashed like mirrors each time they touched his naked skin. Except for the small fire flickering at the other end of the room, this was the only other light. Loff's breath made the only sound, as his bare feet danced noiselessly upon the stone floor.

Concentrating in the silence, he pushed himself through the unremitting exercises. He had been imprisoned for over two weeks now and had barely had the strength to practice, so it was hard going. His body ached and sweat poured from him as he began the last of his stretches. As his heart pounded, he felt the awaited tingle course through his spine, from bottom to top. Yes, at last he had tapped into the source of his strength. A flush covered him as he breathed himself into a calmer state. Already he was beginning to feel much stronger, though it had taken longer than he was used to. Remembering the fear that had seeped into his thoughts several times in the last hour at the prospect of losing his vitality brought another burst of energy up his spine and a sigh from his lips.

If he was going to be able to fight his way out of here—

and fight was what he had foremost on his mind these days; fight or Mistress Ranla, that is—he needed his vitality and his mental barriers to be in perfect condition and immediately available. He remembered hearing stories from the old men of the valley that recalled the loss of their vitality and how he had shuddered at the time. Now he knew what it really felt like. He could never have imagined, until now, what not being able to defend himself might be like. The taste it left in his mouth caused his determination to grow stronger.

When his breathing had again slowed to normal, Loff began circling the room to cool down, and then headed for the bath that awaited him. He had his own tub for bathing, and he had already grown accustomed to it. He insisted, however, on bathing in privacy when Ranla suggested that one of her women would be made available to bathe him. He wanted no woman to distract him—unless, perhaps, it was Ranla—and certainly didn't want to be scrutinized by a guard while being scrubbed by a female. He tugged on the chain of the kettle that hung suspended over the fire. Once the kettle was positioned over the tub, he tugged it again and slowly emptied its contents into the tub. Then he lowered himself gradually into the steaming water. He worked great gobs of suds into his hair and as he washed, his mind went over the speech he had heard just three—or was it four—days ago.

Lord Creedath could certainly be charming when he wanted to be. Loff was able to see beneath all the pomp and flowery words, however. Most of the other "guests" had been deceived, but not Loff. So he was supposed to believe that Creedath had "rescued" them from their fate in the dungeon? Just who was responsible for their imprisonment in the first place? That detail had been left out, as were so many others. Guests, in locked rooms, brought to the brink of death with sleeping potions—not Loff's idea of hospitality. He longed for the Trees and their safety. This morning, even the luxury of his bath could not remove the knots from his stomach, or the clench from his jaw. Something was about to happen.

Loff jumped when he heard the sound of the key grating in the lock, followed by the door creaking open. He had been expecting Mistress Ranla, but Lord Creedath strode into the room instead.

"What!" he exclaimed. "You still luxuriate in the bath. Boy, there is much to be done. Here, dry yourself. Dress and come to the table." With that he threw a towel to Loff and sat down at the table to watch him dry and dress.

Pretending he was still weak from the ordeal of being drugged and imprisoned, Loff stood up slowly, wrapped the towel around himself and just as slowly stepped from the tub, his back to Creedath. Careful to hide himself as best he could while he put on his clothes, Loff kept the towel draped around his stooped shoulders. He wanted to keep his physical condition a secret for as long as possible.

Creedath, on the other hand, was not so easily fooled. His eyes followed Loff's every movement. He had already examined the calluses on his hands while Loff had been unconscious, and he knew what they were from. Loff was aware of a concerned voice saying, "We must have the physicians attend to you. I fear your stamina was greatly affected by your imprisonment. Allow me to have them come to examine you immediately."

"No, thank you, sir . . ." Loff's voice trailed off. He turned to face Creedath, bringing himself up to his full height as he did. The telltale expression on the other man's face told Loff this conversation had been a trap. No word had been spoken aloud by Creedath or himself. Every word Loff had answered had been a direct transmission from his mind to that of his captor, who now stood there with a sinister grin.

"It appears that you are not so clever as you thought. But I like your spirit. You shall be an interesting challenge in the months to come. Ready yourself," he ordered. "I will have the guards bring you to me at the appropriate time so that we can have a private chat, you and I. We are expecting important guests at table tonight, and I want you right there beside me so that you will know your fate as it is spoken.'' With those words, Creedath turned and left the room.

Loff stared at the place where Creedath had stood moments before. So it had all been a trap. For weeks he had been on his guard, and now he had betrayed himself. *Ah well, at least now I will find out just why I am here*, he said to himself.

As Creedath stormed down the corridor to his apartments, a great chortle escaped his throat. By the time he reached his door he was laughing so hard that the sentry at his door stood frozen in amazement. Regaining his senses, the sentry scrambled to open the door, but Creedath pushed the man aside and opened the door himself, slamming it shut in the astonished guard's face. Every few minutes his eerie guffawing could be heard from within his chambers, and it sent shivers up the man's spine.

The guard jumped again when Creedath suddenly appeared at the door. ''Bring Ranla to me. Now!'' he ordered, and slammed the door once more.

Careful not to leave his post unattended, the man called to another sentry who stood several paces away. Instantly relieved of his post, he was off down the hall in search of Mistress Ranla. At this time of day, he knew she would be in the kitchen overseeing the preparations for that evening's festivities. He found her huddled over a great bowl of dough with several of the bakers. Ranla turned when she heard her name called, clearly annoyed at this intrusion.

''Mistress Ranla, the Lord Creedath would have you report to him in his chamber immediately. I am to bring you.''

Summoned in this way, Ranla could tell something was wrong. Creedath usually sent a message directly to her by telepathic contact. She sighed. ''Yes, Jamiel, make bread sticks with seeds rolled into them if the dough does not rise. I must leave it to your discretion. Please don't fail me." Ranla removed her apron and smoothed the front of her dress as she followed the sentry from the kitchen, most of the staff silently watching her back. The room broke into loud whispers as soon as she was gone.

Standing before the ominous chamber, Ranla waited as the guard pounded his fist upon the door. The noise was followed by Creedath's call from within to enter. The visibly shaken guard opened the door and it closed behind her with an echoing thud.

Standing inside the chamber, Ranla's vision blurred, and she felt as if a great chasm had suddenly opened before her. A heavy weight settled over her limbs and she was unable to move, frozen to the spot where she stood. Ranla blinked her eyes and opened them wide as her body, which was no longer under her control, began to move. In great lurches that resembled walking, her legs brought her to the bed. Standing there, spasms lifted her hands and placed them at her belt. Terror gripped her as she realized that Creedath was waiting for her, reclining naked upon his bed.

Creedath fixed his steely gaze on her and reached out to her with his mind. *I have changed my mind, my dear. You are not for Meecha, but for me. Does that not please you?*

As he smiled cruelly, Creedath patted the blankets beside him, continuing to control Ranla's hands as they stiffly began to remove her clothing. She could only watch in helpless fascination as her fingers twitched while they untied the laces of her bodice. Her breath was coming in great gulps now. Her mind tried to put up a fight. She attempted to form words that could somehow appeal to him, but her struggle only increased the intensity of his grip on her. No sounds could pass her lips save for her breath, which came in loud gasps.

Besides, Lieutenant Meecha is dead, he said with satisfied finality. Creedath had seen the anger and hatred she had tried to hide from him when he had "given" her to Meecha as his bride, and now those emotions once more filled her. They seemed to excite him all the more. *Hurry. I'll help you remove the rest of your skirts*, he said as he reached for her and pulled her down onto the bed beside him.

Baffled by what was happening to her, Ranla tried to remember the spell-song that had always worked in the past to calm him down. It seemed to be wiped from her memory. All that remained in her mind was the all-consuming lust that Creedath directed completely at her. His strength was beyond belief. When had he learned to do this? She fought back and realized too late that the pain of fighting was causing her to lose consciousness.

Hours later, when she awoke, Ranla was all too aware of a dull throbbing pain in her head as well as between her legs. Creedath was no longer in bed with her but on the other side of the room, fully dressed and seated by the fire, sipping a goblet of brandy. She pulled the blankets over her naked, shivering body. Surprised to hear herself sobbing, she tried to muffle her sobs with the pillow.

Creedath approached and sat next to her on the bed. In a gesture of what seemed like tenderness, he put one hand on her shoulder, offering her the brandy with the other. He made no attempt to link with her telepathically. "This should ease the pain somewhat. Stay and rest. I want you here when I return. I'll have the servants come and freshen you up for later." He picked up her hand, placed the goblet of brandy in it—wrapping her limp fingers around it—then rose to leave.

"It is time you had a child," he said in a low whisper.

Ranla's breath stopped and her head snapped up.

"Surprised?" he asked when he recognized astonishment as well as hatred in her eyes. "Don't be. That was always my intention for you. You will learn not to fight me; that will make it easier on both of us." He rubbed his temples as he spoke.

He left her alone then to realize her fate. She stifled her crying by drinking down the contents of the goblet in two huge gulps, but it did nothing to stop her trembling. Realizing she was in shock, Ranla called out to the guard while she still could. Very timidly the door opened, and the young man swallowed hard when he saw her.

"Send me my women," was all she could manage. Her hand lost its grip on the crystal goblet and it shattered into hundreds of pieces as it hit the stone floor. Ranla had fainted again.

Creedath hurried down the steps on his way to the main dining hall. Already the preparations were under way for tomorrow evening's banquet. He planned to announce to the Mayor and other prominent citizens his intentions toward those "under his care." That would be his first announcement. Then he would announce his forthcoming marriage to Ranla. She would attend, of course.

A pity none of the other wives survived childbirth, Creedath mused to himself as he walked. *Perhaps Ranla will.* She was much stronger than any of the others had been. Having survived these past five years in his presence as keeper of his house was more than promising. Surviving the cruelty of forced mind-rapport while in the act of lovemaking had driven most of the other women mad within the first week. But that had been in the early days, when he had less control over his powers. Ranla seemed a bit shaken and bruised, but that would change. He made a mental note to himself to consult his book before he did further damage to her. The thought of her body moving rhythmically beneath him caused a warm surge of pleasure to pass through his groin.

An unflattering grimace of a smile crossed his face as he remembered how well he had controlled her movements, especially her hands. After she had gotten the laces undone and her blouse off, Ranla's hands had hardly jerked at all. Yes, he was learning fast how to maintain his dominion over others without damaging them permanently. She possessed the potential to please him greatly, but to do that she must live.

He felt confident now that things were finally under way as he strode into the banquet hall. Even the Honored Couple of the Temple would be here. How ironic that he should ask their blessing on this, his newest union. He had never done so before. What would they say when they knew his real intentions for his flock of "adopted" young men and women? A sharp laugh escaped his throat. It caused the servants busy at work in the hall to cringe.

Passing through the banquet hall, Creedath made his way toward the round dungeon. There were four new prisoners he wished to question himself. Once Creedath had found out that the purse of Lieutenant Meecha had been found in their possession, his orders had been absolute. No one was to touch them until he had personally inspected them. He would find out which of them had been responsible for the death of Lieutenant Meecha and his search party, for he was sure they were not returning. He wanted to know every detail, and nothing would stop him.

Creedath knew he could obtain any information he wished from the prisoners by his brutal mind probing. He suspected another depth of potency lay within his understanding, and he was eager to test it on someone disposable, like the prisoners. If they died in the process, it was nothing to him. All he desired now was information. Suddenly he thought about the female he had held in his grasp in this very same dungeon—that is, until she had been helped to escape by Ranth and Kessell, the stranger who had captured her for him. She was the real prize. *What if these vermin I now have in my clutches know something of her?* he asked himself. His blood boiled at the possibility of mating with the likes of her. Hunger for power surged through Creedath as he began to descend the spiral stairs to the round dungeons below the palace.

Thirty-One

THE FOUR OF THEM WAITED, SITTING TOGETHER IN the dark, sodden, foul-smelling dungeon on piles of straw that were at least clean and dry. Straw, water, and a bucket for waste were all that had been provided for them so far. In the dark, it was hard to tell how long they had been here. Someone's stomach rumbled loudly, and three heads turned in Bimily's direction at the sound. Her large appetite was no secret to them. Since so often her days were spent in the shape of an eagle, her metabolism took a bit more adjusting than the others. But all of them were beginning to show some strain.

"It's this body. Perhaps if I had chosen a slimmer one . . ." Bimily offered with a shrug of her shoulders. A faint shimmer of the air around her caused a visible shrinking to occur around her middle. "There, much better. Now I won't distract you or myself with the noise."

Bimily's adjustment to the physical form she had chosen happened just in time. The sound of boots slogging across the wet floor on the other side of the door announced visitors. Quickly Shunlar checked her appearance. With assistance from Cloonth and Alglooth, she strengthened the illusion that covered her, as they strengthened theirs. Cloonth and Alglooth held hands tightly, concentrating on the mental barriers they had placed around all four of them.

Keys rattled in the lock and the bar squealed loudly as it slid through its rusted metal brackets. Someone leaned

his weight hard against the door and it groaned open reluctantly, the bottom so swollen from the dampness of the
place that it stuck several times in the process. Into the
room stepped a massive individual holding a torch in one
hand and a sword in the other. He grinned toothlessly, and
gestured with the sword for them to rise. As Shunlar's eyes
grew accustomed to the torchlight, she could at last see the
man, and quickly realized he was not grinning; his mouth
was a scar slashed across his face and that dark empty
chamber held no tongue. Behind him, accompanied by
more armed men of the same stature, Creedath himself entered.

"Ladies, gentlemen," he sarcastically addressed them.
"I wish to know how you came to have in your possession
the purse of one of my most trusted soldiers. I assure you,
I can pull the truth from you in a matter of seconds, so let
us be open with one another. I promise it will cause you
less pain," he finished, his cold gray-blue eyes menacing
as he spoke.

Suddenly Cloonth was on her knees, golden hair cascading over her shoulders. "Sir, I beg of you, we had nothing
to do with your soldier. We—my companions and I—were
merely spending an evening at the inn, as we are accustomed to doing, and this person," she turned, casting an
accusing finger at Shunlar, "entered. He bought us dinner
and in return we entertained him in his room for the night.
Please be merciful." She clutched her hands together and
prostrated herself on the filthy floor before Creedath. Bimily did the same. Both women were in tears.

It was clearly Alglooth's turn, and he knelt beside the
two prone, sobbing females, put his hand on Cloonth's back
and with his head bowed low, begged in a shaky voice,
"Please, my lord, my companion speaks the truth. We have
been wrongly accused. Be merciful."

"Enough. Out of my way." Creedath advanced on them
and they scuttled backward in terror, huddling together
close to Shunlar, who had remained in the background,
leaning against the wall.

"Now I ask you, holder of the purse. How came you by it?" He spat the last words at the old man accusingly.

Shunlar reeled under the impact of Creedath's full attention on her. Her shaking wasn't pretense. It was taking all her strength to maintain the physical cover of a grizzled old man. Droplets of sweat formed on her brow from the exertion. Enduring the force of his powerful telepathic bombardment, she was thankful for the sputtering torchlight, for she was certain that her image wavered now and again. Her terror was very real, and her breath soured. She swallowed hard in an effort to keep the bile in her stomach from spilling out. Her knees weakened and she began to slide down the wall in a convulsive, trembling way.

Alglooth reached for her arm in an attempt to stop her from falling all the way to the floor. His touch transferred an instant burst of energy into Shunlar, and she straightened her knees and pushed herself back into a standing position, still using the wall behind her for support.

Suddenly Creedath seemed to leap, and in two long strides he was leering into her face, nose to nose. He grabbed Shunlar's shoulder in a grip so tight she thought her bones would crack. The pain sent her to her knees. Shunlar gave a throaty gasp, but her barriers held as Creedath's mind forced its way against her mind. He saw only what they meant for him to see: an old man rummaging through the belongings of a band of soldiers and mercenaries. The scene was night and the entire band lay dead.

Shunlar was clearly at the breaking point when something made Creedath pull his hand from her shoulder and step back, as if he had been burned, an odd look to his eyes. A sensation in his hand caused a faint itch to spread across his palm and up to his elbow. He didn't stop to think about it, but attributed it to his loathing at touching the old fool who quivered before him. He stood rubbing his arm, forgetting for a moment just why he was here. He blinked a few times, then stared blankly at the old man who knelt retching onto his boots.

Creedath backed his feet away, stamping and shaking

them in disgust. Suddenly regaining his faculties, he ordered loudly, "Bring them some food—real food—and water. I want them alive. No one is to touch them or he will answer to me. Is that clear?"

He whirled around to scrutinize each guard one by one, then stepped quickly from the cell, an enigmatic frown on his face. He hadn't gotten much information, after all. There was also this feeling he was unable to identify, the inexplicable sense that someone or something was pushing him out of the cell. The guards followed close behind him with the same uneasiness, backing their way out.

Before the door had groaned to a close Alglooth knelt at Shunlar's side, soothing her with his touch, pouring strength into her from his deep wells of power. He held her in his arms while she continued to shudder, until her shoulders finally stopped quaking and she slept.

Cloonth and Bimily helped to lay Shunlar down on the pile of straw and pulled her cloak over her, turning her to face the wall. No one entering the cell would be able to tell the form was not an old man.

"Whatever you two did to push him from the cell seemed to work very well. Which one of you began thinking of fleas?" whispered Alglooth.

"Bimily," answered Cloonth. Then all three of them put all of their attention on Shunlar again.

Hours later, when food arrived, Cloonth and Alglooth took no chances and again covered Shunlar with a strong illusion. The eternally grinning, corpulent guard entered the cell with a torch in one hand and a sword in the other. Two other guards stepped in and set down trays that held four bowls of steaming hot stew, bread, honey, cheese, and a skin of wine. Once the food was deposited and they were again left in the dark, they dropped the illusions.

The cell had no windows, save for one slit above the door. A thin band of yellow light from the oil lamps on the other side of the door gave them the barest minimum of light; it merely allowed them to see outlines of bodies and objects. No one was able to see into the cell as they cared for her, nor did anyone bother to look, so terrified were they of the master of the castle. The prisoners were left completely alone.

"Come, my dear one, eat. You will need your strength." Alglooth coaxed Shunlar, her head propped on his knee. He gave her water first, and then Cloonth offered her a bit of bread dipped in honey. Shunlar managed one bite, although the effort of chewing took most of her strength. She swallowed at last, then quickly fell deep into sleep again. This was a dangerous sign. All they could do was try to keep her warm and watch over her as she slept.

The stew was hot, and Bimily began to dip crusts of bread into it and eat. Reluctantly Cloonth joined her and had a few bites. "Alglooth," she whispered to her mate, "eat now while it is hot. It will warm you for a moment and you need to keep your strength, my dear one." She felt, more than saw, the smile he gave her as he rose from Shunlar's side and joined the two females in their meal.

Try as he might, the food stuck in Alglooth's throat, so he picked up the wineskin. He sniffed at it and quickly ascertained that it was not tainted with any drug, but tasting it only soured his stomach. He scooped up a bowlful of water and returned to his daughter's side.

Weak from her ordeal with Creedath, Shunlar sorely needed to rest, but this was different. Her breathing had become very shallow in the last hour, and showed no signs of improving. Recognizing how dangerous the situation had become, Alglooth decided to take action. He reached out to his child's mind, tentatively at first, trying to draw her back to him and the world around her.

He tried to touch her mind, to open it to places long forgotten by opening his own mind to remember, to bring back the memories of her mother. He showed her his true identity as he had never dared to before.

Everything he did was to no avail; very little of Shunlar's awareness remained. There were only faint traces of her spirit left when he reached to make contact with her. He knew then that she had been pushed to the edge of death, and he raced ahead to find her. The openness on this internal plane had a quality that could best be described as very slippery. There were colors, but when he decided what colors he saw they dissolved into gray, and then nothing. But he continued in the direction he thought was forward. At last he saw Shunlar far off in the distance, suspended in the air, a translucent quality to her that grew fainter as he came closer. He called her name.

Cloonth and Bimily sat nearby, monitoring Alglooth from time to time. He had been sitting in a trance for a little over an hour, the strain of his seeking becoming more obvious by the minute. He sweated and breathed hard. When Cloonth and Bimily heard him calling out loud, they linked minds with him, and only with their help was he able to contact Shunlar.

Shunlar floated in a place somewhere between sleep and reality. She drifted in a gray void, calling out to Ranth for help. *Who is Ranth?* part of her wondered. No person came to mind, just a name. In the distance she knew a dark man pursued her, but two female shapes intervened, flying about, pushing him away, leaving a very confused look upon his face. Then another voice, a male voice, called out to her from far behind, and she turned around to find him. A bright flash of iridescent green and blue flew by as recognition sparked her memory.

The flying man came to her and wrapped his wings comfortingly around her. She felt tears on her cheeks as she embraced him, called him father, and began to remember. Shunlar gradually became aware of his touch and, returning from her dream, she clung to his strength as it gently called to her, bringing her back from the nightmare that had nearly become reality.

Shunlar's eyelids flickered open. Before her in the dark cell glowed two sets of concerned yellow-amber eyes. She focused on the set closest to her and said, "Father, I know you." They propped her up and fed her some of the cheese and a few sips of wine. Then she fell back into a restful, healing sleep, this time taking full, deep breaths.

Relieved beyond words, Alglooth knew she was not lost to them. He turned to Cloonth and reassuringly kissed her cheek. "How is your strength, my lovely one?" His concern was for the new life she carried as well as for her.

"A bit low, but the food has helped. Will you eat something now so that we can all rest?" Her attention shifted as she looked to where Bimily stood.

On the other side of the cell, Bimily's agitation was palpable and fast becoming uncontrollable. Shifting her weight from foot to foot, her attention was fixed on the small slit of a window at the top of the door.

Cloonth turned to her and said, "It is time for you to leave and see that the others arrive on schedule. Please go safely. In what form will you travel?"

"I haven't yet decided," she answered tersely. "Sorry, I did not mean to answer so rudely," she checked herself. "I cannot speak and act. Farewell."

A shimmering and wavering of the air occurred around Bimily, and in her place stood a small bird. She flew to the opening at the top of the door and quickly disappeared through it. On the ledge just inside the door, she assessed the room. Strange: There were no guards. Once again Bimily changed her shape, this time to that of a large rat. She ran in the shadows until it was safe to change her form yet another time. Bimily leapt from her ledge in a shimmer.

The form that touched the ground was that of a large, rather angry-looking guard. He grumbled as he made his way up the stairs. When he encountered others he merely saluted, and they allowed him to pass. His garb was that of the personal house staff, and no one questioned him as he stomped through the palace and out into the courtyard toward the stables. The fact that it was daylight confused her. It should be night! Could they have been captives longer than one day? She began to worry as she hurriedly saddled, then mounted the horse.

"I pass under direct order of Lord Creedath, an emissary to the Temple." No one dared question Bimily as she moved through the gate on horseback. Breaking into an easy trot, she was soon at the Temple gates. She dismounted and pulled the bell cord, and she and her mount were ushered inside.

Thirty-Two

IT HAD BEEN A MERE TWO DAYS SINCE GWERNZ and Marleah had entered the safety of the Temple grounds with Ranth. In that time they had been made very comfortable guests. They were treated to as much warm, wonderful food as they could stuff themselves with, as well as the luxury of hot mineral baths. Being given separate rooms in the guest quarters of the Temple, with real beds to sleep in, had been the most welcome part for Gwernz and Marleah. Just knowing they could escape into the solitude of a private room was a relief both of them were reluctant, at first, to admit. Spending so much time traveling together had made both of them secretly wish for quiet and privacy. Mostly, though, it felt extravagant to relax in comfort without having to remain constantly alert to the possibility of danger. Safety had a good feeling that could be short-lived, however. Tonight they were to attend the banquet at the palace of Lord Creedath.

Most of this particular morning Marleah, Gwernz, and Benyar had spent mind-linked with Ranth, memorizing every corridor, wing, and dungeon of Creedath's palace. When they weren't viewing the palace through Ranth's eyes, Marleah, Benyar, and Ranth practiced their swordplay. Marleah was impressed by the strength and tenacity not only of Benyar but of his son as well. Both were worthy opponents. The younger, Ranth, could use some polishing, but he had years ahead of him in which to catch up so he could match his father and herself in technique.

Marleah had also taken every opportunity to learn whatever she could of Shunlar. She had been allowed to see and subsequently memorize her face, her voice, and her movements, thanks to the cooperation of Ranth. He cleverly tried to hide his deep feelings for her, but to no avail. Marleah secretly approved of her daughter's choice.

Benyar was more than delighted with the turn of events. In fact, there were probably no words that could describe his joy. He reveled in the fact that after so many long years of searching, his son and he were face-to-face again and soon would be on their way back to their homeland, to restore life to his wife—Zeraya—Ranth's mother—by returning her stolen Lifestone to her. Their reunion after all these years would be cause for weeks of celebration in the desert of the Feralmon.

Gwernz lost no time at all in acquainting himself with the mysteries of the Great Cauldron and its vital messages. Most of his free moments were spent in the company of Delcia and Morgentur, exchanging information, secrets, and new interpretations of some of the spells they had deciphered from the old texts. Far into the morning they worked, explaining another mystery, solving another puzzle.

But to those who knew them well, Ranth's return had made the most noticeable change in Delcia and Morgentur. They seemed years younger. His story of the winged pair, Cloonth and Alglooth, and the parts they played in this unfolding drama was the most intriguing for them because it gave new meaning, as well as a whole new dimension, to the dragon glyphs in their system of divination.

Yet while the knowledge of the existence of the dragon-beings gave everyone a feeling of excitement and hope, it caused Marleah great pain. She at last knew who was to blame for the abduction of her child; there remained no doubt. For a time she tried to persuade herself that the father had been one of her valley, but now all these years later she knew the truth as never before. She hadn't been wrong. She had seen the faintest glimmer to his skin, even at the dark of the moon. She had seen that his hair was white, not imagined it. This also explained her daughter's unusual gold-flecked eyes, not to mention the green birthmark at the nape of her neck. She hid the anger that seethed inside her behind a facade of excitement. Marleah was excited, but not for the same reasons as everyone else.

No amount of food or hot baths or swordplay could settle Ranth. He paced. Sitting for hours at a time with his father and Marleah and showing them the different passages and hallways of Creedath's palace tired him, but he paced. Despite hours of working out with the swords and learning new techniques, he paced. They all waited anxiously for Bimily to arrive, but Ranth was as restless as a mountain cat in a cage. When the bell at the back gate chimed at long last, Ranth was there pacing, waiting to let her in. He had spent the better part of the afternoon worrying and anxious for news of Shunlar and the others, having expected Bimily's arrival the night before.

Because Bimily wanted to keep her shapechanging abilities a secret, she had prearranged for Ranth to meet her at this gate. His hands nearly threw the gate from its hinges as he pulled it open. There stood a large man with a horse behind him, in the livery of the man Ranth hated with a white hot heat.

"Identify yourself!" Ranth blurted out before thinking, in a tone much harsher than he had expected to use.

"Ranth, it is I, Bimily," the low grumbling tones of the man answered. "Let me in before I box your ears properly, young man." Yes, it was Bimily.

"Apologies, but your appearance and clothing startled me. I have been so worried. You are nearly an entire day late. Tell me," he demanded, once man and horse were within the confines of the stable, "is Shunlar unharmed? Are she and Alglooth and Cloonth taken prisoner as planned?"

All he got for the moment was a chuckle from the imposing guard, whose eyes darted nervously around the stable. Satisfied that no eyes but Ranth's could see her, Bimily quickly changed into a startlingly lovely copper-haired woman.

Ranth blushed upon seeing her, remembering again their first meeting at the oasis. Recovering himself, he bowed to her, saying, "Lady Bimily, our party awaits your orders. I have been sorely worried because you have arrived so late. I trust that Shunlar, Cloonth, and Alglooth are in the palace and remain unharmed?" His tone, once more, was calm and civil.

"Ranth, how rested you look. Yes, they are captives. Everything took much longer than expected. When I left the palace I made as much haste as I could without bringing suspicion on myself. Shunlar is well cared for. Alglooth and Cloonth won't tolerate any harm to come to her." Aware of Ranth's agitated state, Bimily wanted him to be at ease. She didn't mention what had happened to Shunlar when Creedath visited them in their cell.

"But tell me, is your father still under the care of the Temple? Will I have the pleasure of speaking with him before we depart?" she asked with a broad smile, deliberately changing the subject.

It worked. "Yes, Lady. He is here, along with two other guests who you will be surprised to meet. My father and the others will be joining us in the rescue tonight. But permit me to explain in better quarters than the stables. If you will come with me this way." Ranth bowed politely to her and smiled, obviously pleased to see her as he offered his arm. She took it and returned his smile.

Silently he led her through the corridors of the Temple, to the meeting room where the entire party waited. The quiet conversation in the room stopped as Ranth escorted Bimily through the door. Everyone stood as he presented her to them. "Our emissary from the palace of Lord Creedath has arrived. May I present the Lady Bimily."

Delcia and Morgentur spoke their greeting in unison, bowing together. Bimily stepped forward and embraced them both, then bowed. "I am most happy to meet you,

Honored Pair. You have long been the protectors of the weak, hungry, and wounded of Vensunor and are much loved by all. Now that I am in your presence, I understand why.'' They exchanged quiet glances and looked puzzled but remained quiet.

Marleah and Gwernz greeted her enthusiastically, bowing after they did so. This woman before them represented the real possibility of rescue for Shunlar and Loff.

Bimily was stunned speechless when she learned who they were. ''Shunlar's mother and uncle?'' she finally managed to say, as she repeated again, ''You are her mother and uncle?''

In an effort to snap Bimily out of her shock, Ranth gently tugged at her sleeve so that he could introduce her to his father.

Benyar was finally able to thank her in person for rescuing him and bringing him to the safety of the Temple. Having seen her first in the form of a large man, then as a horse, he was taken aback by her beauty. Benyar reached for her hand and lightly kissed the back of it. ''Lady, I thank you for saving my life. My condition was such that I remember only sliding from the saddle of a kneeling horse.''

Bimily finally turned her full attention on Benyar when his lips touched the back of her hand. She curtsied to him and strangely enough, she began to open her mind to him, showing him a part of her that yet remained the eagle. She had seen a similar depth in Benyar when she had picked up his Lifestone, and this was her way of telling him. ''I am relieved to see you recovered so completely,'' was all she replied, coyly smiling up at him. Then she nudged his awareness away from her mind as she took her hand away.

Benyar understood the reason for what she did the moment he saw her images of the scene in the round dungeon when she touched his Lifestone. This sort of testing and sharing of another's powers had been going on ever since he had met Marleah and Gwernz. Accustomed to hiding his real talents from others for so many years, it still made him a bit nervous when it occurred. He good-naturedly bowed and smiled.

Intent on continuing, Ranth spoke up again. "Lady Bimily, it seems we are all to be guests under Creedath's roof this evening. Now it will be easier than expected to enter his palace and release Shunlar and the other prisoners held there. Come here and tell me if my memory serves me right; I have drawn a map of the corridors. When you left today, where were guards posted?" More anxious than anyone else to review the escape route once more, Ranth called Bimily over to a table on the other side of the room, where he hunched over the map of Creedath's palace.

Ranth was about to question Bimily about their part of the plan to free Shunlar, Cloonth, and Alglooth when she told him the most surprising thing. Whispering so that only Ranth could hear her, Bimily said, "The round dungeon contains no other prisoners, except for our three friends. There were not even guards in the anteroom when I left. I thought this to be very strange, but I didn't dare turn back to tell them about it. Now that I think of it, perhaps I should have."

But Marleah had overheard. "Bimily, just how did you manage to escape?" asked Marleah with a strange edge to her voice.

In response, Bimily turned her head with a snap toward Marleah. A small bluish spark seemed to appear around her head for the merest of seconds, then vanish. Something in the way she stared made Marleah look away and bow her head. A sudden intake of breath later, Marleah added, "Forgive me. I do not wish to tread a dangerous path with you. I am simply very eager to find my children."

"Children?" Bimily questioned. "I heard you mention Shunlar; do you have another child imprisoned by Creedath?"

Gwernz answered her by stating simply, "Some weeks ago my nephew, Loff, who is Shunlar's half-brother, was sent here to find her. We know he has been captured by Creedath somehow, and that he remains Creedath's prisoner. You say you were the only ones in this dungeon. Is there another dungeon where he might be held prisoner?''

"I regret that I have no answer for you,'' was all Bimily said, though her voice was much softer this time.

Breaking the awkward silence after a few moments, Ranth suggested, "Perhaps with the noise of a banquet drawing everyone's attention, we will be free to explore the palace and find the other prisoners. That is, once Shunlar is safe,'' he added. As an afterthought to himself, he mused, *If there are any to be found.*

"If there are others, we will find them,'' answered Bimily solemnly. Ranth's face turned red as he realized that once again, in his excitement, his thoughts had been projected to the group, and he slammed his barriers down. A strange silence fell upon them. One by one they left the meeting room, until only Ranth and Bimily stood looking at each other.

"Ranth, if you will show me to appropriate quarters, I would like to bathe and relax in the hours that remain before we leave for the banquet tonight.''

"Of course. Forgive me. If you will follow me, I will show you where the baths are located, and the room where you may rest. Also, I will arrange for some refreshment to be waiting for you in your room. That is, if you are hungry.'' Ranth smiled slyly at her and then escorted Bimily from the room. It took them a while to come to her room, so enthralled was she by the beauty and serenity of the Temple. Everyone they passed smiled and bowed with respect, but kept to themselves.

Later that evening, as the bells tolled the hour, they assembled in the hall with the honor guard. Clothing had been provided for all the guests, and they were resplendently dressed in formal city attire for the banquet. Over their formal clothing they donned long white capes with hoods that conveniently hid their faces. Cloaked this way, Gwernz, Marleah, Ranth, Benyar, and Bimily made up part of the honor guard that was to escort Delcia and Morgentur. After a quick check that all the members were present, Delcia and Morgentur gave the signal. Torches were lit and the gates thrown open. The procession passed through the doorway, each person taking a torch, to descend the steps and slowly proceed through the streets, winding their way to Creedath's palace.

Along the way many of the city's inhabitants had turned out to watch; some asked a blessing, some bowed in respect, some murmured words of thanks for past kindnesses. All who watched showed great respect for the group. It soon became apparent to Marleah and Gwernz that Delcia and Morgentur were greatly loved, as Bimily had pointed out earlier that afternoon.

Marleah marched along in silence. Continually repeating certain particulars of the plan they had formed, she found herself unable to keep her mind from making some of her own when it came to thinking about Alglooth, the father of Shunlar—the man responsible for her pain and loss.

Beside her walked Gwernz, with a very unusual expression on his face. When he reached out to place his hand on her arm she shrank back from him. Gwernz could immediately tell that something was very wrong. They could not risk speaking aloud just now, and he needed to communicate to her how obvious was her rage. Finally, after several attempts, she allowed his touch. She held nothing back, and Gwernz stumbled as the flood of information dropped into his awareness with a thud. He had been so busy the last two days, it had never occurred to him to piece together the puzzle of Shunlar's abduction so many years ago.

My only request is that we learn whether this person is truly the abductor, as well as the father of your child. His fate will be decided by the Great Trees, my sister, not by either of us. You must not allow your loss to poison yourself against what possible good might come from this meeting.

Brother, release your hold. I wish my solitude and I make no promises. Marleah shrugged her shoulder from his grasp, abruptly ending their communication.

Very troubled by her actions, Gwernz sent off a silent prayer for the fortitude to see this journey to its end. In the pouch that hung from his belt, he carried the Lifestone he had found in the hidden chamber of the Temple at Stiga, and in the last few moments he had become increasingly aware of it. This stone, it seemed, contained more power than he had ever before encountered, except during his initiation and acceptance by the Great Trees. As they neared their destination, the pouch seemed to heat up, causing a warming sensation across his left thigh.

He cleared his throat and indicated to Marleah that her assistance was needed, by offering his left hand to her, palm up. After several seconds she placed her right hand into his and instantly knew what troubled him. She forgot her plan of vengeance for the moment and reached out to Gwernz.

This is another reason I will need your strength. Alone I cannot hold off the power of the object I carry. If we are to defeat Creedath, you must be with me at all times. I will forfeit my life if need be, but. . . . He trailed off, waiting for her reply.

Very well. I put aside my vengeance for now; until the children are rescued and the man is dead. For the first time in days she let her temper cool and began to set a pattern to her breath that would further calm her. *I set it aside. I do not forget.*

Of that Gwernz had no doubt. But to whom did she refer when she said, *"and the man is dead"*? He started to ask the question, but took a deep breath instead and stopped himself. His sister was a very passionate woman, and while she was in the midst of such a dark mood, Gwernz knew not to interfere. When her temper was cooler he would ask that question, and not before. There were more important issues on which to focus his attention. His side became warmer with each step, and he lent himself fully to maintaining his strength until he was quit of the contents of the pouch he carried.

Thirty-Three

🍃 "AWAKE NOW. EAT SOMETHING, MY CHILD. I HAVE given all I can of myself. Now you need food to do the rest. You must have your strength to help us fight our way out of here if we need to." Alglooth spoke aloud to Shunlar, his voice echoing off the damp stone walls and waking Cloonth first. For hours he had been in direct mind contact with Shunlar, monitoring her breathing and rebuilding her strength from his great store of energy. But now he too began to tire.

Cloonth stood and picked some of the straw she had been laying on out of her hair, then stretched her whole body, retracting her wings as they scraped across the low ceiling. "This cold has made me stiff. How much longer will it be until Bimily returns with Ranth? I feel that we have been here longer than we anticipated."

"Father," Shunlar's voice croaked. "Water, please." Both Alglooth and Cloonth gladly granted her request, relieved that she had responded to his call and was awake. The long hours were doing their job of repairing some of the damage Creedath had done. How long ago that was, they could not tell. They felt entombed, and the effect of being so deep under the palace was beginning to take its toll.

Alglooth helped her to sit and lean against him. She sipped some of the water from the wooden cup Cloonth handed her. As Shunlar sat chewing some bites of the remaining bread and cheese, Cloonth began to show extreme agitation at being imprisoned. She breathed in great gulps and spoke more loudly than usual, pacing as she clenched and unclenched her hands. Shunlar stopped eating, propped up against Alglooth as she was, and sat upright, so she could focus her full attention on Cloonth's odd behavior.

Aware that both sets of eyes were on her, Cloonth suddenly stopped and pointed at the door. "There is no one out there on the other side of this door. I mean to burn my way out of here now. I will abide this prison no more. It is enough."

Alglooth was on his feet in an instant, but he slowed down his impulse to move fast and took a few tentative steps toward his mate. Something was different about Cloonth; he could see it shining through her skin. She seemed to be glowing from the middle of her body up to her face. Shunlar could see it too. In fact, the cell was beginning to become brighter as they watched her.

Cloonth clutched her middle and gasped as her knees buckled under her. With a diving motion, Alglooth was at her side, gently encircling her torso, preventing her from falling and helping her to sit. Cloonth grimaced and made a poor attempt at getting back up when she realized they were sitting on the grimy, slick stones, but her legs would not hold her and she relented, leaning heavily on Alglooth for support.

Her skin was warm to the touch and covered in a thin layer of sweat. But as soon as Alglooth touched her the pain subsided. Taking his hand, she placed it over her belly. Then she opened up her mind to him, which had the curious effect of pulling him into her thoughts much faster than he would have dared. It caused them both to inhale suddenly, but the feeling of peace that washed over them took away their fears. They became aware of several tiny waves of life stirring in Cloonth's womb. For many minutes neither of them spoke. They were awestruck.

"They are beginning to form into individuals. There is more than one. Can you sense them, Alglooth?"

"Yes, I can, my dearest one," he answered with a tone of awe to his voice. "It is nothing like the first time you carried a child. I am able to sense some strong presences within you; many, in fact. We will, of course, do as you think best, but I believe we shall need more than the two of us to raise these children. What do you think, my love?"

"Thinking only confuses me now. My instincts want to take over. I know we are waiting to be rescued, but I cannot tolerate being in this small, damp room another minute. Algllooth, can we not at the very least break out of this cell and wait in the outside room where there is light?"

"Of course, my dear one. We were but waiting for Shunlar to regain some of her strength. This will take only a moment." Algllooth rose and stood before the door. "Shunlar, come and stand behind me so that my wings can shelter you from the heat."

Without a word, Shunlar got up from the floor as fast as she could. Her body was stiff from the damp and her shoulder throbbed. Algllooth spread his wings behind him and Cloonth stood behind Shunlar, covering her as well by curling her wings forward around her. Then Algllooth inhaled deeply and exhaled a steady stream of fire at the door. The wood smoldered at first, being so damp, but the heat was so great that by his third breath the door began to burn.

Cloonth was correct; there were no guards on the other side of the door. There was no noise, save for the crackle of the fire. Soon the middle of the door glowed white hot. Shunlar could feel the heat in her throat, as well as the tickle from the smoke, but the wings surrounding her kept the fire from burning her skin. She put her cloak over her mouth and waited.

Sensing that the time was right, Algllooth stepped forward and kicked the door at its middle. It cracked in two, one side hanging on its hinges, the other teetering for a moment before it crashed to the floor. Chunks of burning embers scattered, hissing as they slid across the wet stone. Steam rose, putting out the fires, and the heat subsided. Still no one stirred in the guardroom.

"Shunlar, kneel down while we clear out the smoke," Alglooth ordered. She was used to obeying his instructions and, without giving it a second thought, she knelt, covering her head with her cloak. All she heard was the flapping sound of their wings as considerable gusts of air tugged at her cloak. When they stopped, Shunlar stood up. Only a small amount of smoke remained in the cell; most of it had been blown out into the guardroom.

In the stillness Cloonth thought she heard something. "Listen. Someone coughs as he approaches," she hissed.

For several seconds they waited, listening. The hairs on Shunlar's nape tingled, then stood on end, a sign that danger was approaching. Finally they all heard the unmistakable loud thunk of someone's boots running down the stairs, coughing as he came.

A lone guard ran into the room, his sword drawn. The man stumbled to a halt when he saw the smoldering pieces of door strewn across the dungeon floor. His mouth dropped open as from one of the cells on the end the very tall form of Alglooth stepped into view, wings ashimmer in the dancing glow cast by the oil lamps on the walls.

Backing away, the man suddenly lurched to a stop, clutching his heart and gasping in an attempt to breathe, while a look of utter disbelief filled his eyes. His face turned scarlet. The hand holding his weapon spasmed open suddenly, and the sword made a loud clatter as it hit the stone floor. The guard choked for a moment, but he stood, though so unsteadily that he had to support himself against the wall. He continued to stare.

Alglooth took a few steps toward the guard, beginning to touch his awareness with a burst of energy that would render him unconscious. The information culled from the man's thoughts would tell him how many others followed and how soon they would arrive. However, behind him, Cloonth stepped from the cell. Cloonth reached out also, but her mind attacked, and within seconds the man crumpled to the floor. Alglooth spun around with an accusatory look for Cloonth, but kept silent, though several large sparks slipped from the corners of his mouth.

Shunlar stepped through the doorway just in time to see the guard fall face-down. Not able to understand what had happened, she looked first to Cloonth and then to her father. Alglooth slowly moved closer to the guard's very still form and reached out his hand, holding it over the man's back.

"He is dead," was all he said, but he cast another dark look at his mate.

Cloonth took several tentative steps closer to the body, a most unusual calm to her features. "It seems that I acted by instinct. Shunlar, perhaps you should be at your father's side the next time he protects us."

"His weapon was drawn and he meant to harm one or all of us. Don't forget we are prisoners here," she answered quickly. Shunlar seemed to be happy that the man was dead.

But Cloonth was trembling. Her first concern had always been for the lives of other people. Never had she used her powers to kill anyone. There had been times when she had lashed out with her temper, when she was younger, but that had never had such force behind it. And always the first rule was to stun, not to kill. This act of violence she had just performed unnerved her.

Cloonth's voice shook uncharacteristically as she said, "I suggest we wait here for a few more hours. Surely Bimily and Ranth will come soon. We know they are coming and must wait for them. For us to leave before they arrive will only endanger them. Perhaps they will have information about the other prisoners. Come closer to me, both of you. I feel the need of comfort from you. There is a strangeness settling over me and I can't say as I like it."

Shunlar and Alglooth went to Cloonth. They wrapped their arms around her and helped her walk to a small bench against a wall that was slick with moisture. A round brazier in front of the bench held ashes and charcoal that was just as damp as the rest of this miserable hole in which they waited. Alglooth shook the brazier. Quickly he found more charcoal, then breathed over it, and soon they had warmth.

Cloonth sat between them holding her hands tightly clenched in her lap, her face and expression blank as Shunlar drew her cloak over her shaking shoulders. The only sound was the occasional hiss of the charcoal as every few seconds a drop of water fell upon it.

Thirty-Four

As they approached the gates of Creedath's palace, Ranth and Bimily each felt a shiver of excitement run through them. There were guards everywhere, but with the help of Gwernz and Benyar, their eyes were clouded and not able to see two figures break off from the group and cross the courtyard. Once inside, the two of them removed their white cloaks. Bimily changed herself into the form of the huge guard that she had used several times before. His form was becoming familiar to those who stood at their posts along the corridor. She held Ranth's sword against the small of his back as she marched him straight to the round dungeon. No one barred their way.

Smells of damp and mold reached their nostrils as they descended the spiral stairs. At the bottom of the stairs Bimily called out for a guard, but no one answered. The flames of the oil lamps hanging on the walls swayed as they stood waiting for an answer, the guttering noises the only sounds to be heard. In the yellow light of the lamp the prone form of a guard could be seen near the wall. From the way his head was twisted it was apparent he would not be getting up. All the doors of the cells were open, and a fog of smoke seemed to hover near the ceiling of the round room. Then three people stepped out from a charred doorway.

With a sigh of relief Ranth ran to Shunlar as soon as he saw her. They embraced and were instantly reminded that they were not alone as Cloonth loudly clicked her tongue.

"Tsk, tsk. My young ones, there will be more time for those activities later. Now it is time for us to leave these moist accommodations."

Ranth laughed, recognizing where Shunlar came by her unusual sense of humor. "Yes, Lady Cloonth, you are right. Besides, we have a banquet to attend. It seems that Cree- dath sent invitations to the Temple. My father and several others await us in the banquet hall now. Bimily has already informed me that the other 'special prisoners' have been removed. Do you know anything about them?" In his ex- citement Ranth forgot to mention that Shunlar's mother was one of the others who awaited them.

Shunlar squinted as she focused on the faint trails of heat trace that remained on the air. "It seems they have all been escorted out—mostly carried out of here, it looks like. I will only be able to tell what's become of them once we follow their paths up the stairs."

"How do you know they were carried? What do you mean, 'follow their paths up the stairs?' Shunlar, tell me what you see. Please." This last word he added when he realized that everyone else was staring at him.

"Ranth, there is no time to explain now. Time may be running out for those poor unfortunates. Lead us out of here. Did you bring us our weapons?" Shunlar motioned to the stairwell with a wide sweep of her arm. Uncharac- teristic laughter from Cloonth followed as they began their climb.

Bimily noticed instantly that there was a difference in Cloonth, but she attributed it to nervousness. Only when she caught Alglooth's eye did she begin to worry. He put his finger to his lips behind Cloonth's back as she started to climb the stairs, and he reached for Bimily's hand. In- stantly he began to transfer information to her about what had transpired in the dungeon after she had left. Finding out that the guard had been killed by Cloonth puzzled her, but, like Shunlar, she felt it had been necessary. Their rap- port was cut off as soon as Ranth and Shunlar reached the top of the stairs.

As they had planned, Alglooth and Cloonth came to the forefront. Feeling that surprise would be their best defense, they pushed their cloaks off their shoulders and dropped the physical illusions covering them. No longer were they a beautiful young blonde woman and her partner; their hair was its natural white.

Their height alone was intimidating, but when Alglooth unfurled his green and blue iridescent wingspan, and Cloonth her wings of green and gold, the sight of them was terrifying enough to make an ordinary person's heart stop. The scales on their arms and wings reflected light from the lamps. The light bounced off the walls in curious patterns. Walking down the corridors toward guards at their posts, they smiled ruefully at the first two men, who jumped at the sight of them and just as quickly fainted. Alglooth picked up his sword and dagger and Cloonth disarmed the other one as well. At the third turn in the corridor the guard was stunned before he could unsheath his weapon. A small stream of flame from Alglooth's lips was all it took to make him drop to the floor. Shunlar grinned as she tested the weight of his sword, then thrust it into her belt.

Ranth took over leading the small party to the banquet hall, leaving a wake of stunned or unconscious sentries behind them. Some of the men—the more seasoned soldiers— merely froze as they walked by, disbelieving what they saw. When they had passed, the guards began to regroup behind them, following the small party of strange beings but keeping a safe distance.

Thirty-five

🍃 A RUNNER ANNOUNCED TO THE STEWARD AT THE door that the guests from the Temple had arrived. The steward thumped his staff on the floor three times and in a loud, practiced voice boomed: "Delcia and Morgentur of the Temple of the Great Cauldron, with guests, my Lord Creedath."

Engaged in a discussion with a group of wealthy merchants and their spouses on the far side of the room, Creedath excused himself and made his way to the entrance to welcome the newest arrivals. The room, aglow with the blaze of hundreds of candles, ornate hanging lanterns, and a blazing fire in a fireplace whose mouth was taller than a man, hummed with the conversations of the nearly one hundred guests. Food and wine were being served in abundance, and from the bandstand in the atrium the sounds of flutes and stringed instruments could be heard playing a spirited tune. As groups of guests parted to allow him through, Creedath put on his most practiced smile. His oldest adversaries were approaching.

As members of their honor guard filed in and preceded them, Delcia and Morgentur seemed to float across the threshold. They remained side by side, waiting for a formal greeting from their host. The white-cloaked and hooded honor guard lining up on either side of the double doors did not escape Creedath's attention.

"Welcome at last. I had thought your pressing duties

263

might prevent you from joining us this evening," he said with an overly eloquent bow.

The couple bowed back to him, though not as low as custom required. "We have brought guests, Lord Creedath. I believed it would be no great inconvenience to you on an evening such as this. In fact, I assure you, you will be delighted at the special gift they have brought you," Morgentur answered with a barely hidden smile.

Intrigued at the mention of a gift, Creedath asked, "And just who are these guests?" not attempting to cover the impatience in his tone.

"May I present to you travelers from afar, Gwernz and his sister, Marleah. They request a private audience with you, at your convenience." Morgentur gestured in their direction. Gwernz and Marleah stepped forward, pulling back the hoods of their white cloaks, allowing their faces to be seen.

The sight of Gwernz's white hair gave Creedath a start. He recalled the story of a brother and a sister, the only offspring of the female dragon. He recited to himself the poem from the book of his ancestor, Banant, that went:

> "If thee seeks the dragon spawn,
> be wary of those of white hair...."

While continuing to stare at Gwernz, Creedath took Marleah's hand before she could stop him, thus placing himself in instant rapport with her. He began raking at the edges of her mind, probing fast and hard, seeking anything that might give him a clue as to who she and her brother were. Might he finally be face-to-face with the dragon-beings? *If so, the female will be easy to manipulate if this first encounter with her is any indication of her strength*, he told himself. But as he reached out toward her mind with more speed, his confidence overcoming his control, somehow Marleah managed to pull her awareness apart from him, twisting and turning her mind from his grasp faster than he could follow. Creedath reached again, this time nearly closing the gap between her mind and his. He knew she would call for help, and he put forth a greater effort to gain control of her voice.

When Marleah's hand was picked up by Creedath, she was rewarded with such a sudden jolt of mind-probe energy that she lost her breath. She had been warned to keep her strongest barriers in place, but nothing like this had ever happened to her before. He was proving to be faster than she, but just as Marleah felt his touch reach out to silence her voice, Gwernz made his move. He placed his arm around Marleah's shoulder and forced Creedath from her mind with his stronger control.

A gray pallor washed over Creedath's face. Droplets of sweat beaded his brow. He became mute, the force of his own intention turned back onto himself, and now he reeled, completely under the influence of Gwernz's superior powers. No one had ever imposed this experience of terror upon him, though he had routinely inflicted it hundreds of times. Gwernz pressed on, knowing that using so much strength would cost him later. He demanded to know the location of Loff, and Creedath complied helplessly. Having learned the location of his nephew, he released his hold on Creedath's voice and instructed him to order that Loff be brought to them.

"Guard," came the subdued voice from Creedath, "send our guest Loff to us immediately."

Noticing that several of the other guests in the room were eyeing the scene suspiciously, Gwernz reminded Delcia and Morgentur of their part. They bowed, taking their leave as they began to mingle and distract any prying eyes from what was happening to their host, as if this were truly a grand social occasion.

This distraction enabled Gwernz to continue his manipulation of Creedath. He and Marleah, her hand still held tightly in Creedath's grip, walked slowly away from the main entrance to an alcove on the far side of the hall. Gwernz nodded in Benyar's direction, a prearranged signal to bring them some refreshment, and the man responded.

As if he had done this many times—his identity still hidden by the hood of his white cloak—Benyar brought a flask of wine and several goblets to them. He bowed respectfully and began to fill the goblets.

No one seemed to think it was unusual that Creedath would place so much attention on a woman. His physical appetites were legendary in Vensunor. The three of them sat at a small table in a corner, and with Benyar hovering over them it was impossible for anyone to observe Creedath's condition. He shook, and his motions were clumsy. Sweat poured from him with the effort he made to break from Gwernz's control. It was fast becoming painful for him, and that was making him angry.

Showing visible signs of strain, Gwernz spoke to Benyar. "I require your assistance now," was all he could manage, nearly out of breath.

Benyar had been standing behind Creedath, serving the wine, and he merely reached up and discreetly placed his hand at the small of Creedath's back, pretending to offer a goblet to him.

Any semblance of fight left Creedath completely. All he could do now was surrender to the two men who had gained control of his mind. A pitiful whimper escaped his throat.

They placed his mind in a box, neither man allowing him to see anything but blank walls. Every time Creedath had the smallest inkling of a thought it was crushed, and he found himself back in the box, staring at blank walls. At this point he began breaking down—or more correctly, splitting apart. Neither Benyar nor Gwernz felt triumph at what they did, but neither one stopped or let up his pressure. It was necessary and they continued.

Inside his mind, Creedath saw a room with blank walls where two images of himself stood facing each other. The man who had so ruthlessly controlled and at times killed with his powers screamed wrathfully at his other self, the coward, his true identity. In a very quiet voice the coward began to speak to the one who raged, but he could scarcely be heard above the screeching. No matter; the coward's voice droned on and on, cringing occasionally but never stopping. Something in the power of that droning voice began to crumble the stronger, mad persona that shrieked. Gradually the louder voice stopped and stared in disbelief as the coward's voice relentlessly continued in its monotone. He listened, unable to comprehend any of the words.

Gwernz and Benyar continued to control Creedath, observing all that was happening and at the right moment pressing forward with more support for the coward. The image of the stronger but now subdued Creedath gave way under the pressure and began to diminish in size as well as substance. He became transparent and nearly vanished from sight. Both Gwernz and Benyar watched in fascination, pressing on as the supposedly stronger images of Creedath faded to a mere shadow in the corner of the box. The coward self of Creedath continued his whining self-deprecation.

Marleah had remained caught in the middle all this time. Now, her strength was slowly returning, and she began to withdraw her awareness from the midst of the tangled power struggle. When she at last had control of her thoughts, she remembered her part in this.

Marleah asked softly, "Is it time yet?"

Gwernz nodded his assent and she began forming enticing thoughts in her mind of the Lifestone of Banant. She broadcast it vividly to the image of Creedath's coward-self, who remained cringing within the box.

The enticement did what it was intended to do. Creedath's attention became riveted on the vision Marleah projected to him. Every cell of his being called out with greed for the Lifestone. He heard in the back of his mind three voices saying, *Remember that we control you, above all else.*

In the next slow moments Gwernz, Marleah, and Benyar removed their hands from his body. Realizing he was free, Creedath stood and took several shaky steps away from them. Shudders passed through his torso, but he was unable to fully disconnect himself from the invisible hold that seemed to envelop him. He turned toward them with a great

look of suspicion in his eyes but closed his mouth, unable
to speak or accuse. He was subdued, and it was apparent
from the set of his shoulders that the coward in him had
taken over completely. His shoulders drooped forlornly. He
could not raise his head to its normally arrogant tilt.

But at the moment Creedath turned away the doors of
the banquet hall again opened and the steward struck his
staff three times on the floor, loudly announcing, "Mistress
Ranla with her escort, Loff." They caused quite a stir as
they entered the banquet hall, with Ranla proudly holding
onto Loff's arm. All heads turned; conversation stopped.
People stared.

The stunning couple were dressed in the same colors,
Ranla resplendent in the intricately tooled red and black
leather gown that Creedath had intended as a wedding present for her. Loff wore matching red and black leather
breeches and shirt. Both wore highly polished black boots.
Belted at Loff's waist was a sword in a black and red
leather scabbard encrusted with jewels. Ranla carried a
short sword at her side in a scabbard of the same design.
From across the room Marleah gasped at the sight of her
son.

Slowly approaching Creedath and the others, Loff and
Ranla bowed, she so low that Ranla feared for a moment
her bosom might fall out of the dress, so scantily was the
bodice cut. They both noticed Creedath's uncharacteristic
state of confusion and discreetly cast a small sideways
glance to one another as they acknowledged the people to
whom they were about to be introduced. They bowed to
them, though not such a low one this time. Loff blinked
several times in astonishment as he took a good look at two
of the three people who stood before him.

Gwernz and Marleah held their faces in perfect masks of
stone. Neither showed the slightest recognition of Loff, so
he took their cue and chose to play along.

"Please allow me to introduce you to my betrothed,
Ranla," Creedath said in a quavering voice. Not seeming
to notice his condition, he continued, "And Loff, my foster

son. These are guests from the Temple. Excuse us," he said, offering his arm to Ranla. "We have others to greet."

With a gesture that seemed curiously tender, Creedath placed her hand upon his arm and Ranla reluctantly left Loff's side to join Creedath in greeting the awaiting guests. As they walked to the other side of the hall, she shot a quick, confused look over her shoulder at Loff.

"Mother, Uncle," Loff said quietly as he clicked his heels together in a formal bow, inclining his head sharply, pretending for the benefit of anyone in the room that he was meeting them for the first time. He turned to Gwernz and asked, in the language of Vensunor, "Uncle, please include my mother in this conversation."

Gwernz merely smiled as Marleah surprised Loff by tersely demanding in Vensunic, "I can understand you. Now explain if you will what he meant by calling you 'my foster son.' "

"Forgive me, Mother, I should have guessed you would be able to speak the tongue of Vensunor. Now that you and Uncle are here, I am fine. I was captured by Lord Creedath's men. I am embarrassed to admit how." He cleared his throat nervously. "I have been held captive, first in a dungeon, then in a locked room. This is the first time I have been freed from my prison. Just yesterday he tricked me and discovered that I had been hiding my ability to mind-speak. I had eluded him so far, even while under the influence of strong sleeping herbs. Until he spoke the words this moment I had never heard him refer to me as 'foster son.' After the way I have been treated by him, the words are almost comical. He is a dangerous, cruel person and often kills simply for the pleasure of it, using the terrible power of his mind. Tonight, at this banquet, he promised me I am to learn my fate. This is all I know."

"Loff, I am so relieved that you are safe. I have been so worried." Finally Marleah began to believe that her son was standing before her, unharmed as far as she could tell. To calm her emotions she reached out to embrace him.

"Mother," Loff cautioned, "I believe such a familiar

embrace would not be wise in present company. It is very good to see you. Both of you.'' He reached for her hand and brought it to his lips, making certain to protect his thoughts from her as he kissed the back of it.

My son is grown. You have seen some of the world and have fallen in love, thought Marleah directly to Loff. He released the hold on his mother's hand and did not answer the inquiry that was part accusation, choosing instead to look past Marleah toward the place where Ranla stood, close by Creedath's side, never taking his attention completely from her.

Gwernz sensed the tension between them and intervened. "I must ask you to remember the reason for this journey. Have you heard mention of the name Shunlar from Lord Creedath or anyone else in the palace? We now know that is your sister's name. She had allowed herself to be captured again by Creedath just one or two days ago and is a prisoner here in the round dungeon. However, this time she is accompanied by her father and his mate, and travels under the disguise of an old man.''

"My sister? Held prisoner here? I was imprisoned first in a round dungeon but for the last week have been in another wing of the palace. The only people who were with me in that stinking pit were all younger than I. There were no old men. Perhaps if I were to see what she looked like?'' Loff was intrigued.

Gwernz suddenly remembered the man who stood behind him and stepped aside to motion him forward. "In all this excitement I had nearly forgotten. Forgive me, my friend,'' he said.

The man's carriage seemed to set aside any notions that he was a mere servant. "This is Benyar,'' introduced Gwernz. "He and his son Ranth have come to help us find you and your sister. You will meet Ranth later.''

But another commotion at the doorway interrupted them again. The laughter and conversation of the banquet hall was rent by a scream from the far side of the room as all heads turned to see, bursting through the doors, swords in hand, a young woman accompanied by Ranth. Behind them, protecting their backs, followed two white-haired beings, much taller than anyone in the room. They entered, spurting out short bursts of flame from their mouths at any who ventured too close. In the next moment they unfurled iridescent wings and took flight, much to the dismay of some of the guests.

More screams punctuated the air as the crowd turned with what seemed to be one motion and tried to run from the room all at once. Outside the double doors the guards who had been driven back by the flames were unable to enter due to the crush of bodies pushing their way out. Creedath stood mutely, his mouth agape, his head nodding up and down at the utter chaos before him as well as the two dragon-people flying above him.

Standing next to the person whom she loathed with a passion that seethed like fire, Ranla recognized that a chance had at last presented itself. Making not a whisper of sound, she stepped backward two steps, just beyond Creedath's peripheral vision, slowly unsheathing her sword as she did. Loff, who had never stopped watching her from the other side of the room, gripped the hilt of his sword and began pushing toward her through the press of bodies.

Through the melee, Creedath saw Loff fighting his way toward him. His head snapped up, his eyes alert again. He wheeled around, sidestepping Ranla and drawing his weapon as he did, just in time to stop the downward thrust of her sword at his back. She had no real skill with the sword. Hatred alone had driven her to this course of action. Her sword swung down and connected with Creedath's, making a spark as it did.

To say the attack was unexpected would be a huge understatement. Creedath stared at her, his eyes wide in disbelief. Ranla had never so much as touched a weapon. They stood for a few seconds, locked sword-to-sword, and then Ranla backed off under his strength, stumbling with the effort. As she regained her balance, Loff reached her side, his sword challenging Creedath.

From his vantage point across the room, Gwernz was shocked by an awful realization. He had been so involved dividing his attention between the entrance and the commotion in the hall, that he had released his hold on Creedath's mind. One look toward Benyar told him he had also become transfixed, as had most of the remaining guests, on the two beings who flew overhead and breathed fire.

Most, that is, except Marleah. Marleah hunted. She had unsheathed the dagger at her wrist and taken aim at Alglooth, who circled nearby. Just as she was about to throw, cold steel touched her throat. She froze in mid-motion, not even daring to breathe.

"Throw it and you're dead, woman," Shunlar snarled, pressing her sword to Marleah's throat. "Drop your weapon."

Marleah strained to see the face of the person who had stopped her and gazed into green eyes flecked with gold. She complied by dropping her dagger.

Hovering directly overhead, Alglooth touched Shunlar's mind very gently. *Lower your arm, my child. Use the weapon where it will do some good. This woman has only love for you. I know not her name, but I remember her.* Alglooth tenderly whispered to her then, *She is your mother, Shunlar.*

Then he was gone again, assisting his mate in backing the guards nearest to the door out of the hall with long bursts of flame. Stunned by what her father had said, Shunlar obeyed and lowered her sword from Marleah's throat.

Out! All of you! The voice of Creedath boomed suddenly within everyone's skull. Those remaining guests, who could not protect themselves from this intrusion directly into their heads, covered their ears in an attempt to stop the sound. He was in control of himself once more, and seemed to have learned a bit of finesse from his encounter with Gwernz and Benyar.

At the back of the room, Delcia and Morgentur chose comfortable seats and settled into them, as though they were observing a play unfolding.

When the room had finally cleared, only a handful of people remained. Alglooth and Cloonth chose to settle on the floor to stand with Shunlar and Marleah. Loff and Ranla remained together, their swords held menacingly in hand. A small group of guards had managed to place themselves between Creedath and all the remaining visitors. Together, off to the side, stood Ranth, Benyar, and Gwernz. Only Bimily stood apart, next to the banquet table, her dagger spearing bites of food.

Backed and flanked by armed guards, Creedath regained some of his former composure. Brandishing his sword, he slowly eyed the room's remaining inhabitants. He pointed at Delcia and Morgentur, accusing, "You brought these killers into my midst. There is no law that can protect you now."

Very slowly and deliberately they stood and joined hands, choosing to speak in unison for the first time that evening. "We were foretold that this meeting would occur," their voices echoed eerily. "Guards, take his sword and bring him forward."

Bewildered by this turn of events, the group of guards stood looking back and forth from one to the other. Finally, one of them spoke up. "My Lord Creedath, what is your command?"

"*He* has no commands now!" This time the Pair's voices thundered, shaking the furniture. "*We* command here. Bring him forward." Lightning crackled off the walls.

Slowly, one by one, the guards sheathed their weapons and retreated behind Creedath. Hands before them, open palms turned up in a gesture of submission and acceptance, they stood with their heads bowed. None dared to look at Creedath, though one motioned for Creedath to step toward Delcia and Morgentur.

"You will all taste my sword," he spat at them as he reluctantly stepped forward at last.

"Gwernz, your gift for Lord Creedath," the dual Voices ordered.

Feeling great relief at last, Gwernz removed the shiny

black box from the pouch at his side. In the last few minutes it had become painful to carry. "Marleah, I will need your assistance. Benyar, yours as well. Stand on either side of me and firmly grip my elbows."

They both stepped to either side of Gwernz and did as he instructed. Once they touched his arms he covered them and himself with an intensely strong mind-shield. As he readied himself to turn back the lid, Gwernz reminded Marleah and Benyar of the torment in which they had placed Creedath's mind before all the excitement began. He bade them do it again, and they obeyed without question, placing Creedath's mind back in the box of blank walls.

Creedath's body suddenly went rigid as they wrapped the illusion of the trap around him. He made a small guttural sound and dropped his sword. His power and confidence left him as he became the coward once more.

Gwernz pursed his lips grimly and continued, pulling open the lid of the box with no small effort. Bursts of light shot across the room from within the box as soon as the lid fell back. Gwernz's body shook, as he moved his feet a little farther apart to take a stronger stance, bending his knees for additional support. All eyes watched in fascination the sparks spewing forth from the shiny black box.

"This is the Lifestone of Banant, Wizard of Stiga. It bade me bring it to you," Gwernz's voice quavered.

As the words sunk into him, Creedath flushed with excitement. The Lifestone of his ancestor! Did these people realize what they were offering him? First a look of delight spread across his face, then one of disbelief, quickly followed by apprehension. Finally he raised his arms, and with an unusual look to his eyes, he stepped toward the Lifestone. "Now," he mumbled aloud, "now there will be no more fear or doubt. I will truly possess the power I have always wanted. Yes, yes . . ." he murmured over and over as he came closer.

His hands reached out and into the black, night-dark container that had suddenly lost its sheen. He wrapped his fingers slowly around the Lifestone, picking it up. For the moment the lights that had been shooting into the room stopped. Then a faint hum could be heard as blue and orange currents crackled and began winding themselves around Creedath's hands and forearms. He took two steps backward and gave a great gasp as the breath was forced from his lips. An enormous weight pressed against his chest. He could scarcely breathe. Movement was impossible. He tried to drop the Lifestone but no amount of effort could force his hands forward or apart.

Creedath began to panic, realizing that his awareness was again within the box with blank walls. He began to whine pitifully. Stark terror overcame him as the coward personality grasped what was happening. He stood firmly fixed to the spot on the floor as the currents grew in intensity and twisted up his arms, down his torso, and finally down his legs. The currents took on the form of snakes, crawling rapidly around and through his body. Creedath opened his mouth to make a sound, but only iridescent orange smoke escaped his lips.

A not-quite human voice issued forth from Creedath. "I cannot accept this frail excuse for a man. Where is Banant?" the voice demanded loudly. Only the word *Banant* was understood by Creedath, for the language was formal Old Tongue.

Creedath's eyes opened wider and began to glow. Smoke rose from his shuddering body as the blue and orange snakes continued to intertwine. Suddenly he burst into flames. So hot was the fire that his body was consumed before his clothing actually ignited. As Creedath's black leather clothing started to burn, it remained upright, blazing for a few seconds before it crumpled into a heap of flames. When the Lifestone hit the floor, it too was aflame. Then it shattered into hundreds of tiny fires that continued to burn, strewn across the floor.

Everyone waited in silence until the last piece of the Lifestone burned itself out. Wisps of smoke curled upward from small piles of ashes as the last flames winked out. What little remained of Creedath resembled the contents of an ash bucket that had been dumped into the middle of the room. The jewelry and weapons that had adorned his body and clothing were reduced to pools of melted, misshapen metal. A sweet, acrid smoke tainted the air.

Gwernz, Marleah and Benyar remained frozen together. They hadn't been able to so much as move a muscle since Creedath had lifted the Lifestone from its box. But now small white fissures began appearing on the dark container in Gwernz's hands, and a crackling sound emanated from it. Within less than a minute it turned to dust, and he stood holding what little hadn't trickled through his fingers. That disintegration enabled him to move at last, which in turn gave Marleah and Benyar freedom to remove their hands from his elbows.

The soldiers were the next to recover. They efficiently regrouped before Delcia and Morgentur, saluted and then stood at attention.

"We await your orders, Honored Pair," said their leader.

"Am I correct in stating that there are a number of young people under this roof who have been captives here for many months?" asked Morgentur.

"Yes. They recently were removed from the dungeon and placed in rooms in a private wing of the palace. They wait even now, under armed guard, to be brought to this banquet," he answered in a quiet voice.

"Have the guard escort them all to the Temple immediately and leave them under our care. Then go tell the citizens that the merchant Creedath is dead by his own hand. We will put it to The Great Cauldron to decide who will head this house hereafter, since he had no heirs. For now, leave us," came their reply in one distinct voice.

The soldiers departed, careful to skirt the remains of their fallen lord. Delcia and Morgentur turned to Gwernz. "Do you believe anything special should be done with these remains?" they asked, pointing to the dust on the floor.

"Spare no precaution. Scatter it on the four winds so that it can do no harm to anyone living or dead," answered Gwernz solemnly.

"It will be done," they answered.

"And now we have members of this company to whom I anxiously await a formal introduction," said Delcia with a great smile. "Ranth, please introduce us to your friends of the fire-breath."

Ranth bowed to them as he made the introductions. "I present to you Shunlar and Cloonth, foster-mother to her, and Alglooth, her father."

Hearing the man at Shunlar's side called her father, Marleah bristled, her hand instinctively seeking the dagger at her wrist. Finding the sheath empty, one glance at the floor told her the blade was too far away to do her any good. And Shunlar stood between it and her.

Cloonth, however, did not miss the attempt. She walked past Shunlar, bent and picked up the dagger off the floor, then turned back to Marleah and offered it to her hilt first. Her eyes were fierce and smoke curled delicately from her nostrils. "I offer you your weapon back. But be careful, little mother; I guard my mate's back at all times."

Marleah, thus warned twice, thought better of any action she might have wanted to take against Alglooth. She nodded her head gravely, took the dagger and sheathed it quickly. Then she took a stance with her hands behind her back. The air remained taut around her.

The tone in the room had changed dramatically. Alglooth, who stood a few paces from Marleah, came to stand before her. Very gracefully he knelt at her feet and looked up into her face. A wisp of smoke left his lips as he parted them to speak.

"Lady, there is no punishment to fit my crime. I did abduct your child from you many years ago, knowing that she was my child also. But my reason stemmed not from malice but for fear of losing a life more precious to me than my own. A child born to my mate, Cloonth, had died, and she too was fast fading from me. In my blind grief I blamed all full-blood humans, even you, for the death of our child. Bringing Shunlar to Cloonth saved her life, and I had no thoughts for you. That, I know now, was unforgivable." He remained kneeling before Marleah, his head bowed low.

When at last he was able to look her in the eye again, something in Marleah had been touched. A great sadness came over her, and she felt drained of all energy. She swooned and was caught in the arms of Alglooth, who suddenly held her to his chest with great tenderness. When Marleah asked him to release her, Gwernz offered his arm for her to lean on.

"Speak no more of this tonight, please. Tomorrow . . ." and Marleah's voice trailed off, clearly overcome by memories, as she leaned heavily against her brother's shoulder.

Delcia and Morgentur spoke in unison. "Shunlar, we now take great pleasure in introducing you to your mother, Marleah. Gwernz, your uncle, and Loff, your brother—all from the Valley of the Great Trees."

Numbed by the scene that had just unfolded before her, stunned beyond words, yet knowing it was truth, Shunlar could only nod her head and gaze into Marleah's face. They reached for each other's hands, and in their deep rapport there was no denial that they were truly mother and daughter. However, they did not embrace.

"Daughter, I have waited for this day for over twenty years. If you will give me some time, I would have you return with us to the valley of your birth," replied Marleah in a voice husky with emotion. "Your uncle and I are eager to return and would take you with us, if you are willing."

"Yes, very gladly," Shunlar answered, glancing first at Ranth, then at Alglooth, her father. "I request a promise from you before I do so, however. I ask that you withhold your vengeance from Alglooth. In time, perhaps you will find forgiveness in your heart."

Marleah nodded her acceptance of the proposal, saying only, "I will allow time for his explanation to settle in, and withhold my vengeance. For now that is all I can promise. Will that do, daughter?" she asked finally, the word feeling a bit awkward on her tongue. Shunlar gave a quick nod in acceptance.

Ranth could wait no longer. He had been patiently standing next to Shunlar, but now he took her hand and drew her aside, questions tumbling out of him.

"Have you suffered much here? You look pale and thin. I want to know everything that happened in the days that we have been apart."

"Ranth, it is good to set my eyes on you again. No, I haven't been treated too badly," she answered. "Besides, with Alglooth and Cloonth as guardians, how could I have possibly come to any real harm? In time I will tell you all." She embraced him tenderly. "You do understand that I must return with my mother and uncle to my birthplace? As you must go with your father to yours."

He looked at her in silence for a long while. Then he nodded. He had known for some time they would part, but that did not make it any easier to do. His journey, like Shunlar's, was just beginning. He wanted more than anything to return with his father to his homeland, bringing his mother's Lifestone to restore her life to her, but the very thought of separation from Shunlar caused his heart to ache.

They held each other close as he said, "Too soon, my love, we must say good-bye again. We have at most a few precious days together before you embark on your journey to the Valley of Great Trees and I to Kelaven, the desert of the Feralmon. I have many questions to ask about the city of Stiga. Perhaps that will be our home when we are ready," whispered Ranth in her ear as he held her encircled within his arms.

She gave him the most curious of looks. "Perhaps it will be. Ranth, you and I have only to think of one another and we are together. If a message needs to be sent, there is always Bimily!" She grinned a satisfied grin at this last remark, then laughed out loud at her joke. After a few seconds he laughed too at the thought of Bimily, the messenger dove.

Arms entwined they turned their attention to listen as Delcia and Morgentur began speaking to Cloonth and Alglooth.

"For now," Delcia and Morgentur's voices delicately chimed, "the unfolding of the prophecy has come to pass. There were many mysteries we could not fully understand. Foremost, the mystery of why the dragon glyph was so prominent in all of our most recent interpretations."

They turned together to Cloonth and asked in a whisper, "Please our whims, but are you aware that you are with child?"

Her smile seemed to light up her face from within as she answered. "Most definitely, we know that soon we will have a family to raise. I sense the presence of several children."

"We have been urged to tell you that it has been foretold that they shall spend the first years of their lives being raised in the Valley of Great Trees," said Delcia as she stepped forward to embrace Cloonth in a congratulatory hug.

Then Morgentur spoke alone. "At least one other foster-mother will be required to help with the children. And the Valley has so many who would be willing to share themselves with you. You are special beings who have much to teach and much to learn from humans, lest you forget that half of you is human also."

Alglooth received all this information with a bewildered look upon his face. When Delcia returned to Morgentur's side, they spoke once more in unison. "There will come a day when the city of Stiga will again be abundant with life."

At the mention of this, all eyes turned to them; even Bimily's, whose hand had remained busy with a darting dagger at the banquet table.

They continued, "From the Valley, the Desert, from Vensunor and the Caves, all who worshipped there together once will be brought together again. This time it will truly be a city of peace and knowledge. The poison has left the stone and Stiga awaits."

As their echoing voices brought a stillness to the air

everyone in the room knew they had stepped into a new era.

"Our profound thanks to you, Gwernz and Marleah, for your part in bringing all this about. Without the Lifestone of Banant, Creedath would yet live and continue to inflict his tortures upon innocents. It is most fitting that he died as he lived, violently." Visibly shaken by remembering the man, Delcia and Morgentur let a tremor pass through them.

They turned next to Benyar. "Our brother of the desert of the Feralmon," they bowed. "Your perseverance led us all finally to our meeting with Alglooth and Cloonth. We know you are anxious to return and restore your wife's Lifestone to her, and thus restore her life, and we eagerly await the day you and she return to visit us. Know that within the walls of Vensunor you will always have a home within the Temple. Our heartfelt thanks."

Benyar bowed deeply to Delcia and Morgentur, remaining silent, a look of pure joy on his face. He stood near Ranth and Shunlar, remembering similar feelings of young love as he watched them embrace. "I am anxious to return. It has been years since I have seen my home, and longer still since I have held my beloved wife. And yes, we will return when her full strength has been regained, of that you can be sure."

"So now," Delcia suggested, "let us return to the Temple and enjoy some time of quiet. The events of this evening have made us long for the solitude of our own familiar walls. All of you have the future to consider and preparations to make for your journeys. Those preparations would be better done elsewhere."

As all readied to leave, Ranla approached Delcia. A look of extreme sadness was upon her face as she bowed before her. "Honorable Delcia, what will become of me, now that no one is left to head this house?"

"Child, do you wish to stay and run it until the time another can be appointed?" they asked together.

"No. This place was as much a prison to me as to those poor young wretches who were captives of Creedath. I could not bear to spend another night within these walls. I ask sanctuary with you at the Temple.''

But before they could answer, Loff was at her side, saying, ''Ranla, return with me to the Valley of Great Trees. Leave the sorrow of this place behind.'' He held out his hand to her, and as she searched his eyes, she nodded her head, accepting his hand and his offer, while Gwernz and Marleah watched.

''My sister,'' Gwernz chided as he released his hold of Marleah, sensing that she could at last stand unsupported, ''have you long prayed for a large family?''

As the honor guard opened the doors of the hall, they followed Delcia and Morgentur, by twos and threes, out of the palace of the late and unlamented Lord Creedath, and wound their way back through the streets to the comfort and solitude of the Temple of the Great Cauldron.

A new journey and a new way of life was upon them all.

RETURN TO AMBER...
THE ONE *REAL* WORLD, OF WHICH ALL OTHERS, INCLUDING EARTH, ARE BUT SHADOWS

NINE PRINCES IN AMBER	01430-0/$5.99 US/$7.99 Can
THE GUNS OF AVALON	00083-0/$5.99 US/$7.99 Can
SIGN OF THE UNICORN	00031-9/$5.99 US/$7.99 Can
THE HAND OF OBERON	01664-8/$5.99 US/$7.99 Can
THE COURTS OF CHAOS	47175-2/$4.99 US/$6.99 Can
BLOOD OF AMBER	89636-2/$4.99 US/$6.99 Can
TRUMPS OF DOOM	89635-4/$5.99 US/$7.99 Can
SIGN OF CHAOS	89637-0/$4.99 US/$5.99 Can
KNIGHT OF SHADOWS	75501-7/$5.99 US/$7.99 Can
PRINCE OF CHAOS	75502-5/$5.99 US/$7.99 Can

And Don't Miss

THE VISUAL GUIDE TO CASTLE AMBER
by Roger Zelazny with Neil Randall
75566-1/$15.00 US/$20.00 Can